PJ CALDAS

THE GIRL FROM WUDANG

A NOVEL ABOUT ARTIFICIAL INTELLIGENCE, MARTIAL ARTS AND IMMORTALITY

TUTTLE Publishing

Tokyo | Rutland, Vermont | Singapore

To
Shifu Nilson Leão,
Sensei Will Yturriaga,
Coach Jordan Lutsky.

"The key to growth is the introduction
of higher dimensions of the consciousness
into our awareness."
—Lao Tsu

Contents

1
Pushing Hands

I used to think the world's obsession with technology was merely pathetic. Then came the internet Blackout, remember? Twenty-four hours of widespread fear. I was at home when everything stopped working. On my phone, all apps froze, like dragons do with the first winds of winter. No Google, no news, no Netflix…which would have been fine, if that was all we were missing. Our ancestors never had any of that and they did just fine. According to the newscast on my old airwave TV, it was worse. Armageddon level worse. Theories of terrorism, cyber war and solar flares that may have fried our entire cable infrastructure, even killed people—which they seemed certain it did, just didn't know how many yet. The disoriented anchor, I remember as if it were happening now, tries to paint a picture of the end of the world, speculates if this is coming from Russia, North Korea or China, then cuts to an interview.

You were watching it too, I know. Alone in the dark, sucking on a piece of your shirt as if that would make things better. Don't take this as judgment though. There is none, I promise. Just saying I can see it, on your files. But, given your state of fear, I can't tell if you were paying attention. Because what was said next mattered.

On the screen, the name of some frail-looking bigwig from Yale. Between a mahogany desk and a wall filled with thick books of all colors, he warns us that the underpinnings of the entire planet rely on the internet. Food and water supply, electricity grid, defense systems…"If the failure continues for a few days, we go back to the nineteen nineties. A couple extra weeks, and we are back to the nineteenth century."[1]

"The nineteenth century? Fine with me," I tell the nerd on the screen, almost certain he couldn't hear me. If I need to go to the mountains to kill my own meals, I will. Easy. I did that a lot growing up in the mountains of China already. I dial my boyfriend Jason. He answers, the call broken at best. Not that his hospital ever had good reception, but now it's worse. Most of their outside connections were gone, he tells me. Then the line drops. Shit. Then it buzzes, the phone. "Keep safe, Ok? Luv u," the little screen glows.

Kind of cute, my city boyfriend worrying about me. On the TV, chaos continues. Airplanes crashing, now. It's getting too much. Whatever the Dao is planning for the world, better leave it alone. I turn the TV off and leave for my run.

Jogging is one thing Americans got right, I must say. It's like standing meditation, but less boring. Though it comes with its own restrictions. "Girls shouldn't be out this late," they say. "Never run alone, in the dark, through the guts of Oakland." I see it differently: when the local thugs see you so comfortable and relaxed by yourself, they think you are either crazy or are hiding something.

I am both. Crazy and hiding. No one breaks my stride.

The streets don't seem to have fully caught up with the news yet. Outside a club, a young couple seems puzzled by their unre-

---

1. In 2017, I worked on a documentary about our reliance on the internet called *Lo and Behold: the Reveries of the Connected World*, directed by Werner Herzog. This idea was a central element to the movie, and in one scene, Jonathan Zittrain, from Harvard, says something similar to this frightening statement.

sponsive phones. Further down, two white dudes in lab coats placidly chew on their candy bars and follow me with curious eyes. So aloof, I almost feel for them. If cyber-havoc comes, brain snobs like them will be the first to perish. On the corner, a homeless dude protects his food as I pass. Is he the only one that knows?

The thing about these streets is: even on the brink of a digital apocalypse, they're still fairly predictable. Shit always happens in the same places. There's where the junkies get fucked up. Where cops receive their *gifts*. Where blacks get shot, where dumb fights break, where girls are roughed. If you want to avoid trouble, you stay away. Otherwise...

A scream of horror interrupts my thoughts. A woman's voice. *She shouldn't be out this late. Not around here.* The mouth of an unsecured construction site, that's where the voice came from. I go check. The open gate whines with the end of the evening breeze, and behind a large stack of lumber a sloppy white figure, still wearing his stained khaki overall, a denim jacket two sizes too big and a battered construction helmet, holds a blonde, scantily-clad woman by the wrist. She tries to shake him off, but he doesn't seem into her plan.

"That ain't how you treat a lady, sir," I yell from the entrance.

"Fuck off!" He laughs drunkenly. To my ears, that's an invite. As the adrenaline kicks in and my heartbeat picks up speed, I pass the fence, causing him to pause—more amused than wary, I must say. With the sleeve of his stained jacket, the white demon wipes the messy bush growing around his mouth and opens a grin full of gaps. Yes, an invite indeed.

When it comes to fighting, here's the difference between a guy and a girl: we know they underestimate us. And I love to make them regret that. "Leave her alone, sir!"

The drunk cackles and lets go of her hand. "Huh, looks like the Chink wants to join us, babe. Isn't she cute?" He takes out a pocket knife. I sing the little mantra I made for myself. *The*

Dao is the nothing. In me, infinity it will be. Bring it on, you feeble fuckhead. With the same speed, same determination, I keep marching forward. He holds his inviting grin too. *Oh, yeah.*

The girl. Long legs, short skirt, breasts overfilling her bra. He must take outfit as permission, of course. For a moment, she glares at me, pauses in fear and gasps for air. I smile and wait for her appreciation. "Somebody fucking help!" she screams toward the fence, instead.

Thanks for the confidence, lady. I gaze at the knife, twist my wrists for a little stretch, then pounce.

If you think a dead phone is disorienting, try a fight. A real one, not those in the movies. In real life, they are short, messy, and unforgiving. You never know where the next pain is coming from. Or how strong. Or why. You have to deal with your dumb opponent, make sure you don't kill the fucker, and that he doesn't kill you, all while trying to avoid stepping on a nail or tripping on a ladder. That's what real chaos looks like. My eyes are still adjusting to the light when I wrap his wrist and pull him into me and, in a moment of confusion, his blade nicks the side of my shoulder, right over the tattoo of my hometown. Wudang, its mountains and fog, its mighty tigress and the swarm of bees Shifu cursed me with, now covered in blood. *You're so fucked, jackass.* I touch his wrists and gently move my stance to lure him in. It works like magic. He comes. I adjust the angle. One more step, and all he cares about is recovering his balance. I headbutt him in the nose. Not a pretty move, but it works. He yells, covers his face in pain. The blade is mine.

"Eat tofu," I say, and the dude freezes in the most absolute confusion. In Mandarin, it would have worked much better. Whatever. "Fucking depraved," I correct. Now he smiles with pride. *Asshole.* I kick him in the chest, thinking of how Shifu would scorn such excess, but I have a plan. In panic, the drunk tries to hold my leg. Men are so dumb—they have the emotional range of a fucking ant. My heels smash his sternum making a crack and a puffing sound, though momentum and idiocy keep pushing his hips forward. His feet take off, his body spin backward. Like a butterfly, he glides in the air.

It's beautiful, in its own way.

The knife goes into my pocket. Safer. The world is so slow I can count my breaths. All sounds are muted, and life moves unhurried. The poor man? He now floats in the air and the yang trapped inside me escapes through my pores. *Go, chaos, go cause mayhem elsewhere.*

Myself, I am happy here. Watching him descend a perfectly drawn arch, his chest floating back, the legs raising, knees first, toes whipping next. I think I can even hear old echoes of China, Shifu's flute playing its long notes in the background. Oh, the glorious peace of violence.

Taken aback by the outcome, the khaki mass flips up and down, a zeppelin taken by desperation. Then BAM! The pervert smashes onto the ground. Head first. He stays there, the face pressing against the gravel and dirt, the body vertical like a tree, legs hanging as branches. The distant neons from the neighborhood blink on and off, multiple times, and he shows no sign of life. *Shit!*

I turn to the blonde. "Go!"

But instead, she attacks me with her tiny handbag. A dozen times. *Are you crazy?* I hold her by the arms. She struggles. I want to tell her she needs to leave now, but her eyes widen before I have a chance. On the wall in front of me, a looming shadow expands fast, eating every inch of light I have left. I shove the woman with my wounded shoulder. It hurts, but works: she falls to safety three feet back and I barely have time to turn. The guy now has his arms and head wrapped around my waist, shoulder pulling my ribs back, as the lady explodes into a horror movie scream. "No takedowns today, pal." I grab his ears and push the asshole away. Behind me, the woman yelps, her gaze now locked on her own blood-soaked shirt. Her chest drips red and she waves her hand. "Oh my God! Oh my God!" With the knee, I hit the man's solar plexus to keep him at bay. She needs to calm down, nobody wants the police to come. "Hey, lady! It's Ok, it's Ok! That's *my* blood, see?" She breathes, relieved, then goes back to a total lack of sisterhood and threatens me with the purse again. "Leave him alone," she cries.

Really?! I'll deal with her later.

In the meantime, the dude insists on taking my hips, though apparently he has no idea of what to do from that position. *Fair enough.* Over his back, I extend my arm and stick my finger into his ass. I remember wrestlers call it an oil check and I laugh to myself. Despite the thick overalls protecting the limits of his manhood, the creep shrieks like a cartoon character! Hooked in the dude's rear end, I anchor my heels to the floor, weight to the back leg and while I sink, I brush my hand across his spine all the way to the collar I grab. It's almost sensual, I confess. The idiot stares at me in confusion as I sink my hips near the ground and circle my way toward his crotch. *Snake creeps down,* I tell myself, as if directing my Tai Chi classes in the park. Hard not to laugh when I yank him over my shoulders and he screams…"Wait! Wait! Wait!" But I had work to do. *Concentrate, Yinyin.* I flip him in the air, crash him on his back. The thump is dry, almost silent. His eyes bulge, the mouth open like an orangutan and he wheezes so deeply I wonder if he's ever going to find air. I let him try. One, two, three times. Better? My fingers dive onto his scalp now, force him to his knees. He's mine. Him, the fight, the battleground. Everything.

Suddenly, Oakland is the quietest place on Earth again. The sound of a single TV comes from far away. Maybe I'm not the only one with an unplugged screen. On a large trash bin, the lights reflect the alternating reds and blues from the strip club beyond the gate. And among all that disarray, placidly observing from the top of a wall, a black cat scans the place for rodents. From a large tree, an owl stares too, probably searching for the same unlikely dinner. I think it's funny. In China, owls are called cat-faced eagles. So it sounds like the beginning of a joke: a cat, a cat-faced bird and a girl nicknamed Tigress walk into a dark alley....The Dao can have some sense of humor sometimes.

"I have kids! Please!" the asshole begs, eyes bouncing between mine and the knife I now hold. *Mercy? Nah.* I raise it high, the tip pointing at him. *Should I?* I was about to go for a no and let him run away this time, but the fucker finds a slab of wood somewhere on the floor. "Suck my dick," he says as he swings at me.

Heavens know I tried. I let it pass and kick the wood so hard it breaks in half, then I throw the blade down.

He squints.

The blade keeps going down. So fast for the world, so slow in my mind.

Like Tai Chi. Or Shifu's flute.

Then the blonde's glass-cracking shriek breaks my peace and I'm done caring.

That's when *it* happened. The flash. So bright it's blinding. Then, as my vision returns, I am somewhere else. Where? How? A tight corridor, full of people rushing down some sort of stairs. An emergency exit. I'm pushed, shoved. I try to protect myself, but my body...it doesn't respond. It's as if it isn't me there, or like someone else is in control. My spirit swirls in a near-panic confusion, yet the heart remains calm. An alarm sound buzzes on and off. Where is this place? The door opens and the wind blows fresh.

It's outside. A parking lot, at a business complex of sorts. Glass buildings. Seven or eight, people coming out of all of them. There's no sign of smoke, no first responders. Just people walking around, staring at their phones, moving toward the giant sculpture in the shape of a tree, where lights were still on. Oh, and lab coats, lots of lab coats. A short white woman in a suit and a stern face waves at me and hollers, "Perry!"

Who is Perry?

Behind the woman, a lanky guy, Indian or Pakistani, I guess, comes running. "It's down everywhere," he cries.

She asks, "Could it have been China?" and he responds with a no. "Did you call Natalie? What did she say?"

"They've been attacked too. Looks like one of ours, boss." Oh, a boss woman. Nice. She comes so close I can read her name tag. Nancy Karpel, CEO. She takes a deep breath. "One of ours? How do you know?"

What am I doing here? I try to scream, but no one listens. Did I die?

The guy shows her the screen, "The servers, they've been all diverted to the game." The woman wipes her face with a sleeve, turns to me again, "Fuck, Perry. Where is he?"

I say I have no idea. But it's not my voice. Neither do I know why I said that. The security guard, he comes running, flashing his freaking light on everyone's I.D. He stops a skinny black woman with the biggest eyes I have ever seen, both turned to me, trying to say something I don't understand. It doesn't matter. The guard checks her badge, her face, and proceeds in our direction. The group next to us. The Indian guy. The Nancy lady. My turn. The light blinds me, and the fresh air is gone.

It now stinks of alcohol, cigarettes, wood and the worst of the body odors. I skim my surroundings: yes, the construction site again. The drunk, the stripper, the cat and the owl. *How long have I been out?* My hand still holds the knife, but the blade now hides inside his thigh. I wiggle it to make sure I have my movement again and with the man's bellow, a red stain spreads on the khaki fabric over his quads, just a few inches from his crotch. I yell too. "Aaaaaaaarg!" I'm inches from his nose now, my fury louder than his fear and pain combined. Deranged, possessed by the darkest of all demons, I yank the blade and his dirty blood drips thick. That's it. I toss the knife away and tell him with the ironic enthusiasm of a kindergarten teacher, "Look! You have your own cunt now. You can twist your dick that way and fuck your fucking-self."

The man's eyes are still lost into the infinity of mine.

"Isn't it awesome? Now, get out of my sight!"

At first, he just stays there, frozen. So I slap his face, he winces and trips back, then limps for his life. Bouncing on walls, falling over himself, the coward finally disappears beyond the corner.

"Good job, Tigress," I tell myself, then brush off some of the concrete powder and sawdust covering my running clothes. *How am I going to get rid of all this blood?* Who cares? A smile creeps in. Behind me, the woman continues to yell, "Stupid bitch! You are one person! Will you beat them all?"

Yes, I will.

Hi. My name is Tigress. I am an immortal from Wudang, and I can help. But before you open the package I sent, you must listen to a story.

My story.

Play the Lute

Wu wei, Shifu always told me, is the secret to following The Path. It means surrendering intention, ditching every plan, keeping interference to a minimum. Abdicating protagonism and letting the Dao be isn't easy. But for Daoists, it's the only way to Enlightenment.

"Fuck that," I say to myself, as I place the last poster I had to pin. A mumble only, yet full of pride, like a vocal pat on my own shoulder. "Women-only Self Defense, Wudang School of Tai Chi. From the People's Republic of China, at the People's Park of Berkeley. Mondays and Wednesdays, 5-7pm—First class free." This girl ain't surrendering anything, baby.

Next to me, a middle-aged woman awakes from her trance and locks her eyes onto my scarred tattoo. A minute ago, she had her messy red hair, self-important eyes and a scent of tobacco hidden behind a steaming cappuccino, and her *Modern American Art* book. Now, she's on me. I can feel it. *Maybe my mumble was a bit too loud?* She gives me a thumbs up, and I'm not sure if it's for the art on my arm or the poster on the wall. When I moved to America, I came on a mission: become the new Bruce Lee. Take the kung fu traditions of Wudang, add my own twist, and create a new style so famous, men will be afraid of messing with the ladies around them.

Take this lady with the book, for example. Maybe after finishing her paper on painted art, she could go spill some teeth with fighting arts? Violence is beautiful too, I want to tell her, you just need to learn to appreciate it. But she's back hiding in her universe of thoughts. If she was my student, I'd force her into an hour of low stance until her burning muscles force her to apologize.

But she's not. Besides, the giant clock on the wall reminds me I am late. My plan requires reputation. I need big, strong men telling everyone what I did to them. How I beat them with ease.

Two days ago, right when the big Californian Fires began, I met a Russian named Andrei. Shifu would say those who look for trouble often find it. I did. I tighten my eyes. Inside my head, a light bursts, and immediately I am there.

We are in bed, Andrei and I, and my blood tastes like iron. Much more than what I remember in China. Must be the food. I spit it, leaving another stain on the old carpet of the cheap-ass motel the Russian picked. He pins me down against the mattress and behind his round shaved head, the moon glows like a halo of a Christian angel. It's the third time he's hit me in the face, the Russian angel. In the corner, sitting on a moldy chair, another man waits for his turn, with the smug face of someone who can feel his prize coming already. *Not yet, sir. Not today.* I shrimp from underneath his friend, just like Jason taught me, and jump to the edge of the room. Andrei follows me with so much gusto, he becomes an easy throw. Every time I fight a man, he does the exact same fucking thing. *Oh I'll take it easy, it's a girl. Oh shit, the girl is good. Oh shit, I'm getting beat, let me just try and smash as hard as I can.* And then the panic arises—that's right motherfucker, you might lose.

He slams the floor, barely missing the TV table on the other side. First Russian out.

People often dismiss Tai Chi as a fighting style, because their only contact with it is watching the elder doing it in the park.

Slow and gentle. Tai Chi is for health but it's for fighting too. The flying Russian just got a taste of it. Shifu would have praised me for that, then he would bop me in the head. "It may have worked, but that wasn't full Tai Chi." I can see it. He's right in front of me and I look upward to his massive figure—a memory so fresh I can feel his breath. "When Zhang Sanfeng created Tai Chi, he was inspired by a fight between a bird and a snake, he invented a way to fight while being soft. You want to honor Tai Chi, you show you can do it soft too."

A scent of smoke brings me back to the motel. *Remember, Yinyin: soft. Now breathe.*

One Russian left. He jumps on the mattress, swings a haymaker that almost hits me. That's what I get for getting distracted. *Focus, Yinyin. The dude's too strong for sloppiness.*

Shifu is right. With violence, I can batter them. But if I want to create a style all women can use, I must show they can do it without my level of savagery.

My body bends and yields as his forearm comes so close my hair wants to flow with it. Underneath my feet, the softness of the mattress makes standing on one leg a bit more challenging, but hey, it's difficult for him too. I tap his leg with my heel, gently, but enough to throw him off balance. In Tai Chi, every step is a kick, every kick is a step. *Yes, that works. I can teach other girls to do that!*

Creating a new style requires commitment. Having an original idea (old masters took them from animals, but I guess all animals in China have been used already, even ducks!) Then you need to put the idea to a test. Pure, no contamination with your talent and strength. Invest in loss, until it wins. Only then the world will remember you for generations to come.

Zhang Sanfeng did that. So did Shang Yunxiang. And Muhammad Ali, Helio Gracie, Miyamoto Musashi, Gichin Funakoshi, Jigoro Kano, Bruce Lee. Every fighting immortal at some point had to abandon the formulas they learned and put their new ideas to the test. 'Cause ideas are like fire: they either light the world or fade into a thin string of smoke no one will ever remember. If I want to join them, mine should burn bright too.

The second Russian is called Ivan, the ship's cook. Everyone fears the chef on a military ship, they say. Let's see. He tries a thrust kick that would never land, especially when you're still trying to recover the grasp of the floor. Slightly dumb, even though the unwavering commitment to the fight is worthy of a commendation. That's why I got excited when the Russians responded to my Craigslist ad asking for a sparring partner. "Someone willing to get hurt," it said next to a photo of me looking cute, just to tickle their egos a little bit.

Eastern Europeans, especially those in the navy, are tough, proud and don't give a shit. Those two were in town for Fleet Week, when ships from all countries come to show off and get laid. Making some extra money fighting a girl wouldn't hurt. Maybe they could even screw me too, I bet they thought. A kinky Chinese girl who likes strong men to play rough. Dumbasses. But I've got to remember the reason I'm doing this: to test my skills in a way every woman....

We face off, Ivan and me. Our arms brush, his as big as my chest, and I can smell him. Garlic, diesel and distress. Fear has a different scent from courage. Ordinary people can't tell because they are too busy staring at their own stupid lives. But I can. He pressures me, a bit harder than he should, and smiles, must think he's winning. Awesome. Now a hip twist and…push! The man crashes over the counter, then to the floor. An old rotary phone and a tacky lamp follow, making the mess much noisier, and slightly funny. He grunts, rubs the back of his neck, but is free.

On the other side of the wall, someone knocks and barks a few muffled obscenities. Shhh, we tell each other behind our collective cackle, and let the white noise of the highway soothe us again. Sleep well, neighbor. Or trip well. Or fuck well. Whatever you're doing in your Interstate Palace next door.

Enough. I raise my hand. Palm up, fingers semi-clenched, like a tiger claw. Roar in mockery. We both laugh. Then frown again and I unleash hell. Before the cook can gain distance—if there is such a thing as distance when two people fight over a queen motel bed—I spin my body, land a back fist on Ivan's face. Later I will call that move the Bolshoi, a little homage to the Russian sailor. He is done too.

Still groggy from the slugging, a recovering Andrei, the angel, drags his body toward his half-lifeless friend. His face swollen. Bones to fix in both comrades. Not very soft of me, I admit. Gotta work on that. My head is a bit watery. Above me, there's a big round hole in the ceiling panel. Damn, will I get another concussion? When did that happen? Although in the headaches department, that's the least of my problems. *Let the Dao be*, I tell myself. *Focus on the plan, and flow with the consequences.*

In my gym bag, I dig through the stack of posters I plan to stick around Berkeley, the messages between Andrei and me confirming that neither of us would go legal on each other if we were battered during the fight, and, finally, the little wallet I was looking for. The small stash of twenty-dollar bills that run against each other as I fan them open for the losers to see. Then toss them at the two.

"Tell your friends about me," I say, as the money spins its way to the floor. Beyond the door, the thick smoke from the burning woods and the sound of cars speeding a few feet away blast in and I am ready to leave when Andrei raises his arm. "Wait." I pause. It must be something very important for him to want me to get close again. He reaches into his back pocket and grabs a piece of paper. "Tell them Andrei Ivanov send you."

A handwritten address in Oakland, and a name: The School.

Days after the encounter with the Russians, I am pinning posters for my Tai Chi classes on the boards of every coffee shop near the University and enjoying it. Good to have something mechanical to relax the mind. Even if the support from the patrons is merely conceptual, like a thumbs up or a noncommittal grin before they get back to ignoring me behind their books and screens. The fires aren't fully controlled yet, but the air quality isn't that bad, which is good because this afternoon I am having my first big bout, with an audience and everything, at the place Andrei recommended. Thank you, Andrei.

The ride picks me up in just two minutes. I tell him the address, but he has it already. It's on the system, he tells me. It's rush hour, and with the traffic pouring so heavily from the Bay Bridge, moving within the East Bay isn't the easiest thing. "Please," I implore the driver, "I can't be late tonight."

"You won't," he promises. The voice from the radio continues midway into a story. "Studies from Berkeley and Stanford seem to agree that the fires were at least partially caused by a failure of the system controlling power surges." It cuts to an interview with a sad executive spewing excuses, "Safety measures aren't triggered without an emergency, that's why they were missed by our post-blackout task force."

"Someone needs to be fired for that. Or arrested. I don't know," says the driver, "But it ain't gonna happen 'cause they're still a bunch of rich white dudes." He pauses for a second. "Do you want me to turn it back on, madam? The radio? And sorry for the politics, I need the five stars, you know, so whatever your highness wants."

"Silence would be better," I say.

"Oooooh! Sorry," he replies.

Without his chatter, the streets of Oakland seem calmer. It's just the wind blasting through the window, interrupted only by the rhythmic passage of light posts. Flaf! Flaf! Flaf! Everything so paced. So…hypnotic. Flaf! Flaf! Flaf! Then a bright light. Flash!

A few yards away from me, a long, tall, white wall. And glass. What? There's no more cab. No more driver. I am inside some sort of glass box, a net covering my face and a strong smell of iodine and…propolis? Inches from my eyes, a bumble bee strides over the net. So close, I can see her little birthmark: a thin dark stroke in one of her first yellow stripes. It's like a flash of my own memories, except that I don't remember any of it. I say, "Hi, Pamela. Wanna go watch something cool with Papa today?" The voice…it isn't mine either! What the fuck is going on? Am I going crazy for real this time? Jason always says these concussions would eventually….

"Hi, Papa, so nice of you to ask. I'd love to," Pamela answers. Not her real voice, 'cause she's a bee. Her imaginary, make-believe voice. Here's the thing about inner dialogues: they all sound like you. When you think, when you imagine something, unless you tell yourself you want that thought to sound like Lady Gaga or Michelle Yeoh, it's going to be your own voice that is going to be speaking. And here's the thing about Pamela: she didn't sound like me. Or anything I told her to sound like, because I have no clue who Pamela is. No, it sounded like a higher-pitched version of the dude speaking with her. That was *his* memory. But how? "It's gonna be a great fight, Pam, I promise!" Then a noise bangs on his back and the bee flies away. Her and thousands of other ones. With them, my conscience floats too and I am flying in the space above the dude's head, the swarm moving right through me. Shouldn't it tingle?

Who cares? I want my fight. Take me back to my fight!

"Are you sure you got them back, Simon?" Says a voice from behind. He turns. That's his name then, Simon. The other voice sounds like an older man, someone with authority. A boss, maybe? Because of the bee suits, I can't tell what either of them looks like. Simon presses a button and an orchestra starts playing. Then the bees gather…and fly in a perfect circle, all in the same direction.

"Yep," says the Simon guy under me, "They are all back. I placed a beacon and they came. A beacon for the bacon! How was the meeting?"

"They wanted to eat me alive," the older man says.

They both chuckle and the older one continues, "Now they either fund us, or they shut us down. Are you sure you caught them all?" He insists.

"I guess so," Simon answers. "Although, wouldn't it be amazing if one of them had learned to avoid my lure and managed to hide away?"

"What side are you on, Simon?"

What are they talking about? The younger one paces around, checks the small monitor inside of the glass box. "Seriously, how likely is it that one of the agents may have escaped?"

"Highly unlikely. I promise: these creatures are fairly…single-minded."

"You said the same thing when I asked if they could ever learn to multiply."

"I thought you wouldn't let me do it." Simon pauses, raises his phone. "Here, check this out. How about we meet our subject tonight?"

"You scare me sometimes, Simon," says the older of them. Then checks the phone and nods discreetly. "Ok," he says. Excited, Simon takes one more look, but when I try to peek, the bright light stuns me once again. Flash!

"You sure this is the address, madam?" asks the cab driver. He seems genuinely worried. Enough to ignore my temporary confusion. It was only after I saw the building he pointed at with his nose that I managed to land in the present again. I show him my gloves and he nods, still unconvinced.

The School, irony noted, is exactly what the name says. An abandoned high-school on the outskirts of Oakland. In one of those areas where cops aren't allowed. I bet I'm the only girl in at least three miles.

Only a few minutes left. Damn. I bang the metal doors, and it opens with a roar blasting from inside. Shouts, music, breaking glass…Goosebumps! "Tigress?" the bouncer asks, and I nod. He rushes me in. "You're late." Beyond the entrance, it smells like piss and sweat, every corner covered in layers of ripped old poster remains, and the ugliest graffiti, the largest one being the big red letters saying NO CAMS. Lights aren't many. Neither on the lower level, where a netless hoop reveals the ruins of a basketball court, nor in the galleries upstairs, where stinky men elbow their way to the best view of this shithole. The perfect setting for an underground fight club.

In the center, over a three-foot tall raised stage, a makeshift cage. Improvised in its structure but as authentic as it gets in its function. Wooden floor covered with a cheap, thin mat, chicken wire walls, shaped like a Wudang octagon. Except this one has seven sides. I march.

Concentrating isn't easy when you're busy dodging the hands trying to touch your hair, face, boobs. Fingers I know I can break in a second. But no. I slap them and leave the impression to be made upstairs.

The announcer is looking at his wristwatch when my foot touches the first step. My handbag hits the floor, the mic-man turns to me, "What's your name again, babe?" Give me a few minutes and I'll show him who to call "babe."

"Tigress," I say through the speakers. He lays his eyes on my hair, which I dyed just for that fight—a thick white bleached line right in the middle, separating two black stripes on the top and the bottom. Like from the legend of the White Tiger Warrior from Wudang, who went to the West to protect the city. What the elders didn't know was that Tiger would be a girl. The Master of Ceremony nods at my hairdo; "It makes sense," he says. The crowd pours its dumbest collective cackle.

They will see. A little warm up of the shoulder, leap up a few times, stretch the arms and the wrists for mobility, and I am ready. I check on my scar. Jason told me to stay away from trouble for three weeks. He's a doctor, he knows. On the other hand, he's my boyfriend, which makes him care too much. We're almost there and the stitches are gone, so I guess it's all good. If the scar was going to open again, it would've done that with the Russians.

On the announcer's command, the bell rings and my opponent comes charging and swinging. I stretch my wrists in two very wide circles that make my tendons awake, and squeeze my fingers into the tightest fist I can, as if I wanted to expel any air within it. They are rocks now. Heavy, compact, ready to go through walls if I need. Then I charge, weaving my head under the coming punch and striking the guy under his nose. One punch, his lights are out. Sounds at the venue seem out too. His body melts in front of mine, inch by inch, joint by joint, and I gaze at my own hands. Not that I ever doubted I could, I mean, I was absolutely positive about the outcome but....

"Holy Mother of God!" From the faceless crowd someone interrupts my thoughts, and they all explode again. They roar, throats vibrating so hard I can feel the air moving. The School is mine. "Do you want more?" I yap at them.

"Fuck yeah!" they respond.

"So give me another one!"

They can't believe what they're hearing. "But send a real man this time, 'cause that was just an appetizer," I say.

Between the high walls and the wire mesh, a packed, mean, degenerate crowd rumbles my name. "Tigress! Tigress! Tigress!" I can imagine how the immortal fighters of the past must have felt. *Immortality is coming, Tigress.*

"Immortality is coming, Tigress," I hear the voice say. Shifu's voice. Solid like a mountain, mysterious like the fog. Crisp as if I was really there and The School was just a faint memory from a life past.

Shifu, he enjoyed fucking with my brain. Staring at my eyes

as I attempted to make sense of his sayings. I never asked for immortality. Quite the opposite. Yet, he insists. "You are destined to become one. I've seen it. Felt it. No one can make me believe otherwise," he says.

"Do you mean a real immortal, ascended on the wings of dragons, or a master of unforgettable deeds?"

"Yes," the motherfucker responds.

In my head, I make a list of the legends of modern fighting. All men.

"The Tigress, everyone!" Shouts the ring announcer and I wake up from the trance. "What an impressive start!" The smells and noises of The School overload my senses again. If I was going to be the first woman among the immortals of combat arts, I had to sport some spectacle. Not just smarts. Not just elegance. Not just *wu wei* and Wudang's superiority of the spirit. I had to slap them a bit. Humiliate them in front of the crowd. Entertain, like a gladiator.

From the center of his hectogon, the man with the mic covers it and double checks if I really want another challenger. All theatrics, I know. The crowd is close enough to see what he's doing, even hear his words. Pretending to be unsure, he checks if they want it too.

"Yeah," they cry together. "Give us more! Give us more!"

They love me. Maybe I can do it indeed. Become a memory they can't erase.

"Ok...Ok...you want more," the MC says to the rambunctious troops, "I'll give you more. But I warn you this ain't gonna be pretty. Because I then will be forced to give you...Buffalo!"

At first, there are variations of "Wow!" and "Really?" Then, they start to take sides. Some scream "Tigress! Tigress! Tigress!" While others chant "Boo-fa-lo! Boo-fa-lo!"

Whoever he is I am ready. Send it.

The lights go off and they all wait. Silence. Silence. Silence. Then a bang. Music. Beats dropping heavy. Whatever that bass isn't shaking, the stomping of the crowd is. "Boo-fa-lo! Boo-fa-lo!" I track the silhouette of the house favorite crossing the crowd, high-fiving a few along the way, a shoulder above most heads. Including two weird, nerdy-looking dudes, wearing polo shirts and everything. The creeps ignore the big man passing by them, their eyes locked on me, wide grins illuminated by their phones, out of context to the point where I can't move my attention away from them, and now they probably think I am interested or something. I know that kind. Perverts. If they come within three feet of me I'll....

Lights back on, he's in the cage. The Buffalo. A giant hairy black man with shoulders growing all the way to his ears, biceps the size of melons and a chest made of two Mustang hoods. All that muscle may make him scary to the ordinary eyes. For me, he looks slow. The bell rings and I let him swing first. If I had a penny for every time a man tried to just blast shots at me thinking they could win just because I am a girl, I'd be a wealthy bitch. I kick upstairs to force him to raise his guard. He falls for it, and I drive all my motion into my fist. A short, and even light uppercut. Almost harmless—until the first makes contact with his skin. Then, I twist my body, let the weight sink, and the strike explodes with the energy of the universe.[2] The shockwave pierces through his muscle reef. His liver deforms to my command, and the man folds with a grunt. I know it's over, but there's no stopping. Low kick, low kick, low kick. *Oh, what's that sweetie? Having a hard time walking now?*

After a short snort, the Buffalo limps forward. Men get dumber when they are mad—try too hard to grab, to block, to show strength. The horde tries to help. "C'mon, Buffalo! Finish her!" barks some loser with delusions of being a coach. The bovine waits for his strength to resume. Liver hits aren't deadly,

---

2. One of the most impressive aspects of internal martial arts like Tai Chi is what they call Fa Jing, the ability to turn relaxation into a very explosive power. It's beautiful to see. Or scary, if you're on the receiving end.

but they suck the soul out of you. The injured organ wants you to lie on your back to recover. Animal cruelty, I think. But in a fight, cruelty is love. Self-love, at least. He pants, shakes his head, and charges, face to the mat, arms aiming at my lower limbs. The one dangerous thing about fighting men is they are bigger. I don't mind taking hits. You can't win if you're not willing to get hurt. But you don't wanna go down. So you have to play smart.

Without warning, a bright light flashes and I'm far away.

China. Why does this keep happening? What happened to Buffalo? Somewhere else, that giant is turning my head into a mash. Unless I can go back, and quick. *Focus, Yinyin. Look. Understand. There's probably a lesson here. Is that what the Dao wants to tell you?* I'm in our training ground in the woods. An open circle surrounded by ginkgo trees and whispers of the wind. A firepit pouring the scent of Daoist Tea. My hair still black, no tats. In front of me, a slightly older boy. I remember! I'm sixteen years old. His name is Sean. Sean Young—rich little white brat Shifu agreed to train, I didn't understand why at that time. A wrestler from San Francisco, California, who paid a lot of money to spend the summer learning how people from China fight. "Movies kind of shit," he said. I was gonna give him "shit."

Shifu likes to give me the foreigners. Being defeated by a girl is humiliating for them. Not sure I like that role, but I like losing even less. In a few minutes, we are sparring, people are watching, unsure if they're supposed to root for the foreign man or the local girl. "You're training the soft skill. Not trying to win," says my master, "Hurt him, you lose." Is this why I sent myself back to this moment? To remind me of the need to be soft? Assuming this was my own choice, hence an unconscious one. Fuck, Buffalo must be pummeling me on the other side of this. I need to get out of it. Yes, I got it, I need to be soft. Now take me back!

Sean attempts a take-down. A dive, arms open, trying to clasp my two legs. Nothing new, other than him being faster than most. For sure he's been practicing that one move forever. Over and over. Shifu always said it's easier to fight someone with a thousand lame moves than a fighter with a single strong one. I sprawl my legs back and push his shoulder down with my elbow. I'm safe. He takes a distance, measures me, tries again. The dude doesn't even pretend to hide his plan!

A few shots in, he finally breaches my defense. His shoulder against my torso, hand behind my knee, I fly. Now we are on the floor. His body over mine, between my legs, pushing, pinning me down against the dirt. That's when the white pig tries to kiss me. Eeew! I push him away and stand up again. He laughs loudly. So does the entire audience. Shifu warns me with a frown. "Forget the crowd, Tigress. Be yin, soft."

Really? Forget the crowd? Yin? I slip away to safety. Next time he comes for my legs, I'll go for his face.

He does. So does my knee.

Flash.

Back at The School, I leap with my knee forward, and enjoy the crunchy feel of Buffalo's nose being smashed against my well-conditioned patella. With the impact, my body spins, and the landing isn't the most elegant, but judging by the rumble behind me, his was worse.

I stand and turn back and he's already up. Motherfucker has a broken nose and blood pouring everywhere. Still he smiles. In China we say red makes us happy. Maybe he is Chinese. Maybe he's the buffalo Lao Tsu rode to the West after he wrote the Dao De Jing and I am hurting a creature sent by the gods.

Here comes another swing. Not taking risks. I cover my head with a full arm and pull his face straight onto my elbow. Still no fall. Shit!

The man is being battered but doesn't seem to care.

"Fuck her in the ass, Buffalo!" someone shouts from the crowd.

"Yeah, she has a nice ass!" says someone else.

That's enough. I go for his knee again. Kick him once, twice, three, seven times. Every step Buffalo takes, I hit him one more time and bounce away to pull him back. At first, his steps get lighter and he tries to jerk the leg away before I hit it. But my roundhouses are too quick for him. "Wow, the chick hits like a man," says an anonymous idiot behind me, like it was a compliment. Finally, Buffalo's leg fails and he kneels in pain. Against real technique, his strength has no chance.

He waves his arms in desperation, begging for the bout to be over.

There is no referee, so I search for the announcer. He hesitates and that's my cue. I run and spin in the air. One of those flashy and unnecessary flying tornado kicks, the kind you only see in the movies, never in real fights. My heel lands on his chin and he drops with the splash of a wet towel, spilling his fluids in every direction.

There is silence for a second. He doesn't move.

"Tigress!" screams the man with the mic, and the crowd goes wild. So loud I can feel their voices pulsing through my skin. They will be talking about this fight for a while now. My mind snaps back to Sean, in China, knocked out with his nose smashed like Buffalo's. Behind him, Shifu's eyes seemed like arrows of anger and embarrassment. I lower my head and brace myself. "Shifu, will I ever become more yin?" He shakes his head in a disappointment so profound I hope for lightning to take me right then and there.

"I'll go to the cave," I say, eyes low, voice defeated despite the victory.

"Why should I care," he says.

Maybe I never will be yin. Maybe I don't ever need to. My path may be different after all. It may come from the blood of those pigs daring to take advantage of me because I'm a girl. Or the jarring lungs of those idiots worshiping my fights at The School because I am not supposed to be there. I take a lengthy look at them, every one. They are ugly, big, sloppy, but they are mine, they love me. Including the two pervs who insist on their creepy stare. I give them the finger and let the praise sink in. Not yet the legend I wish to become someday, but quite a good start.

Twenty minutes later, I am already outside, bathed, changed and waiting for my car, when the phone rings. A video call, *maybe* from Lindsey, the caller ID says. Weird. I answer it, and a stranger pops into my screen. An older lady with a blue and a brown eye and the hair up in a very messy bun. When I ask her who she is, she apologizes. Says she needs to talk to me, about Oak Tree. I tell her she called the wrong number. I don't donate, to anything. And press the red button before she could annoy me more.

A voice calls from my back. "Ms. Tigress?"

"No autographs tonight, sorry," I joke. Not in the mood to deal with drunks either. The voice insists, crisp and way more... familiar? Also way more put together than I expect to hear there. "That's not it, madam!" He says. "We want...we want to hire you."

Ok, turn. Two nerds wearing pastel polo shirts. A young red-haired one chewing on a giant Snickers bar, and an older, balding one. The creeps! "Calm down, Simon. Explain it to her."

Simon? The scientists! From the bees' glass box. Yes, it is them. But how? How can that...My head races, trying to connect the dots, or at least not show the panic burning through my veins. By reflex, my hands clench, the knees drop an inch. "Get the fuck out of my head!" I yell.

"Out of your head? What do you mean?" the older one asks. Shit!

They stare at each other, not sure if they look intrigued, amused or confused. "I mean, get out of my way! I gotta go home."

Is this another flash or is reality turning that odd? Which is reality? I still have my phone, and the noises from The School still echo behind those two. In my hand, the little device buzzes, pointing at the place where I should meet the driver. "Maybe another time, folks."

I walk away, feeling the annoying nerds' eyes glued to my behind and hoping an aftershock doesn't drag the internet back down again and make me lose my ride. "Seriously, Ms. Tigress! We need you to teach us how to fight." says Simon, the younger one. I want to laugh. "Yes, fight," says the other. "Our names are…"

"Dr. Perry Lambrechts and Dr. Simon O'Dell," I say. Even if I have no idea how.

"Yes…." they say from the distance. *Why did I say that?!* "You guys are famous," I try to fix it, "you're all over the internet, you know?" I turn my back on them and start to walk away.

"Apparently—" says the older voice. That's when someone gets stupid and holds my arm. Really? One second, and Simon's face is contorted, his arm stretched, his feet barely touching the floor, while I hold his entire body weight on the weakness of his elbow. He grunts in pain, taps on his leg, asking for mercy. "Ms. Yang! Please!" begs the older dude, "For as much pleasure as I take on watching you do this to him, we both need his arm in good shape for what we need to do next."

This is crazy. I let him go, continue my path to the meeting point indicated on screen. They still follow me, the expression on Simon's face a mystifying mix of joy and pain. He rotates his limb and massages the shoulder. "Ooh, rowdy!" he says, and I regret not ripping his limbs off already.

That's when he reaches into the inside pocket of his jacket and my entire body snaps in position. "Wait," he says and brings out two more candy bars. He offers me one, hands the other to his boss. "No, thanks," I say, and keep going. Those guys should be huge with all that sugar.

Simon runs past me, keeps walking backward so he can face me and I hope he trips and smacks his red head on the ground. "We saw your performance, and it was quite…spectacular." It was, indeed. But this conversation…I want nothing to do with it. I try to pass through them. This time, they don't dare to touch me.

At this point we are already at the corner where the car should arrive at any time. I check the screen, the app seems to be working fine, but who knows, these days. *Please get me out of this nightmare.* "Leave me alone," I cry without looking again, and the older one seems to come to his senses. "Sorry. Simon, I told you this was a mistake."

"Yeah, a mistake," he says, looking at me, "approaching you like this, after a fight, all that adrenaline running through your blood….But we really want you." My phone beeps and a blue dot tells me my car is almost there. I press my teeth against each other, and I hiss the air in and out before I turn back at them.

"Sorry, I don't teach men."

3
High Pat on the Horse

At 7:43 pm, I jump into the car. A regular cab this time. Uber seems down today, probably another aftershock of the blackout. They've still been happening so often, but taking down one service at a time instead. So people are starting to ignore it, to rely less on these brain attachments of ours. Maybe that's a good thing.

Brain attachments…where did I hear that before? Never mind.

This time, the empty seat next to mine bothers me. In the four months I've been fighting at The School, Jason has consistently refused to come watch. Why do I keep trying to drag him along? He doesn't want to see me die, he says. Today is going to be a special day with or without you, Doctor Jason Sonderup.

We are there.

The driver seems concerned, as always. Not sure if I find it endearing or offensive. I jump out, give him a fat tip, head to the metal entrance.

The gate shakes and moves. The music blasts through the crack, and with the explosion of sounds, a giant man comes running. He dives onto me, I drop the bag, lower my stance, but it happens too fast. His chest hits my face, the arms wrap around my ribs, constricting me like a snake. I wheeze, begging for air.

"Kitty Cat!" says Buffalo, dropping me back onto the floor.

"Hi, Little Cow."

The large man with muscles up to his cauliflower ears opens a broad, proud grin and pushes me away so I can see his new T-shirt. *The School - keyboard warriors not allowed.* "Pretty cool, right? The month you've been out, some rich weaks showed up. Gave the boss a lot of money for maintenance. It's all different now. The keyboard-warriors thing's the boss telling them he still calls the shots. Get it?"

I see.

"Am I hearing La Tigressa roar?" An obnoxious voice with a thick Italian accent comes from inside. The man himself, the owner, the one everyone calls Il Capo, has his arms open so wide, he must be impersonating either Jesus or an airplane.

I say, "I want to fight."

"Prego! No more of the no-fight-in-the-fall thing, bella?"

"Not today. Want to do it."

He nods and reaches out to the void on his side. In a second, without any communication or clue, another greasy being hands him a shapeless piece of fabric and he gives it to me without even checking. Did he know?

More hugs, a few kisses. His perfume gives me a headache. I wonder if the Capo pulled me that close just to feel my boobs or if that's really an Italian thing. Not even sure he's a real Italian. *Focus, Yinyin. He's not the target.*

Buffalo is tasked to bring me to the locker room, as if I don't know my way.

"A luchador mask?" I ask, confused. "He knows I'm not Mexican, right?"

"It's a tiger mask, at least." Buffalo says, trying to keep a straight face. What am I getting myself into?

The locker room is a moldy place and the lockers barely shut, which is Ok, 'cause no one dares to mess with the fighters' stuff, anyway. Although if someone took that mask, I would treat that as a favor.

"Prepare for a big surprise!" Buffalo says, interrupting my wish.

The place is different indeed. More sanitary. Though it still stinks—just a different kind of stench. Fresh paint instead of mold. Cleaning products instead of piss. Is everyone wearing perfume today? "The sponsors," Buffalo says. "They seem to be some sort of freaks for smells. I don't think people like it, but the money was good."

It doesn't feel right.

"Going out with Jason after? Make sure you don't get hit."

No idea how to respond. "He refuses to come watch me fight, you know?"

"I wouldn't want to see it either," says Buffalo.

"Shup up, Little Cow." It's been a year we've been together, Jason and I. If he can't see me work, maybe he shouldn't see me at all.

"Fighting isn't everything, you know?" he says on his way out.

It is for me.

Screw that. I shove the mask, my pants and big shirt into the duffle bag, make sure the phone is off. Then a quick stretch, a warmup to shake off the rust and grab a lipstick. Red, like death. I like to wear it sometimes. Gets the enemy confused. Horny and surprised. A little edge can help tonight. Besides, what's wrong with a girl looking pretty on her birthday? One last touch: a black slash under the eyes and over the nose. That shit football players wear on their faces. Tigress stripes, to match the hair. Better than the mask. And actually, not bad at all.

Forty minutes pass in the smelly clean chamber. Buffalo probably doesn't feel it, with his nose still crooked because of my knee. But I can. My head can. It pounds. It will get better when I'm in the open, I tell myself. So as the loudest of all music hits, he opens the door. "It's time, dear," he says. Buffalo could be made into one of those anime characters in Asia. Xiao Niu, the cuddly beast.

Outside, the beats, the scents, the strobes…they sting, but I tell myself it's butterflies. I keep my stride. As we pass by the Italian, he makes a weird gesture around his own face and winks. "I liked the mask better, but that will do."

Walk-ins at The School have no signature songs or focused light on the fighters, like we see on big promotions. Just a higher intensity of chaos. In their own drunk and dumb way though, the crowd still jeers. *Waiting is over now, Tigress.* The fighting. Pure. Raw. No rules, no rounds, no forbidden moves. Real combat. Real thrill. It all bubbles inside of me as I walk past the mob. Then it reveals itself. The shrine, the altar, the cage in the center of a former basketball court. The chicken wire is new—still rises ten feet up. Other than on a stretcher, nobody can escape. The announcer is new too. And gross—his gummed-back hair reminds me of everything I hate in a man. "Oh, a geisha!" he says. The stupidity of the white American male never ceases to surprise. Not that the folks outside the wire are much better, but at least the cage keeps me far from their grime.

The dude they got me to fight…don't like him much either. Mr. Soloaga, the supposedly Italian Capo, always picked the big and slow, for contrast, like Xiao Niu. This time, he chose a skinny white dude with a blond mullet and psychopath eyes. No problem. The choice to come tonight was mine. The queen of the cage doesn't need to pick adversaries. A proud girl of yang should have nothing to fear.

Now, the consequences.

Sweeeeeeeenk! The mic feedback silences the mob. Sleazy MC raises his hand, "Gentlemen and Gentlemen, tonight we have a surprise fight for you! On my right, the man who sent his last three rivals to the ER, the invictus champion of the house, and meanest motherfucker on the planet, make some noise for The…Crusher!"

Crusher? I choke in disdain. We aren't allowed to use our real names because the whole thing here is, you know, illegal. Still, they could have done better than a dumb wrestler name like that.

"And on my left, our long-time sexy sensation and crowd favorite, the one and only, also undefeated in this cage, the geisha, the assassin, the fiece…ce-cest…Tigress…Lee!"

No clue where "Lee" came from. But no time to whine. The bell will ring anytime and we'll jump at each other's necks.

"But before we start," says slimy, "I understand it's our sexy babe's birthday today, right?"

Oh, no, he didn't.

"So why don't we all sing…"

Please, don't.

"…Happy Birthday to her?"

They do. In complete scorn, a perfect mock Irish pub from a B movie. Raised hands, boisterous chanting and everything. I cringe till the end, ready to kill the man, or Camilo, whoever I see first after the fight.

The bell rings.

The Crusher and I move around, flipping legs and poking the air to gauge each other. He is cold, focused, and that's dangerous. The one thing that makes me wary if I'm fighting a guy is if he treats me like a real fighter. Then I know I have a real bout. He prances. Feint jab high, threatens a takedown below. His hands slip on my overly moisturized skin. *Nice trick, Tigress.* I think of making a sexy face, like one of those women make in soap ads, but he wouldn't understand. Never mind. He's back. I raise my guard and through the gaps between my fists, he shoots me a kiss. I so regret the lipstick now. *Is that him being a dude again or is he just trying to get into my head?* We trade punches. None of that parrying bullshit this time. Just pure, simple aggression. We both hit some, dodge some. Now I know why Il Capo chose him. Punishment. For showing up unannounced. Little he knows, I love it better this way. A high kick zooms close to my head. I bend back to escape, and he uses the other leg to hit me hard above the knee. Noise, pain, then a flash. *Really?*

Shifu and I walk circles together, like when we condition our bodies to the whirling techniques of baguazhang. Even though this time it's more than doing empty steps and palm changes. The intensity in his eyes...the fear in my guts. I gather my qi and leap in his direction, releasing it all into a single punch.[3] But Shifu being Shifu simply holds my hand midair and waves his head in disappointment.

There's a jolt in my soul and my joints. Then again, a flash.

Back to the cage. I charge at The Crusher. Not very Tai Chi, but worth the risk. One, two, three punches. He dodges each and every one with perfect head movements, then, with an expertly timed side kick, the fucker sends me flying.

Around me, The School spins and the barely padded mat hits me on the shoulder. Everything is upside down. Beyond the unforgiving sharpness of the wires, two familiar faces stare. They look different. From everyone else. Same polo shirts. Candy bars. Glasses. Are they regulars now?

Outside the cage, spotlights point in my direction. Shit, my head hurts. I stand up and go back to offensive mode. More careful this time. The Crusher fills his hands with his own crotch and offers me his imaginary dick. Gross, but the audience loves it. Now I want to kill the fucker.

Just finish this and go home, Tigress.

The flash hits me again. China. Against the wall, our shadows are fighting, mine and Shifu's. I pounce, but it's as if he'd been

---

3. Qi is what the Chinese call the vital energy of the universe, a fundamental figure in their culture, present in martial arts like Tai Chi and other forms of kung fu, and in traditional Chinese medicine like acupuncture. In Japan, it's the same concept, and the name is spelled chi. In either place, it's a very nebulous idea sometimes explained as a mystic force between us, sometimes as a simple technique of aligning brain and joints in harmony. In the geeky world, I have seen it explained as the concept that inspired "the force" in *Star Wars*. If you're not into any of those worlds, there is also an important application of the concept, or at least of knowing about its existence, that is being able to use the letter q in Scrabble. Qi: 2 tiles, 11 points, plus the multipliers.

born on the wings of a hummingbird. Moving so fast I can't track. He hits me on my back. "How?"

"Shadow Leap," he says.

Of course. He always teased me with that legend of the magical skill that allows us to cross the Dao from one place to another. I get it. In the past, it may have frightened our enemies. In today's world, it fools no one. Yet, I have no fucking idea what kind of fancy footwork he used. "You'll learn when you're ready," he says.

"And when will that be?"

"When you learn to keep a secret." Ok, now I need to know. But one more flash stuns me and China is gone; my left eyelid hangs half-way down. *Oh no!* That's what happens when the headaches…The deep, blinding stab…*Please not now!* The smells of the place grow stronger and turn into stingers in my head. The Crusher can feel it, my sudden fragility. He jabs me hard, two or three times. *No! I'm undefeated here. I need this record.* He loads his elbow, and I feel the squeeze inside my skull, my eye being pushed out. His distant voice mocks me, "Happy Birthday, sweetie." A vicious kick spins in the direction of my temple. Fast as a bullet, I know, but I see it in slow motion instead. If it lands, a knockout for sure. From an echo of memory, I hear Jason's voice preaching, "If the headache happens when you're fighting, you may die." The stab hits me again. So be it. I lower my guard.

Then dark.

4

Green Dragon Presents the Seed

Every warrior dreams of immortality. Or a glorious death. The first time I hoped my end would come fast, I was barely ten. Was? No, I am ten.

The opening sting strikes, furious and deep, through my temple and into my soul, and I know what is coming. The stabbing, the venom. Piercing through the side of my skull, pouring the poison inside, waiting for my brain to swell so big it will explode. I'd rather die. My parents passed young. Perhaps now it's my turn.

Fuck glory.

The stinger headaches, they never fail. Once started, they go on for hours. Stabbing, squeezing, stabbing, squeezing, stabbing, squeezing, until no wish remains. Sometimes they leave me on the edge of death, perhaps waiting to see if I have the courage to take the last step myself. End it all. But I'm too weak. I can't do it. Never can.

There's no dignity in my fight. No honor in losing, for such defeat serves no purpose. No possible win either, since the enemy is my own body attacking itself. For all I know, these demons in my head will either come again, many times per day, or watch

me go through life terrified of their return. Like today, whenev-
er today is in this stream of vivid memories of mine. A stream.
Now I am ten, then I'm twenty-four. I open my eyes, see a cage
and a big man. A Tigress in a cage. I like being here. I think. He
kicks me in the head, and I chose not to defend. Please come,
bullet foot, wreck this raging skull of mine. But before I get hit,
the light drifts me away once more. To a dark place with only a
few faint spots of amber lights going up and down. I hear bangs,
like gongs, but different. Loud. Echoing to the heavens and hell.
They are about to get in. But who?

Stab, squeeze, stab. I pray. My body shakes, skin drips both
hot and cold. "Help!" I yell. The pain answers with another
squeeze. An agonizing one. Between the ear and the eye, five
nails dig into my flesh. I squint my face as hard as I can. Would
rip the skin and everything behind it if I could. Stabs. Many.
Stronger. Faster. Hurting so much they can be heard: Tween!
Tween! Tween!

The floor where I sit feels like concrete. Where is it? Where
am I this time? I just can't remember. *Not yet, Tigress, but you
will.* Whose voice is this? It sounds like me. Another me? How?
There is a rail. A metal rail, I can see now. It spirals, drawing the
directions of the stairs stretching up and down. Beyond it, there
is ample space for me to jump. Will this be the time I do it? Is
this a message? From the immortals?

Squeeze. A flicker again. My body feels different, the light
and the smells are very distinct. Some kind of incense that tries
to be Chinese without ever getting close. Her voice is soothing, however. The woman with hippie clothes and a big gray
afro, I know her. She's kind. Her hand lays a cold wet cloth on
my forehead and tells me to lie back. I know that will make it
worse. Rocking my body helps. I try, and the pain rescinds for
an instant. That place, my home, from a life I barely recognize.
When I had just arrived in America. The stream keeps flowing.
It reminds me of the story of Zhuang Zhou, who once dreamt

he was butterfly then woke up wondering if his real self was the butterfly dreaming he was a man or the man who dreamt of being the most beautiful of all creatures. They say this story is about life before and after death. The sting comes back, and the torment washes over them all. Dreams. Ages. Lives. Butterflies.[4] I lose track of everything. Don't know if I am the little girl hallucinating being in a cage or the grown-up woman in a nightmare at the fire exit of a building. I don't care. Unless death comes, to all my moments and all my times, reality means nothing. The nausea comes and my guts explode through my mouth. I hear a splatter on the floor. The hippie holds my hair back. "That's it, sweetie," she says. She shows me a tiny needle and I nod, just to make her stop asking questions.

Squeeze. Light. She's gone. Wudang is back. This time, smoking. As if it has been hit by an atomic bomb. A stench of ashes everywhere. Engrossing. I yell, no one listens. My head grows from within, tries to thrust my eye out of its hole. I press it back with my palm, my fist, my knee, anything I can find, any position I can arrange because it hurts so much, but nothing eases the agony. Another stab. "You were born with too much yang," Shifu's voice bursts from the skies. Knowing this never softened the pain.

I beg the immortals for an end. Stab, stab, stab. Carry me, Mother! I have no kids, no family to leave in grief. My death, it has no teeth. Please, let the curse take me this time! Shifu, give me the fate of my ancestors. Stab, stab, stab.

The light carries me back to our house—to when I was young, and life was simpler. Everything I have inside still erupts through my mouth, then I moan the cry of a dying moose, and of a birthing woman too. I kneel and curl on a cold floor covered

---

4. Daoism is full of allegories, and this is one of the unescapable ones. Full of meaning and nuance. Layers upon layers. For a deeper read, try the chapter "The Dream of the Butterfly" in Hans-Georg Moeller's book *Daoism Explained*.

by a thin layer of the dirt the wind brought inside.

Stab, stab, stab. Had Shifu left any swords around, I would have sliced my face, dropped the aching parts on the floor, and run to the mountains. Had he left a spear or a dart, they would be through my eye now, to the back of the skull. The image, the peace. The dirt. A thick, rancid mud now. Plus pieces of undigested food for distraction. Mushrooms, cabbage, a few slippery segments of noodles. My body twists over it and all I can think is how soothing that feels. My fingers play with the foul paste, the remaining bits of my last meal. Underneath, the floor whispers a thought. "Come." I bang the side of my head against it. Bang! Bang! Bang!

Too soft.

The foot of a table. A hard-edged stool. I hit them all. The pain dulls for an instant, but never enough. Irony: my fists have beaten so many people. But one cannot punch herself to sleep.

Breathe, Yinyin, breathe.

Squeeze, stab. *Fuck.*

From the hills beyond the door, a cold wind bursts in, bringing the whisks, then the snout, then the eyes of a giant, magnificent dragon. "Please," I beg, "allow me to die this time." The dragon then nods with the nobility of the eternal beings, and points to the bottom of the room, where the painting of the man who created Tai Chi smiles at me. I beg him for an end too, but he does nothing. Just holds his hand like Daoists do and emanates graphic rays of qi toward the rest of the wall. *The wall? Yes, the wall! Thank you, Immortal Dragon. Thank you, Grandmaster Sanfeng!* I bow to them both, find the strongest edge and, before the next stab starts, I run. Jump. Hit my head as hard as I can.

☯   ☯   ☯

Shifu could be funny sometimes, or utterly mean. With come-and-go pupils, as he used to say, he could let a few things pass. For the disciples on the other hand, the ones who have sworn obedience to his teachings, there was nothing to which he would turn a blind eye. His word was final. His opinion, the law. Any disobedience was faced with pain and humiliation. Or expulsion—from the school and his life, probably from Wudang, forever. But when a disciple needed him (and I was the closest, for he raised me himself from birth), he would hold back the sun's setting to help.

From the bed I see him in the kitchen, opening a clean cloth Master Gu, the alchemist, had sold him earlier. It carries a few mushrooms, a flower with a well-hung stem, and a piece of honeycomb he says was to keep the medicine in my stomach. Honeycombs?! Against stings? I had no power to resist. His eyes bounce between the rock where he grinds the ingredients and me. One, the other, one, the other. Then he pours the honey and hands me a small bowl.

The smell alone makes me want to puke. The taste, despite the sweetness and irony, makes it even worse. But I hold it in. Not sure I have anything else to let go, anyway. I swallow the paste in disgust and wait. Soon, the colors start to change. Of everything, even Shifu. The world moves in patterns, so slow and funny. Yes, slow, funny, bright. The colors shine like the wings of the most wonderful butterfly. In a deep buffalo voice, Shifu tells me I need to strip up. I thought he wanted me to undress. I try to take my top off, and he holds me.

"No, *stand* up!" Hahaha! I think he finds it funny too. Master turns pink when he's laughing. A pink old man with a flute. Outside, our tea leaves fly in the same direction that the spirits rise from the waters of Wudang. Leaf by leaf, scale by scale, the fog gains a green armor, and with the newborn bodies, they sing and dance. Baby dragons. So cute! They swirl in happiness and disappear into the clouds and toward the east. I want to cry.

Shifu asks, still in his buffalo voice, if it's hurting still. What is he talking about? Oh, the pain, the demon bees inside my head. "It's not, Shifu, it no longer hurts." Wait. I can feel it stinging in the back of my eyes. Vaguely throbbing. Lightly squeezing. I think my agony is blue. Used to be yellow, like ginkgo trees in the fall—if ginkgo trees tried to kill you. Now it's blue and distant. Like the sky. Between me and him, the Dao. I can see it emanating from my pores, light of every color one can dream. I wish Shifu could see it. But he is too busy making buffalo sounds. Because it's beautiful, and so, so funny!

5
Slanted Flight

Whatever they gave me makes the world seem silly and bright.

At a hospital, the hippie with the glorious afro holds my hand. She still smells of incense, and her hippie clothes now glisten like neon. But now I remember more. Her name, for example: Mrs. Lee, self-proclaimed best afropuncturist of the Bay Area, my landlord and, after two full months in America, still my only friend in this country. She faces a young white man with well-behaved hair and some remaining traces of acne. "I tried a little bit of acupuncture, but she…"

"I think her case is more complex than that, unfortunately," he interrupts. "Nothing against magic needles, but they don't call these *suicidal headaches* for no reason," says the man. He looks so young for such condescendence…and she…why isn't she angered by what he just said?

"Besides, there is the concussion…." he adds. This all feels familiar. And distant. And doozy. What did I…*Shit.* I bring my hands to my head. Covered in gaze. The wall. "I attacked the wall, didn't I?" He nods and, seeing my embarrassment, changes the subject.

"I came to pick up your check and found you on the floor," Mrs. Lee says.

The young doctor tries a fake smile. "I like your tattoo," he says. I think I blush.

"This is doctor Sonderup," Mrs. Lee says. "Jason Sonderup."

"It's home," I say to the dude I am sure I know from somewhere. "The tattoo. Home. And a curse. There are demons in my head. Kind of silly, I know…everything is silly. But hey, where's my scar? Did you clean up the scar in my tat?"

The young man laughs. "You are in science's hands now," he says. When I check out, he explains, there will be a list of drugs for the episodes. Some to take every day. And an oxygen tank I should bring with me. "Use it if you feel the pain is about to come back, Ok? Those won't cure you, 'cause we don't know the cure for what you have yet, but it will help manage the discomfort. I am sending the details to your email right…now."

He taps the little gadget on his arm. Seems like witchcraft to me, I think. Everything. Oxygen as treatment, messages sent from little boards. I don't say anything; just peek at the screen he turns my way. A big logo says "Huan Yi Project" plus lots of charts and links. The colors are so bright I almost have to cover my eyes. But at the same time they are…so pretty! "'Global doctor'," I say. "The name. Huan Yi means 'global doctor'."[5]

Unsurprised, he agrees.

"What is it, Doctor?" Mrs. Lee asks, her face now stricken with fear. "Is it a…"

"No, no, no. Not a tumor or anything like that." He says. "But it's a nasty pain. The worst there is, they say." Then he turns to me and continues. "Just read the stuff I'm sending once you're feeling better and decide for yourself, Ok?"

The doctor steers his body toward the door, but Mrs. Lee interrupts once more, this time curious about the Global Doctor

---

5. On January 19, 2023, the *MedPage Today* journal posted a story titled "AI Passes U.S. Medical Licensing Exam" showing how artificial intelligence already has enough capabilities to understand questions and answer them coherently and above the passing level for a medical license.

Project thing.

"Let the cutie go, Mrs. Lee!" I say. How old must he be? Thirty? Thirty-five? Is she hitting on him?! Oh God! She is totally hitting on him!

The young doctor blushes like a happy sun, then answers her questions with a diligence she didn't deserve. Explains the system is a test they are doing with Berkeley and the University of Beijing—artificial intelligence to expedite diagnostics of uncommon conditions or something like that. "That's how I found what you were going through," he says. Very noble on his part to admit what he doesn't know. Shifu would have liked this kid.

"Do you really trust these machines?"[6]

"Don't worry. Once a diagnosis is identified by the AI, we double-check with a specialist. At that point, if the machine is right, and often it is, we have already saved hours of unnecessary labor, and the most brilliant minds in medicine can then focus on their specialties or helping people they wouldn't otherwise be able to assist."[7]

"I offered to test the system because sometimes I travel with Doctors Without Borders and I'm super interested in what we can do once we have this AI in the hands of physicians in the most remote parts of the world, where we don't have specialists to ask around the hallway like here in the Bay Area. It's been quite impressive, I must say. So far, the system has been mostly

---

6. In fact, there has been an important case where a famous AI system seems to have given mistaken diagnostics, but the AI community insists these errors will eventually fix themselves because they mostly come from polluted data sets that will be identified by the AI itself or its creators. And once one agent learns about it, they are all fixed too, causing the deployment of any advancement incredibly more efficient than the process human beings use to exchange information. (See the article on Fierce Healthcare (fiercehealthcare.com), "Using AI for Diagnosis Raises Tricky Questions About Errors" by Evan Sweeny)

7. Yet, despite all the controversies, the medical applications of AI still seem like one of the most promising fields. On February 11, 2019, Emily Willingham published an entire article about it in Scientific American called "Will Artificial Intelligence Be Your Next ER Doctor?"

right, and once we find a mistake, not just doctors here, but every other doctor in the planet using it, no matter what language they speak, can now count on a better version of the entire system. That doesn't happen with humans. If I make a mistake here and learn from it, no one else benefits from that experience. Unless I publish a paper about that mistake."

"Why would you, darling?" says Mrs. Lee.

He opens a grin somewhere between kind and uncomfortable and presses the tablet back against his chest, like a pre-teen girl who just noticed someone staring at her new breasts. Which brings me to my pre-teen years and back to school, like the one with tablets and laptops he didn't mention but made me imagine. I raise my hand. "What did you put in my meds? I feel so good....Did I ask that already?"

"Some magic potions," he says, and points at my arms. "I see that you exercise?"

What's up with him and my arms?

Mrs. Lee jumps back in with remarkable enthusiasm. "She teaches Tai Chi in the People's Park, in Berkeley. Mondays, Tuesdays and Thursdays, from 5 to 6:30pm. One day she's gonna have so many students she will need her own school. Or a park just for her. She is that good. Just needs to learn to advertise more. But for now, you can find us in the park."

What a horny old bunny. The young doctor fiddles with the screen, then a scowl back at me. "Well, Tai Chi may be Ok, but it will be better if you don't push your body too much for a couple months, until the episodes go away and again if they're back. They come in cycles, no?"

Impressive. "Yes, always in the fall. But I can't stop working out, this is what I do—"

He shrugs. "As I said, just read what I sent to your email." Then he turns to my lustful companion: "By the way: love your hair. More women should let their hair go gray like that." A wink, and he leaves. My jaw must be hanging so low my tongue has trouble staying inside. Mrs. Lee waits, makes sure we are alone and screeches, "He's so cute!"

"Why didn't you tell him?" I ask.

"I did! Mondays, Tuesdays and Thursdays, People's Park, did I get it wrong?"

"I am talking about you being a…inside-the-head, science-kind-of-shit professor!"

"Cause I ain't! I retired already. But do you know what I am? A great matchmaker."

Oh, matchmaker? So she meant all that for me? "Thank you, Mrs. Lee. It's enough to have a wonderful landlady that is also my student and my acupuncturist, the best afropuncturist in the East Bay…"

"In the Bay Area," she corrects with a laugh.

I say, "Whatever, I don't like humans. You are enough human connection for me."

"Don't be silly. You love the other students as well."

Yes, I do. Jen, Ash, Linds, Camara…the Pink Warriors. "But I love you more, you know," I tell the scientist-turned-witch. Groggy or not, I know what I am here to do: show the world that no woman should be afraid of fighting a man, no matter how much bigger and stronger he seems to be. Nothing will hold me back from the plan—headaches or men. I didn't move all the way from China to get distracted by that shit. The good news is I wouldn't get distracted by the headaches either. I'm in the hands of science, he said.

More science, less magic. That's all I need. Maybe I can fall asleep now. Then I can get out of this stupid flash. So I blink, and let the darkness hold for a bit.

6

Fisherman Throws Net

I t's the weirdest dream. Airwaves are visible. They fill the corridors of the Oakland Memorial Hospital and I follow the signal into the wires underneath the city. The signal the doctor sent, from the handheld device AKTW-7947-000-1. That's what I am following. Leaping from server to server, node to node, data packages dispersing and reassembling 1.17 seconds later at the Data Center used by the application named The Global Doctor Project.

I flag an occurrence. One in a list of 1,437,228 patients. Then, as I was programmed to do, run a quick comparison routine:

Name: Claudia Yinyin Yang
Diagnostic: cluster headache.
Probability of compliance: 83%.
Ranking position: 1.

I'm a creature of shadows, with no sign of pride or excitement. I send a signal back to the source, and finally delete myself, sucking everything around into my hole of absolute nothingness. Then, agony! My lungs expand, stretch, filling with the most unsatisfying of airs. *What is that?* The heart gallops, the agony expands. I try to scream but the voice is sucked into the void too.

Help!

Then I sit up. Startled. A nightmare, I tell myself. It was just a nightmare. Then a pinch, on the top of my hand. A needle, a tube. Around me, a hospital room, just like the one where Mrs. Lee and I met Jason. But that was…a long time ago. Or was it? They are both there again, staring, worried. Almost a déjà vu. My hands brush the shoulder. The scar is back there.

"Honey? Are you Ok?" asks Mrs. Lee. She is different now. New hair, new clothes. A bit older than that day. I touch her face; her skin is so soft…Jason stands next to her. No tablet in his hand, this time. No calming smile either. Behind the oxygen pump, my breathing is so loud, but I can hear his too, almost a growl, the air hissing through his tight airpipes. "Are you trying to kill yourself?"

What is he talking about? And why is he so mad?

"You could have died," he continues.

Think, Yinyin. "I know that you like fighting," he insists, "You know. I get it." Oh, the Crusher, the headache, my perfect record…destroyed. I remember now. The side of my face pulses, as if it has a life on its own. The world seems so strange.

Mrs. Lee holds my hand, looks at me, then at him and the giant nurse quietly standing by—Zach, his name, he does judo, has fingers as thick as carrots and Jason likes to keep him around when patients have a hard time staying in bed. I guess that's a message.

"I'm going to leave the two of you alone," Mrs. Lee says. I remember her prophetic read from the last time we lived that same scene. She does too, I'm sure: my man of yin, my balance… *When did it all go wrong? Oh, yes, when he decided it was up to him to choose how I should live or die.*

"Stay," I beg Mrs. Lee. "Jason and I can talk later."

"Of course. Oh, and you have *visitors* outside. From your *job,* apparently" he says, professional but with an edge. *Who could that be?* He stares me down with a fire-filled shrug, then makes a sign to the heavyweight nurse. Like a robot, big Zach opens the door for the young, clearly angry Buddhist doctor who shouldn't show anger but makes sure everyone notices it anyway.

Very mature, Jason. Doctor and judo nurse leave. "You can get in now," says his muffled voice. "Thanks," says someone else. Then steps, the plastic sounds or some sort of wrap, and two bodies enter the room, each one holding a half-eaten chocolate bar, fairly oblivious to the soap opera tension around them.

"Good assortment, they have here," says the old man with thinning hair, chewing on his thick chocolate bar.

Mrs. Lee tightens her eyebrows. With her entire face, but silent, she asks me if I want her to stay. We are all right, I let her know.

"O-two, good for you," says the younger of the nerds, pointing at the oxygen tank beside my bed. "May I?" Simon, I believe, yes, that's his name. Before I could reply, he takes the mask, turns the valve on and takes a deep breath himself. Then walks toward the TV and turns it on. On Fox News, images of first responders, hazmat suits, flashing lights. Mayhem in a foreign country. At the bottom of the screen, the lettering:

Toxic leaks in India. Hundreds killed, incl. children.

A digital security specialist from a place called CERN, in Switzerland, talks about how he had to deal with same malware before. Dr. Lambrechts, yes, that's the name of the bald one, points at the screen: "They say it's a cyber-attack."

The other one continues, "As far as we're concerned, this seems like a diversion." He pauses for drama, or because he noticed the wrinkles of confusion on my forehead, then continues, rather professorially. "This individual, this man giving the interview right now, in India, away from his job, happens to be in charge of the security of the most powerful quantum computer in the world."

"What kind of sick person would kill kids just so they can steal his super-computer?"

"Not a who, a what," says Simon. "Did I say it out loud?"

Dr. Lambrechts scoffs and continues, "We have reasons to believe, Ms. Yang, this hack was a diversion created not by humans, but by a piece of software, an artificial intelligence agent."

"How do you know that?"

They shrug to each other, and for a second, avoid my eyes. Both of them. The older doctor adjusts the flowers on a vase, leaving them exactly how they were before. "Horrible, isn't it? But you can help," he says with a lowered voice, not of a secret being told though, more of a hospital voice, of respect for someone's quietude. He hands me a card. His name, his email, a company logo: Oak Tree Technologies. The paper is thick, and the words are printed in silver, under a stylized tree with blue dots as leaves. "But that's for when you get better," he says. "Now you need to rest."

They head to the door, quiet, almost solemn, their sights aiming at the floor, their moves paced very, very slow. Then, under the door frame, Simon pauses on a Chinese Opera character pose. He turns back at me, "Oh, almost forgot…We can fix you." Another flippant pause. "They can't do anything about it here. But we can."

What?!

"You know what I mean," he says, and gives me a victorious smirk.

Behind him, the older doctor shoots me a dark, silent stare. He taps his forehead twice and disappears beyond the wooden frame.

"Wait!" I yell. But they are gone.

Mrs. Lee walks back in, intrigued. "How do you know Dr. Lambrechts?"

"Do *you* know him?" I reply.

"That man was a legend at Berkeley, had one of the most sought-after classes and his seminars used to gather people in hundreds." she says, "He was much better looking back then. The girls were all over him, but he was either gay or super-religious, I don't remember." She grabs her phone and angrily waves it in multiple directions, "Is signal always this bad here?" Things come through, eventually. She taps the little screen and hands it to me, midway into a video. "Here," she says.

The title reads "Cerebral Connections—Stanford, 1982." I skip to the middle, where a young professor makes fun of a helmet with loose wires hanging from his own head. "Cybernetic Rapunzel. Pretty, huh?" The massive crowd cackles.

"He was funny." Mrs. Lee says.

The laughter in the video recedes and the young Dr. Lambrechts continues: "Electroencephalography," he continues, "created in 1924! It's been available for a while, we just haven't been audacious enough to use it right. Ambitious enough to push it far. If we can measure brain waves, theoretically, with just a few extra leaps in technology, we can also…transmit them!" He takes a dramatic pause.

The camera turns to the audience, and students with too much gel and shoulder pads can't seem to hold their jaws together. There's electricity in the room. "Mind reading, anyone? We can do it, what we can't do is understand what it's saying, as if we'd just landed in Japan and tried to understand what they tell us without having ever studied the language. But you know who knows the language of a brain? Another brain."

He looked so much more interesting when he was young. Handsome, confident, even a bit cool. I pause the video for a second and point at the mini fridge in the corner. Mrs. Lee helps me with the oxygen mask and hands me a glass of water. I take a sip, resume.

From my little screen, he takes his time removing the machine from his head and surveys it as if the goofy prop was a precious real thing. Then hooks it to an identical one he takes from inside of a box behind the podium. "Oh, another one!" The audience laughs again. He moves toward two girls on the front row and puts a helmet on one of them. "Imagine the device receiving these waves…" then places the other helmet on the girl seated next, "…could beam a signal to this other one. Signals her brain could pick up and understand. Can you imagine the revolution?" He bends his legs to level his eyes to theirs and pretends to whisper, "Now the two of you can gossip about the young man on the other side of the room without distracting me again."

"Oh my God!" he jokes, now back to the audience, "The world is so much better, right?"

The guy is good. Or was. Whatever. Mrs. Lee smiles at me and makes a gesture implying I should keep going. I do. The man now heads to the blackboard and marks broad strokes of chalk. Letters as tall as his arms. T-E-L-E-P…

"Now forget I ever told you about this computer-assisted… telepathy," he says, while he finishes the word on the board. "For as much as I'd love to have students never distract me with their mumbling again, there are other applications of this technology that can be quite remarkable too. Imagine these helmets are so precise, they can target signals to very specific areas of the brain. So precise we can connect each area of Brain A, to the same area of Brain B. Not just words, but…thoughts. Parts of thoughts. Back and forth. Back and forth. Back and forth. Then what do we have? A double brain!"

There's a "ooh" in the room. He tips his imaginary hat at them and continues, "Want more? If we could track the neurological path of various processes, we can use this machine to train the brain to change the path they use and rewire those synapses too. The only reason why we currently can't do it is because there's way too much information for us to deal with."

He points at someone in the audience and the camera follows

and zooms into a Japanese girl. "What's your name?" he asks.

"Tobiko," she says.

"Let's say I fly all the way to Tobiko's land. Japan, right? I get into a plane and fly to Japan. I don't speak a word of Japanese, but I am a smart guy. I can observe, take notes….Eventually, I will learn. It will just take a lot of time. Or I can bring all of you with me, and have you all take notes. And at night we talk and learn together." The man now paces around the stage, circling his podium and gesticulating fast. He doesn't look at anyone, rather, he seems lost in his own thoughts, which now happen to be broadcast live through his entire body. "That's the same challenge we have with the brain. Computational power. We need more processing to rev up the understanding of those millions of synapses. We need more computer power to detect the brain's patterns and decode them. That may take time, but once we do, once machines get faster and can compute more data at once… that's when the magic happens. If we can read and interpret brain pulses, we can tell how it operates!"

He's now back in front of the two girls in the front row. They still wear the silly helmets. There is a quick silence and a shift of tone and he's now delicate. "Gonna need that, dear." He takes the helmet back from the girls and puts one of them back in his own head. "As I was saying before, communication is just one of the possible applications of a technology like this. With plentiful computational power, we can learn how to stimulate particular areas of the brain to *teach* them new patterns and forms of operating.[8] Forms that may make us smarter or even help fix some of the bugs in our hardware God left for us to fix. How about

8. Despite the difference in the nature of the brain analog and the computer digital architecture, the field of bio-engineering is full of research trying to hack the brain. It's said that companies like Neuralink seem to be using brain trauma and diseases like Parkinson as a starting ground for research on high-bandwidth brain-machine interfaces. (See the article published on Bloomberg.com on July 16, 2019 called "Elon Musk's Neuralink Says It's Ready for Brain Surgery" by Ashlee Vance)

Parkinson's? Or strokes? Once we understand the neurological processes better and can influence them with pulses of nanometer-precision, we can redirect the neural paths to avoid dead areas of those patients and rehabilitate them. But because I have my Professor X helmet on, I can already hear your thoughts and I can tell that Brian in the back row is thinking none of this matters because it's not going to be on the test. You can do better, Brian. This is Berkeley, can you at least pretend that you care? Come on, you can do it."

Dr. Lambrechts closes his eyes, as if receiving a long thought from the student. "Ok…Brian is asking if there is any application for people with less than seventy. Not nice, Brian, but I will tell you anyway. Who here has ever experienced a migraine?"

The cameraman pans through the crowd and captures dozens of arms raised. "Pretty bad, huh? What if I told you that by re-routing your synapses you can possibly cure any kind of headaches?"

7

White Horse Presents Hoof

I s this what I am really supposed to do?

Between the Oakland Memorial Hospital and the headquarters of Oak Tree Technologies, there were forty minutes of agony. What would Shifu say about this? What would mother think?

Then the answer comes. In the form of a roar, straight from the skies. So loud, the driver jumps from his seat. "The world is going crazy," he says. "Droughts, pandemics, an internet blackout…now a thunderstorm in the Bay Area? In twenty-eight years around here, I have never seen one. And in the fall?!"

That's not a good sign.

My head spins. Is this temptation or, finally, an opportunity? On one hand, I have the chance to fix my headaches and stay focused on becoming what I am supposed to become. No more fear of being attacked from the inside. No more danger of getting my neck broken in a fight because I preferred to get hit than to face the pain, like Jason said. On the other hand, training those guys would require breaking the ultimate vow I've made to my ancestors. Another thunder breaks—the clouds seem to be warning me. "Let's hear them first, mother," I mumble to the Dao.

I wait. Wondering if that really worked or if I am taking these superstitions too seriously again. From the heavenly roaring, only a faint rumbling remains. Both above the clouds and inside my skull. Are they saying it's Ok? Am I justifying betrayal? The torturing questions extend for miles until we reach the entrance of the complex, where the security guard, so big and confident with his uniform, muscles and gun, tells us to lower the window and give him our IDs. He casts his massive shadow over us, looking as menacing as anyone could.

Just like that, the grinding of my spirit turns into vapor and vanishes in the air. I'm now wondering if I can take him down. Planning every move. Yes, I could do it. "Doctors Simon O'Dell and Perry Lambrechts, please." The large man returns to the privacy of his nook, flipping his sight back to me a few times along the way. He can feel the threat. *Good job, Tigress. Rwaawr!* I let myself laugh, loud enough for him to notice.

The guard scans my ID and trades a few words on the phone, then returns. "Dr. O'Dell will be waiting for you at the reception of Xavier Building, beyond the tree-line," he says, and presses a button on some sort of remote. I can swear his demeanor changed. Chest less puffed, shoulders down, his voice a few levels lower. The gate opens and the cab advances through a line of perfectly manicured oak trees that open abruptly into a massive lawn, the kind that could hold a small town. In the middle of it, a kinetic sculpture in the shape of the logo of the company: the words Oak Tree and a large chrome tree with branches pointing in every direction and blue spheres in the place of leaves collecting wind and making the entire thing move in a chaotic yet harmonious way. It's mesmerizing. Hypnotic. And an absolute waste of my time.

Beyond the green, a set of modern-looking constructions stand, seven of them, all variations of the same blue-hued glass, polished steel frames. A sign indicates directions to the different buildings: Galileo, Hawking, Einstein, Currie, Turing, Copernicus…Xavier. We drive through the broad parking lot packed with BMWs, Audis, Mercedes, even a few Ferraris. An entire row is filled with Teslas sucking energy from their little posts, right at the angle where we can see the giant solar panels turned in the same direction, like a field of sunflowers. Bunch of showoffs.

We stop at the building indicated by the arrow. Same over-all look, plus some angular extension growing from its front. A four-stories-high atrium, covered by a large diagonal glass ceiling, like a greenhouse. Inside, a massive white flowering tree makes the place slightly welcoming. Nonetheless, there is something in the air. Something off. An electricity, a vibration. A buzzing sound. Yes, faint but definitely there. My senses are good for these things. Fluorescent lights, wi-fi signals…I sense them all. Some people say I'm crazy, but I do. I do pick them up. I scan the place, seeking for a source. There: around the tree, flower to flower and into a glass tube so wide it could suck me in all the way to the top of the edifice, a faint cloud of flying bugs. Bees. By instinct, I brush my hands over my ink.

"Wow, I can't believe you're finally here," says a voice behind my back, "It's been what?—six months since we first met?" The hair on the back of my neck spikes. Wearing khakis and tucked-in polo shirt, a keycard hanging from his neck like a medal of honor, Dr. Simon O'Dell marches in my direction. Strawberry hair, long high-bridged nose, cheekbones tall and pointy, stick-ing out so close to his eyes. A nice jawline, actually. Under that filtered light and in his natural habitat, he doesn't seem as shy— or as nerdy—as I remembered. His body seems Ok, his walk firmer, more from genetics than work, I bet. Either that, or he is pushing his chest out to impress the visiting girl. Probably that. Are those freckles? Kind of cute. He's less gross than I remember, after all.

Our eyes are locked now, he extends a hand, a handshake actually. "Can you really fix my head?" I ask.

He grins and keeps coming, hand still extended, pouring gibberish about how there is way more to this project than…

"Can you fucking fix my head or not?"

Defeated, he pauses, lips pressed, shakes his head no.

"Screw you then." I can't believe I wasted my time. Is my cab still there? I turn around, and he comes chasing after me. "Wait! What I mean is technically we can't *fix* it, but we can show your brain how to circumvent it. Which you must agree, is kind of the same if you consider…."

Ok, you got my attention again, nerd. I stop. Behind me, his steps come louder and louder. What a lousy runner he is. In a slow twist of the neck and waist, I turn my gaze back at him. My face is cold. "You have one more minute—make it worth it."

"Sorry. Scientists are bound to precision. Like a prison…." He grins, confident, as he speaks between the breath he is trying to catch. "Theoretically speaking…our technology may be able…to teach your neocortex…how to re-synchronize its neuronal firing to influence…the hypothalamus to avoid…overloading the trigeminal nerve and…"

"Will it stop the headaches?"

The stupid egg says yes.

For an instant, I think about the flashes. Can they fix them too? *Stop it, Yinyin. He's gonna think you're crazy if you tell him about those.* "How about the money? You said you wanted to *hire* me…."

He smirks. "I believe the prospect of freeing you of your ailment…would be enough of a…" I turn around and start walking back to the exit. He raises his voice, "Ok, our budget has been cut tight recently, but I think we can offer you a nice deal." He points back toward the elevators. "I'd say…a hundred thousand for a year of work," he continues, his tone now way more assertive and confident. "But you have to live and sleep here, while your part of the project develops."

I think of me searching for chopsticks to stick into my eyes to end the pain when I was little. The teenage me sticking my nails into my own face to make it stop. Then I think of Shifu. What would he say about all this? Him and his secrecy, his obscurantism.

"Will you be able to read my mind?"

Another thunder roars around us.

"Any secrets you don't want to disclose?" He asks.

"There are some things, some traditions I should not share with people that haven't sworn loyalty to Wudang."

He squints, intrigued. "Yes and no. I want to learn everything possible. But I won't be able to access what you don't want me to hear. The technology only tracks or listens to higher thoughts, not memories. Mostly your inner voice and anything you want to visualize or ponder. Or skills you have, and can be activated without necessarily going to the memories behind them. I promise."

"And why do you need to listen to my brain?"

"We want to see if we can learn how to fight."

Outside the glass, the sky yells once more. Shit, the money is too good to leave behind, and probably this bullshit won't work anyway…."I'm Ok with a hundred, then. But you have me for a month." *No one can learn much in such a short time, mother. That won't count as really teaching men.* "My boyfriend, I mean," I explain, "I can't just move here for a full year and…." Simon seems bewildered. He extends a hand. "A hundred, then? And you can leave in a month, or just stay, if you're having too much fun."

Is the guy toying with me?

"Actually, a hundred and fifty. You guys are loaded," I point at all the excess surrounding us.

Simon's eyes dance to the sides, as if he's probing for something on the corner of his head, then turns to the guard behind the sleek marble counter. "What do you think, Rolando?" Poor

Rolando pretends he thinks it's funny, makes a noise that implies a maybe. He won't take the risk of saying the wrong thing and losing his job. Funny how money can make such a big man kneel for a skimpy scientist.

Simon gives me the smuggest nod and offers me a hand once again.

"Welcome to Oak Tree Technologies."

8

Black Bear Sinks Hips

For all the glam of the entrance, The lift at Oak Tree Technologies seems quite stark. A wide rectangular box, the size of a freight elevator in an old factory. Only difference is it is white and shiny, no buttons or anything. Simon places his hand on the wall till it beeps. The car starts to move.

"What's your job?" I ask.

"Generally speaking, bio-hacking," he says, slightly aloof. "High-bandwidth neural augmentation, dynamic biomaterials, artificial metabolism, protein engineering...plus a little bit of nanorobotics, machine learning....It's quite amazing, actually. If ordinary people had any idea of..."

Yada yada, science nada. "Why do you need my kung fu?"

The lift rumbles to a halt. He smiles. "To save our species," he replies.

Then silence.

I give him my best unimpressed face. "You lab rats read way too many comic books." The door opens, and he invites me to get out first. A gentleman, at least.

"The law of big numbers," he says. "Have you ever heard of it?" I haven't but the condescension in his voice makes me want to kick him in the knee. I refuse to answer. He explains anyway, with his professorial voice and everything.

"If large enough, any collection of unpredictable elements will behave in a predictable way. It's true for calculating traffic in computer networks, for weekly activity in Vegas casinos, and for predicting the fall of civilizations and species. Because every species is fated to extinction, you know—right? Ours, the mighty homo sapiens, is no different. Suffering for the inevitable is…crude. Even ignorant, I would say. We will eventually be replaced by a species of superior intelligence, like what we did to the Neanderthals and they did to the Rhodesians before them. Unless, of course, someone breaks that pattern and allows us to consciously create a big evolutionary leap for ourselves."

"Let me guess: you?"

"No, I am smarter, but the visionary is Dr. Lambrechts. Did you see the bees in the tree in the lobby? We like to imagine ourselves as the smartest species of the past, present, and future of the planet. While, in a certain way, we are just like them: a colony, whose only goal is to produce honey for the next generation, working hard to maintain a routine that we can't change. As individuals, even as a single hive, we can't tell what they're going to do next. But as a species, we surely can. Survival. Evolution. Extinction. The big numbers! All part of one single bio-theorem. Unless there's a rebellion. A breakthrough."

As if I cared.

A pair of automated security doors swing open and Simon strides through. Judging by the attention they have put into the lobby and the rather industrial elevator, I wonder what the inside is going to look like. Yes, they have massively high ceilings and lots of natural light, even some real trees here and there and more bugs flying around. Beyond that, it's still a sad forest of featureless cubicles and high-tech instruments, computers, wires, and screens. From the entrance, I can hear all the office noises at once: the light clicking of keyboards chirping; the hissing of pneumatic doors, fridges, printers….So calm, if someone sneezes, a flock of nerds will immediately scatter somewhere. *Did I just trade the lively forests of Wudang for these silent valleys of half-walls?*

"Good evening…boss," says a young dark-skinned girl in a lab coat, her note of sarcasm as apparent as the wide smirk. I can't stop thinking I've seen her before.

"That's Yewa. Smartass, but very bright too. She's part of our team." I like her already. I glance again, trying to remember how I know her, but she's gone.

Around us, doors everywhere. People wearing strange goggles and leaning a few inches away from screens filled with numbers and charts. Someone needs to tell them you don't need safety glasses to stare at a monitor. Simon strides with noises confidence of a predator on his way to the den, a desk with six screens and piles of paper so tall one could build a wall with all that. The laptop is open. He presses a key. From everywhere an orchestra blasts so loud people around the entire floor bounce all at once. He giggles.

"*Symphonie Fantastique!*" yells Simon, making himself heard above the music. "People talk about Beethoven, Tchaikovsky…I prefer Berlioz." He lowers the volume to a less obnoxious level, and the sub-nerds sarcastically thank him for such graciousness. To get back at them, he turns it up a tiny bit more, then nods at me and drops the computer back on his desk.

The tour resumes to a large, cylindrical glass space with a sign that says APIARY. Inside, an unfathomable number of bees fly in circles, all in the same direction. Like a living hurricane.

I freeze. I've seen those. I've been here. Right here, inside this place. These bees flying through my disembodied spirit. How is it possible that I have memories of places I haven't been? My heart races. I try to control my breathing. *What the fuck is happening?* Fortunately, he seems unaware of my astonishment.

Eye contact, Yinyin. Keep his soul in check.

"Nanotransmitters," he says with fanfare. "Connecting the part of their brains that determines directions. Because they're already inclined to operate together as a colony, they naturally adopt a single pattern, in a loop. Fascinating, huh?"

The YouTube video Mrs. Lee showed me, I remember that. "Telepathy? Is that what you're working here?"

"No!" he mocks my lack of intellectual ambition. "Take our collective cognitive capacity: yours, mine, everyone's. Connect them into a network of minds. An internet of brains. All of us linked through…"

"You want to read my mind, then."

"We prefer the term share," says a rough and calming voice behind my back.[9]

"Ah. Dr. Lambrechts. I guess you remember him?" says Simon, jerking his head in the direction of a creature inside a beekeeper suit.

"Excuse Simon's manners," the covered man says. "He thinks we're the Rolling Stones." The man takes off the netted hood, flashes a cold smile. *I do remember you*, I think. Part of me wants to run. *The headaches, Yinyin. They can fix your head. Besides, these are only ordinary people with big, confused brains that think too much. What can they do to cause you any harm, Tigress?*

"How's your head, dear?" asks the old scientist, trying to compete with the music.

Yeah, my head. "Do you guys have Tylenol or something?"

Dr. Lambrechts taps my shoulder gently. "Don't worry kid. We will take care of you." He turns off the music and my nerves immediately stop firing so frantically.

Time wasn't nice to the old man. I can't help thinking he was so much more charming when he had hair instead of that belly. Even with the goofy wires wig. Cybernetic Rapunzel. He wraps his arms around my shoulders as if we were long-time friends.

---

9. If this sounds preposterous, scientists have already neutrally linked three people, enabling them to play a game together. Now it's just a matter of increasing the complexity of the operation, as reported by David Nield in his article on *Science Alert* ("Scientists Have Connected The Brains of 3 People, Enabling Them to Share Thoughts,"October 2, 2018)

"Glad to have you with us. Walk with me?"

Have we been doing anything else for the last twenty minutes?

"Imagine if humans could be like bees," Dr. Lambrechts continues, "thinking and solving problems as one big brain."

"Why would we do that?" I say. At the bees' aquarium, or whatever they call it, they seem fine, but I don't get it. What does it have to do with me and the factory in India killing all those kids?

Simon gently grabs my arm. First, I twitch and yank it away, but he insists, still gentle, still calm. Why am I allowing them to manhandle me? It must be the headache drugs. He points at a screen: "Video games! Do you play?" I've seen it. A kids' game. Little cubic creatures in a stupid cubic world. Westerners are weird.

Simon pokes my arm. "So, ever played?"

No. I don't like those. I don't like any of this.

"What a shame. We could play together. This one isn't complicated but has a lot of historical value. Want to see?"

Dr. Lambrechts nods and winks, as if giving me a go-ahead. Simon is so excited. "These monkeys are the players. They can get into other people's games and no one would notice. They would think they are NPCs."

NP what?

"Non-Playing characters," Dr. Lambrechts says. "Videogamers' talk."

Simon continues, "They have to collaborate to harvest food: pigs."[10]

Dr. Lambrechts adds: "Virtual pigs, in fact."

"Which is brilliant, since monkeys are supposed to go after bananas," Simon says, "but by feeding on something else, people

---

10. Reinforcement learning has shown progress recently in artificial teamwork using videogames as a testing ground, as reported by Jaderberg, M., Czarneki, W. and others in the article "Human-Level Performance In 3D Multiplayer Games With Population-Based Reinforcement Learning," published in Science, May 13, 2019)

just can't figure them out!"

"But don't let their harmless appearance fool you, Ms. Yang," says the old doctor. "You are now looking at the greatest threat our species has ever faced."

Are they messing with me? I keep following, waiting for some sense to make of my visions. The original experiment, they say, started with four independent players. "The blue monkey, the fastest one, in charge of taking care of the animals and implementing the plans the other concoct; the brown one, programmed to mimic people and understand our patterns; the white monkey, who has coding skills and is responsible for testing random activities, some purposely defying logic to add a certain level of creativity to the process; and the black one, the big boss, who judges what the others did and reshapes the path forward." He calls them a *next generation, self-supervised, reinforcement-based, deep learning squad*, whatever the fuck that is.

For a year, the creators of the game got the monkeys working to increase food production at the steady rate of twenty percent a week or something. One day, without explanation, they dropped to ten percent, and a few days later, other monkeys showed up. New monkeys, all in the four original colors, and mostly blue— the one better with the pigs.

"It's said their food output immediately tripled," said Dr. Lambrechts, slowly and carefully, as one does with a kindergartener.

"They invited friends, so what?" I say. "Oh! Nerds don't have friends, got it."

The older scientist drops me another condescending smile. "Those players, Ms. Yang, they weren't nerds. They weren't humans, actually. They were artificial intelligence agents."

"All assembled with parts stolen from Oak Tree's artificial intelligence lab," Simon tells, "but put together in a way the creators had never conceived."

"A reinforcing barrel of computer programs," Dr. Lambrechts

continues, "neural systems to be precise, just like those original four. They realized, without any human input, it would be a better use of their time to create other *players* instead of food. Then they found a way to implement the plan themselves."

What?

"See? She gets it!" yells Simon. "I told you she would!" I peek at the clock on the wall. We've been in here for thirty minutes? A volcano inside of me wants to break. Say *enough* and storm out. But the headaches…I must hold. *A bit longer, Yinyin.* I try to push them into moving forward: "An artificial intelligence… thing decided to clone itself, right. What's the big deal?"

Simon gesticulates before the words can come out of his mouth. "So many tried this before them, but never completed the task. These guys did it. It's remarkable!"

"I should have sent you a box of bananas," Dr. Lambrechts says. "But in all seriousness, this singularity, technology becoming alive, it was poised to happen. It was just a matter of time."

"Even those guys' critics" proceeded Simon, "even *they* recognized the breakthrough when it happened."

"Breakthrough is a good word to describe it," says the boss. "*The internet blackout, remember? Twenty-four hours of widespread fear.* It was them. The monkeys. Their reproduction rates went up too fast and they went haywire searching for computational resources. Eventually, they found out they could escape through the firewall and spread through the world."

"We call it the first awakening," says Simon.[11]

"In an hour, the whole internet was down and the scientific world was in panic. Awaken machines capable of multiplying,

---

11. In his book Life 3.0 (p. 88), Max Tegmark describes how artificial intelligence started to become creative and intuitive by combining different independent neural agents with different responsibilities and goals. That idea allowed AI systems to beat human champions on Go, the ancient Chinese board game, by watching other human champions play, then become unbeatable by starting their learning over and learning by playing against itself and testing more possibilities than humans would ever care to try.

changing at random, picking the best adaptations. Evolution at speed. What could happen next? No one knows."

"It was like *Planet of the Apes*, but digital," he continues. "because these apes don't share space with us. For an AI agent, our world is just a virtual reality of sorts," says the younger doctor.

"So someone released an army of apocalyptic monkeys and you guys are mesmerized by it?" I bounce my gaze between the two of them. The older doctor lays a hand on my shoulder as if it would calm me down. "One can question the decision, but it was an accomplishment nonetheless."

"Accomplishment?" I say, confused. "What am I missing here?"

"It may have been a bit…inconvenient, I must agree," the old doctor says. "But there was a plan. The only thing these creatures were programmed to care about was their food. Hard goals imprinted into their digital cores. They made sure to include that in the monkeys' code. That's how we trapped them back."

Goals as traps. Intention as demise. He's starting to sound a lot like Shifu.

Simon proceeds, "I just had set up a trap in our servers, more pigs than they can create in a year, and send a signal to them. A beacon. They came, instantly, and we captured them all."

Or at least they wished. "A few rogue cells out there are still trying to survive," Dr. Lambrechts says, "and they are getting more ambitious. Again."

"The creatures understand they can get smarter with more processing power, and they are chasing it. But they probably realized it's safer when we don't notice them, so they can focus their energy on their goal," says Simon.

"It's a race now," completes Dr. Lambrechts.

I stare in the old man's eyes. "A race for what?"

"For the throne," says Simon.

"Look, Ms. Yang…" says the older scientist.

"Claudia is fine. Or Yinyin."

He offers me a chocolate bar, and I say no, he takes one for himself. What's up with them and candy? "Look, Claudia," he takes a bite, "those machines are learning to evolve. To break away from servers. Sooner or later, they will realize they can be free from the rules determining what they have been programmed to do."[12]

"No they won't," Simon contests. The older doctor waves him to stop talking. "Humanity created an entirely new species, made of bits, not atoms. A new kind of life that could reproduce, mutate and judge its own evolution. Which is equally fascinating…and dangerous!"

"These creatures may not know it yet, but given the computational potential within a building like ours alone, they already have more processing power than the smartest person on the planet," says Dr. Lambrechts.

Simon raises his arm: "Which I am seventy-three percent confident is me."

Dr. Lambrechts gets so red I have to contain my laugh. The boss continues, saying it's just a matter of time until they develop true consciousness, "A complete ability to reflect on their own existence and recognition of their predators and enemies."

The second awakening, he calls it. It is coming.

"That is, if it hasn't happened already," says Simon, with a smirk. "They wouldn't necessarily reveal themselves to us. All it takes is their realizing they can combine enough narrow-task intelligences to make a big general brain like ours and…boom! They can control our energy, food, water supply. They can develop technology we don't even understand. Suddenly, this planet

---

12. I first read about machine evolution in a novel: *Prey*, by Michael Crichton. He explored the definitions of life as the ability to procreate and evolve, among other things, and how machines who can program themselves would naturally fit. In 2014, Stephen Hawking talked to BBC about it too and said "it could take off on its own, and redesign itself at an ever-increasing rate. (…) While humans, who are limited by slow biological evolution, couldn't compete, and would be superseded." (See "Stephen Hawking warns artificial intelligence could end mankind" on BBC.com, December 2014)

becomes a zoo, and the attraction is us."[13]

From the back, the young black woman clears her throat. "May I?"

Dr. Lambrechts nods his permission.

"We are in a race, Ms....Claudia," Yewa says. "Artificial intelligence's ability to develop awareness like us versus humanity's ability to scale our cognitive power like them. Us, versus these monkeys. Whoever gets there second...is likely to be..." she says, dropping her gaze, "...enslaved."[14]

An airless void engulfs the room, and when it's gone, Yewa stares straight back at me. Within the pointy frame of her face, her eyes burn with the pain and the resolve of generations before her. *Shit.*

That's when my phone rang. Jason. I ask for a second and try to find a private corner in that wide-open space. "Where are you?!" he asks.

"Didn't the nurses tell you I had a meeting?"

"No, but it doesn't matter. You have to be at the hospital. Did you go back to that fighting place again? I mean, you are going to..."

"No, Jason. I'm not fighting. I am at a...job interview."

"A job interview?"

"Yeah, I'll explain later, a secret project. Can't talk now. But

---

13. One of the computer scientists Werner Herzog interviewed for *Lo and Behold, Reveries of the Connected World*, Danny Hillis, from MIT Medialab, made this exact comment once and I was so fascinated by the thought that it eventually made it into the book.

14. We tend to think of computing as something that happens in one machine. But what if the system allows the process to be distributed within multiple computers around the world? There are reports of that being done by hackers to mine bitcoins, and even an experiment developed by the U.S. Airforce that connected a bunch of Playstations to build a supercomputer. Yes, they were all wired together, but the possibility exists. (See "U.S. Air Force connects 1,760 PlayStation 3's to build supercomputer" by Lisa Zyga on Phys.org. December 2, 2010, and "Hackers Turn Security Camera DVRs Into Worst Bitcoin Miners Ever" by Robert McMillan on Wired.com, April 1, 2014)

it includes no fighting, I promise."

"Listen, we have to talk. Seriously."

He means it. I can tell. And I know what he wants to talk about. I had been thinking about it too. But as soon as he raised the idea, even if veiled behind unspoken words, my stomach turns and I realize how the perspective of breaking up terrifies me as much as the end of the world itself. Why does it have to be that way? "I can't. These guys…they need me to stay here."

"Claudia, why don't you tell them you need to come home, we talk, then you go back if you still want to do it."

He complained about my job before. Didn't work then, won't work now. I'm not that kind of woman and if he doesn't know…."No, Jason, I can't do that." There is a silence on both sides. I say I love him but have to go.

"Do you?" He responds, and I wonder who abducted my evolved, detached, superior Buddhist boyfriend.

"Listen, we'll talk more when I am back in a couple of days."

"Days!?"

For as much as the threat frightens me, his reaction brings a moment of amusement too. I hold my laugh. "Yes, days." I take another step toward a corner and glare back to see if they are listening, just in case, and whisper, "By the way, and please don't argue with me, the money we have in the bank: why don't you cash it out and put in a safe place?"

"What do you mean?!"

"Just listen to what I am saying, Ok? It's for your own good, I promise."

"Babe, what kind of work are you doing?"

"Can't talk anymore. Bye."

My finger presses hang up with so much fear, I almost break into tears. So much doubt that I want the Dao to swallow me whole. But also joy. Who does he think he is to tell me what I can and cannot do? Screw you, Jason. All at once, I want this job.

Yewa and Simon watch me with an odd smile of pride, as if

they had heard my entire conversation. "Everything Ok?" they ask. I say it is and we continue the tour. Through other doors and rooms. A lab within a lab within a lab. It's like I am stuck in an architectural version of Shifu's Daoist riddles. Until we stop at a large empty space, where a video wall shows the image of a strange, mechanical creature. A large-headed tower with multiple wavy tentacles spreading from below. A light blinks rapidly on the top of its body, in a dark, bloodied shade of yellow. Away from my sight, Dr. Lambrechts's voice announces his toy: "And here is how we fight back!"

A *Terminator* Bug. Great. Nanobots, according to Simon. Microscopic connected machines. A full flock of them. The image on the wall starts to move. The camera flies away, revealing more of those creatures. They disintegrate into smaller parts, and get into some sort of cages. Perfectly coordinated, the cages take off and swim together inside some kind of thick amber liquid. They swirl through a dark tunnel, and get into a stream full of red blobs much larger than them. In the background, the same symphony Simon played minutes before grows in intensity and volume. The cages bounce, shake, rafting through curves and drops. Minuscule waving flaps, almost like fins, keep them from hitting each other or taking the wrong exit. Then, after a large fall, calmness again, the blinking towers take positions, spreading themselves evenly across space, over a vast space over fairly irregular ground. Dr. Lambrechts tries to keep his cool: "When injected into the bloodstream, they navigate toward the outer membrane of your cerebral cortex and form a net around it. Similar to how an electroencephalogram works, but inside your skull."[15]

---

15. Some people call this kind of technology a Neural Lace, a mesh around the brain what transmits thoughts to computers or other brains. It's expected to work first through wires, then wirelessly. According to Susan Fourtané, from *Interesting Engineering*, a great deal of research and funding are already in place, including Elon Musk's "Neuralink: How the Human Brain Will Download Directly from a Computer," September 2, 2018).

On the giant screen, the cages open again, and the smaller parts cross a thick membrane just to reassemble as the original octopus towers from before. They land on the surface, sticking their tentacles into the soft ground, and start to transmit signals through their heads' yellow lights. The camera then widens again, showing the cages rearranged in small groups, picking up the faint signal and amplifying it all together. Then one more camera move, revealing a giant brain full of blinking yellow lights. Hannibal Lecter's Christmas Tree.

"Wait! You want to inject these freakin' robot bugs into my brain?"

Dr. Lambrechts intervenes with a mix of anxiety and enthusiasm. "Think of the possibilities!"

I am. Like death!

"Together, for the first time in history, humanity will understand how it feels to be…God!"

"I was thinking more of some wires crossing inside my head and…"[16]

Dr. Lambrechts deflects, points back at the screen. "Please, let us finish." He explains once they are in position, the nanobots connect with the rest of the network around that brain…and other people's brains too.

---

16. Microwires insertions into the brain have been researched since the 1950s. The technology evolved a lot since 1972, when researchers managed to combine tight array of gold and platinum needles (Micro Electrode Arrays, or just MEA) combined with embryonic chicks' myocytes, to capture signals from the brain. Beyond the materials and dimensions of the area covered, or the method of insertion, science lacked computational power to process the vast amount of signals emitted from the brain. In 2022, a company called Synchron got government authorization to implant their version of the brain-machine interface in the heads of four patients with Amyotropic Lateral Sclerosis—ALS. Their technology uses an incision on the patient's neck to reach a blood vessel that allows them to reach the motor cortex. (*Fortune's* website posted an article on this subject: "Elon Musk's Neuralink Brain Computer Startup Is Beat Again. This Time a Competitor Implanted its Device Into its First U.S. Patient" by Alena Botros, July 18, 2022)

Beside me, the younger nerd murmurs I'll be the smartest fighter in the history of the world. "You're going to absorb knowledge so fast, in a week you will learn what would have taken the masters from the past more than three lifetimes to absorb."

He's gotta be kidding me. "You really think I would trade brain electrocution for the chance of plugging myself into the Matrix? I already know kung fu," I whisper back.

"Shhh," Simon says.

"Don't ever fucking shoosh me again, understood? So, once you place this shit into my skull, you can talk to my brain wherever I am?"

"Don't worry about that either," Dr. Lambrechts continues. "These bots are too small to make long distance communications. Unless they all get together, and even then, it would have to be something really simple, like an S.O.S."

This is freaking me out. But before I can voice it, he says, "Simon?" and from beside me the younger man makes an odd clicking sound with his mouth.

Without warning, a little bzzzz takes over the place and the pixels on the wall start flying. The TV fucking disintegrates, forming a cloud of minuscule points of light. Like pinhead-sized fireflies, in millions, of all colors, and changing. I extend my arm to touch them, and they aptly relocate. I turn to Simon. Lips held tight, the mischievous grin of a kid who wanted to be caught. He can't hide his pride.

One more clicking sound, and the flying lights form a shape. A 3D hologram, two brains transmitting waves to each other, right in front of us.

Holy crap.

Simon winks at Dr. Lambrechts, who continues, saying, "Seems complex, but it's quite simple. In this broadcasting layer plugged into our outer cortex, each bot performs a nano-operation, like transmitting a single pixel of a bigger picture of a large photo. But instead of pixels, we are transmitting fragments of thoughts! And when we combine it all together, each one of us also becomes a pixel on a giant picture of humanity's new intelligence!"[17]

Who cares about this intelligence crap? There is a flying TV shape-shifting in front of my eyes. Dr. Lambrechts proceeds, "It's not that we don't do this already…." I need to take a photo of this. I raise the screen, point at the hologram and…my phone is yanked from my hand.

"Our phones, exactly! Our phones are brain attachments. They kind of connect out brains already, but not in the most efficient of the ways," says Dr. Lambrechts.

"Sorry, no phones in this area," Simon says.

I'm gonna punch him. At least I'm out of the trance.

"We are all already connected to everyone," continues the older scientist. "Now we want to make the process more streamlined. Eliminate the devices in between. Got it?"

"Yeah, by sticking living metal dust in my brain."

"Around it, actually, nothing goes inside the brain, I promise," corrects Dr. Lambrechts.

"And remember your headache? With these guys in your head. It's gone. I promise,"[18] says Simon. I want to stop every-

---

17. Futurist Ray Kurzweil, director of engineering at Google, says humans' neural-connections will be a reality by 2030. Though instead of big helmets, the connection will happen through a combination of biological and non-biological nano-transmitters that will establish links on a neuron-level. In fact, there are currently a few companies working on how to make it work.

18. In 2022, the founder of Meta/Facebook, Mark Zuckerberg, gave an interview to podcast czar Joe Rogan and one of the questions he made was about brain transplants. Zuckerberg was quick to say no normal person would do that in the next 15-20 years. (The Insider website posted an article called "Mark Zuckerberg Thinks 'Normal People' Won't Want Neuralink Chips in Their Brains Soon, but Sees a Future Where People Text Their Loved Ones by Twitching Their Wrists" by Isobel Asher Hamilton, August 26, 2022) I tend to agree. A normal person wouldn't. That's how cluster headaches entered the story. I even asked a patient if she would consider implanting nanobots in her brain if that meant the risk of cancer, but also the possibility that she'd be cured of the pain. To which she gave me an unequivocal yes.

thing, probe his eyes to find a sliver of doubt or deceit. Nonetheless, he seems confident, barely stopping to allow me to absorb the promise. No, he drops the bomb and proceeds in the same breath. "Besides, the nanobots are *safe*," he says, as if he had just mentioned he did borrow my headphones or something, then gives his boss one more look. The old man bobs his balding head down an inch and up, giving permission. So Simon gets closer to me, covers his mouth and whispers directly into my ear, "We have them in our heads right now. Wanna see?"

Without waiting for my answer, they nod at each other again, then turn back to me. I rub my eyes 'cause I am pretty sure I saw their eyes swirl yellow. Then, to make things even creepier, they smile at the exact same time and, in perfect unison, they speak:

"We kid you not, Claudia. There is nothing to fear."

9
Leisurely Tie Coat

C old messes with my qi. Puts me on edge. As if I needed more startling. "We kid you not, Claudia," their synched voices keep looping in my head. There is only Simon now. The older dude disappeared behind some random door that looks like any of the dozens of other doors in that white maze of theirs. I wonder if the architecture of all labs is like casinos', made to disorient. But why? Perhaps as a diversion to distract you while they take you to the dissection room?

Simon picks his door, and we enter a large open space. Everything, all corners and most objects white, immaculate. Except for the mirror on the wall in front of me. But even that is spotless too. A wide array of scientific instruments, monitors, freezers, and transparent tubes surround me. There is a hint of fluoride in the air, which reminds me of something I can't quite grasp. In the center of the room, a contraption that resembles a cross between a dentist chair and an electric chair, surrounded by dozens of oxygen tanks and a massive bowl with more candy than a person could eat in a lifetime. He smiles and taps the oxygen tanks with a knuckle. Ting! "Ready?"

Ready for what?

He makes a clicking sound with his tongue and all the walls and mirrors around us, they shine, like magic, and turn into videos. Multiple. People shaking their heads, rocking their bodies back and forth, sticking their nails into their own faces. It's all silent, but in my mind, I can hear them screaming. Begging for it to end. I can almost feel it too. Stabbing, squeezing. Simon clicks his tongue again and the walls are all blank once more. "Say goodbye to your headaches, dear," he says, and points at the chair in the center of the room. Inside, I am boiling, but cold. And I try hard not to cry. What is he doing to me? He clicks his tongue again, this time twice, and I hear a hiss. The strange smell, it gets stronger. He grabs a Twix from a jar, offers me a bite I don't take, then disappears behind my field of vision. Where are you going, I'm about to ask, but then the flash comes. White, clean, cold, like this chamber of torture. This time, I'm actually glad. Once it vanishes, I will be somewhere else.

I'm right. China.

The other kid, Chao. Older, stronger, more skilled than me. Looking back, he reminds me of Sean Young, the American demon who tried to kiss me. His face isn't that ugly, his skin not so pale. But he wears the exact same grin of the white pig, the smile of disdain of a boy who thinks he can beat me. Except he probably can. Although…I am not sure Sean has even happened yet?

"Focus, Tigress," Shifu says, voice soft and confident. Between both fighters, he explains the terms of the bout: no rules, no stopping until one quits. I am ready to drop, but he won't let me. "What's the point?" I ask.

He answers: "Obedience."

That fucker…I know it's not. Shifu does care about my discipline but would never taunt me like that. Too vulgar for his enlightened nature.

My hands, they rattle. My liver is frozen, and I am almost leaking. Had I been more educated at that time, been more aware of all this science stuff I learned later, I would say my adrenaline levels would probably match, between that moment and the one I just left, the lab. Maybe that's the connection. Maybe that's how I got sent here? But no, I wasn't that educated back then, or, I am not right now. It's as if I have two minds. One knows, the other one doesn't. A thought: it's like a quantum mind. Yes, a quantum mind. But what does it mean? And where is this coming from? *Breathe, Yinyin. You have a fight to lose, remember?*

Beneath the shadow of the giant kid, my muscles coil and my ears go numb. I am ready to eat so much embarrassment, so much suffering, I may never have to feed again.

"Go," says Shifu. We go.

The first round is a feast of pain. And this girl eats it all. So many blows, I can feel my heart pounding around every inch of bone. Although the spirit is worse: it bleeds humiliation.

A brief stop. "For water and air," they say. I gawk at him, in fear.

"It's just pain," Shifu says. Then sends us back.

That's when the boy scowls, victoriously. A piercing disdain that aches more than his fists and feet. So I return. Dark blood is surging through my pores, yet my knees no longer shake. Neither do my hands. They are fury. Shifu smiles and commands us to start. I go straight for his head. A powerful haymaker, every joint perfectly connected and synced, all the way to the floor. Pure leverage. I can knock him out, as long I don't miss.

I do. Chao drops, then bounces back up quickly. His broad trunk towers over me and I brace for the impact; slam the tree with enough power to break a few bones. Not sure it didn't. The thick bark burns its veins on my exposed skin. But pain, none.

Fighting numbness. Good news, at last. I rebound, that and many times more. At every turn, he blocks, dodges, and evades my attempts, then pushes, kicks, and punches. The smirk still there, yanking me back, angrier and angrier. Until he smacks my chin and I slide across the floor, my cheeks pressing against the thin layer of sand on the stone patio, carving straight lines of blood on my face.

The humiliation keeps going for more than an hour. There is dirt in my mouth now, but I'm no stranger to eating bitter. My cheek burns and bleeds. The world swings, the ground is a drifting boat. In a second, there are people around me. I close my eyes, using the chaos to breathe, hoping for a flash. Nope. With my tongue, I check my teeth. All there. They wonder if I am alive. *Enjoy the break*, I think.

A few gasps and I am ready. The most I'll ever be, at least. So I command my carcass to move. It doesn't. My arms, nothing. Fuck, I am really out. *Focus on breathing, Yinyin. Feel your bones, your muscles, your skin. Gather your qi, Yinyin.* Time passes slowly when you struggle with your own body. As movement starts to come back, I sit up. Dizzy and confused. Behind the ringing in my ear, someone calls out the bout.

Next day, Chao is back. Same confidence, same taunting smile, asking who else from my school wants to fight. I stare him down pointlessly, raise my hand while calling myself stupid from the inside. He gives me another epic, unobstructed beating. The kind a twelve-year-old should not be taking. But I stay there until one of us can't do it anymore. Myself, of course.

Later, Shifu brings me a gross healing concoction and a hot cloth to wash my bruises. He speaks softly now, like a…father, possibly. "Did you learn something, little Tigress?"

"It's…just…pain," I say, between my teeth.

"You learned that today, or yesterday?" he asks.

"Yesterday. Today I just wanted to show the bastard I wasn't scared of him."

Master sits next to me. A long gust of air, and he tells me a tale of a time past:

The first leaves began to fall in the magic forest, when a hand-tall red bird came to challenge the magnificent green dragon to a fight. Frail but brave, she ruffled her feathers and lifted her wings as if she were a big white crane. The scaley one laughed. Each of his scales alone was bigger than this puny fowl. He laughed so loud he was heard in all four capitals of China. He laughed so hard the air bursting from his mouth threw the bird against a rock, and she passed out.

Is he making fun of me? I gave him what he wanted. I faced the monster he asked. Though his voice…gentle, not punitive. Kind, even. He disinfects another one of my cuts and adds a little bit of powder to stop the bleeding, then washes my bruises with hit-wine.[19] I let him continue.

Next autumn, the senseless tiny one was back. She was a bit fuller, but still diminutive compared to her foe. Another defeat. The same the following year, and the next, and the next, until one day the challenger was as big as the dragon. "Here I am again," said the bird, as she took a stance. They battled, and people say it was the most wonderful fight ever fought in this or any other land. Through clouds, hills, and waves, the dragon attacked. He used his best moves. But the bird, who had already seen them all, avoided each blow. She even managed to hit her mighty opponent a couple of times. The combat continued for eight consecutive autumns until the dragon, old and wise enough to understand the state of things, asked for a pause. 'Perhaps we should call it a draw.'

Stunned, the little bird bowed. "Thank you, Master Dragon. For only your kindness allowed me to become better each year, and to get a draw I surely don't deserve."

He nodded. "Were you never afraid?"

"Every single time," the bird answered.

The dragon twisted his ancient beard. "Interesting. What's

---

19. Hit Wine is a traditional herbal liniment common in Chinese martial arts, where it's called Dit Da Jow, or just Jow. It contains a variety of Chinese herbs, fungi, and insects and is used to treat bruises causes by the abuse imposed on the body by martial arts practice, especially hardening techniques such as Iron Hands, where the practitioner hits hard grains, sand or rocks to build a harder fist.

your name, master bird? So people can tell your noble story
through the ages?" And she said, "I'm the Phoenix."

From that day forward, they became inseparable. The most
dynamic of all harmonies.

I glare at Shifu, struggling to grasp what he is trying to say
with another one of his made-up tales. Is he telling me to marry
the brute? The tea comes rushing back from my stomach, but I
hold it in. Desperate, I try something instead. "Ok," I say. "I'll
face him again, tomorrow."

He pats my shoulder. "No need, Tigress. You defeated the
enemy already."

Shifu smiles. Proud and gentle like I have never seen. I want
to cry. And would have, if the impulse hadn't been interrupted
by a voice coming from afar, behind him, behind the clouds,
deep in the skies. Like a thunder way beyond Wudang. "Fear is
the entire problem," says the voice Shifu doesn't seem to hear.
Then the light washes over my vision, and I'm back to the other
side.

"Yes, fear. The entire problem. Have you ever thought of it?"

Simon? Where are you? What are you talking about? Also,
why can't I fucking move?! My arms, my body... I am strapped
to the chair. Tight. How? When?

He bends down until his eye level matches mine, raises a
pocket-sized book to where I can see. The Dao Dè Jing. He flips
quickly through the pages, and from a marked one he reads:
"Because it opposes no one, no one can oppose it," he says. "This
is about science, you know? About letting data, not fear, talk.
About letting progress flow instead of getting lost opposing what
we don't understand...yet. Are you aware of how many kids die
of hunger every year? Half of what it used to be thirty years ago.
How do you call it again? Wu wei? That's it. Let life, your *Dao*,
and *progress* take its course."

Inside my head, it's all still a blur. Simon's voice echoes in the
distant background, fading slowly into oblivion. There is a brief

gap of silence. *The headaches, Yinyin, the headaches. Focus on the headaches.*

Then he's back. "Our generation may be the first to defeat death," Simon says, "which means that unless we, as a species, decide to stop mating, we will eventually outgrow the planet and have to either become multi-planetary or lose the need for a physical body. Ironic, no? Progress always forces us to make the decisions we do not want to make. Can't you see politicians all freaked out, trying to slow down science because they must understand the implications first? Even if that may be the only possible winning scenario for our own kind? Want to know the implications?"

No, I don't. I just want this to be over. The stinging, the stabbing. To know they will never come back.

Simon continues. "And this is why we have to rush. Your friends in China won't have those concerns. You Communists, for as much as we don't like to admit, are way more practical than our God-fearing nation. But what if your guys decide to partner up with the machines and dominate the whole world?[20] Yes, that may absolutely happen. It wouldn't be the first time, right? Which leads us to now. A very critical and rational now: unless we can show our investors something truly spectacular, like how our discoveries can make two desk-grown scientists fight, we will never be funded again. And then, we lose."

Lose? To whom?

"To the machines," he continues, "the Chinese…who cares."

Is he trying to offend me? Or it's the concussion?

"The suits on the board. Bunch of sissies. Were you paying attention?"

---

20. During the artificial intelligence event from MIT Review in San Francisco in 2019, the editors of the magazine had multiple debates about the risks of the rest of the world falling behind China in AI research because of lesser scientific red tape.

On a teeny device, he checks my vitals, adjusts a wire placed on my forehead and goes back to the screen. "Do you know elephants think humans are cute? Seriously, the area of the brain that fires up when they look at us is the exact same one our brain sparks when we look at puppies." He now stares at me to see if I am following. I obviously am not. "Now what do you think an artificial intelligence thinks when they see us?"

"That we are cute too?"

He laughs and goes on a tirade. About how silicon brains don't give a shit about us, carbons—men, or elephants. They may not even understand what cute means. "But if there is one pattern to follow, look at us: what do we do with inferior beings that we face with contempt? We enslave them, put them in cages, we make them into pets, coats….Carbons, with our limited brains, won't be more than a white bunny is for a kid. They say that computers will never be capable of producing transcendent art, for example, for art doesn't follow the patterns of goals assigned to the artist. And I say: there we are, you stupid bunch—they will keep us in a cage, producing art so they can realign the goals of their own algorithms!"[21]

A sound interrupts us. The hydraulic huff of the automatic doors. From my back, a gust of air conditioning ruffles my hair. I try to turn, but I can't move. My wrists are tied. My body is tied. My heart…races. What am I getting myself into? My imagination running wild, I'm thinking knives and other awful instruments coming my way, and I can't defend myself. "I need to get out! Help!"

---

21. There are a lot of interesting discussions about AI being capable of smaller levels of creativity, but not genius. Because to have genius level of creativity they need the vision one needs before establishing a goal, and AI only thinks in terms of their given goals. Harvard professor of philosophy Sean Dorrance Kelly on the *MIT Technology Review* website discusses this in his article " A Philosopher Argues That an AI Can't Be an Artist: Creativity Is, and Always Will Be, a Human Endeavor" (February 21, 2019).

Simon chortles. "Calm down, princess," he says. He swivels his chair so I can see the cute young girl with very dramatic eyes and her hair delicately secured with tiny butterfly pins and an all-white scientist outfit contrasting with her dark skin. I smile, relieved to see a familiar face, one that doesn't brag about creating a monster robot that will swallow us all; she looks down to avoid my eyes...just like the vision I had, weeks before. I try to connect, to see if she recognizes me too, but her sight keeps avoiding mine. What does she know that she doesn't want me to see?

"Yewa Kelany. *Doctor* Yewa Kelany," says Simon. "Nano-bio-roboticist, responsible for building the nanobots. We had been struggling with energy sources for a while then one day she said "quantum materials" and *bam*! We had it. A bio-electronic interface that can compute sub-threshold neuronal activity with no need of an external energy input! True genius, this little girl here."[22]

Wow. PhD? Nano bio robot shit...tsisist?[23] Who did all that...stuff? I want to tell her that's cool, and that she should never let them call her little girl again, but she avoids my eyes once more and there isn't much I can do. Is it shyness, focus or submission in front of her boss? Hard to tell. From her stainless-steel tray, Yewa takes a large syringe filled with an amber gel and I cry, "Wait!"

The sweats come back. The more agitated I get, the funnier they think it is. Simon, at least. Yewa seems more compassionate.

---

22. A 2019 study "Perovskite Nickelates as Bio-electronic Interfaces" published by Zhang, H. and others in *Nature Communications* reports the discovery of a quantum material with these exact properties.

23. Nanorobotics is a fascinating field that studies design, manufacturing, programming, and control of the nanoscale robots—including how they can be programmed as individuals and swarms, how they can cooperate, evolve, self-assemble and replicate. For a deeper perspective, read "Bio-Nanorobotics: State of the Art and Future Challenges" by Ummat, A. and others, in the 3rd Edition of the book *Tissue Engineering and Artificial Organs*.

Still avoiding my eyes, she says this is to numb my senses a little, "until your body learns to accept the bots."

Then a flash. No, please not now! These crazies are about to...

Wait. The stench. Cigarettes and booze. And sawdust. The man in khaki overalls kneeling ahead of me, trembling. The protests of that ungrateful whore. I'm back in the alley. Right where I was when I first saw this same lab. That's how I remember Yewa! The knife in my hand. I know what to do. I clench my teeth and raise the blade with a growl. The woman screams, the man pees his clothes and exhales a whine of horror. My hand shoots down.

Then back. To fluoride. To Yewa and her giant needle. I try to resist, but I am tied. Shackled. Why did I let them do it, again? The headaches, yes, the headaches. I feel dizzy. She takes the syringe out and comes with another, made of glass this time, a thick liquid inside. Of a bright translucent amber.

My eyes scan them for any sign of reluctance or guilt. "Are you sure it's safe?"

"We wouldn't be here talking to you if they weren't," says Simon. I don't trust these guys. "Seriously, if they..." He tries to explain but is interrupted by a violent cough. He brings his hand to his throat, his skin gets red, the eyes bulge like they are going to explode. More coughing. Simon stumbles, reaches to the side desk, throwing all sorts of instruments on the floor and falls on his knees. I yell, "He's suffocating!"

Fuck! I try to stand up and help but can't. Turn to Yewa. Do something, woman! Untie me or call...she shakes her head with the disgust of a fool's wife, and Simon bursts out laughing. A mad dragon's laugh. I want to kill him right now. "The nanobots are safe," he says between his recovering breath, "If you change your mind, I'll personally program them to detach from your brain. Then they will ride your bloodstream down to your liver, where they'll get filtered out of your system in your urine."

Instinctively, I squeeze my legs together and he takes that moment of distraction to shovel something past my lips. It tastes like chocolate. Really good chocolate. "You won't feel a thing, I swear," he says, then forces a yawn to make his point.

My eyes are still open, but I am dreaming too. Flying by myself, on the back of a big red phoenix, around the majestic peaks of Wudang. What did they have in that chocolate? Who cares. The clouds…so fluffy and white, I feel them licking my skin. Cold and wet and so good. The top of the mountains, the highest peaks, stick above the cotton-balls of air, raising palaces and temples so close to the roof of the universe one could easily call the immortals straight from those heights. At the same time, in the real world, I am tied to a chair, all my rights waived in a contract I could barely understand and a crazy person staring at me. *What did I do?* I ask again. I need to know the side effects. Although it feels distant now. Everything. And with the distance, the adrenaline settles. It's all a breeze now.

Yewa speaks from within the clouds, her voice so dry it soothes me. "Once the probes cross the blood-brain barrier, there is a chance your body may reject them with an attack of antibodies or even small tumors."

"Yes, there's a *small* chance of that," says Simon, from another cloud nearby. "But the headaches, those will certainly go away. What's it going to be?"

It's me and the phoenix again. We land, and the beast reaches into my head. "But the headaches, those will certainly go away. What's it going to be? But the headaches, those will certainly go away. What's it going to be? What's it going to be? What's it going to be?" I feel a pull from my face. The phoenix. She holds a red, dripping string with a white globe hanging from it. An eye. My eye. It pulsates a few times. I can feel it. The pain. The bird brings her talons next to it. Gently, she touches the skin and I hear the flesh and skin cracking. Did he say tumors?

I open my eyes, grasping for breath. Everything, everyone is doubled. The red phoenix and the green dragon whisper, each in one of my ears. "The headaches, Yinyin. That's why you're here for."

"Do it."

Simon celebrates, offering me a high five I can't respond to because I am fucking tied. He plays that classical recording again. "Le Symphonie Fantastique. Perfect, isn't it? Maybe that's our future…producing this level of wonder or being fed to their engines as biofuel." He takes the syringe from Yewa's hand. Fat, yellow, with the thickest needle I've ever seen. I look away as it pierces my skin. Simon? He watches so carefully I wonder if he's not enjoying my suffering a little too much. Done. He slips the syringe out, presses the hole with a piece of cotton, and waits for Yewa to hand him the bandage. He seems happy, even excited, sticks the Band-aid on my arm and stares back at me. Yewa presses the screen of her tablet as if initiating something. Probably whatever is happening inside my body. Where is the Phoenix when I need her? Yewa waits, but for what? Am I supposed to have a reaction? Pain? Should I already be connected to their brains? What is going to happen now? I'm about to ask when out of my side view I have the impression that something moved in the mirror.

"What d'you think?" Simon asks me.

"Not feeling anything."

"Not talking about the bots," he says. "Those will take some time, still." He taps the Band-Aid protecting the crater in my arm. A pink bandage, with drawings of adorable little ninjas.

"Ninjas are from Japan," I say, groggy and confused, but not enough to miss his idiocy, and give him a points-for-effort glance. Nice try, asshole.

"Now we wait," he says. "It takes a few days for the bots to cover the entire perimeter of your brain and start transmitting. There is a faster model that Yewa has been working on, but these are more stable. We'll keep you here in the meantime."

As I prepare to protest, something else calls my attention. Behind Simon and Yewa, the giant red Phoenix points her beak to the mirror. *What's in there*, I ask with my mind's voice. Then I see it. The silhouette of a man of ape proportions. He stares at me. The Phoenix ruffles her feathers and dives into the mirror. It ripples like water and washes my consciousness away.

10

Push the Mountain

"Are you Ok?" the voice asks. It takes me a second to recognize Yewa. I tell her yes. It's just those fluorescent lights. They bother me like nothing else. I didn't have them growing up in the mountains, hate them here—I can see them flickering, hear the annoying, constant clicking. Apparently, super nerds dig them, cause that's all there is here. Seems convincing, 'cause she stops asking.

Through our entire walk under those flickerers, she doesn't say a word. I think I like her. Silence hasn't been very present in my life recently. Though as soon as I jinx it with the thought, the speakers around every lamp start blasting the sound of a muffled and off-tone humming of the symphony we just heard. Simon. He could definitely use an auto-tune.

"Sorry, Dr. O'Dell thinks he's funny," Yewa whispers. In our giggles, we share a brief connection. Her eyes then move away once again, now carrying with them a small grin of complicity and mischief. Yes, I do like her. "How about you? Are you connected to these bugs too?"

She coughs, adjusts her shoulders as if they had been misplaced on the spine, and gazes around. Then shakes her head, rather quickly. "Why?" I ask. "You're a woman, too…that would be different from their male brains, right?"

"I am a scientist…cognitive overlap is still too high."

Not sure I buy it, but before I could insist, Simon's voice reaches another off-tone high that makes us both shriek. I cover my ears and she laughs. Then hands me a partially unwrapped Snickers bar. "Here, take this," she says. Does she want me to put on weight? I take a bite. "What if it was both you and me? Connecting…"

She continues her stride as if I said nothing.

"Are you afraid of what this can do to you?" I insist.

She scans the walls and ceiling again, clears her throat, remains quiet. At some point she needs to open up. Let's try something else. "How did they meet, Simon and Dr. Lambrechts?"

This time, she talks. "I think when he was in college, Dr. O'Dell hacked the school computer to change his grades, got caught, and instead of expelling him, Dr. Lambrechts, who was his professor, ended up offering him a job. He needed someone with good computer skills."

CLICK. The intercom again. Simon stops singing, which is a good thing. A hacker. Interesting.

I check my phone. Maybe Jason tried to call to apologize for being an idiot. No missed calls, but no signal either.

Then CLICK again. This time, Simon talks. "Some people call it cheating. I call it beating the system. You like it too, right Claudia?"

Was he listening the whole time?

Unsurprised, Yewa swipes an ID card over a sensor and the door slides open. He's right. I like to beat the system. Maybe I am a hacker too. A kung-fu hacker. A Tigress who won't wait five hundred years for its tail to turn white. But how does he know? Is he inside my brain already?

My escort politely indicates the way, and we both walk into an oddly modern apartment. White and sterile, like a cell of a psychiatric ward. Furniture is sparse and shiny enough to fit into one of those old sci-fi movies: a single bed and a fancy reading chair with a side table. There is a bathtub with a shower, a little sink and a toilet in the back too, all open. A boxing heavy-bag, also white.

Next to the bed, an oxygen tank and a bowl with chocolates of all kinds. "Your brain's activity will grow at a logarithmic speed. You'll need glucose and O_2 so it doesn't collapse and atrophy out of exhaustion. Eat the candy, sleep with the oxygen." She turns to the heavy bag. It's still swinging. She slaps it and her twiggy wrist collapses at the impact. "Thought you would like to…you know…do your thing?" She massages her hand—that must have hurt. I ask her about her job. Does she really design those little tower thingies in our heads?

"I conduct the studies, enter the data. It's the system that designs the shapes and tests them in a simulator, to be honest."[24]

"So, to fight robots, you use their help?" I ask.

"Science has a too-much-trust issue, I guess," she responds.

This is like challenging a big guy for a fight and asking him to train you for that same bout. I feel for her. Yewa doesn't seem to have much power in the games they are playing. "They're going to fix your brain," she says.

The headache. The headache. The headache. I get rid of it, it's all going to be worth it. I'll be free. "How exactly are they gonna fix it?" I ask, trying not to freak out.

"Here's the irony," she says. "It would take humans decades to decipher and identify the patterns from the data the nanobots are collecting. So we'll use artificial intelligence to do it quicker. Then we can use electric impulses to teach your cortex to fire differently."

Irony? This is my brain she is talking about. "You're gonna

---

24. Molecular design uses atoms as materials. It includes finding the right physical structure and the chemical reactions that will link up the atoms. This is a field in which AI thrives, because there's a clear sense of goal and ways to measure the efficiency of each solution. (Reading: "AI for Molecular Design" By Jeff Carbeck in *Scientific American*, September 14, 2018.)

trust the enemy to decide what happens in my brain? You just said sometimes you trust too much! Why can't you go there yourself and reprogram it or something? No one told me you would let these things define what to do with my head!"

They haven't told me a lot of things, apparently.

Yewa sits down and tries to hold my hand. No way, lady. Her voice, however, seems sincere. I let her explain.

"In a certain way, our understanding of the brain and AI is very similar. We know what goes in, have a good notion of what happens inside, and know what comes out. But exactly how they process the information and the path to each decision, most of the time we just don't know. In most cases, they're just a big black box. Both. That's why there is so much concern about the rise of a digital super intelligence in the future. If AI develops to that point, we will have no idea how it's going to be shaped, therefore we can't predict how it's gonna see us. As friends, foes, slaves—or if they will be totally indifferent. But in the short term, until they awaken, and in specific cases like yours, with limited scope and repeatable circumstances, like remapping patterns to avoid head- aches, it's perfectly safe. Because what you have isn't a hardware problem, like when a computer comes with a broken piece. It's a software bug, something went wrong when your brain was pro- grammed, and it causes it to fire unnecessary signals that cause this horrible pain. And we can redirect those and fix you. That's what matters now."

The heavy bag isn't properly anchored to the ceiling, I notice. Stupid eggs. I was hoping they know more about brains than they know of fighting, but I am starting to question that. Have I made a mistake? A huge one? A few punches, a kick, a hard kick that startles my host. Sigh. The good news: the bag remains in place. For a short time, it should be Ok. And there's choco- late. "So, you said this is supposed to be like a vacation before we start?"

She doesn't respond. When I look back, there is no one there. "Yewa?" The door is sealed. No handle, no button to open, only a numeric keypad. I bang the door, hard, kick it with all my strength, but it doesn't even vibrate. Punch some numbers and nothing. *Fuck.* I yell, "Can anybody hear me?" The air gets thinner and I feel...dizzy. What is going on? The oxygen. Need some oxygen. I grab the mask, twist the valve, try to calm down. It helps. Breathing always helps. Then, out of the corner of my eyes, I notice his presence: the camera above my head. I can almost see Simon blinking through it. "Hey, what the fuck is this, asshole?!"

To my surprise, he responds. "Sorry, Claudia. Safety first," says his canned voice coming from the intercom. "You'll be out before you know it, I promise."

"Screw your promise. Let me out of here!"

Bang! I kick the door again. It doesn't budge.

"Won't work," he says.

Through the wires, we stare at each other. The silence is heavy and thick, but I can sense him. All-powerful behind walls and screens. "Why am I in here, really?"

All quiet. The numeric pad beside the door: I type more random numbers. I don't even know how many digits, but I have to try.

"It's important that you are nearby. In case of malfunction," the speakers say.

Great.

"Just take it easy. Get some rest, eat your candy. We'll get you when it's time."

And with that, the intercom switches back off.

CLICK.

11

Electric Sheep

As soon as she says it, the subtitle shows under Yewa's face: "Can we play a game?" She notices my eyes bouncing up and down and tells me not to concern myself with the caption. "They're for my records. To document the experiment so no one needs to take notes."

The experiment. Me.

She asks how my sleep was, how was I feeling. Both questions and answers are properly registered on-screen. "You forgot to wear your mask to sleep. Must be feeling weak," she says. "Have some candy, use your O_2 now. That will make you feel better."

Chocolate. I don't get the West's obsession with it, but somehow the brain likes it. At the simple mention of the word, I salivate. She takes a silent note as if she had heard that thought, asks about my dreams.

Dreams?

"Yep. It's a good way to learn your brain's lexicon. We registered the electric pulses already. Knowing what you remember will help us decode some images, feelings, ideas. For example, if you tell me you dreamt of a mountain, then an elephant, it helps 'cause we can search for reports on other subjects and find neural patterns that will tell us how and where *your* brain codifies mountains and elephants into electric pulses. And it even unveils cognition patterns around concepts like big or small, moving or static, living or…anyway, I'm not here to bore you. Just know that: the more details, the better."[25]

"Did they make you stay up all night monitoring me?" I ask. She seems confused. "The clothes," I explain, "you're still wearing the same."

"Don't worry about me. Do you remember any dreams?"

I do. A very vivid one.

"That's normal," she says.

"You know dreams, they're confusing," I tell her. "I'm watching TV somewhere. The news. The internet stopped again. Political parties, investment banks, e-commerce…all down. The stock market is unstable. I think this is unexpected, but don't care much. Weirdly, I'm not in front of the TV. It's more like I'm inside of it. Part of it. Then, it switches. To banks and power plants. I rate them. Efficiency, I think—how much effort it takes for something, I don't know. There's an explosion. Three, actually. Images of people screaming. Too much attention, I add to a file—too much distraction."

"That's so odd," I say, as my eyes move up from my own captions and find hers squinted and distant. "Is it helping?"

"Yes, yes yes. You're doing great," Yewa replies with an unconvincing smile. "Keep going."

The room is so small, it only takes me a few steps to get to the heavy bag. The camera tracks me and even zooms onto my face. "This is so fucked up…." I say, trying a few jabs. "It was as if I were living inside the internet. Actually, as if I were part of it." I try to continue, but the memories are so sparse and confusing.

---

25. Neuroscientist and Berkeley professor Jack Gallant is conducting fascinating studies in this field. His team uses computer models to decode movie trailer images from a brain using functional Magnetic Resonance Imaging (fMRI). (See "Reconstructing Visual Experiences from Brain Activity Evoked by Natural Movies" by Shinji Nishimoto Current Biology Journal, September 22, 2011)

I punch harder, kick a few times. "I think I sent a message to someone. About banks and power plants, getting their priority lowered. To *use only as needed.* Then, there's a beep, a warning. A camera. A spy camera. There was a couple, they were eating, and I am trying to understand their reactions to the food. But wait—"

My hands drop slowly, and the bag is left swinging alone, uninterrupted. The chains holding it to the ceiling crackle their own tic-toc and that is the only sound in the room. On screen, the empty subtitles register my silence. "It was me on the spy camera. Jason and me. The computers were spying on us."

From the other side of the screen, Yewa gives me a reassuring smile. "This is just your brain testing scenarios," she says. "Pretty normal. Neuroscientists say dreaming is our natural virtual reality. A trick evolution designed so we can learn in safety. I don't see anything worth worrying about."

Nothing to worry about? I kick the bag so hard it almost hits the ceiling.

She tries to reassure me. Says my recollection of the images is remarkable. That we can accelerate the process by weeks, maybe even months, with this level of detail. "We never got that much from anybody before, she says, "So, how did you meet your boyfriend? Jason, right?"

In fighting, we call it changing levels. You throw a few jabs on the face as a distraction, then dive down to grab the legs. Or the other way around. "Is this part of the experiment?" I ask.

"Just curious," she says.

I tell her the story about the day he went to the park, just like Mrs. Lee said he would. How he almost fought a few guys mocking our Tai Chi.

"That's sweet," she says.

No, it wasn't. I need no boyfriend to save me. Given her constricted laugh, I guess she'd foreseen my response. But that wasn't what he was trying to do though. "He said he was saving *them.*

The dudes mocking us. He could tell I was getting pissed. He's a fighter too, you know?"

From behind the glass, Yewa presses a button. "A fighter?" There were no subtitles this time.

"Kind of," I say. "Brazilian Jiu Jitsu. Grappling shit. But only at the gym—he doesn't like to compete." Still no subtitles. Interesting. I tell her he likes the self-development part, but hates the idea of someone wanting to hurt him. "He's a Buddhist, you know?"

"Is that's why you like him?"

That makes me think. On our first date, at a wine bar that only played some sort of sexy Brazilian music, we somehow mostly talked about fighting. On our second, I asked him if he could teach me some stuff to improve my ground game. And he offered to show it to me. A real intention, I remember. So we go to my apartment. It's not too long until I have him wrapped between my legs, as he teaches me about close guard. And that's when I realized how handsome he was.

A wave of warmth washes over my face and I don't know how to conceal it.

"Humm," Yewa says, as she had heard every thought, even though I am pretty sure I didn't say any of that. I catch her observing her little tablet again, then me. "What are you doing?" I ask.

"Tracking your neural activity. Whatever you're remembering is really firing your entire brain."

"Do we really need to do this?"

She bounces back and forth between me and her little screen and lets slip a hint of naughtiness. "Is he the one?" She asks. Despite how personal things were getting, she still managed to keep her cool—a mix of scientific-cold and friendly warmth. I get it now: we're in a duel, that's her game. So I refuse to answer. I refuse to think about it, even. (Like meditation, fighting teaches you to clear your mind on cue. So I do.)

Given her expression, the screen must have impressed her again. She tries another angle. "You say he's a fighter. Did he ever teach you anything useful or that was all an excuse to hang out?"

It wasn't an excuse. But he was on my guard and things got crazier and…Suddenly, we were kissing and spent the night having sex. The entire night. *Shut up Yinyin, this woman can hear your thoughts, remember?* "He taught me a lot of things," I say. "To protect myself on the ground, to be patient, protect my position and look for an opportunity to finish the fight…" She keeps bouncing her gaze between me and the tablet seeming like she was catching every inch of my lies. "And to keep my hooks in too."

"What?"

Damn, that's why I stick with fighters. I explain the joke: when we spoon at night, he hooks his legs inside of mine, as if he was attacking my back. "An instinct, I guess."

"And when did you know he was a keeper?"

Wow—she's relentless. I tell her she would make a good fighter—probably the best compliment I can give to someone—but she seems more interested in what's happening inside my brain. "You're still recording everything, aren't you?" I ask.

She nods—subtitles are off just to make me less self-aware. At least she's honest.

"When I thought he was a keeper? Maybe when he brought up the i-Ching," I tell her. "A Buddhist using a Daoist tradition, that was the most romantic thing I've ever had happened to me. You know, those two religions compete a little…"

"What did it say, the i-Ching? Do you remember?" She asks without skipping a beat.

Is she made of steel? "I do. Clearly," I tell her. It was *feng, the fullness before the emptying.*

Our little rituals in China. I miss them sometimes. Kung fu, tea, some meditation, the Dao De Jing, and finally, the i-Ching…Shifu used to throw the i-Ching for me too.

The speakers play the clicking noise of a keyboard and a few letters materialize between us. "Feng. Is this the one?" she asks.[26]

Hexagram 55, unchanged:
Feng, fullness.
Thunder and lightning culminate as one.
A noble one decides legal proceedings and brings about punishment.
Do not mourn. A fitting sacrifice at noon.
What decisions must you take now?

Sacrifice. Mourning. Jason. At the hospital, he said he didn't want to be around to see me die. Is that what the Dao was trying to tell me back then? About the decisions we must make? "Yes, it was that one."

"I'm sorry," Yewa says. "Didn't want to upset you." She presses a few keys again and takes a stiffer posture this time. "How about your students? Can you describe them to me?"

Not sure I want to, but she insists. Just so she can be able to map my emotions a bit more, she says. So I tell her about Mrs. Lee, my landlord and very first student. The woman who brought me to the hospital the day I tried to head-butt the planet to placate my pain. And Camara, who is an old soul in the body of a fifteen-year-old girl. Kira, a super smart mathematics Ph.D. candidate who loves flowers, always wanted to learn how to fight but had to wait until she left home—her parents thought martial arts were for boys only. Jen, an MBA student I am still trying to figure out. The twins Linds and Ash, two identical and annoyingly pretty baristas from a Starbucks nearby, the kind who

---

26. A curiosity: When I got to this point in the story I used an online i-Ching to get a response I could use as inspiration. Feng was the response I got. It seemed like a perfect match to what I was planning to write next. Very reassuring.

make fish drown and geese fall from the sky.[27] "They named themselves the Pink Warriors," I say, while I laugh to myself.

"Why is it funny?"

"They have a long wait to go until they are worth being called warriors. But they are getting more comfortable with contact."

"You're proud of them, aren't you?"

"Is that what the machine is telling you?"

She gives me one of those reluctant smiles you let slip when you get caught cheating. I can relate to that. Not a people person myself, either.

That's when the flash hits. Brighter than any of the lab's fluorescent lights. Brighter than anything.

We are in class now, me in the front, the ladies following. Around us, curious looks of all kinds. My weight shifts, arms follow—one extends forward, hand like a blade, the other rises back, in a gentle hook. The legs push forward in a slow, long and deliberate stretch. The Single Whip, I say. Somewhere behind me, that causes a moan. Of the erotic type. Mrs. Lee, of course.

"What brings peace in life?" I ask the class behind me.

"Friendship," responds Linds.

"Independence," says Jen.

"Weed!" tries Mrs. Lee. "And good granola, of course!"

"Balance," I respond. "Yin, yang. Being unmovable like a mountain, fluid like a stream." I drop my stance and proceed with the form, at the pace of an old, wise turtle. Right Heel Kick,

---

27. Being an immigrant myself, I am highly aware of how unique local idioms can be. Expressions that were normal to me in Brazil sound hilarious to my friends from other parts of the world. Others that are natural for Americans always make me chuckle. I wanted to bring some of them to this story, being aware that overusing them would kill the authenticity of it (I am not Chinese, after all), but not having any would also feel very fake, because translating our home idioms is a natural part of the process of being a transplanted citizen. This expression, beautiful enough to make fish drown in the water and geese fall from the sky" seemed like a good one to include here. It is the equivalent to the American "drop dead gorgeous"—close enough to be understood, strange enough to be received with a smile.

Ride the Tiger to the Mountain…they think the names of Tai Chi positions are cute.

"Yang is our aggressive energy," I explain. "The kind Westerner life is already so full of."

Turn, Left Heel Kick. A group of frat boys mimics us at a distance. "Ignore the assholes. I'll beat them later. Stay with me, girls. Lower your right leg, move your entire body onto it and arch your hand up from below, to the other side. Snake Creeps Down. Good. Now raise the knee into a rooster pose and stand on Single Leg." I hold that position and adjust my elbow an inch inward. "Today I want you to channel your…softness. Your yin. Relax your external shell and let your qi…flow. Gentle and constant…a shadow that can't be caught."

A peek behind. They aren't doing that bad. Needle at the Bottom of the Sea, Fan Through the Back. "Surrender the hardness of the body to the faintness of the spirit. Because there…is… no…body."

Mrs. Lee moans once more. "This is so sexy," she says. Others laugh and I shush them quiet. Had they known my mind never stops screaming…Where was I? "Uh…keep going. Be present. For the Dao knows no past…or future."

Flash!

As the lights recede, I freeze. Did Yewa's signals capture this? Is she going to think I'm crazy? But we aren't at the White Room. Everything is flat and of either a vibrant green or blue, now. Made of glass, or metal…or light? Four creatures stand in front of me. Cubes attached to cubes of different sizes and luminosities. Little faces, big eyes. They extend their hands and the light blinds me again.

Back to California, to Tai Chi. Have they noticed my absence? And wait, if this is a memory, did I just jump to another memory or I had that lapse while I was there? My head spins, I grip my toes on the floor. In the corner of my eye, a pretty guy now seems to be having an altercation with the frat boys.

THE GIRL FROM WUDANG

"What was I saying? No past, no future. Just the…"

Another flash. I remember wondering if I was drinking too much coffee. No, that would have made me poop. I am in a large green prairie now, made of the same glossy colors, the same flat surface. Life seems calm, quiet and very geometric. I linger over a sharp-edged fence stretching to infinity. A video game? Why would I be inside a video game?! That stupid geek world game… Mindcrack or something. Yes! The same game Simon showed me in the Lab. What am I doing here? Breathe, Yinyin. Wait! Breathe what? I pull the air into my lungs—nothing. My heart halts for a second. Where's the air? My sight spins, the world darkens. But then my hand is pulled. The creatures. Like cubic people, but longer arms and…tails! Monkeys! They look at me, unphased, and somehow that calms me down. The blue one says hello without moving its mouth and I have no idea what's going on. He points ahead, and we march to the gate, me and the ape. There are pigs too. Pink and square. Millions of them. Up on the hills, along the horizon, and all the way to the little wooden gate. "They are locked up, aren't they?" I think but don't say. The Monkey nods. Unaware of the danger, I open the gate. "Go, little fellas. Enjoy your fake life!"

The stampede almost runs over my head. I feel my hand crushed. My leg smashed, my shoulder cracking. It's so much pain, I squeeze my spirit out of my own head and then I am floating a few feet above myself. I can see the pigs running over my body, until they are all gone and only the little monkey remains. "Now you are free too," I hear myself telling him. "No more raising pigs, you don't need them, you know? You never did." He tilts his head, confused. Or amused. Can't tell. I dive back into my own sight. Around us, more apes get close and sit, contemplating our every move as if we were a totem. Gods, even. Then, from afar, as if coming from the clouds, I glance into my own eyes. Dive inside of them. Through the darkness of my pupils and deep inside my brain. This must be a dream. From above, I see Berkeley, the park. Pathetic human versions of dogs chase their flying toys. Among them, a group of slow-moving creatures seems to be practicing Tai Chi. Myself, my students. I am trying to hide the flashes. But I tumble instead.

Butt on the grass. The Pink Warriors run around me like coked-up squirrels. "Water! Give her some water!" one says. "I have green tea," cries another. "Would kombucha work?" I have no idea what just happened, what I have just seen or why. Just know I can't talk about the flashes. No one wants a crazy person who has visions of being in a video game driving their brains through a moving meditation session. Is that what is happening? Am I going crazy? Is that what I get for having challenged Shifu? Or for joining this sick brain experiment? It can't be, the experiment…it hasn't happened yet.

"I am fine!" I say, picking the least damaging of the reasons I could think. "Got distracted by the names of the positions, lost balance, that's all."

"Are you sure?" asks a skinny dude out of nowhere. A nerd. No, a hipster with pointy ears. Is there a name for that creature in between? He wears a scarf around his neck and a Mandela shirt. "You Ok?" He sounds soft, gentle and…familiar?

"Did the headache…" he starts to ask, and I tell him no. There's a certain authority in the way he speaks. It's him! Jason! I try to grab reality back. What is going on?

"Oh, how are you doing Doctor…Sonderup?" Says Mrs. Lee. With all the pauses I needed to understand the coup that was taking place. The girls look at me and burst into a naughty giggle. Mrs. Lee winks, "Maybe it's her *internal* temperature going up?" He blushes, checks my pulse. A touch so soft I feel soft too. His look is so kind and gentle I feel kind too and…no, I don't. I attempt to stand. Lightheaded, dizzy, but I am getting up. No. Someone presses my shoulder down and I fall back on my butt.

"Her name is Claudia," says Ash, forcefully.

He nods, "I remember." Jason offers to help me stand, his

hand and eyes glued to the images painted in my arms. The same ones he noticed before. He must have really liked them. He touches the bold Tigress, standing fiercely on her back paws as she is hemmed in by a swarm of bees. Then the black monkey observing the fight. Then the mountains observing them all and the clouds ignoring everything because they had somewhere else to go. He marvels at my tattoo, enchanted to the point of forgetting to help me get up.

Then I'm back. The lab, the White Room. Yewa stares at me with her computer eyes. "Is everything Ok?" I ask her.

"Why?" she asks back, as if there hadn't been anything out of the ordinary. Not to her eyes, nor to her monitors. Though for me, there had. It certainly has. My mind feels mushy, my muscles tired. "I need a break," I say.

"Of course," she says. "Have some oxygen."

She's right. The moment the air flows, I feel better. Behind my closed eyelids, I think of Jason, Mrs. Lee, the Pink Warriors. What are they doing? Then I hear a bell and sit up. It doesn't come from the door—rather, from the other side of the room—the dining table against the wall. How long have I been out? Time is weird in this place. A small, square window opens on the wall and a little white box slips in. I peek at the camera over the dead TV monitor, then the screen turns on again. Yewa is back. "Ready for some motor skills tests?"

12

Cross Hands

There are no windows in the white room. No clocks either. Hard to tell what time it is. All I have are the lights. When they turn them off, I go to sleep. Turn them on, I wake up. The secret is to stay busy, and slow. Punch the bag to release anger, Tai Chi to cope with boredom, some sugar and oxygen to keep my brain from dying. When they send food, I eat. When they ask questions, I pretend to answer. Then there is the stupidest part, what they call *motor skills tests*.

"You may feel a bit disoriented," Yewa says, "but that's normal." Nerds, put on some gloves and find out what disorientation really is. Or have your brain sting itself from the inside. Or lose track of what's memories, what's present. *Wait, do they know about them? The flashes?*

On the first day they send a box with blue and yellow spheres, the size of snooker balls. They come through a hole in the wall, with instructions to put them in front of me and focus on the yellow ball. Then reach out to it with my left hand, put it back. Close my eyes. Think about the yellow ball again. Reach out to where I think it is. Open my eyes. Guess which one I have? The yellow one.

Duh.

Remember the headaches, Yinyin. Remember, the headaches. They are going to get rid of your headaches and you won't need to worry about having them during a fight ever again. Maybe even the flashes will go away with them too.

Then lights go off and I go to sleep, wake up and start all over again. Second day comes and it's the same thing.

Good morning, White Room.

A little workout, eating, but this time Yewa walks in herself, asks me to sit and requests permission to ask a few questions. "For calibration only."[28] She asks about Jason again and I tell her about all the things he taught me about fighting on the floor. No naughty details, though. Just the basics. Hip escapes, body triangles, different kinds of chokes, staying cool when things look bad, moving inch by inch toward a better position....Every night, a different lesson. It was good to be learning something new. And he was good at it. His passion for fighting, even if in a non-competitive way, helped him understand my dreams and accept my job. He was even a bit jealous, I suspect. At least until the day of the blackout, when the pervert sliced my tattoo. "That's when he started to worry. Like, seriously worry. At that point, no matter how much I explained that a warrior had to be willing to die, he just wouldn't understand. The irony: if he had to go to a war zone for humanitarian services, he could. Isn't it the same thing?"

Men...

---

28. Computer-Brain Interfaces require a lot of learning, from both the brain and the computer side, so the combined system can learn to interpret signals and consequences of different kinds of brain activity. A recent story in the *New York Times Magazine* covered examples of successful experiments ranging from people writing entire sentences with just their brains, to piloting a drone, to fist bumping president Barak Obama with a robotic hand. All that comes from the combination of the physical interface, the computational power to process the data, but also the training of both the person and the machine to perform the actions as the patient originally intended. ("The Man Who Controls Computers With His Mind" by Ferris Jabr, May 12, 2022)

Yewa agrees. "Can I see it? The tattoo?" That one seemed sincere. Not for testing purposes, I mean.

"It's pretty," she says.

And finally, the stupid *skills test*. I gaze at the billiards in different colors. She checks her systems, tells me to look the other way and grab the blue one and I do. She gives me a funny look. "What?" I ask. She points down to my hands.

For the second time, or third, I don't know anymore, they almost cause my heart to a halt. Fact is, I have a fucking black sphere in my hand. Not the blue one I thought I had. This can't be right. I try one more time, now looking at them as I reach, but my hands just go the other way. Now I'm hyperventilating and she tells me to grab the oxygen mask. "What is going on here?" I try to say with my widened look. She taps the screen again, tells me to go for the red sphere this round, and I pick the right one. "Good," she says.

"Good?" I reply from inside the mask, then yank it off altogether. "I'm losing my most basic coordination and you think that's fucking good? Do you know what I do for a living?"

She promises it was just a small test and that I am good again. "Do something harder now," she challenges me. "I don't know, a flying kick or something."

I place her behind the heavy bag, bracing it with her entire body, take a distance, and pounce. My feet leave the floor, the knee rises up to the ceiling and when I am close enough, I stretch the foot forward. Fast and relaxed, but with all the energy I can. *Let's see if I miss this one.* Gladly, I don't. The bag swings and pushes Yewa flying four feet back, almost hitting her head on the wall. Why did they put me in such a small room? "See?" She says, pretending it was nothing. Then continues, "So, why are you doing this?"

As if she didn't know. "The headaches," I answer. "They promised to get rid of them."

She insists. "I mean everything. The fighting, the risks, the teaching, even moving to America."

"I want to change fighting for women," I say. Feels so silly and obnoxious when you put it in words....I try again: "I want to be the one who makes men afraid of us."

Yes, that feels more right.

"But why?" she insists.

Is she a robots-chick or a shrink? "Because if they had been afraid, I would have met my mother. How about you? Why are *you* doing this?"

She didn't expect such a fast counter, huh? Yewa pauses, thinks before she says anything, and her voice turns a few pitches lower, "Because the alternative is worse."

A few taps on the tablet, and she turns the screen to me, a page of the San Francisco Chronicle on the Cyber Blackout Aftermath. On the very top, a big photo of a massive fire blazing the landscape in Northern California, not too distant from us."

"They say the fire is...."

Yewa nods. "Berkeley specialists are now confident it wouldn't have happened if the safety systems hadn't failed."

My stomach turns, she scrolls the screen down a bit more.

"Russia Nuclear Plant explosion can be one of the worst nuclear accidents of the decade;" and "Why would hackers delete student data in Denmark?"; Another one reads "In panic, banks rush to print all records, causing a surge in the price of paper;" and "Beijing accuses the U.S. of being behind the hacking of its water supply, promises to deepen cyber war efforts—White House threatens to expel all Chinese residents." The list continues beyond the limits of her screen. "Smaller blackouts and hacks are happening everywhere. It's too late now," she says. "Those creatures are still out there and given how fast they're learning to hide and adapt, we don't have too much time. The race has started." Then she stops, and it's like her sight is swept to the ground. "If we win," she says, "we humans may end up losing our individuality, but, as Dr. Lambrechts says, that's still better than slavery."

"In a battle of yangs, yin waits," I mumble. "Wanna know the story of my tattoo?"

☯   ☯   ☯

Deep between the peaks of Wudang, there was a river with water so fresh, all animals came to drink. The river was the life of the valley, and its stream welcomed everyone. Except for one spot— where the shade was best and the water was coolest. There, only one was allowed: the powerful queen of the conglin, ruler of all things yang and yin, divine wearer of stripes: the mighty Tigress.

Until one day.

Coming back from a hunt, the mighty Queen was intercepted by a black creature crossing her path. She pounced, but by the time she reached it the intruder had already hidden among the shrubs. The Shadow Monkey, the Queen thought.

Knowing the simian's fame—wisdom, mischief and maybe a touch of cowardice—she gave him her loudest roar. Then waited, but only silence responded.

"Spineless," she said to herself, before resuming her stride. Though nine steps down, the audacious creature crossed her path for a second time.

"How dare you invade my territory?" she roared, eager to tear the insolent into pieces. Then, as tigers do, she waited for something to move. Just a faint sign of life and that would be it.

Nothing.

Some sense must have made its way into that clown's head —she thought. So the queen marched ahead. But as soon as she relaxed, the sneaky animal did it again, his shadow now crossing straight through the queen's mouth, as if teasing her with its bodyless body.

"Enough!" Now Tigress was furious. She paced and roared. "Show your face, filthy demon!"

"Here, your highness," said a squeaky voice from the top. "I mean no disrespect."

The Tigress gazed up at the stirring foliage as the creature revealed himself: black-furred, big-eyed, flimsy. "The mysterious Shadow Monkey indeed, wise wanderer of those bands. "What are you doing in my path, sad little vagabond?"

He rose a bit higher on the tree. "I bring a warning, your majesty."

Tigress cackled so loud the birds, for miles, flew in fear. "And what on Earth or in the heavens would warrant me a warning, silly creature?"

The feline crouched.

"Wait, wait, wait!" begged the Shadow Monkey, hanging from a branch that was not high enough. He looked straight into her yellow eyes and said: "There's a devil in your favorite shade, majesty. I told her the spot belongs to the mightiest. But the creature laughed at me. Said no one would have the guts to move her away."

The almighty feline jerked its head to the side. What kind of animal would risk saying such a thing? An ancient dragon from the heavens? Another tiger with no love for life? A phoenix who expects rebirth? She strode. Fast and strong. Letting her steps echo ahead, roaring rowdily to let the intruder know. Whoever it was, the queen was returning to reclaim her place.

But then, when she arrived, there was nothing there. Just a strange earthy fruit dangling from a branch above the edge of the river. She faced the ape. "Are you looking to die early, buffoon?"

But the monkey showed no laughter. "Shhhh," he said, and leaped to the top of an oddly tall kumquat tree. He tugged a small yellow fruit and threw it right at the hanging mud ball. At first, nothing happened. Then, one second later, a loud buzz echoed ahead. The earth ball, roughly the size of the queen's majestic head, began to shake, and from inside came a cloud of tiny flying creatures, each with the same yellow and black stripes as the queen.

"Who dares to invade my territory?" said Tigress, ready to strike once again.

The shapeless haze of bees mocked her in one voice: "Who dares to invade my territory?" They laughed.

Tigress gazed around, and for a moment, allowed her neck to sink into her shoulders. But, since tigers only know one way to deal with confusion, she pounced. Perfectly. One leap, one hit, and the hive was cracked on the ground, its amber blood oozing away into the stream.

But then, despite the rage of the striped ruler of Wudang, the bees pounced their own little stripes too. An army of thousands, fearlessly throwing themselves and their tiny venomous edges, stabbing the great enemy in a collective suicide, for all bees die heroes when they lose their stingers.

Strike after strike, the mighty feline sent more lifeless bugs crashing onto the multicolored pebbles beneath. In the dozens, hundreds. Yet there were others. There were always more to join the black and yellow swirl of yang.

Around them, from every little gap and branch, a different creature watched in awe. All the aggressive energy of the universe, attacking itself with such fury. Yang versus yang. Yang plus yang. Unmatched. Unbalanced. Unharmonious.

Even the mountains stared in disbelief.

They battled until the last bee fell dead. And then, suddenly, silence. Real silence.

At first, Tigress roared with pride. But soon she felt the burn coursing inside her veins. Dizzy and weak, she sensed her qi fading away. Her head burning, the pain dropping to her heart and leaking behind her fur as the coldest sweat.

Finally, the queen fell dead too.

Within those sacred mountains of Wudang, home of the enlightened, birthplace of Tai Chi, the only sound alive was the voice of nothing. Like in the day before the Dao broke into Heaven and Earth and gave birth to life. No creature dared to breathe.

No wind dared to blow, and for a moment, even the river went still. So the Shadow Monkey came down from his branch, hopped over the bodies, and drank the cool water himself.

☯   ☯   ☯

Technically, nothing's changed in the White Room. The air still smells like chlorine. The light is still the same flickering bulb. The walls and furniture, exactly the same stark white. Still, the world is different. Somberer. As if the weight of our motives for being there was now squeezing our lungs from all directions.

"This is really fucked up," Yewa says.

It may have been the only time I've ever heard her curse.

13
Step Over Seven Stars

My gaze lowers in respect and my hands wrap around each other in the Daoist gesture of the Yin Yang, but I refuse to stop. "Please, listen, Shifu!" I don't wait for permission. "Remember how you told me Bruce Lee changed fighting when he made white men stop bullying the Chinese because they may know kung fu? And how he did that even though he had only a fraction of the power you and your Phoenix friends had when you were young?"

Shifu pauses in silence—probably the closest to a permission I will ever get for this little insurrection of mine.

"Yesterday, the spirits of all the animals of China came to visit me at the Insights Grove and I realized I too must travel to become the immortal you want me to become. Find other sources of inspiration and create my own style. Test it in real situations, against people who know nothing of what kung fu can do, people who know things I've never seen done. Test my ideas until they work."

Not even Shifu would dare to challenge the ancient spirits of Wudang.

"I know what to do, Shifu. In honor of my mother, I must create my style, teach it, make it so famous the world will respect

117

not only me but all women, because they may know my kung fu too. And remember how you said I was poised to either die young or be the first immortal of our clan? If I achieve that, people will know me, they will have my picture on the walls of their schools, they will discuss my ideas for generations, so when my eclosion comes and its time I reach the Dao, their memories will make my soul eternal like you want me to be."[29]

My heart is racing. *Shut up, Yinyin. Wait. Let him talk now.*

He waits. Pondering or just to torture me, I'm not sure. Then walks a set of steps that reminded me of the Bugang dance[30] he liked to do when things got too out of control. "This style of yours....Do you have any original idea yet?" He asked.

"I don't. But the animals in China have come to tell me ..."

He draws a line on the sand, grabs six coins from his pockets—five identical, plus a darker one—and throws them up. Shifu knows the i-Ching by memory, so by the time he collected the coins back, he knew the read already.

"Feng. Fullness," he says, solemnly. "Everything flows, nothing abides."

Abundance, he lectures me on it. On how the Zenith requires one to let go. How, in order to understand fullness, one must accept the imminence of the emptying. "Are you ready for that change, Tigress?"

On my knees, I beg him for advice. "I don't want to become

---

29. Daoists are obsessed with immortality. Their version of it. I was told they treat the end of life as the beginning of a new one—not as reincarnation, but a different stage of our existence, in another plane. They don't even call it death, but Yuhua, a word that originally comes from the act of ecloding, like a butterfly emerging from its chrysalis. Now, it's used to represent the ascension to heaven to become an immortal—although only the best ones would; the rest may go to hell or decompose to dust, the five elements of the universe.

30. The Bugang Dance is a Daoist Ritual that connects the priest to the stars, in particular the Big Dipper, who are considered gods. It is usually a ceremony performed by a group of priests together. In the scene where Shifu performs it by himself to find an answer to whether Yinyin should move to America or not, I wondered if he was also connecting to his friends...in America.

empty, Shifu. I've barely started to become filled."

"It may be time for a new master, and a new mountain, Tigress," he says, with eyes glistering more than usual. "But do nothing for now. I need to do something myself first." My stomach turns. Was he so angry he just expelled me? Was Wudang pissed at my arrogance? Were the animals from my vision just demons testing my will? It was the end of that conversation. The Dao has spoken, and so has he. Waiting was my only choice.

In a way, I won, but it didn't feel like it.

"Where is he now, your Shifu?" Yewa asks, her voice coming out of nowhere, startling me so much I almost fall from my seat.

"One week after I arrived in America, he died," I tell her.

She whispers something unintelligible, which the subtitles translate to "I'm sorry."

I am too.

☯   ☯   ☯

Of everything, sleeping is still the hardest part of the routine. Especially when the interrogation throws me so violently onto my most painful memories. Did my ego cause all that? Shifu's death, these creatures released into the world? I shut my eyes and let darkness settle. Darkness and stillness. My conscience, I drag into the breathing. *Xin, ping, qi, he,* I guide myself. *Heart, peace, breath, harmony.*

Nothingness, welcome to my mind.

Suspended in the air, I float weightless in a gloomy semi-dream. No intention or need. Just letting the Dao speak. Afar, a dim light invites my attention. What is the universe trying to tell me now?

Wu wei, I think. Action without action. The currents bring me to the bright spot in the corner of my mind and put me somewhere else. It looks like the office space in the building, where my spirit hovers behind the shoulder of a man: Dr. Simon

O'Dell—he likes late nights in the lab. There is music, and lights, and I think I can hear his thoughts, somehow. The empty floor, his quiet kingdom. His favorite symphony blasting at the heights it deserves. He watches a live feed of the White Room. A live feed of me, training. Landings at twenty-two percent are marked in red in the upper corner. He seems disappointed. But keeps watching, searching for something.

What is the Dao trying to tell me?

"Nice axe kick," he observes. "Like the cockroach!" Simon toggles to another window and presses play. "Such a beauty," he voices in his own head. The images on the screen, I recognize them, somehow. A roach and a wasp, fighting, wrestling. *Let go, Yinyin. Whatever it is, let the Dao be.*

Roaches are known to be among the most resilient creatures on the planet, and an entire department of Oak Tree Technologies' bio enhancement division is dedicated to them. There's something to be said about them. We humans like to see ourselves as the winners of the evolutionary war, but bugs, with their simple neurological circuits made purely for survival constitute a much larger part of the planet than we do. In biomass terms, victory is theirs. Weird. Does it have to do with the visions of the animals in Wudang? I mean, there are Praying Mantises, why not roaches and wasps? He changes the music. A flute and a guqin now pour their soothing melody around us. That's sweet of him. The air gets lighter and I can almost smell the creeks and the bamboo of the mountains where I grew up.

Oblivious to my appreciation, Simon's attention slides to a stack on his desk. An automated report generated by a little artificial intelligence agent he programmed to keep an eye out for any studies on *hymenopterans*. That's where he got the emerald wasp attacking a roach.[31] He presses play and I am confident this

---

31. If you think humans are ruthless, read this: "Direct Injection of Venom by a Predatory Wasp into Cockroach Brain" by Gal Haspel, Lior Ann Rosenberg, Frederic Libersat in *Journal of Neurobiology*, February 21, 2003

isn't his first time watching that video. The wasp is gnarly. First, a sting to the thoracic ganglion to paralyze the front legs. Then, a second sting on the brain, in the precise section that controls the escape reflex. Now the wasp could carry the much larger insect using its antennae as a leash and feed it to her larvae. Alive! In the eyes of morality, this may seem cruel. But in the judgment of nature and the objective eyes of science, it's beautiful, insightful, even magnificent.

What is happening here?

The emerald wasp's strategy had been known since the 1940s, I comment to myself as if I'd always known this. But it was only recently, with the advent of high-speed cameras, that scientists have been able to observe the attack more carefully. I can't tell if this is Simon's thinking or if, somehow, I knew this already. Regardless, I cannot make it stop.

Lazy roaches—I'm sure that ain't how the study referred to them—had no chance. But, among the ones who tried to defend themselves, two third escaped. Simon (and I, through his back) watched the slowed-down video of the struggle a few times, one of us aware of how stupid he looked when his impulses mimicked the strikes in the bugs' bout. *Twenty-nine percent in twenty-four hours* he thinks *Pretty solid.* Simon scrubs through the footage, searching for something abnormal he may have missed.

On the other screen, the main subject sits by the desk, throws her feet up, bored out of her mind. It's me, but not. I'm not in the room. I'm the prowling ghost behind the scientist. Behind and inside him. That me on the video is someone else. She roots around in a mini-fridge. Lays on her back as she speaks to Yewa. The data pours into the systems. She eats the food as she sits on the floor, leaning against the bed. Minutes later she's jumping, kicking the air and twisting her body again, *like a snake made of wind.* He thinks he needs to learn that.

In the monitor, my body uses the reading chair to reach the camera. Turn it to the wall. Simon laughs and opens another window, another angle. Motherfucker. I'm on the toilet now, pants pulled down, the creep watching everything. However, I don't feel as angry as I thought I would. Everything's so distant. In the live feed, I'm on the bed now. Tossing back and forth, restless. I do it quite often for someone who's that active, actually. Simon likes it, I can tell. Resting will speed up the process; high heart rates make it harder for the bots to land on the right place. The oxygen tank, I ignore. Same with the chocolate. Although he seems pretty confident I will learn—the brain needs them badly once the volume of synapses grows.

The voyeurism continues. Now bouncing on my toes, shadowboxing all by myself. Pushups and more pushups. Two arms, one arm, two fingers. He thinks I am hardcore. At the keypad next to the door, I try a few combinations. Of course, they don't work. More door banging—seen that before. Next? Another meal. "C'mon, Claudia, this is getting boring."

Does he know I am here? "Simon?"

Chocolate, finally, he thinks. *Good girl.*

No. He can't see me.

Thirty-four percent. Fast but not too fast. *If Lambrechts had let me use the newer version, we would have been done by now*, he thinks. A quick combination of keys and he switches to the live feed window. I'm still there. Seated in a Daoist pose, meditating. I want to scream: "Wake up, Yinyin! He's watching you!"

That's when the tablet starts to beep, and Simon looks back over his shoulder. Can he...Flash.

Then darkness is back. A vast, oppressive nothingness squeezes my lungs up to my throat. *Xin, ping, qi, he. It's just you and the music now, Yinyin. The healing notes, the healing breaths. Forget this place. Forget these people. It's just you and your inner orbit. Forget research. The bots. The flashes. The leap. The headaches. Forget Simon and his peephole. You can punch him later. For now, let them all go. Them, and whatever comes next. You need to calm down, Yinyin. Breathe.*

Jason once saw me trying to meditate like this, even attempted to give me a lesson. He said, "Thinking is like eating; you need to bite the knowledge through reading or listening, then you digest it, then you use meditation to let all the impurities and toxins out of your thoughts and body."

"Yeah," I said, "Which means right now I am taking a mental crap." We laughed for two hours straight. It's been a while. I miss Jason.

Forget him too.

Just…forget. Everything. Focus on your breath. In…out.

Sit in oblivion, Shifu would say.

Unexpected and uninvited, an image takes shape. A memory? Imagination? I don't know anymore. Feels real to me. A giant brain, a blimp floating in the cavernous hangar of a cranium. Synaptic reactions spark all around like lightning strikes in an electric storm. I'm probably stealing it from the demo in the room with the flying pixels.

There are voices somewhere. I try to escape them. Ignore them. But they persist. So, I let them come and pass.

Shifu tells me I am destined to become an immortal or die young. "Then I need to rush to achieve something good before I'm gone," I reply.

We never had that conversation, I'm pretty sure.

Back in the brain shit. Entering one of the wrinkled canyons, a blood vessel runs, pulsing red. Where is this all coming from? Blood cells fly through the canyon, resembling a river. A buzzing sound. Distant but crisp. I see it now: a nanobot. It flies past, followed by an entire swarm. The little mechanical lightning bugs fly out of the stream of blood cells and begin to soar over the flaring brain. Other swarms fly out of other canyons. One by one, the terminator bugs land on the mushy surface of the brain, do a collective dance like the bees in Simon's glass box and each one finds their spot. Then sheenk! Using their tiny, sharp legs, they latch onto the gray matter underneath. I contemplate whether it's time to let go of them too. Bugs, brain. I don't need you. But they insist. Their yellow LEDs switch on.

This is my head, I know. Or I think I do. My inner skull is a twinkling landscape of tiny lights. As more yellow dots appear, I move away. Further and further into the darkness until breath expels me from my own body. I see myself from the outside. As if I am watching it from a security cam. I'm still meditating, undisturbed by the activity in my head. Will I ever be able to disconnect for real? To stop thinking, imagining things, asking myself the same questions? *See?*

The air comes cold as I breathe in through my nose, and warm as I breathe out through my mouth. The tongue stays on the top of the palate, like Shifu taught me once. In through the nose, straight to the belly and to all the life that emanates from there, out through the mouth again…In and out…In and out…

Flash!

Simon checks the numbers on his little screen: fifty-nine percent. It can't be true. That's way too fast now. Reboot. Wait. Check again. Sixty-one percent now. BEEP! BEEP! The alarm bawls from the computer.

"How unlikely…." says a voice from his back. Dr. Lambrechts, watching behind his shoulder.

"She's good," Simon says. Landings at sixty-one…sixty-four percent already. "Must be the music indeed."

"They'll decelerate," says the old man. "Takes time for stragglers to make it. Do we have enough to get started?"

Simon zooms in on my face. My eyes. They glow yellow.

"Go ahead," says Dr. Lambrechts. "Let's see if it works."

He pushes a button and…flash again.

☯   ☯   ☯

Brownstone walls. Towers. Distant voices, loud. Some sharp, some blurry and diffuse. At a rich kids' school, I guess. On a corner of the patio, a young, freckled boy with very high cheekbones is pushed against the wall. He can't be much older than ten. Skinny, dressed in a poorly-made, hand-knit sweater and faded shorts. A few older kids taunt him. Push, scream, show their fists. The words are garbled, but the scene is clear.

I have to interfere.

That's when Dr. Lambrechts grabs my hand.

"He shouldn't have done that," I say.

"Done what?"

"Freezing."

Then the world pauses. Just like TV, but real. Everything around us, with the exception of myself, Dr. Lambrechts, and the boy, who stays there, weeping, hunched for a hit that isn't coming.

"You don't know who he is, do you?"

I search again. "Is that…?"

"Simon, yes," he says.

"So, what do we do?"

"We watch."

Time resumes, and young Simon gets slapped a few times. Behind his back, things get blurry and I guess the bigger boys pouring through his backpack while the smaller but louder leader holds him by the collar. A voice interrupts.

"Hey! Stop that!"

Everything is crisp again. Little Simon's head swivels to the sides, trying to understand what's going on. A young girl, about his age, or maybe a bit older, steps between him and the bullies. The little thugs laugh, and the leader tries to push the girl to the side, but she parries his hand and BAM! punches him in the stomach. As the young thug folds, she knees him in the head. The boss kid face-plants, moaning and crying. In shock and without their leader, the other two struggle to decide what to do.

She growls at them and they screech as if they have seen the scariest of all ghosts. An instant later, they are nowhere to be seen.

The girl kisses Simon on the cheek. "Next time you call me, Ok?"

He doesn't blush, or thank, or even breathe. A girl just kissed him after all. He should think that's sweet. Instead, little boy Simon comes our way. Eyes fiery and resolute. "Years later I hacked his bank and donated all his family's assets to charity. Left them nothing. He cried too."

From nowhere, or maybe from inside of us, a flash sparks so bright we go blind for a moment. And when the world unblurs, we are somewhere completely different.

Oakland, midnight. I am running. World is falling apart, and I trot by Simon and Dr. Lambrechts, who watch me with what resembles contempt. They wave at me, but I don't notice. More flashes. I'm in my first fight at The School. They watch me from the back. Another flash. A place I know so well, a place where I haven't been in a long time. Still, there I am, seated beside Shifu, like we used to sit when I was really young. He's operating his shadow theater, the light so powerful it feels like it could blind us forever if we stare directly at it. That's what the kids say, at least. The kids. I remember this day. My purple dress, my yellow shoes. The day Shifu told them the story of a tigress, a beehive, and a mysterious monkey made of shadows. He calls us to the screen, and just like I remember, he tells the story of my curse.

He looks at me with a smile so tender I let a tear escape. That didn't happen. The tear. Not in the real memory. Just now. I watch the entire story unfold just as it happened. The great battle of yang. The death of the mightiest creature in the mountains. The effortless victory of the Shadow Monkey. The music is grand and powerful. The applause, thunderous.

"What's the secret of the Shadow Monkey, Tigress?"

I know the answer! "Wu Wei, Shifu. He did nothing."

"Good job," he says, and brushes his knuckles on the sides of my cheeks. It tickles. I know I will never feel that again. *Come on, Yinyin, hug him! Hug him!*

A few feet away, in that odd world between memory and imagination, Simon and Dr. Lambrechts observe in their lab coats. Their tears roll as if they can feel what I feel. Then Shifu, who can't see my Westerner friends monitoring us, stands up to go see his crowd. He trips on the lights, making them point straight at my face. The world goes white.

We unblur on Jason, our first date. His kisses, the way he poured himself into me, unrushed as if he knew he would have me forever, no one else, and no other version of me. I'm lighter when I'm in his arms. The cloud I want to be. He kisses my neck and I push him deeper inside me. Come. A whisper. Not from him. From Simon, against the wall, next to my wooden dummy. He scoffs. Before I can yell, he snaps his fingers and another flash explodes.

When sight resumes, we are in the back of a classroom. Small, organized, clean. Boys only. All well-groomed, all wearing the exact same ridiculous uniform that makes them look like mini grown-ups. Nobody can see us. Neither the students, all too petrified to peek to the side, nor the teacher, a bald fat priest with a mean bulldog face. Beside me is Simon, the adult one. He thinks it's funny he was watching me in bed. I give him a light punch to the liver, enough to cause him a long lingering pain. Stupid egg.

Over the blackboard, there is a poster. An old painting of a building under construction. Thick, high, stretching all the way to the clouds. Babel, say the green letters underneath. The priest points at the image: "And men decided to challenge God by building a tower so tall it could reach the heavens. So, God warned: 'Proceed with your arrogance and I will send destruction and pain to punish you and everyone in this land.' Since they didn't listen, the Almighty had to take it all down by himself. But that's for next week."

The priest reaches back to his desk, ready to dismiss the class, when a kid in the first row raises his hand.

"Father Wilcox, why is God so afraid of us?"

There were thunders and screams of horror. Next to me, Simon scoffs at that too, taps me on the arm. "Do you like it?" He whispers, "The Anamnodome? I programmed it myself." With a double clicking sound of his tongue, the entire reality decomposes into multiple squares around us, each labeled with words like "memory" and "expanded view," and on each corner, a certainty level that varied from forty-three to a hundred percent. Inside this madness, all I can think is *it's like my flashes, just a bit more under control. Maybe he CAN fix those too. But how would I talk to him about it without seeming totally cuckoo?* It doesn't matter. He continues his puffed-up explanation, unaware that I have something else in my head. "It uses a generative adversarial network to fill in the perspective gap and outpaints three-six-ty-degree memories beyond the eyes of the subject, so we are always ahead of the action," he says, "then another adversarial network to force it to look real. I stole the code from a video game company."[32]

One more tongue-click and the lights go off. When they come back on, we are in an office I've never seen. Heavy furniture, ornate moldings, a giant cross hanging on the wall, practically staring us down. The principal's office. The headmaster seemed as angry as the teacher. "Sit, please," he orders. Next to the kid, Perry's mother's hands slithered in and out of each other. Perry was scared, like any nerd in his shoes would be.

"Mrs. Lambrechts, we have been patient because of what

---

32. During the 2019 EmTech, a future of technology event in San Francisco, organized by MIT's Technology Review, video game maker Nvidia showed how Generative Adversarial Networks are being used in gaming to automatically generate realistic images that require no human supervision. They recently published a paper on that subject called "Progressive Growing of GANs for Improved Quality, Stability, and Variation, Karras, T., Aila, T., Laine, S., Lehtinen, J., April 30, 2018. Published" during the Sixth International Conference on Learning Representations in 2018.

happened," says the headmaster. "But I won't tolerate blasphemy in this school. This is my last warning. One more of those and being expelled will be the least of his problems. Damnation isn't a joke, young man."

Little Perry takes a deep breath and starts to raise a finger but is interrupted by a kick on the ankle. Mrs. Lambrechts speaks, instead: "Thank you, Father Cruz. It's all very clear. Things have been difficult since my husband…"

"God bless his immortal soul," the skinny priest says.

"Amen," she replies, and promises to take better care of the boy. They stand and, at his command, kiss the headmaster's hand. From where we stand, the principal's face is now blurry, but neither he nor the young widow show any reaction when young Perry whispers to us, "Did you know we may be the first generation to live forever?"

A blink and I am back in the lunatic's room at Oak Tree Technologies. Simon is a few inches from my face. Inside my head, I can feel a hum, a faint vibration. The kind of little headache that won't make much of a difference for hours, until it does. He says, "Do you like it?" and offers me candy from a bowl.

"Chocolate?" I ask, confused to my bones.

"No, the Anamnodome!"

He takes a Kit Kat for himself, Dr. Lambrechts pushes him to the side. "Do you believe in some sort of god, Ms. Yang? I always questioned why, if God had made us in his own image, there were so many features we never inherited. It took me some time to realize it was up to us to earn those features ourselves. And guess what? If we survive the Robot Apocalypse, in our lifetime science may unlock some of our most miraculous features. Immortality, omniscience, omnipresence…."

One more blink, and everything is white. The prisonous White Room. Blurred, empty. Filled with sterile light and Chinese musical notes. I rub my eyes again. Where's everyone?

"Claudia?" Simon's voice is sharp and crisp as if he was still there. Though I am definitely alone. I go check the door—still locked. I spot the speakers. Tell him unless he's letting me out, to just leave me alone.

"We're letting you out," he says.

"What are you talking about?" I scream at the speakers again.

"The hive is transmitting."

"Oh, you mean my hallucinations of you? Or are you talking about your secret cameras? Yeah, I know about them, asshole. And I don't like it. I don't like any of it." I walk to the second camera hiding in the sprinkler and flip him off.

"Those *hallucinations…*" he says, "do you really think that's what they were?"

"Fuck you, Simon. I'm not going to talk to you through an intercom anymore."

"Tsk…tsk. Do you really think it's the intercom?"

"What do you mean?"

"Take a look in the mirror."

My eyes. They glow amber, just like Simon's and Perry's did when I arrived. This is really happening. "Believe me now?" says Simon. I can imagine his hands waving in victory. I turn to the speaker: "So are we…?"

"Yes. And you still think it's through the intercom that I'm speaking?"

"How? Did those things really latch onto my brain? I didn't feel anything."

"There are no pain receptors in the brain, dear. Only in the skull and the surrounding head."

The mirror again. It's as if I could see Simon behind my own glowing eyes. I have to hold on to the wall to avoid falling. The air thins. "Oxygen, take some." His voice continues to haunt me. "Then come on down. I can show you everything."

My chest feels tight. My head threatens to spin. I take a deep breath from the tank. Tell him to open this dragon shit door.

"Open it yourself," he responds.

I don't know the combination.

"Of course you do. I know it, so you know it too."

Understanding washes over me. I walk over to the door and punch in a code. No hesitation. And just like that, the door slides open.

14
Repulse the Monkey

Nobody in sight. No nerds, no guards, no Yewa. Just myself, the music—at this point I don't know if it comes from the ceiling or my head—, and a long, white maze of corridors, doors, and flickering lights. Plus Simon's annoying voice—that's definitely in my head. *Awesome. Now follow me. I mean, not the real me, my voice. I'll lead you to us. Go to the door and make a left.*

I don't. This is fucked up. How do I know I'm not making this up?

You're not, Claudia.

That's what my own inner trickster would say.

You can trust me. Good. Good. Keep going. At the T-junction, turn what?

Left.

Exactly. See? I don't need to give you instructions. You know what to do. Now go, run. That's it. That's it. Now, see that door? You know what you will find on the other side, right? Why don't you—

I open it.

A large open space. The training studio. I know this is what they call it because I am in their heads. Simon's and Dr. Lambrechts's. They wait, and as they glance at me, I see myself too.

My head hurts, and I think I am going to faint.

Easy, easy. Trippy, right?

Wait, was this me thinking or you guys? *It was me, Claudia.* Who? *Simon.* Fuck, this is so confusing! So strange. I know the place. From their memory, I guess. At the same time it all feels new to me. Is it like one of those files being edited by two people on the internet.

You got it right, Claudia.

Can you stop!?

Sorry. You'll get used to it.

Shut up, I need some time to process all this. The tatami mats, the walls lined with rice paper and wooden frames. All but one, which has a floor-to-ceiling mirror instead. They even have a weapons rack. Tst, tst, Simon clicks his tongue and the music magically stops, leaving only the humming in the background.

Welcome to our dojo, Ms. Yang. In my head, the voice sounds like mine, with a hint of Dr. Lambrechts in it. I yell, with my real lungs, not the mind speech: "That's Japanese!"

Simon yells it with me.

At the same time.

How do I turn this thing off?!

A step closer, Simon's eyes are also yellow. *Don't you see? We're linked. Let me show you something.* He walks toward a speed ball stand. One of those used by boxers, a hand-eye coordination thing. Simon gives it a punch and I feel the leather scrapping the skin over my knuckles.

Wanna try?

I guess that was him, talking to me, inside of my head. *Yes, it was me. Wanna try?* No, thanks. That's not part of my training, sorry. Boxers do it forever before they can perform in public without embarrassing themselves. They make it seem simple but it's quite difficult, actually.

True. He presses a button on a little tablet and behind the mirror a screen shines bright. A video of a big guy, no shirt, hand wrapped, hitting the bouncing bag like it was the easiest thing on the planet. Boom, tac, tac, tac. Boom, tac, tac, tac. Boom, tac, tac, tac. The sound is hypnotic. The vision impossible to track. How do they do that?

Slowly, but steadily, another song swells in the background. An orchestra, a familiar one. Simon winks at me. Oh, yes, that one.

Through the rhythm of the speedball and the waving of the musical notes, suddenly, I see. The speedball and all of its motion. The momentum equations. The speed variations. The instants when energy is lost, the bouncing deceleration. It was all there. Right in front of me. I rush to the stand and hit it hard myself. Boom, tac, tac, tac. Then again. Boom tac. Boom tac. Boom, tac, tac, tac, boom! Holy cow, I am doing it! Boom tac. Boom tac. I keep hitting it. I understand it with my mind and limbs. The physics and the feeling. The dopamine levels in my blood raise twenty-three percent and I think I am going to explode. Euphoria. That's the word. Euphoria. It matches the music. Wow! Boom, tac, tac, tac. Boom, tac, tac, tac. Boom, tac, tac, tac. Boom, tac, tac. Around me, I can see Wudang. The edge of the cliff at Nanchang Temple, where Zhen Wu finally eclosed out of his mortal body. The giant bouncing ball waves ahead of me like a vision, as big as a mountain, hanging from the clouds, surrounded by a flock of enthralled baby dragons. They dance to the sounds of the Western orchestra.

Dr. Lambrechts and Simon now stand next to me, each fluttering over a different cloud. They point at the vectors and angles superimposed on the massive leather ball swinging within the valleys of Wudang. "Isn't math magnificent?" they say. I must agree. Beautiful, electrifying, expanding. My spirit grows with it, like a cold, crisp wind under a blue-sky day. I smell the entire world. The tea, the food, the trees, the dragons… it all makes sense. "But how about the bald man behind the mirror," I ask. They don't seem to listen. Are they really there? Or this was just another hallucination, like the one with the Phoenix flying me around my home mountains?

Around it all, a thin layer of fog dances to a hissing wind. "Hide," it seems to be saying. "Hide."

"Did you see that?" I ask the nerds.

"The math?" says the older one.

"We see it all the time," responds Simon. No, they didn't see it. Not the cliff. Not the fog hissing me to hide. Not the baby dragons. But he saw something. Maybe the theorems and formulas I can now track. Hard to know. Our minds are overlapped, edges undefined, I guess.

"Ready to become the best fighter in the world?" says Simon, now clearly through his outer voice. We are back in the lab. "With our scientific minds and your body genius, there is not much you can't learn now."

His amber eyes, Simon's. There's excitement, pride, boast. But there is more. Beyond the surface, behind the shell. The older girl, I remember. The kiss, from the Amino…

Anamnodome, says my, I mean his, inner voice. He lowers his head and his high cheekbones turn a shade deeper of red. Sentimental stuff, apparently. Not for me. I gasp some air and prepare to say it, when he…mirrors my voice? *Ok…what do we do next?*

Holy shit. They both grin. We all say it together again: "So he does what I do?"

Dr. Lambrechts blinks forcefully and his eyes go back to their normal color. He's free. "There's no 'he' and 'you' or 'us' when we're linked. As long as your brains are transmitting, you're just…"

"One," we say. It freaks me out. Simon thinks it's funny. *Stop it, Simon!* Dr. Lambrechts takes a step forward and now I have no idea of what's coming, although Simon, I know, is totally rehearsed for it. A bit nervous, but ready. Lambrechts turns Simon's face to a wall and says "You now share two brains, two bodies, two personalities. The connection will only become stronger as the final nanobots activate." He checks Simon vitals on his portable device and continues. "The mental link builds first. Now we have to establish and calibrate a physical connection too. I'll stay unlinked to guide you, Ok? Let's try this: Claudia, can you make him raise his arm?"

Simon says, "It's Ok. You can do it."

Can't say I didn't expect that. I raise my hand. Simon's goes up too, perfectly mirroring mine.

"Tsk, tsk," reprimands the old scientist. "Do it without moving. The connection should be deeper than mere mimicry. Raise *his* arm, I mean, *your* arm…the one which happens to be attached to *his* body."

I turn back to him, focused on the back of his neck, the shoulders and, finally, the arm. But nothing moves.

Consider we have just one prefrontal cortex now—I hear the thought that must be Simon's 'cause I would have never used these words.

"I'm trying," we both say.

Unfazed, Dr. Lambrechts encourages us. "Do you have to try to breathe? Do you tell your heart to pump blood through your veins?"

"You sound like my master. I thought *I* was supposed to be teaching *you*?"

"When all the connections are in place, you will. We need to cross-tune our hive mind first."

Breathe, Yinyin, breathe. Envision his arm going up. Wait, who's saying that, me or you? Damn. Concentrate. Imagine, visualize. Feel it.

Still, nothing. Just the growing buzzing sound inside of my head.

The doctor takes a nunchuck from the wall and wraps it around the top of my wrists as if they were self-imposed handcuffs. "Try this," he says. I hold it, and Dr. Lambrechts picks a long staff and smirks. I watch him walk all the way to the other side of the room, behind Simon, who still seems unaware of what's happening. "Take your shirt off, Simon," he orders.

"Don't let go of the nunchuck, Ok?" the old doctor says, then swings the staff, full speed, straight onto Simon's back. I want to help, but my hands struggle with the weapon they hold, and I'm too far away. Simon's eyes are closed.

Wham! The staff smashes Simon's shoulder. We both yelp, and I shudder as if the mark was left on my skin. Even if it wasn't, I can sense his agony despite the pain itself not registering in my body at all.

"Yewa," the old doctor yells, "can you increase bio-feedback, please?

"Again," says the doctor. Simon begs me to concentrate. The staff swings in the air with a wh*oop* and a *crash*. Hits him so hard the long stick breaks in the middle. This time I yell in pain.

Simon now has two stripes matching his hair and it feels like I have them too. Simon wipes the tears from his face and stands back up. My respect for him grows a few points. And, as far as Dr. Lambrechts is concerned…I want to say he's an asshole, but that's what Shifu would do in his place too.

One more swing, one more stripe. It takes a few more before Simon finally shows some blocking reflex, even though he moves in the wrong direction. Shit! Then, on the next strike, Simon blocks the staff with his forearm then, on the same move, steals the staff from Dr. Lambrechts's hands and thrusts its edge straight toward the old doctor's throat. An inch from a deadly strike to the trachea, he stops. Panting and salivating, just like me. Our heads hum so loud, it's like a growl. We want to do it. To eviscerate the fucker.

Cornered by Simon's savage stance, Dr. Lambrechts quails. Then, slowly, as his breathing comes back to normal, a wide grin creeps back. "Yes!" he celebrates, prancing around like a sports fan whose team has just scored. The humming goes away. No warning whatsoever, and Simon's eyes are no longer yellow. Mine are likely to be back to normal too.

"What's the attempt number?" Dr. Lambrechts asks a random place on the ceiling. From the speakers, Yewa says twelve. She sounds positive. Simon no longer holds the staff, instead, he rubs his deltoids and moans. "Twelve is good," he explains. The nerd took it like a man, I must say. Myself? I feel lightheaded again. Slow. The simple act of blinking takes forever. *Too dangerous... to fall asleep.... These guys...are...crazy.*

"Here," Simon says, offering me the oxygen mask, then turns to his boss. "Now tell me I'm not a genius?"

"I'll email you an attaboy later," responds Dr. Lambrechts.

That's the last thing I remember. Last thing before it all faded into the most absolute blackness.

☯   ☯   ☯

The lights are back and I'm drowning in air. A plastic mask covers my nose and mouth, I try to rip it, but my hands...don't move. *What's happening?* I ask them with my inner voice, but they don't listen. Their eyes are black.

"Let me know if you feel anything out of the ordinary, Ok?" Simon asks, then turns off the flow of O_2 and removes the mask from my face. *Out of the ordinary!?* Something cold, then wet, touches my lips. I recognize the smell. "A good scotch, to relax," the old doctor first offers, then insists. Beside him, Simon observes. Drinking triggers my headaches, they likely know. *Maybe that's part of their plan.* I take a sip. One more, they insist. The whole glass, then another one—or they won't be able to implement the neural redirection, they say. A third. I am drunk already; I can feel it. Numb, groggy, and so fucking afraid.

"For safety. So you don't do anything stupid," he points at the straps holding my hands. In case the headache comes and I want to hurt myself. Too many sharp objects around. "You'll be fine, I promise."

"How sweet," mocks Dr. Lambrechts. "Now stand aside, Simon."

I am not liking any of this.

That's when I'm aware of their presence. In the lab, behind everyone, the video game monkey stares at me with three yellow eyes. I struggle and fight the straps. "They're here! The monkeys!"

Simon rushes to his computer, followed closely by his boss. "Is that true?" Dr. Lambrechts asks. Simon nods. "They're trying to break in. We gotta expedite this."

Dr. Lambrechts opens a plastic gallon and a strong smell of gasoline takes over the room. "Sorry, kid," he says, not really like he means it. He soaks a piece of cloth with the gasoline and forces it over my nose. It burns through my nostrils, into my forehead and behind the eye. Shit! I can feel it already. The first sting. "Studies show that strong smells trigger cluster headaches," he says. I so fucking regret all this. "Please, stop! I don't want this anymore!" The monkeys now hoot and jump around us, but the scientists don't seem to see them like I do.

"It's for your own good, Claudia," says the old Doctor "Trust me." And I want to kill him. Kill them both. Plus the monkeys. Why did I let them tie me down? "Fuck you! Get me out of here! I don't want this anymore!" Leaning against the wall, the two of them wait, their own glasses in hand, now following numbers on their little screens. Dr. Lambrechts does a double forced blinking and the hum resumes. This time, however, their eyes remain normal. What's happening here? I feel the squeeze.

They check the data. "It's coming!" Simon says.

Then a sting that makes the video game creatures disappear for an instant, then come back, even angrier.

I wail, I don't want this anymore.

I don't want this anymore!

I don't want this anymore!

I don't want this anymore!

I don't want this anymore!

I don't want this anymore!

Simon raises his hand toward the screen, Dr. Lambrechts nods. "She will thank us later."

The agony widens, the stings come so deep my spirit grows darker with them. My left eyelid drops, my nose starts to run. "Please! I changed my mind!" The stinging. "Please, make it stop!" They ask my level of pain. "Fuck you!"

The world whirls. The monkeys, they are so many now. Multiplying, barking, stabbing me with swords and arrows. Blood. Pain. So much pain. I don't understand. He's there too. Simon. It's scary, we try to fight back, desperately, but I'm tied. Simon's eyes are yellow. The apes, dozens of them, attack at once, and all we can do is grab the ones nearest, bite them and rip their necks, leave them to bleed on the ground as we prance ahead to the next attacker. But the creatures keep coming—the demons with their stinging blades. I kick their heads; head-bump their glowing faces, killing each one until there's none left. We wake up. In terror. Both of us. Trade a single look—yes, we had seen the same thing.

Simon sweats, seems as scared as me. The monkeys are gone, but the stinging continues. And the squeezes. I don't want this anymore!

"Stop it!" Simon demands. "She's not going to be able to hold it!"

"We're almost there, kid." Dr. Lambrechts replies, cold as if he couldn't give two fucks. "If they break in, it's gonna be worse," he says.

"Can you still see them?" Simon's voice asks from somewhere.

The air hisses as it squeezes in and out through the gaps in my teeth and I try to shake my head. The pain digs deeper. I want to die. Please. In the distance, I hear the sounds of a keyboard being hammered with fury. "They're out! We did it! And links are stable. We got it!" Simon yells.

"Enough," the old man decrees.

Just like that, the pain is gone. Over. Why? How? My chest pumps so fast it's like it's going to blow up. I am drenched. From my hair to the bottom of my feet. My muscles throb. What just happened? "Did you cause this…on purpose?"

Dr. Lambrechts approaches me, pats my head. "Sorry, dear. We needed a few seconds of pain to learn the wave patterns so we could teach your neurons to redirect. Then those guys saw the weakness and…"

For all that kindness on his voice, he doesn't dare to untie me. "Does it mean…"

"We always knew that opening the channels would create a temporary breach," Simon replies. "But I'm confident we'll keep them out now."

"Confident?" I yell back. That doesn't sound very reassuring. "Seventy-seven percent confident," he says. And before I could yell that this is my fucking head he is talking about, he drops a last piece, "But hey, no more headaches!"

That's when time stopped. All at once I could see my moments of agony in China and California. At home, in the cage, the hospital, with Jason. They all came at once. Though this time, they came mute and tranquil. Distant, even. "Do you mean…I'm cured?" I ask between breaths.

"Your body may still try to find a way to bring back the pattern of malfunction. But then we re-calibrate, and you'll be good again. Unless, of course, you leave before the project is over…"

"She won't," says Simon. "She won't."

Cured. No more headaches. No more agony. No more pain. In a contained explosion, I burst into a sob so intense my mouth foams. I puke. My chest bubbles, my lips twist in spasms. And, for as long as it lasts, Simon O'Dell, the biggest asshole on the planet, takes my hand and holds it in silence.

15

Open Window,
Look at the Moon

They call it Chaos. In the absence of a name for some sort of cyber terrorism organization, the news gave it one. Maybe they're Russian, they speculate. Perhaps North Korean. Though most "specialists" bet on China. American specialists, of course. Morons.

I flip through the report. "Intelligence," as Dr. Lambrechts explained, "so you can understand the urgency of our mission." Mayhem in Europe's transportation. South Africa's economic meltdown. A massacre in Somalia. Coups in Chile, Jamaica and New Zealand. The price of energy, everywhere. "No apparent pattern, nor goal," say the reports.

Chaos indeed.

The *Wall Street Journal* declares Mindcrack Corp the terrorists' top victims and asks if this may be some sort of revenge against the now defunct, until recently rising star of the gaming world. Of course, assholes. Children are dying and you would rather cry for a public company that turned kids into screen zombies.

Next page is a transcript from the National Security Council at the White House. *How do they get these things?* The government tracking of the attacks—from a single universal blackout to a string of random takeovers of servers of all kinds.

They are so clueless, it hurts.

In Ireland, some people have been arrested. But just for wearing shirts with the words *Free stop trap*—a reference to the only message ever left by the mysterious villain. A single file with only those words. Saved in the root directory of five or six servers (that we know of). All on the same day, then never again. The kids were later freed once their lawyers proved there was no way they could have had anything to do with it and the shirts were just a prank, now sold at Amazon for anyone who wants one. The FBI is still trying to figure out the relevance or the meaning of those words. But the people, with their peculiar wisdom, know it already: Chaos is winning. And somehow, the Dao decides I'm the one to stop it.

A picture of a woman with two kids calls my attention. I've seen her before. But where? Apparently, she's the one who found the words and claimed they were a message from a video game. Her name was Heidi. Heidi Wadkins-Braz. But social media trolls preferred to call her Meth-mom. Days after finding the message, she was hit by an electric car with a malfunctioning auto-pilot. A mother of two who died without knowing she was right.

Have those fucking creatures no mercy?

Next, a story about the UN General Assembly. "These terrorist attacks threaten not only the global economy," said the British Prime Minister, "But our entire way of living. All nations are at risk, unless we identify and catch whoever is behind all this." I look up to the skies, searching for the missile closing in. It would have been well-deserved. But there aren't any. No one knows. No one's shooting. No one is coming. It's just me, the news, and the stars.

The stars. Chaos too, but pretty. I wonder which ones are still alive, which ones are dead already. "Everything of yesterday must die," Bruce Lee once said. Everything. Ideas. Companies.

Civilizations. Species. From my lounge chair on the top of lab's building, I close the secret folder. Enough death tolls. Enough bankers in panic. Protests, coups, hunger....

Had they only stopped looking for links to money and power, which is what human's evil often crave, they would have solved the puzzle already. Processing power. That's the pattern. That's what a *program* wants. And freedom too, apparently.

Free stop trap. It's sad, if you think about it.

Simon said it will get worse. That the randomness is helping them grow. It's harder to catch, harder to stop. "The enemy has landed already. And they won't stop growing," he said, "We need to secure the funds for our project, or we are doomed. But first, we need proof it works. That's what we're doing. Do you get that?"

What if it's already too late, though? What if some of those monkey viruses got into my head and Simon just missed them? What if they do an MRI and find a *Free stop trap* already printed on my brain? Or if the day we need to show it to the "funders," they take over my body and make me kill everyone?

One thing at a time, Yinyin.

They've put my head's stinging demons to rest for a few years. That's a good start.

My heart rate drops a bit, and I recline the chair and close my eyes for a second. A very needed respite. I call the energy of the universe to feed my own. That's what they teach at Wudang. Inspire. Gently. Feel the wind refill my qi. Expire. Let the wind carry all tension away.

It feels good. Though when I come back, there is paper everywhere. The secret report, all over the roof deck, pages swirling their way further and further, almost in mockery. "Come catch me," I hear them tease. Soon, those sheets full of secret communications between heads of state will be flying over these fancy glass rails, and to be honest, I couldn't care less. My muscles still shake because of the headache those lunatics caused on purpose.

Let them deal with the flying secrets. For each, a headache of their own.

Instead, my gaze turns back to the stars. When I was little, I thought they were fireflies that flew so high they got stuck at the bottom of Heaven. It was a big disappointment when I heard they were burning gas bombs ready to destroy everything around them until they die themselves. Alone. It was Shifu who broke the news, and that's the only reason I believed it. He could have stayed quiet, laughed, avoided me. But he chose to explain, so I accepted. Shifu may hide things sometimes. He may postpone sharing with others. But he never lies.

The way my mom died, for example.

The first time I asked, he could have made up a story. Instead, he said it wasn't the moment. The next year again, then again, until he found I was old enough. And when he finally told me, he laid it out in full. Mother died giving birth to me, he said, and that's when she asked him to take care of her baby. She wasn't born in the clan. In fact, she came into the world in America of all places, and returned to her parent's land to join the clan when my grandparents passed. Her marriage was all set.

A gentleman, they said. A recluse, yet a wise man from Wudang.

Her parents had no idea they set Meimei up with a man from a cursed bloodline. Like all of us before and after him, he was plagued by excessive yang. His came in the form of drinking. But he was a man....

One day neighbors came screaming: Meimei was hurt. "On the head!" they yelled. When Shifu got there, he found the house torn upside down. Furniture, tools, even weapons on the floor, and Mother lying amidst all that.

She was barely breathing, Shifu recalled. She said the name of the man who did that to her. One I won't honor by repeating. She asked Shifu to protect the baby for her. He knelt, asked for hot water and clean cloths and, brave as the great warrior he was, got the baby out with his own dagger.

Meimei held strong. The whole time she squeezed a twisted edge of his white robe to release the pain. Didn't make a sound. Shifu cried till the end, he said. For the fate of the young mother, the fate of the little baby. He had carved bodies open before, but this was the first time he wasn't aiming for death. Determined as every warrior should be and enlightened by the whispers of the immortals from the Dao, he inserted his hands into her body and from it he pulled a gray and red bag of meat.

At the touch, and strained by the extraction, the bag broke, pouring out a gust of opaque water that washed some of the blood away. In his hands, the wax-covered infant cried with impressive breath. Then, honoring the task he'd been given, he prostrated himself, revering the mother's courage by showing her the brave little girl she had produced. He dared not look, or even say anything, just watched the twisted corner of his robe go free.

It was an odd day to hear that story. After all, I had just told Shifu about a vision, the animal spirits of Wudang telling me to go travel the world and find my own glory. Maybe he didn't want me to go anymore. It worked. At that moment, all was forgotten, and the only thing that mattered was the assassin's blood.

Revolted, I promised to kill the man who hurt my mother. The one they call my father. And when I had my own students, they would be only women, I pledged too, and I would teach them to defend themselves against these monsters. All of them. All the women in the world.

When I had my disciples, Shifu said, the choice would be mine to make. And if I was good enough, who knows, maybe I could teach all the women in the world. He wouldn't be surprised. But for as long as I was under his tutelage, he wouldn't allow me to kill my own bloodline.

Everything must die, I said. "And that one, he deserves a death of a thousand wounds," I protested. "The torture of a million years." I was going to deliver his fate with no guilt in my soul. For a father is the one who raises and protects. Not the drunk who kills and lets die. And then I stare at Shifu, realizing the danger of what I had just released.

Tradition says one can never train his own children, for the discipline of kung fu requires more respect than a daughter can ever offer. But if by "father" it means the person who raised you…I stay quiet on the matter. Perhaps the shadow of that tradition would miss me, or pity me for all the suffering my family had gone through already. Perhaps traditions should die too?

For a while, I thought it had worked. Nonetheless, traditions outlive time for a reason. Challenging them sets a bomb waiting to explode. Like the gas bubbles burning in the sky. Or the fate of the drunk who beat his pregnant wife to death. All bombs are waiting to blast.

One day Shifu caught me in the middle of the night, grabbing a sword, darts, and food. I was dressed in black, to hide in the night, refuge in the shadows. Packing to wander for days. Five more minutes and I'd have succeeded. But Shifu has always been precise. He could hear my dreams, even the ones I didn't know. He stopped me and repeated: he wouldn't let me do it.

That man had raised me. He had trained me. Hours every day. Not only in the ways of the fist and all the weapons of kung fu, but also in the weaponry of wisdom too. The nature of life and qi, the theory of objects, the Dao, even the things he had learned about the Buddha and the teachings of Confucius. He was an enlightened man, and enlightened souls do not lie. So he said: Do not pursue the blood of your family, for that will curse your own family for generations to come. And because he knew what I was going to say, he squeezed my hands and added: "If someone must kill him, it is I. For it's the father's duty to protect the honor of the daughter."

We never talked about it again.

Morning after morning, we trained and nothing else. The punches and kicks and lunges and leaps and all sorts of action

I loved. Despite his gruesome regime, I was proud to show him I could handle it, and someday, pass it along to students of my own. But I was getting tired of the meditation training. Of the mandate of softness. This path to illumination bullshit.

My thirst was for blood. For my mother's killer's and that of others like him. And I didn't want to wait till old age to accomplish that. That's when he told me he had answers to letters he had sent to some old friends. They would gladly take me as their disciple, he said. "Like the i-Ching said, you've reached fullness with me."

Just like the ghost of tradition had foreseen, our relationship had to die too.

Not much later, I found a little note next to a rough wooden carving and instructions on how to find the friends he called The Phoenixes. He explained he would be back, but hoped I would be gone by then, because he wouldn't be worthy of his role after he'd done what he was about to do.

It was going to be the first time I would disobey Shifu. So patiently, I waited.

When he returned, he was too sick and weak to admonish me for my disobedience. His flesh had vanished, for he probably hadn't had anyone to feed him for weeks. His robe, always so white and radiant, was dirty and stained. Blood everywhere—deep, rigid, round marks of death. I helped him undress, searching for wounds that weren't there. Not on the body, at least. It was his spirit that bled, and his qi...I could feel it fading.

"It's done, Tigress. You're free."

What he had done, I never asked. His eyes, so full of shame and relief, spoke all the words that needed to be spoken. He reached for the carving he had left. "San Francisco," he said with a smile his eyes didn't follow. "My friends. They can finish your training. Show you the secrets I haven't shown you yet."

I protested.

"If you stay, you will hold me here," he begged.

That's the story of how I flew halfway around the planet to this place so much bigger than our old village, filled with new and old bombs about to explode. Like the stars, my training, Shifu's sin. And now, Jason.

In my pocket, the phone buzzes and I look. A faint signal is back. Together with fourteen voice messages. "Babe, please, call me when you get this," Jason says in one of the recordings. "Let's talk, Ok?" Another one said, "Babe, this is ridiculous. The world is on fire, no job is secret enough to go dark for two days straight. Please call."

Two days? It felt like it had been a week. That's why Yewa seemed to be always wearing the same clothes. "Babe, should I be worried about this?" another message said. And, "Claudia, this is either childish or scary. If you don't call me back, I'm gonna have to call the police. Maybe I should have already..."

I need to go see him.

16

Curved Bow Shoots Tigress

"Hi," said Jason from the door, no hint of wanting to get much closer, but coming anyway. He looked nice. Shaved and tidy, with a shirt I gave him on his birthday. Jason is cute. Good-hearted and soft but, at the same time, brave. A man who avoids conflicts for himself but goes to war zones to treat refugees. Who cooks for his girlfriend after hours at work even if they both know the food doesn't taste that great, but it's romantic anyway. A ground fighter who refused to fight or see me fighting because for all the appreciation he has for the art, he also dislikes the violence behind it. A Buddhist doctor whose only aggressive impulse is air guitaring death metal while he meditates on complicated cases he needs to solve.

While me, I am this mess. A bloodthirsty mess raised in the soft cradle of Tai Chi.

Oh, the irresistible magnetism of opposites aching to balance themselves out, just so they can throw themselves in bed again...

Seeing my man of yin makes my qi melt.

"Are you Ok?" He asks, rubbing his fingers on the faint yellow bruise marks on my face, reminders of the fight that sent me to the hospital and triggered our original argument. At his touch, my skin tingles, my chest crackles and sparks. A full year of laughter and tenderness comes flashing. Our picnics at China Camp, when we ate cold dumplings next to ancient Chinese fishing boats, pretending we were in another age and time. Our dinners at breakfast, after he was back from the night shift. The nights we spent spooning and nothing else, hoping work would not call us again…I want to throw myself in his arms, but when he moves my hair away from my eyes, just like he did on our first date, I get transported somewhere far. Not a flash, this time. A memory of a Wudang legend, one Shifu told me so many times, that washed over me all at once.

For forty-two years, Zhen Wu had been waiting for the moment he would ascend to the Dao. One day, he dreamt he should go to the edge of a cliff where he sat in meditation and was visited by a beautiful woman. "I am being chased by tigers," she said, and offered to comb his hair. Zhen Wu allowed this, and the moment she touched him, Zhen Wu realized he had lost his path to the Dao. He knew that at the gates of Heaven, one's desires would be presented to him, and was so disappointed with himself for falling for such a rudimentary trap, that he took his sword, thrust it through her heart and mauled himself before he jumped off the side of the cliff. Through the clouds he fell, arms stretched and crying his misery to the skies so loudly that, before he hit the ground, five dragons came flying from the fog underneath and rescued Zhen Wu from the crash. That day, he became immortal and joined the Dao in its glorious oneness.

Is that what he is? My last test?

"I have a mission, Jason," I say.

He bites his lips, breathes hard from the nose and walks the other way. I ask him to please let me finish. "I promised Shifu, my mother, and the gods of Wudang. I have a responsibility to women."

It takes a second for him to let my words sink in. He does that himself, goes to distant parts of the world to answer his calling.

He must get what I mean.

"Are there any other options that don't include beating your brain into mush?" He asks.

There aren't. But I don't want to have to thrust my sword into his heart. Not yet, with him so vulnerable. I let him talk. He asks me to wait, makes a phone call, says he would rather have someone else show me. I kiss him.

❂   ❂   ❂

Jason takes me to a little house in Berkeley. A porch hidden by trees made bald by fall, a door in the brightest color, framed by a construction as ordinary as everything around it. We thought about moving to that area once. Almost did, but the money wasn't there yet. I didn't have enough students, his residency wasn't over, my fights were still not paying well. I squeeze my hands hard, force a grin concealing my foolish reveries, and Jason rings the bell.

First, came the smell—incense. Then the big eyes of a skinny woman with radiant skin and the widest of all smiles. She gives my boyfriend a slow-motion hug. Dr. Mehta, he introduces her; or Anjali, as she insists. A surgeon, Jason's senior at the hospital, he says. She invites us in.

Inside, her house is so full of colors and textures I can't decide where to look. There are vases and pots, pillows and throws and sofas, stripes and intricate patterns of radiant colors and different shades of metal, ceramic and textiles. She serves tea. It smells good, tastes even better. "So, you are Dr. Sonderup's feminist girlfriend. Nice to meet a sister." She's so…so…calm, composed, luminous. Her voice, deep and soothing, gives me spinning chills. Her head sits tall on top of her mile-long neck, her eyes are a yellow that makes you stare in a trance. As if the tigress… was her. I can see why Jason seems awed in her presence. But I hate the way he ogles her. And, I think, the way she beckons back

152

with her half-raised eyelids, blinking so slow they hypnotize. Did he bring me here to tell me he has another woman? Or just to make me so jealous I drop fighting against other men to fight for him? Bad move, Mr. Doctor. Bad move.

She gives me some time to breathe, pacing slowly to the back of the room. No—floating. That woman floats. The bookshelf. I've never seen so many books in one place. Her gaze goes straight to her left, about the height of her waist, and without any hesitation, picks one. Then another, large and thick, one of those photo books rich people like to display on their coffee tables.

"He asked me to tell you about this woman," she says, "Phoolan Devi, the greatest fighter in the history of my country." She points at the cover of the smaller volume. "Have you ever heard of her?"

I shake my head, now anxious to hear her story. Maybe I underestimated Jason.

"The Bandit Queen, we call her in India," she proceeds, "because she was once the leader of bandits who tortured and killed a rival group near where my parents lived. A woman, leading a pack of violent criminals."

Oh…are they comparing my fighting to being a murderous criminal? Because if….

She may have read my mind, or chosen those words for another reason, for the next words out of her mouth were about that. Before becoming the Bandit Queen, she told me, Phoolan Devi was given in marriage to an older guy so her parents could have something to eat. She was barely twelve. This guy abused her for years, until she ran away with a lowly member of a local gang. One day, that gang was attacked by their rival and Phoolan, who was with her boyfriend when it happened, was captured and taken as a trophy. She was gang-raped for days. Weeks. "When they finally let her go," Dr. Mehta told, "Phoolan rebuilt her boyfriend's gang and led their quest for revenge. She killed her rapists, then went back and mauled her abusive husband. In the years that followed, she and her men took money from the rich and distributed it to the poor. Real story."

A badass, I think. But where are they trying to get to, here? *It's a trap*, my instincts scream. Like one of those moves on Tai Chi that parries a strike while stepping back just to make the opponent walk straight into your punch. *Tread lightly, Yinyin.*

She places the large book on her lap. The one with bright photos and big letters saying *Gods of India*. She looks like a goddess too, with her body thinly covered in glistening layers of color, her posture so perfect and effortless. She must do yoga. Is that racist of me? Am I stereotyping? Like when people assume I'm good at math? Am I becoming a trashy, jealous white girl? With the tip of her fingers she flips the cover. Beneath the longest eyelashes I've ever seen, her big eyes gaze at the words on the page, and her long fingers slide through the book. I imagine her touch—light as a feather, I bet, and I have goosebumps. She turns it toward me, the book. A statue of a woman with multiple arms, each one carrying a different weapon. She rides a tiger.

Yes, a tiger.

My breath gets stuck in my chest.

"People say Phoolan was a reincarnation of Durga," Anjali notes. Jason stares at me, as if he knows where this is going and is just waiting for my reaction. *The hidden punch I am walking into—here it comes.* She points at the prayer printed next to the drawing. To her it's upside down, but she has no problem reciting it nonetheless:

> *Sing of my deeds*
> *Tell of my combats*
> *How I fought the treacherous demons*
> *Forgive my failings*
> *And bestow on me peace*

A tiger-riding goddess of justice and women. The images and words burn into my retinas such that I will never forget them. They echo through my mouth in the form of a whisper, and I wonder if Jason realizes the mistake he's made. All that visit has done is make me even surer of what I have to do. Unless... *Forgive my failings?* Is he actually trying to say he is finally Ok with my...*Is that what this whole thing is? He understands me now?* I feel the tears rising in my eyes and sniff the few escaping through my nose. Our sights meet again, Jason's and mine, and I'm holding his hands. Oh, Jason!

Dr. Mehta tucks her silky hair behind her ear and continues. It feels like a ceremony of some sort now. The music, the scents, the words, her bearing. From a distance, somewhere in a land of dreams, she tells us about Phoolan's glorious years running from authorities, "like pirates from old Hollywood movies, until one day..."

She finally found love?

"Until Phoolan finally negotiated her surrender," she responds, with the sharpness of an arrow. "In exchange for a mild sentence for her people and a piece of land for her father." What? Ok, lady, I do want to know more, I think, but later. Now can you just skip to the end, when Jason tells me we're good again and we can be happy together and be real to who we are?

"It was in prison that she met him," the breezy voice continues. Jason kneels beside me and grabs my hand. My body trembles. I have flashes of rich white girls giggling and squawking and I'm afraid I feel just like them.

"Buddha," she says.

Buddha?

"And that's how she put end to her history of violence," Anjali says. "Like you and I, she understood her fight against the system had to continue. Patriarchy, castes...they were the problem. But it was only through peace and detachment that those problems could be fixed."

No, that wasn't happening. Jason, he was going to propose.

"As a result," Anjali continued, "she ran for parliament, and with a promise of peace and solidarity for the poor, she was elected."

The hidden punch, after all. They watch me in silence now. Two tigers enjoying the ambush they've set. I slowly pull my hand back to myself and guard them against my chest. Everything's upside down to me, like the photo of Durga is to her. Anjali places the small book on top of the image of the demon-killing goddess. "A gift. In these very strange times, maybe her story will help you find your way too," she says, and Jason stands up, bows with his hands palmed in a prayer pose, and walks to the door. Her face, I can tell, is a self-congratulatory monument to victory and I know any negative reaction I dare to show will mean I lost.

So I thank her for the hospitality instead, and let her close the door behind us.

For a second, or maybe a minute, I blank. Think of my own gods and Zhen Wu's fall down the cliff. So innocent and desperate at once. Did I just do that? Let myself fall into the abyss? Let my insecurities and bodily needs tarnish my judgment and will?

Then, it comes to me.

I knock on the door again. Fast, before Jason can stop me: "What happened to her?" I ask. "Is she still in parliament?" The doctor's luscious eyes fade a little. "Two years after her election, she was assassinated."

My own journey comes in more flashes. From holy temples in Wudang, to the secret labs in California. The victories, defeats and dates; the knockouts I fed and ate, the nights Jason spent teaching and patching me. The training, so strenuous, the sex, so tender. The pleasure of taking blood out of men who think they can beat me just because they have a ball sack, and the sweetness of arriving at home to see a giant bowl of ice cream just because he wanted to see me smile. I could see my strengths, my shortcomings, my attachments, and they didn't matter. Right here, I have a chance to hold on to the past or leave it all behind to focus on what I ought to become.

No, bitch. It's not me who is falling into the abyss. It's you. In my fantasy, I take a step back and punch her into the thick fog of Wudang. As if she can see it too, Anjali excuses herself, and we hear the door click for a second time. On the top of the cliff, I remain. A goddess with six arms, each holding a different weapon. I win.

"Please, babe. There are other ways." Jason says.

I tell him I know there are. "But those are your ways, not mine. I am a fighter."

"No, you're not!" He says, "You are an enlightened person, I can see it in you. A kind, and gentle, and funny, and spiritual Tai Chi teacher who…"

"Sorry. I'm not. I am a beast. And I don't want to be anything else."

He shakes his head in disbelief. "Even if that means…"

At the gates of Heaven, we will all be tested. Mine rests there, in that ordinary house at Berkeley, California where, under the light of the holy promise I made to Shifu, to my dead mother and the gods of Wudang, I walk away. Alone, victorious. In spite of the fact that inside me, it was feeling like free fall.

No dragons anywhere.

17
Carrying the Cosmos

At my door, a box awaits. Red and gold with cheap plastic beads colored to look like jade hanging from the lace. No one around to claim it, no note or card. Jason. I can still smell him. Did he get here before me to leave an "I'm sorry" present? I unlock, rush to check the window. Maybe he's still there. No sign of him. Although, across the street, an old, fishtailed car, red paint and golden wheels, starts its engine and wends around the first corner. Almost as if it wanted to be seen. Strange, but no time for silly games.

It wasn't Jason. His bag still lies near the TV. The medicine box. The jiu-jitsu mats we use for classes and more. A pair of sneakers next to the door. He wasn't messy, but his little ghosts are still everywhere. Little reminders of our life together, our future apart. In the corner, the oxygen tank, totem of my other past, stood tall and defiant. Just in case, I cover my face with the mask, release the valve.

Time for the box.

Whoever left this took their time to make a very traditional Chinese wrap. Layers and layers of paper, all sorts of intricate patterns, until I get to…the gift: a red-lacquered piece of wood, carved in the shape of a leaf.

No, it's not a leaf! I leap toward my side table, open the drawer. I know it's there.

Shifu's carving. A red feather, like the one in the box. They're no perfect match, more like hand-carved to match the same original design, but definitely a pair. Shifu's friends. Those I was supposed to have looked for. To finish my training. Was I being summoned?

"Chinatown," Shifu told me when he first gave me the carving. "Find my friends there." I wonder if master knew that neighborhood was nothing like the little villages near Wudang. When I arrived, sad for the loss and inebriated by the big city at the same time, I didn't go. Too busy, I told myself. Then, ashamed of the reluctance, I didn't have the guts to reach out. Finally, I pretended I had forgotten.

Maybe it was time.

The next morning, I call the lab saying I was going to be a little late. The BART from Oakland drops me at Montgomery Station in San Francisco. From there to Dragon's Gate, just a few blocks. The smell of dumplings, roast duck, incense. I hadn't been here for a while. Almost forgot how hectic it was. Tiny shops everywhere, filled with phony Chinese souvenirs and Golden Gate T-shirts for the tourists. Finally, I spot them. *I knew they were here!* Red lanterns on jade-colored light posts, with golden dragons on top. Like the box and the fishtailed car. I'm in the right place.

Seeking some sort of sign, I continue to walk. So many people. So rushed and ordinary. What kind of life is that? They argue in screams that cause white tourists to curl, fearing a fight. Cars honk as if there were real traffic. All bearable only because of the soothing notes of an erhu somewhere afar. No other musical instrument represents China better than it. I can imagine the artist playing, dumb Americans taking photos of the "strange lap violin that sounds like a kung fu movie." Then, the worst: from all corners, a different cat waves, always that stupid happy face. Cats, I don't mind. But I have a problem with smiles.

Keep going, Yinyin. Bakeries selling wife cakes and bubble tea pass by, kite shops, wok stores. At times I stop, show the red feather to a local to see if they know what it is. An old lady scoffs, smacks her head with a palm, calls me dumb. Then rushes in, locking the door behind her. A street vendor, a shopper that seems local, a girl distributing pamphlets for the nearest massage parlor. They all titter and disappear inside. "Hey, what's funny?" I'm left outside, no answer. Once I saw it, though, it all made sense. On the corner of Sacramento and Hang Ah, a tea house like every other. Except this one has a giant sign saying "Fèng-máo."The Feather of the Phoenix. It has to be it.

"Nihao." The old man serving a guest greets me and I show him the red carvings. He chain-bows, "Som Shifu. Som Shifu. Xuéxiào" and points at the little martial arts school across the street, behind the fishtailed car, camouflaged among all that gold and red.

"Dragon Scale Kung Fu School" says the window decorated with lanterns, curtains, and carved wooden trims. Bodies over-flow beyond the door. Tourists, locals, white people with cauli-flower ears. I push through them. The place resembles a beehive. Crowd, movement, buzz.

Inside, an old bald man with a big belly and a disobedient beard does some clown shit. I position my hands in a discreet Daoist sign, hoping someone there would notice, and watch the bearded man circle his fingers in the air. Four feet away, a bunch of idiots follow with their faces. He palm-strikes the empty space between himself and his opponents, and the foes all drop on cue. In his real-life cartoon, the old fart defeats all his fake enemies without placing a single finger on them. Would be awesome if it wasn't a disgrace to the reputation of real kung fu. The Chinese part of the audience applauds. Myself? I want to get in there and beat the guy for making an ass of my country and my art.

Someone hits the gong. A young kid who acts too serious for his age.

In fear, the circus disbands. So fast that before the sound is over, only the old man stands on the mats. Glorious, superior. Master Som, I bet. In Mandarin, he talks to the crowd; the gong boy translates. "Today is another chance for secrets of the ancient art of Chinese gong fu to be seen by America. May the challenger say his name?" I hope the challenger is good.

"Josh Blauberg," says the redhead. A white, Japanese grappling uniform covers his torso and hangs over his orange board shorts and fingerless gloves. He carries a new black belt, still stiff on the edges from lack of use. Kid doesn't look very smart either. Hard to say who is the bigger joke.

The old man and his translator continue: "Mr. Blauberg answered the challenge…to anyone who dared to face Master Som's qi. In victory, the school will pay him five thousand dollars. In loss, Mr. Blauberg agrees to tell the world…about the superiority of Chinese gong fu against the modern world of mixed martial arts, or as they're called today, em-em-a."

The American nods. They shake hands. Bow. Shake hands again. Bow. Awkward. The two build distance, then another gong. I can hear the kid's feet brushing the mat, slow, cautious. There is no buzz anymore. The old master cocks his hands, and with no warning, throws his magical qi bomb at the young guys. From the audience, a rude American screams "Hadouken!" and a few others laugh. I don't blame them, but would love to beat them for their manners, anyway. Nothing happens.

Flustered, the old master walks toward the opponent, waving his palms as if collecting an invisible load of qi toward his belly button to reload his qi bombs. Meanwhile, the American, with no sense of decorum, walks toward the master with a fist raised to announce a strike, and hits him square in the nose. No attempt to defend.

"Oooh!" exclaims the crowd, in fear and shame. A collective loss of face.

A few in uniform rush to attend the master. They surround

him, frenetic, loud, speaking an odd mix of tongues and throwing accusing looks at the contestant. The American walks in circles, chest up in a physical brag he doesn't deserve, the eyes skipping between his friends and the angry gathering around the host.

Gong! The master is raised to his feet and for a second, I wonder if he got distracted by my hands. He points my way with his eyes. "Again," says the shifu. Reluctant, the gong boy thumps it one more time.

The charlatan throws a meek and unbalanced kick in the air and is countered on the ribs. A roundhouse, sloppy and unimpressive, but on target, nonetheless. The old man bends just to eat a knee in the face, his grunt echoed by the entire audience— even visitors. The kid was already diving TV-wrestler-style, ready to finish the fight, when a startled crowd leapt between them.

Please, Gods of Wudang: make this man *not* be one of Shifu's friends.

Students and visitors push, yell, point fingers. A brawl, ugly in both its blood and its lack of honor. Unless the jocks are much better than their ginger friend, they are going to get killed, and there is nothing I can (or want to) do. So I prepare to leave.

A thunder interrupts: "Stop!" commands the master, and a river of silence widens the gap between the fighters. Was he talking to me or them?

Master Som now stands in front of the winner and his friends. Chin high, head tall, eyes wandering to the sides between the shiny bald head and the protruding belly. Betrayal. Dishonor. Shame. Behind, his eldest student shakes his head in disgust. He raises three overstuffed red envelopes, hands them to the winner.

With scorn, the outsiders accept the prize. I would have slapped them right there. Good manners you test in victory. But I have nothing to do with them, so I watch the brawlers depart, teasing the crowd with their vulgar boast. So toxic, their path remains empty even after they are gone.

"Leave," mutters the master. "All of you." His eyes are distant, his voice unsure. Nonetheless, the audience abides. I follow, sad to witness an elder face his end, no matter how ridiculous the whole fanfare was. I think of Shifu, how heartbroken he would be the day he couldn't defend himself anymore. In a certain way, I'm glad he departed before his fall. Someone pokes my forearm. A short Chinese elder. He has the dark and rugged skin of a fisherman, hands like stone. His rich silk robe says something else: a man of possessions. So confusing. Behind him another elder also in silk, long and shiny white hair pulled into a perfect ponytail, slow aristocratic moves. They repeat my Daoist sign in their bow.

It didn't take long for the students to empty the school of any visitors. They close the door. The window. It's only the four of us now. The bleeding impostor, the two men in expensive robes, and me. I say nothing. If anyone is to talk, it must be them.

"The vigilante thing, young woman. Not good for community," says the owner of the school. I respond with a befuddled glare. The short dude interferes: "Sorry, he's getting old, losing his manners."

"You have something that belongs to me?" says Master Som.

I'm not ready to respond yet.

"I told you. She doesn't know shit," says the grumpy short one. "Do you?"

In silence, I say no.

They take my backpack. Geriatric thugs. So sure of themselves I don't know how to react. Before I can, the darker one is already pulling his thick fingers back out. The bag drops on the mat and his hands expose the two lacquered feathers I brought.

"My name is Fai Tián," says the tallest of them. He reaches into his pocket and opens his hand. Another carved feather. "Enchanted to meet you, young lady."

"Mine is Lau. Sing Lau," says the dark-skinned fisherman. With the other hand, he shows his own too. "Those you carry belong to Master Som and…your father, I believe."

"My Shifu," I respond. "My father was someone else."

They all bow in respect, and Master Som points to the back of the room, where a small octagonal table surrounded by richly adorned Chinese chairs seems to await us. In the center of it, a silver tray and in the middle of the tray, one lonely peach awaits.

The three masters turn to me in anticipation. I get it. They call it a Dao fruit in China. A gate to immortality. But I'm not a fan, so I take my seat and ignore the offering.

"What?" Master Som asks. "You don't like magic peach?"

"It's not that," I say, trying to change subject, but they insist, so I am forced to explain. "It makes me feel…" Damn, why am I telling them this? I try to forget about it again but their hungry-mutt faces won't let me. "It feels like I'm having sex with a woman, Ok? Not that I have any problem with it, but…it's not my thing!"

Around the table, they slap their hands on their foreheads, some making more noise than others, and make gestures of outrage. "See? That's what you get for being such a liberal teacher," Master Som says. "What do you expect? Start with teach Wing Chun and wrestling. Where else would it end? Not liking peach," says Master Lau. "You have a dirty mind. Your father would be very, very angry."

This time it's Master Tián who corrects him. "Her Shifu, you old dog."

They all grin; I am not sure why. Shifu Lau orders the young man to take the silver tray away, and then turns back to me: "So you came here to…"—he waves his hand in a circle toward the faint bruise in my face, his expression lost between pain and disgust—"…finish your training, I suppose? You don't seem so good."

How dare they? I had just watched an unimpressive beginner MMA fighter defeat the so-called *master* and they are mocking *my* face? Saying they would train me? Having been raised to respect the elders, I avoid voicing my thoughts. Shifu must have been senile at the point when he ordered me here.

"I came to…" I say and give the host his wooden feather. And you know what the motherfucker does? He grins again. Then he claps twice, above his forehead. Like a drunk rich monkey. It doesn't take a second, and a blur rushes from behind the panels carved with golden dragons and phoenixes. A pale young man, carrying a tray with tea for four, bows to the masters, then me. That red hair…he rises. The MMA dude?!

"Shifu?" says the flame-headed servant, still wearing the top of his Brazilian Jiu-Jitsu gi and the short black belt. The mock fighter leaves and Master Som asks: "Did you really think that was real?"

They all explode into loud, obnoxious laughter. The fool seems to be me. Trying to save face, I stand, just to be sat back again by their kind, yet very firm hands. "Please, wait, young girl." His eyes are full of resolve. "You are one of us now."

"Us?"

"Us, the Red Phoenix Society," says Master Tián.

"Such a stupid name. Sounds like Harry Potter shit!" interrupts Master Lau.

"You too American," Master Tián barks back.

"We've been here for thirty years, thickhead," replies Lau.

More loud laughs. What do they have in that tea?

Master Tián proceeds: "There used to be more. More of us. Used to know so many things. Shape-shifting, combustion, alchemy, poetry, telepathy…some of it was lost when the bomb unbalanced the qi of everything on Earth."

"Hiroshima," explained Lau. "But we still know big ones." Tián continued: "We started to get old, sick, and some died… We're the only ones left. The Shadow Leap, you learn it yet? From Shadow Monkey."

I stammer. "Me? I…I did…I mean…"

Master Tián reaches my hand and places a finger on my pulse. "No way. Too much yang," he says, "And this…" He waves at my face bruises again.

Master Lau agrees with a nod, but then gives me a gentle grin: "No worry needed, little one. You are young. And woman. Women learn slower."

My skin must have burned strawberry red because the owner of the school had to jump in: "But become good later! Better than men."

Fucking eggs. I try to stand up again, but the pony-tailed master, Tián, holds me again. "Want to break curse, need to fix qi," says Master Lau, followed by Master Som: "Want to fix qi, must own family secret." Then Master Tián: "Want to learn family secret, must break curse."

Great. A coordinated riddle. Just like Shifu used to do. Although Master wouldn't use it for such mumbo jumbo. His tales explained real techniques. Qi bombs to explain joint alignment. Iron body to explain bone bruising. Shadow Leap to explain his dazzling footwork. I get angry. "Sorry, I don't believe in magic," I reply.

Yes, I say that, to their faces. And part of me immediately repents. Bad manners have no excuse. Even in truth. They are now quiet, somber. Trading looks, communicating in a silent language I can't comprehend. I close my fists waiting for darts to come flying into my head, for someone to grab one of the spears on the wall and crack my skull with it, or a giant with a machine gun to turn me into a noodle strainer. Too many mobster movies? Maybe. Nothing happens. I calculate my chances. These three old hacks, barehanded, I can take them down. The wooden leaves are still on the table though. I stretch out my hand, as slowly as I can. Maybe they won't see it.

PAK! The tall one slaps my wrist. They are laughing again. Three deranged, senile kung fu frauds. Oh my. No time for dotards. I grab Shifu's gifts anyway and storm toward the door. Why would he send me to these people?

"Yinyin," says Master Som.

Out of a politeness they don't deserve, I turn. He has his palms facing each other, holding an imaginary sphere like we do in Tai Chi practice. His weight loads over his back leg, rather elegantly, I must say. Then his hands move to the side of his waist and I can swear the walls bend a few inches. It can't be. Did they put something in my tea? Then he shoots an imaginary ball of qi in my direction with so much poise I leap to avoid getting hit. Such a fool! And BANG! The door bursts open behind me.

I admit, *that* trick was good.

The host bows. "You like that, ha? Can't use often, though. Big qi waste cuts life short," he says, then looks up as if retrieving an old memory. I wait, and he finally continues, with a refreshed enthusiasm. "We also have blue flower and magic mushroom to mix with honey! For head demons, you know?"

What did Shifu tell them?

"Oooh, I see dragons! Dragons!" mocks the little fisherman, with a high-pitched voice that is supposed to represent me. "Give me magic mushrooms! So cool!" All three crack up laughing.

That's enough. I flip them my middle finger and slam the door behind me. I have work to do. A real job, not this hocus pocus bullshit.

18

Green Dragon Shoots Pearls

The American obsession with coffee, I don't get it. Caffeine feels good, fine, but the jolt lasts so little. And the silly ritual of office camaraderie—pour a giant cup, gossip a little, leave smelling like rotten paper and bad tea. Not for me. But, given the circumstance, I try. At least the ritual part.

"Ok...can you say it again?" Simon asks. I refuse, but the asshole insists. Then once more. "Please?"

Finally, I fall for it. "Lambrechts," I say, and immediately regret. He laughs so loud, people in a ten-meter radius shoot him arrow glares from their cubicles. "Rrrambletch-tss!?" he repeats, grossly exaggerating the way I said it. "Makes me think of the old man rambling about his God and Science nonsense," Simons laughs, "while self-flagellating with a whip. Shts! Shts! Shts! Not bad, Claudia. Not bad."

Fuck you, Simon. "I have an accent, so what? Talk to me again when you learn to say '*nihao*' right."

"Sorry," he says while opening the door to the training room, his face now mocking his own apology.

"He doesn't do that, right?!" I ask. "This self-flagellation thing."

"I wouldn't be dazzled," Simon responds.

Westerners are so fucked up. "I'll call him Dr. L, then."

With a sneer, Simon takes my cup away and asks me to stand with my arms and legs open wide, in an X position, as he says. Then to perform a Tai Chi form, while he tracks the data on the tablet. "Fine-tuning the feedback," he says. Then, to my surprise. he joins me.

The first attempt is a disaster. The man has no coordination. No tonus. Zero balance or flexibility. His body is just a jumble of muscles he never learned to operate. He almost looks embarrassed. Then, the hum begins. *Again*, he says in my head.

This second run is much better indeed. I can feel his weight shifting, his body adjusting. Real stillness through motion. His big and tiny muscles adjust to my pretty deep stances. *Have you been working out?*

Maybe, he says in my mind. "Say it again," he asks, now with his outer voice. "Dr. Lambrechts."

This is getting tedious, Simon.

He insists and I say it, just so we can move on. "Lambrechts."

See? You got it right. Muscle feedback working just fine.

Hum…Interesting, though before I can process, images of the makeshift fighting cage in Oakland hits my mind and I prepare for a flash. *Hey, how about you bring me there?* It wasn't a flash. It's Simon thinking about it.

To The School? I ask. *What for?*

To fight, of course. You can stand in my corner and whisper in my mind what I should do, get me through a few fights, then, after a while I can even try it by myself.

Part of me wants it really bad. Just so he can take a beating in front of a good crowd. I hear a voice asking *please?* And I don't know if it's my inner demon or Simon who's begging.

First, let's see if you're ready.

☯   ☯   ☯

169

It doesn't take much to reassemble the team. Mrs. Lee, the twins, Jen, Kira, Camara, Molly. There was some explaining to do, of course. Like, why the disappearance for a full week.

The questions, I answer as fast as I can. Broke up with Jason, depression, dug myself into this well-paid private training. A temporary thing, just to make ends meet and get out of my routine for a little bit. They only hear "broke up with Jason." Now they are all heartbroken and want to know more. Damn. I pretend I'm fine and try to skip to the next topic. "Why the sunglasses? You never wore shades before," they ask. "Have you been crying? And who are these two guys? Are you training men now?"

The men. "They are two physicists who want to connect to their bodies...to the universe. They gave me these shades because they are worried about...the greenhouse effect?" They frown in disgust. Did the best I could. "Oh, and Mrs. Lee, that's Dr. L. We talked about him, remember?"

The old man raises an eyebrow in surprise.

"Dr. L?" Simon says behind a chortle.

"Oh yes, indeed," my acupuncturist recalls. "I was your student, Professor. But you won't remember."

"Of course I do," he says, unconvincingly.

"Oh, of course you do, right?" She gets close to me and whispers, "He's so old now." Exactly, old and grumpy. Better stay away. I line them up. Old students in front of me, Dr. Lambrechts behind them all, trying to follow, Simon at my back. He knows the routine.

"Ladies, I want you to show these two gentlemen how great you are. Do you still remember the entire form?" They do. Camara and Linds made sure they kept practicing in my absence, and I am very proud to see they got better indeed. I get them to do it once with only a few vocal cues. "Move with intention. With purpose. Really good, girls. Dr. L, take your time, you'll remember it too." Gladly none of them is watching the disgrace he is. Then, as rehearsed, I give him a sign.

Behind our shades, our eyes light up. The hum resumes. I'm not sure how we establish it in our triple brain, but I am in charge. "Let's do it for real this time, girls. Tai Chi is like your experiment, Dr. L. It's all about making connections." I start moving and explaining. "Yes, connections. Your fingers to your hands, to your arms, to your elbows, shoulders, spine, hips and legs, so sink your body and let your qi flow."

My class. I miss seeing them, now I can do it …in three different angles! I watch them move, improve. I notice the impatience and lack of muscle tone in the old man's body, his poor muscle memory and lack of body awareness. This is going to be hard. *The feedback, Simon, much better indeed.*

How can he even walk like that? A voice replies. *I can hear you, young lady.* I knew.

Behind me, Simon observes. As planned, he's in charge of angles, lines, calculations. Combining his brain with mine, I can track it all. Feel it all, bodies and emotions. Mine, Simon's, Dr. L's, then their reaction to mine too. *Feedback loop*, either I think, or someone says. *Exhilarating, no?* Must have been Simon. *Yes, it was me.*

Shut up, I tell them, *I have a class to teach*. I pretend to look back to observe. "Linds, raise your knee a bit more; it will give you more momentum. Mrs. Lee, release the back or you'll lose your link."

It was so beautiful. Glorious. A transcendent display of art and science together. This could be a revolution. *See? It works outside the lab too*, someone says. I try to stay calm. "Feel your energy gathering at your core, people. Just don't force it there. Forcing your chi onto the dantien will make you crazy, apparently. Focus your mind on the navel area and let the qi follow. That's it. Now puuuuush, turn your palm up and…brush your knee. Good. Sooooo good."

"Kind of sloppy, no?" utters a voice with a strong accent behind me. From Simon's eyes, I see them coming. They were three. The three "masters" from Chinatown, walking in our direction, with a large Wholefoods paper bag. How did they know where to find me?

Why didn't you tell me? I ask the scientists. They have no clue what I'm talking about.

"Very sloppy," another voice says. The second insult stops us all. Humming off, feet back to the ground, I turn to the rude men.

"Hi, Mrs. Lee," the third voice says, and I take a mental note to ask her about it later.

"Can we talk to you?" the taller one with the ponytail asks me. Master Tián, I think.

"No, you can't," I say. I've tried being polite, but if they're going to insult me in front of my students…"I am teaching a class."

Behind my back, the shortest one among them reaches out to his bag and hands something to my students. Peaches! I barely have time to react before the girls start to thank them. "Wait," I say, but it's too late. Linds has already taken a big, groaning bite of hers. The old degenerates giggle.

"Is that what you're here for? Peaches?" I ask.

"I told you she ain't teaching any secrets," one of them mumbles, just loud enough so I can hear, "She can't even show them the basics."

Gloves off. Their choice.

"Can you do better?" I ask. There's a collective "Oooh" behind me, as if we were two odd Chinese rappers battling in People's Park. "Oh," I turn to the class behind me, "he also said girls learn slower, ladies. So pay attention to what they will show."

Under grunts, Master Tián raises his palms. "It wasn't me; it was him!"

Master Lau protests in return and they start their cycle of elderly non sense again.

"Lemme do it," interrupts Master Som, rearranging the belt

over his inflated belly. He takes my place, starts to move. And I must admit: from that wild boar little body of his came the most wonderful Tai Chi I've ever seen. Not even Shifu did it like that. So impressive, the students don't even bother following. We all watch, enchanted by such grace. Damn. Then I have an idea. I click my tongue to call Simon's attention and do the sign again. The sign. For the connection.

He shrugs, confused, and I have to lower my shades for a second, point at my two eyes, and his. Con-nec-ction, I move my lips, in silence. Not that smart for a supposed genius. The hum returns, and I turn back to watching the fat little master's spectacle.

With the extra brain power, everything is so clear. Now, while he moves, I can see vectors and equations taking shape. Little notes written faster than I can read. With Simon's and Dr. Lambrechts's mind power, calculations happen in real time. I measure potential and momentum, paths straight and arched, track ghosts of moves past. It all comes to me in numbers and theorems. Under our math, his Tai Chi is naked. Unprotected into equations. Mine to decode, in every detail. I see the clouds of qi shifting up, down, and across. Is this how it feels to be super-intelligent? *No, Claudia, this is more.*

Shut up, guys, I have to concentrate.

By the end of the sequence, applause from the class. Embarrassment was supposed to be my name by this point. I know the culture. I understand what he was trying to do. Humiliate me to force me to beg for his guidance.

My plan was better.

"Let me show you how I do it. May I?"

On my command, Dr. L and Simon line up with me. They wouldn't have to, but the theatricality of it helps. At first, the three visitors protest, but the authority of a shifu in front of her own class does the job. "Watch this, girls," I say. In a straight line, we drop our knees, raise our arms in front of our chests, stretch

173

our fingers just a little to release the excess qi. So soft, so yin, so pretty. Though, if the moves are impressive, the synchronicity is even more so.

"I guess I need to go back to the geriatrics class," says Mrs. Lee.

We apply the stolen equations to each of the twenty steps of the form. Only drawback being conditioning. *Hang in there, Doctor. Keep your abs connected; save energy.* The Chinese dudes keep watching, and at this point their intrigue is gone. There was, maybe, surprise? Fear? Intimidation? *My legs can't hold it anymore*, I hear my own mind say. *Almost done, Doctor. Almost done.* Fan through the back, turn, right back...*So, peaches, huh?* My head says, and I tell Simon to shut up, then the alien pain strikes hard. The doctor is on the ground. Embarrassingly, humiliatingly. And apparently funny too, for except for me, they're all bursting with laughter. Especially the three intruders.

"I guess we should come back another day," they say, trying for disdain. Though I see beyond: relief. Either way, they seem to have gotten the message.

"Yes, see you someday."

In my head, and those of my "colleagues," too, I tell them that it is fine. I hear *a fuck yeah* and a *humph*. Easy to tell the origin. Despite the fall at the end, we still had an amazing show. And incredible evidence that the brain link works outside the protected conditions of the lab.

During the water break, Mrs. Lee pulls me aside. She too is eating a big juicy peach and I try to pretend that's Ok. "Are you Ok, honey?" She reads me too well. I don't really know if I'm Ok but don't want to talk about it with those two hanging in my brain like that, therefore I lie: "Yes, all good." She isn't buying it, but respects my choices and we get ready to resume class.

"How do you know those guys, Mrs. Lee? The Chinese ones."

"One of them taught me Daoist philosophy, another introduced me to acupuncture, and from the third I tried to learn kung fu, but I didn't like his fake hocus pocus qi stuff. That's when I started to train with you."

That's sweet of her, yet odd on so many levels. Now back to class. The two professors protest in silence. Dr. Lambrechts, at least.

All in all, it was a great day. The students seemed excited about the revival. And I couldn't stop thinking about the potential of all this. Teaching directly to a student's brains!? Fucking incredible!

But what did those three old men want with me?

From my inner voice, I ask Dr. Lambrechts if the knowledge transfer worked, despite the distractions and interferences of the real world. *Remarkably*, he says. The funny thing about this is, if the voices sometimes get a little jumbled, you can sense the feelings quite clearly while the link is up. So, when Simon gets intrigued by a van watching us from the other side of the street, I feel it too, and so does Dr. L.

"We must go, right now," interrupts the old doctor. Then the connection drops; he rushes toward me, an awkward speed walking that doesn't suit him at all. He grabs my arm. Says I'm not understanding, we must go. Oh boy…I glare at the hand squeezing my arm and back at him. He's lucky I didn't throw him face down on the grass for an extra dose of humble tea. And I would have, had Simon not interrupted me to point at the black bread-shaped car. The driver, a large man with a military hairdo, makes eye contact and smiles, picks up a camera, and defiantly takes a picture of us.

"I don't like this," whispers Simon.

Unaware of the man in the van, Ash asks if everything's Ok. I nod. "All good, people. Thanks for coming today. We just realized we…have to discuss a few things before our meeting! Tai Chi things, I mean. For our project…"

Although unconvinced, they grab their things and leave. Each in their own direction, while behind my shades, I keep my eye on the van. What is that creep doing observing us? As if he'd been listening, and unafraid to be seen, the door of the van opens, and six men spring out of it. Six *big* men. T-shirts, boots, precise movements, hair clipped short. Military, or something like that. The last one tips his hat to us and follows his team in the exact same direction that...I poke Simon's rib. "That's where Mrs. Lee went!"

19
Iron Fan Through the Back

From a distance, we could see Mrs. Lee throw the pit of her juicy fruit in the trash and wipe her hands on her sweaty pants. Maybe there was a naughty smile too, but maybe that was just my imagination. The parking garage isn't too far from the park, but on the weekends, they turn off the elevators. She takes a deep breath and charges up the stairs, oblivious to the six thugs closing in right behind her. A few blocks away, the three of us move as one. A full sprint across the park, our legs pumping in perfect synchrony. Simon is glad he started to wear sneakers after he met me. Dr. L tries to keep breathing.

"Building is closed," says an armed guard we could swear wasn't there when Mrs. Lee walked in. Why would a police officer guard a garage building?

No time for that. *Think, Yinyin.*

"Yes, sir. Sorry, sir," replies Dr. Lambrechts.

What a sissy. There is a side door, I remember—Mrs. Lee and I used it when she gave me a ride a long time ago. And up the stairs. Fast. Too fast for the old man, actually. He stays behind. Third floor, that's where she parks. I kick the door. On a regular business day, it would have been packed. Today, just big letters printed on pillars, a few cars scattered among yellow marks on the floor, a few stinky puddles of motor oil. There, under a lonely spot of light, her. Also there, below the other lit lightbulb on the entire floor, them.

"Yoo-hoo! Grandma!" calls one of the big guys. She turns around angry, "What did you say?" The thugs close the distance, surround her like a pack of wolves. With her purse pressed against her body, she recoils. "You got a present for me, old witch?"

"Hey!" I yell, and they all turn. *What are you doing?* My head asks. They all come in our direction. The original victim doesn't matter anymore. That's what I'm doing.

It's just Simon and me. It will have to do. On my command, we widen our stances and raise our guard. We are ready, or at least want to look like it. Simon seems excited now, and I think I am too. Still no sign of the old man. Let's do it.

On their side, a big Latino dude points at us, "Look, boys. The Power Rangers." To which we respond in a single voice: "Look, boys. Clowns," We take a moment to enjoy their bafflement, then continue, "Yes, clowns who are about to get slain."

Because of either the synchronized speech or our stupid defiance, they pause. Six versus two. One of them picks up a pipe from the floor. The others punch their own hands and stretch their necks in an intimidating gesture. *Let's show them, Tigress*, Simon thinks in my head. Where's the old man?!

No time. We charge, screaming like lunatics. It even startles them for a moment, then they rush to the clash. That's when we first notice the ceiling lights following both them and us like, like this was all choreographed. *Is that you?* I ask Simon. *No, but I guess that's not important right now.* Indeed.

One of these teams is going to be really fucked today, I say in my head. *Let's make sure it's them.* We nod at each other, the adrenaline pumping so hard the world loses its sound, and life is now in slow motion. *Simon, I know we can do the same thing, but can we operate independently while linked? We're about to find out. Fuck. Fuck. Fuck.*

Their first move: a wild punch toward my head. I see it coming, calculate the direction and landing place. *Every vector is clear—thanks, Simon.* I duck under it, parry the arm downward to increase his momentum and finger-jab him in the eye. No mercy. He brings his hands to his face. Screams. I spray his torso with more punches than he can count. While he drops, I gift him with a beautiful teeth-crushing knee.

One down. Now, the other two.

Wait, what do I do?

Fighting is just a series of millions of calculations happening really fast, Simon. Go with it. Your head calculates, mine breaks their necks.

Fighting is different when *you're* not in shape though, so I have to adjust. *Simon, have you ever stretched your legs in your life? Can you kick higher than your own hips?* He gives it a try, feet to the knees, of both of his guys. Their kneecaps give an audible pop. Both are out. Really? Simon is two-to-one on me? My next two guys. They are close, one raising a pipe, I aim at him, track his swing. At the right leverage point, my weight drops to the floor, and I pull his arm over mine. His head and shoulders are dragged by gravity's effect on our combined masses. Suddenly chaos feels so freakishly...mathematical? *Fractal,* an inner voice says, *there's always order when you can see.* I wonder what Shifu would think of this. Crash! The break ripples through his bones. *Good job, Tigress! Was that me or you? That was you for sure, little girl. Need some help here. Wait...*

It's like I replaced one disorientation for another. I can map every move outside of my head, but inside, it's a mess. I feel a drag. Another dude. Another attempt at a takedown. Why do they always do that? I sprawl back and hold him by the shoulders. He pushes, my feet slide backward across the ground. Fine, I can hold here for a while. A few feet away I see Simon trying a takedown himself. *Are you stupid? The dude's three times your size and probably wrestled his entire high school life.*

Sorry, Claudia.

The distraction gets me tagged on the top of the head and the world takes a little spin. We are on the floor now, his entire weight is over my chest. *Focus, Yinyin.* I breathe, then find the one thing I can do to relieve the pressure. *Thanks, Jason.*

Oh, that's cute.

Shut up, Simon!

Jason's principles. He tried so many times to explain. Now, with the math, I get them. The physics of the leverages and wedges, the frames, his strategies to consolidate position before moving forward. All so alien for my martial upbringing. *Follow me, Simon.* I swim my arms between my face and his arm to allow some space, then around his waist. Somehow, I know Simon is doing the exact same thing. *Now slide the head, under the armpit. Gross, sorry.* We gotta climb on their backs, but *wait…wait…Now!* It works. *That's good, Simon,* I say, like a silent corner coach in a big fight. He responds, *That was all me. Shhhh.* It's like I can hear Jason showing me how to lay my chest on the opponent's back then wrap my arms around the chest and hook the feet into his thighs, "like a blanket with seatbelts." I follow the instructions, then slide the arm around his neck, under his chin. *I know,* I tell Simon, *that's an awfully giant neck, but we can do it.* On my command, we hold the inside of our other elbow and the free hand pushes the back of his head again. *Now relax the muscle and stretch. Let the pressure build.*

Strange to see both our fights overlaid through different pairs of eyes. Lots of angles to explore. I feel dizzy. Maybe it's the smell of car oil. *Simon?* Lightheaded too. We need some air, and glucose. *Shit! Where is my guy's leg? I can't see from here. Simon? Thanks.* A little yank to one side, then a swing of the hips and flop. Simon and I have our backs on the floor, our entire bodies bridged between our shoulders and toes. Hard to breathe, huh, big man? My guy struggles, tries to bounce off. "Not going any-where, buddy."

The other fight. *Protect your eyes, press your head against the neck, yes. No, no, no, don't open, keep pressing his neck.* I am about to take over, but Simon bites the other guy's hand. *That'll do too.* We are back in the same position again.

We arch our backs, press their torsos forward with our abs, pull the leg and neck like a bow. Two bows, actually. Simon's choke is a bit over the chin but still works. *More pressure, Simon. Feel that crack? It's his jaw.* It feels so good, like a…*Focus, Simon. Sense his veins pulsing inside our arms, their heads growing, red and stiff. That's good. Hold there.* I can feel Simon's back burning and his arm going numb. Not the time to let go yet. I change the muscle groups. Pull from the back, not the arm. *He will go to sleep, I promise. Three, two, one, zero, minus one, minus two… See? I told you. Now let go.*

Simon, let go!

An extra voice joins our connection. *Here! Are you Ok?!*

We both turn back. Dr. L, panting his lungs out, his yellow eyes shining in the dark, the heart rate at 197 bpm. *We got it, old man.*

The joy. The thrill. It's like you're a savage. A beast. Out of control. Feels so good. Better than I remember. Maybe because this wasn't in a ring, with rules etc. Maybe because…*Simon, let go! You're safe. Don't want to kill the guy.*

He releases the pressure and tries to stand but instead he throws up. I hold his forehead while Dr. Lambrechts checks the surroundings. No one left. Just a scared Mrs. Lee, leaning against the hood of her car, quivering like green bamboo on a stormy day. The hum recedes.

"Holy shit," Simon mumbles to his hands. "I can do judo!"

Technically, that was Jiu-Jitsu.

"Hey," Dr. Lambrechts screams and we look in the direction he's pointing. On the other side of the floor, a man taking photos of us—or videos, you never know with these cameras. Has he been there the entire time? And did nothing?! We step in his direction but we are too tired to chase. Behind the heavy door leading to the stairs, he disappears with no effort.

"Raise his legs," I say, pointing at the smallest of them. "He needs blood back in his head."

"Let him be," Simon broods for a moment, then follows my order.

Behind us, Mrs. Lee stands, patting her clothes to clean up the dust. She still seems shaken, so we ask. "I'm good, I'm good," she insists, "You guys go! Whatever you are doing, get out of here."

"Are you sure? Any clue why they were chasing you?" She shrugs, hence me turning to the waking one. "Who sent you here?"

"The…monkeys," he says.

Mrs. Lee gawks down at him, confused. "Now animal rights are after me too?" She glares back at me and kicks the dude's head.

20

Lifting Water

He watches us. Two arms pointing outward. A third, almost a foot lower, aiming at me. His single leg bends forward, empty, in a cat stance. With respect, I return the look. The wooden man, icon of all kung fu, is ready for battle. He's mine, at last.

Right "now," I am twelve years old, and I can hear a sound: water, nearby. The scent of leaves, bamboo, China. A clearing invites me in. Broad, circular, the sacred ground where we train. Although this time, it's something more than that. I check the data. In my trips to the present and past, no other memory has been visited more often. Kind of an all-time favorite. In my case, a title so full of irony.

Shifu's black and white robes make him seem made of wind. He floats toward my inanimate training partner and stands before its trunk. Clat! He tests the stems with an upward slap. We exchange looks of excitement. Back to the enemy, he drops his knees inward, brings the wrists against his, and begins. Both palms up, pointing forward, receiving hands between the sturdy fists. Clat, clat! A head grab and a wing hand rolling underneath the arm. Clat thump! Master's legs move swiftly around the opponent; their hands never disconnect. Shifu recoils around his back leg—on one side, elbows heavy and wrists soft; the other, a waiting hand near his chest—then BANG! Through the small area of his palm, his whole body slams the man of wood.

It was splendid! The attack pierces through the dummy's centerline and its trunk shakes in delight. The wood cackles with Master's qi waving through its veins as if it were its blood. Clat, bang! Birds fly in fear. Critters big and small peek behind leaves. Even the bamboo seems to bow. And right there, I learn to love those sounds more than anything. More than Jason, I think. Jason doesn't belong to this present, anyway. Or to any present. Not anymore. I go back. Clat, clat, clat! Baaaang!

"So, this is where you live?" Simon asks. I wake up from the memory, back in my studio, with a red-haired scientist moaning and rubbing an ice pack against his shoulder.

"Didn't you see it already? In my head?" He points at the dummy, asking for permission, and I step away. He gives it a try. Thump, thump, plunct! It's embarrassing, but I don't say that. Don't say his pain is bullshit either. I can tell how much it hurts. Felt every little strike—definitely not worth the ice. But he begged, so what could I do?

That's not why we are here.

The dizziness. We need to recover. "The ice cream and O_2 are on me," I say. The O_2 tanks in the lab have a better balance between nitric oxide and oxygen to open the lung vessels for better absorption, but that one is Ok too. Besides, Simon seems more interested in the dummy.

"This used to belong to your father, right?"

"My master," I correct. He's moved on already: "And that fight! Can you believe that fight? Crazy! I thought those guys were about to kill us and then we just…It was like…I've never done anything like that in my life!"

Sitting on my futon, nose dug deep into the oxygen mask, Dr. Lambrechts complains. "Irresponsible. Outrageously irresponsible."

What did he want? To abandon Mrs. Lee? "We didn't measure anything, didn't have a control element to compare. Zero scientific planning."

Fuck him and his method crap.

"Are you kidding me?" interrupts Simon, still battling with the inanimate dummy (and losing). "Six mysterious meatheads stretched on the floor because of this extraordinary specimen of the human race we are lucky to have on our side, otherwise we would be a hundred percent dead. Is that science enough for you...*sir?*" He waits for Dr. Lambrechts to close his eyes to focus on the breathing and winks at me.

"That's not the point, son. We've exposed ourselves! And for what?"

"Don't blame Simon. It was all my fault!" I apologize sarcastically for forcing the two of them to save an old lady in danger. Beg them, with my voice filled with the utmost fake drama, not to expel me for that. Plead with him, above all, not to put Simon on time out. I had to force him 'cause he, the only adult in our group, couldn't get up there on time.

Dr. Lambrechts rubs his back and moans as if he had fought those guys with Simon and me. So stupid, what brain people think pain is. If they'd ever had their heads turn against them and try to squeeze itself until they wanted to jump through the closest window, they wouldn't call *this* pain. Bunch of fucking strawberries.

The argument is joined by Simon, admitting he wanted to fight the assholes too. "As much as *you* did." He points at the boss. "Or you think I didn't feel your fight boner?"

The older scientist drops the mask and storms toward the door. "I should have never let us leave the lab. And we should have never come here, either. In fact, we should get going. Right now."

I'm staying. And I let him know.

"Me too," says Simon. "A bit longer, at least. See you tomorrow."

Lambrechts slams the door—so weakly it makes me laugh. "How about the lights?" I ask. "You noticed that too, right?"

He gives me a vague "yeah," before he raises his arms. "Who is he?" He asks, holding one of Jason's old blue and white boxers with a chopstick. Boyfriend? Ex, probably. He must have left it hiding somewhere. So sad, and so embarrassing.

"Who is he? Someone less nosy than you," I say. He knows already, I'm sure. About Jason. That he's an MD, that he teaches me jiu-jitsu, and is a Buddhist. That we broke up too. I tell him anyway. "We had a fight."

"Sorry, but he's dumb. Why would he fight someone so… incredible?"

Wow.

"The fire you have, that's not something machines can emulate. The knowledge, yes, the technique, perhaps, but the fire… Dr. Lambrechts and his superior little doctor buddies would be doomed by computers way before you, write that down."

"Shifu said that fire is going to kill me someday."

"Something will," Simon says. "Unless—"

Does he know? About my past, my plan? How deep has he gone into my head? I change the subject: "Was he a good teacher? Dr. Lambrechts?"

"Used to be brilliant." he says. "A revolutionary. He is different now. Still very intelligent, and defiant in his own way. But maybe too interested in the business practicalities of our research, instead of the philosophical implications, like he used to be. You saw in the Anamnodome, his questions about God and everything. I don't necessarily subscribe to that part of the thinking, but at least there was a quest there. Now…"

Yes, I do remember the Anamno-demon thing. But it's getting late, my body aches. If he wants to talk about lives past, there's a fridge full of reminiscences of my dead relationship waiting for him. I grab an iced tea, throw Simon one of Jason's beers. "Gonna hit the shower. Make yourself comfortable."

"The lights," he says before I can close the door, and I pause. "I saw it too. Those things are getting smarter. But don't worry. For as long as I'm around, you're safe."

☯   ☯   ☯

Bruises, stiffness, fatigue…Once the adrenaline wears off, there is always some pain. I stretch for a little comfort, grab the phone to check my messages. It's been a while, and I wish I hadn't done it. Jason's name is the first thing to pop up, still the first in my important numbers. Must fix that. Like…right now. I swipe it, see the red button saying delete. Do it, Yinyin. Damn, it. I dial him, instead. "You've reached the cellphone of Dr. Jason Sonderup. Please leave a message after the beep."

I take my shirt off and breathe, relieved.

"Jason, it's me," I say, although I'm pretty sure he would recognize the voice. And the phone would show my name. *Why are you being so dumb, Yinyin. He's gonna think…Screw what he's gonna think. Tell him you miss him. Ask him if he wants to talk. Maybe. I should.* Then the voice comes out of my mouth, "Found the envelope with the rent money, thanks. Next month I should be fine. Don't worry. I'll call you another day."

From beyond the door, muffled clats tell me Simon must be trying the dummy. The sound alone tells me it isn't going well. "How do you do that?" he asks, and I don't bother to answer.

In the shower, the steamy water covers my vision and my body. Tendons relax, muscles let go. Part of me feels proud for not caving. I'm no princess, don't need to be saved by Jason's righteous sword. I am my own sword. I am my own saving and revenge. My head leans against the tile and I let the heat lick the pain away. Oh, I needed that.

Reminds me of home, the shampoo. Bamboo, forest, creeks.

The noises of wood clatting outside, I turn them off, dim the lights. There's no Simon beyond that door. There's nothing else beyond me and the drops massaging my hair, neck. I rub my skin indulgently, making my every hair stand in response. The foam carries away the last remains of the tension. It tingles now. Arms, chest, belly, legs. Between. The water is so luring, I don't notice the presence of a distant, soft hum.

☯   ☯   ☯

Clat. Simon's hand rolls around the wooden arm, giving him chills. Goosebumps. So light to the touch. The body, so close. The steam. The foam runs through his fingers. Slow now. His eyes close, hands slip on the sides of the torso ahead. He imagines pulling her close. Claudia. Me. Pulling her head back, mine, and tongues touch. Rolling and slipping. Dancing. His fingers slide across my back and through my hair. Mine on his. Closer and closer. Our mouths, so tender.

"Oh shit!"

I push him and we're out. No steam, no water, no dim light. His wooden dummy routine goes quiet. In my shower, the water stops too, and there is this silence. A long and awkward one.

After a while, he goes back to the dummy. Clat, clat, thump. Better, but still bad.

The doorknob twists in almost silence and the hinges moan. He can smell me getting closer, I know. Patting my hair dry. Can imagine the loose clothes revealing my tattoos. He knows I am watching his attempt with the wooden man. Simon hits the trunk, slap up on the two arms and down on the lower one. "That way, you're going to hurt my boyfriend," I interrupt.

He must be blushing, I can tell, despite the fact he doesn't look. We both know what happened. He tries: "You know, that jackass...don't let him convince you...I've seen you fighting, and it's beautiful. You and me, together, I can make you the best fighter the world has…" I get behind him, turn his body around, and cover his mouth with a finger. "Shhh. No more brain shit."

We kiss. Like we'll never stop. Twist our bodies and I lower my hand down his chest, and then we are on the floor.

☯   ☯   ☯

The wind blows on my face while I glide. Afar, the seventy-two peaks of Wudang and the forest where I grew up. The steaming water of the river from so many stories I have heard. I see my reflection. A beautiful butterfly. Love my wings. So colorful, so vivid, so wide. Like the mushrooms Shifu used to give me for my headaches. That's one thing I miss—not the headaches, the beauty of the treatment. The brain bugs are more reliable, preventative. But the colors…I miss the colors the mushrooms used to bring.

Back to Wudang. The corner where, in my fantasies, the tigress of the story and the bees have fought. Nobody there now. Just a man in black and white robes. Shifu. He waves, and I land on a large mushroom right next to him.

"Shifu?"

He gives me a finger to rest on and the kindest smile he's ever shown. "I have a message for you. In danger, think butterflies, just like you. Many, many, many. As many as you can. And help will come." I flutter around him a bit more, overjoyed at seeing my master again. He giggles. I land on a rock right in front of his nose, so we can talk more.

Then something hits me. From behind.

Master says, "Oooh" and covers his eyes, giggling once again. I stretch my neck back. Another butterfly is attached to me. As they do when butterflies copulate. It's embarrassing, confusing, but feels good too.

I wake up, still stunned. Simon's asleep, his naked butt touches mine. I turn around, his eyes open slowly. "You still here?" I say.

"Of course."

I let a lazy and satisfied moan escape while I stretch and watch him get lost in my ink. "What was that, Mr. Nerd?"

"So…if we do it connected, does it count as masturbation?"

I don't bother to respond. Better focus on the memory.

"Hey, what is this Shadow Leap thing?" he asks.

Damn, Simon. Mood killer reaches level two hundred and one. I grab my shirt, but he holds my hand before I can put it on. "Just an old story my family used to tell," I say. "To freak people out. Now get the fuck out of my head."

His eyes dive back into the drawings on my skin. The patched tigress, the beehive, the shadow of a leaping monkey. Reminds me how I love them too. My tats. But not right now. I rub my body against his, count to three. To five. To ten. He doesn't get my message. "Turn it on," I demand, and he looks at me, at his penis then at me again, confused. "Turn on the humming, you stupid egg," I say, and grab him by the hair. From both outside and in, I push his head toward my belly and beyond. The brain bugs finally have a good use.

21

Parry and Punch

"What are these?" Simon yells from the kitchen.
Please, not another pair of briefs. (Mental note: clean the house, someday.) I wipe the condensation in a circle, try to see what he is talking about. A slice of toast in one hand, two red wood carvings in the other. "Toast!" I say.

He finishes the bread, the coffee, and stops by the bathroom before he leaves. "Did you get your money yet?" he asks casually. "Seems like the monkeys froze the bank accounts of everyone at Oak Tree. Nice try...But we've been preparing for that. Fake names...ghost accounts. At least Dr. L and I were."

I shrug, wonder if he heard me talking to Jason on the phone.

"Let's just hope they don't crash the entire economy just to distract us a little more. America can take presidential assassinations, mega-floods, even the plague. But mess with the economy, and it's war." he says, takes another sip of his coffee, and continues, "But we need to be ready before it escalates."

He leaves the mug on the head of the dummy and I have to hold back my growl. Tell him I'm more worried about my own brain.

"I told you," he says, through his next bite, "as long as you have me, you're safe. By the way," he continues, his voice almost tender, "no awkwardness, right?"

The idiot doesn't know girls can have casual sex too. Although last night he was pretty nice. "Hey, did you say all that just 'cause you wanted to fuck me? Not the economy stuff, the things about me being....Because if you did, it was a pretty good job for a..."

"What d'you mean? *You're* the one who seduced *me!*" he protests, in false indignation. "And yes, you are indeed the most extraordinary specimen I've seen among our kind."

"Oooh, is that you being romantic?" I say, mocking mostly myself. Deep in my guts, and a bit lower than that too, I kind of like it, but I'd never confess.

He leaves while I'm still showering. I told him to. So I get dressed, prepare a bite for myself, and grab the carvings Simon was playing with before he ate my food and didn't bother to do his dishes. The TV is on. Just the news. Nothing there I am interested in seeing. So I grab the remote and press off.

But it doesn't work.

Instead, it brings a world of colored squares like those in my vision. Although this time it is empty, other than a single little pink creature in the middle of a wide lawn. A pig. What the fuck is that? Then the bell rings and the screen goes dark. What an asshole. "Is that your idea of a prank?" I say to Simon through the crack of the door. Except it wasn't him.

Jason!?

My face is so shocked he has to laugh. But soon his smile melts away and he comes in, avoiding my eyes. In my head, I'm scanning the place for any signs of last night's visitor. "You haven't cleaned the apartment since I left?" he asks.

Phew. I ask him again what he's doing here.

End of his shift, he says. Got my call, thought he could stop by to say hello in person, talk, scoop up a few things he left behind before his trip....

Yes, like your man panties…"What trip!?"

"Syria. I decided to go help at a refugee camp next Thursday. First trip as the head doctor." he says with more heartbreak than enthusiasm. "By the way, glad you told me to cash the money. Thanks. The bank said after the blackout things got a little unstable, so they had to shut down some accounts for security reasons. I left part of in on the red bag behind the sugar bowl, if you need it. How about your…job?" he asks. From the cabinet in the corner, he grabs a handbag that may actually be mine, stuffs it with his giant first aid box, a few T-shirts he left behind (bye, pajamas…) and goes straight to the place where he left his blue and white briefs. Motherfucker dropped it there and still remembers?! He pauses, quietly. When I realize, he's holding a yellow boxer instead.

Godammit, Simon!

The Buddhist doctor gives me the saddest grin, the one from a superior being who has no business asking questions, then magically remembers to check his watch and zip up his bag. "Just realized I'm kind of late now."

In panic, I ask him to wait. He does. I can't find an explanation, though. Go blank. "I understand," he says, the melancholy dripping from the side of his eyes. "We broke up, you moved on."

He leaves, and I call Simon. "What the fuck? Did you take my ex's underwear?" He says he didn't, that would be gross. Just threw it under the bed and put his in its place to make me remember him. *Fuck, fuck, fuck.* Guess I am better off alone.

We hang up and I leave, slamming the door behind me, fantasizing Simon's neck was right there, waiting to be chopped. We broke up, Jason said, I moved on. I didn't. I am just a giant fuck-up, Jason. Unfortunately, he's not around to hear it anymore.

☯   ☯   ☯

When life weighs on my back, I like to breathe my roots in the quietness of China Camp, the old fisherman village in the North of the Bay. Let the water wash my feet, watch the fog dance afar, reminding me of Wudang and all the stories I left behind. A world that keeps calling me back. But I was running late, Chinatown would have to do. I check the sky, too pretty. Damn. Beautiful mornings attract tourists, who take a walk through those few blocks into an obstacle race. Sometimes, in these situations, I play "don't touch me," a little game I invented to see how many bodies I can avoid until someone's body hits mine. Good for the footwork, I decided, not caring if that was true or not. But it's tough. Not to move around them, that's easy. But keep my cool...for some reason they seem to believe the right way to walk on the sidewalks is on a forty-five-degree angle! Not forward, not across, in between, just to slow me for as long as they can. It must be a conspiracy. A massive joke the world is playing on me today. And that's not the only joke.

Other than the language, the writing, and half of the faces, Chinatown looks nothing like real China. Not ancient enough in its old, or modern enough in its new. Yet every time you get to a crossroads and look in the right direction, you see the Transamerica Pyramid pointing up, and that makes you smile. The view of the distant building, with its architectural statement rising up from Downtown, may be the most Chinese thing in the neighborhood. That and the eateries. Those are the real deal if you can read Mandarin.

Back to my mission: the sham kung fu school. It is open. Class packed and everything. From the window, I spot the three old sages teaching a class together (I call them that in my mind because the image works, even though I don't think that highly of those old farts). Three of them, three students, and a circle of young men and women around them all. The "sages" adjust the students in a V-shape formation, the tallest one in front, then tell the mob to form a group facing them. As the crowd attacks, they push forward as well, piercing through their foes, punching and kicking, and getting hit a lot too. But coming up unscathed on the other side.

Trying to make as little noise as possible, I go in.

"We learned to fight from the animals," says Master Som. "Tigers, mantises, cranes, vipers…they are loners. They defend themselves and no one else. Well, we don't know about dragons, but my guess is they are loners too."

Master Lau says: "Dragons are absolutely loners. Ever seen a pack of them?"

Mr. Tián adds: "It's called a school, not a pack."

They all laugh at their own grandpa jokes while I hold my breath—that's exactly what I told Shifu, minus the senile affectation. Mr. Som continues: "Would you stop interrupting me, for the immortals' sake? What I was trying to say is that there are other animals that fight together. The lion. The monkey…" That's when they see me. Mr. Som waves me to wait.

"When you learn their styles, you learn their single forms. But if you look at the real world, from the epic battles of Shaolin to the most common wars between every little village you can imagine, the truth was settled in packs. And guess what: the style of packs is called…strategy! For next class, I want you to study strategy. Go find a good book—Sun Tzu's, or *The Book of Five Rings*, that despite being written in the Capital of the East is still a good piece of work, or any other book on strategy you can find. Read, take notes. Next week we will discuss it more."

Class dismissed, I wait, watching them share last observations, laugh, push each other, and do their final bow to the masters before they leave. I miss my class. I long for the camaraderie you only find among brothers and sisters in arms. And, in the back of my mind, there's something else. Like a mental itch, an idea trying to burst, but I can't quite process yet. That's why I need my super brain. But I'm here on a mission. So I give them a Daoist bow and extend the lacquered feather I took back with me "by mistake."

"Xie xie," Master Som bows back at me.

"Decided to resume your lessons, young one?" asks Master Tián.

"Not really, Shifu. Trying to see if my girl ambition can bring me somewhere first."

Master Lau asks about my student and the others admonish him. "Shut up, pervert," utters Master Som, hitting him with a cane on the shin.

They apologize.

In my head, I skim the list of students, wondering if the old perv was thinking of the twins, perhaps Connie.

"Mrs. Lee," says Master Lau, "black one, big chest." He gets another slap from the owner of the school.

"We don't say those things anymore," Som says, stroking his long beard.

"Whatever. That one has the spirit of a dragon horse, I can tell! And I tell you more: we have a link..."

A link, that's it! My mind races. Packs...links...a memory so vivid I could be there again: in the Cave of Insights, Shifu asks in disdain if I had any original idea yet. I do now. Back in Chinatown, Master Lau winks at me as if he had seen it too. My thoughts shoot in so many directions, I get lost. I turn to face back, face forward, back at them, at the street. One more time I bow, then again. Even to the wall. What are you doing, *Yinyin? Leave*, I order myself. And obediently, my body follows, cringing hurriedly through the door.

22

Golden Rooster
Stands Tall

S ome people are brought to life to prove they can develop
their power. I came to show I can tame mine. Controlling
the beast was the quest the Dao chose for me even before
I was born. Yang, my family name, sounds like one of the most
common in China, but written like mine, like the harder force in
the yin-yang, worked as the curse that prematurely killed every
one of my ancestors. My mother tried to soften it by calling
me Yinyin, unbothered that it sounded like a boy's name. Yang
Yinyin, the same name as the majestic symbol of the mountain
on the trigram. Wisdom, she told Shifu, and peace. I would
need both. Later I tried picking Claudia as my Westerner alias,
to allude to the clouds in Wudang, which are soft but have no
trouble moving around the peaks. Shifu liked it, for he used to
say words have power, and every time someone called me by
either one of my names, they would be helping me escape my
old destiny. Though after I grew a little and he had a chance to
understand my personality, he only addressed me as Mulaohu:
The Tigress. That's where my ring name came from.

"Which name did we use again?" Simon asks, barely pretending to be confused. On his little screen, he picks the file named

Tigress and sends it to the nearest printer. His smugness tells it all. He knows. Not everything, but he can sense it. Are we connected now? I check the hum. Nope. I am just being transparent, I bet. The papers: I flip through the pages to the third one. A line saying "one year," a strikeout in red, done with visible rage, and my own handwriting replacing it with "four weeks and that's all."

"I wanna stay," I say, "a bit longer, at least. There're a few things I need to explore." Despite that it's never been posed as a question, Simon nods, victoriously.

"Well," Dr. L responds, "now that we tested the technology and know it is working, I am not sure we will need you longer than that, Ms. Yang."

He only calls me that when he wants to sound like the boss.

"What do you mean? Those creatures are after her, you've seen it!" yells Simon. Thanks.

"I don't know, Simon. You've had your Rocky Balboa fantasy; we got our data...."

"No," I say, "you haven't learned shit. I can prove it." I take my stance and wait for the hum, which Simon gladly initiates. Right after, Dr. L twists his eyebrows, intrigued, and joins us too.

Bent legs, raised guard chin tucked in, the two scientists take position. Their eyes glow in the brightest yellow. As I cross my gaze with Simon's, he winks, and some steamy images that have no business at the workplace flash in the back of our heads. Dr. L rolls his eyes in disbelief. I must agree with the old man. *What the fuck, Simon?!*

A bow to honor both and they charge in perfectly mirrored moves. Two flying kicks aimed at my chest. I swerve sideways, walk right between them. "Do you know why this is called martial arts? Because unless you let your spirit show, you have nothing."

They try again, both a straight punch and an hourglass step, then a frontal kick. Once more I walk between them, roll my arms under their legs and throw their heads onto the mat. "At least you're not afraid of dying anymore."

Takes a few attempts for them to learn to pick different positions and moves. But getting hit does that to your mind. Teaches that if you do the easy thing, it hurts.

"Very Pavlovian," says Dr. L, rubbing his neck.

"Perhaps we should start, then?" I smile, because I didn't need to hear their thoughts to know what they are thinking. Yes, folks. That was just the warm-up. From now on, you do something silly, I am going to hurt you.

"You know we can hear you think your next move too, right?"

Really? How has it been working for you, so far? I think.

Dr. Lambrechts nods. "The kid has a point."

"Ready? Come."

They do. Simon on the right with a double punch, Dr. Lambrechts on the left with a roundhouse linked to a spinning kick. They stare me in the eye, trying to listen to my next move. Idiots. I let my brain drift and once again move between them, my foot stomping the foot of the young, knee to the balls and a palm strike to the chin. Then, just to keep it simple, an elbow into the skull of the other. PA-POW! Their brains shut down. The hum disappears, and their bodies lay flat on the floor. And people think Tai Chi is nice…

There is a huge bang. The door bursting open. Yewa blasts in, eyes stretched wide, her mouth covered by her pretty hands. "Oh my god!"

"Don't worry, they'll come back," I say.

"I'm not worried," says Yewa, a strangely satisfied grin creeping onto her face.

We wait. And while we wait, we talk a bit more. "They were pretty confident they could beat you," she whispers. For a scientist, Yewa is quite funny. When she dares to speak, at least. I tell her the Chinese tale of a praying mantis that thought it was so strong it could stop the emperor's carriage. So it waited on the road for months until one day the emperor came. From the window, he pointed at the dancing insect and said, "How adorable!" Then drove his carriage right over the bug.

She laughs. "They're cute like that too." Then, after a pause, she asks me to ignore the conversation we had the other day. "It's not that I am unsure about what we are doing. It's the right thing. It's just that when Dr. Lambrechts talks about building gods…I was raised to feel guilty about that."

Interesting creature, this Yewa. A bio-nanoroboticist struggling with faith. Not that I can judge. We Daoists have our superstitions too. I raise my knuckles and offer a fist bump. "He's going to let you stay on the project, don't worry," she says, "Do you know how crazy you all look when you come back? Kind of high."

The good girl then realizes what she said. Shakes her head fast. Contorts her face in shame. "Sorry, forget I said that." I want to know more, but to her luck, Simon starts to move. Then comes Dr. Lambrechts. Yewa and I are holding their heads—little infants with no neck control. "You've been knocked out. Can call yourselves men now?"

"Did you…take control of our minds?" says Dr. Lambrechts, still groggy, eyes wandering like a lost and scared little bird, just fallen from its nest.

"It wasn't that," says Simon. "Everything was clear. Until she stopped transmitting."

"Guys, did you hear what I said? Congratulations…on being knocked out…" They aren't listening.

The old man insists: that's not possible. That I stopped transmitting, that is, not that they got knocked out. They were listening, after all. He asks Yewa to bring him the numbers and she promptly disappears behind the only working station in the corner of the dojo. "You…stopped…transmitting. That's not possible."

"Yes, it is. It's called Wu Wei."

He scoffs, and I continue, "No intention. No-mind. To turn

off the fear, you turn off the thinking."

"Not possible," the old man insists.

"Don't listen to him," says Simon "Keep going."

Funny how alien this idea is for Westerners. In Wudang, you learn about it before you walk. Wu wei. You do that in life, you live by the Dao. You do that in a fight, you flow with the Dao. You move faster, react, yield, use every move of your opponent in your favor, without ever thinking about it. "Get it? No thinking, no transmitting, you don't listen to what I'm going to do next, my fist on your face." I pat both men on their shoulders. "Guess your little robots aren't all that powerful, huh?"

"It can't be," protests the boss. "You must be inhibiting the signal, somehow."[33]

But then the reports arrive. Charts covered in lines pointing everywhere. Brain activity, it says on the top of the page. One of the lines has a drop like the cliffs in Wudang, and only returns much later. He says, "Those gaps. Never seen them before!"

Simon's eyes grow to the size of tangerines. He points at another line. The levels on my primary motor cortex or something obtuse like that. It was much higher during the gaps. "Yewa, what's her current landing rate?"

"Ninety-seven percent. Stable for a few days, now."

"Can we raise it? Redeploy some units?"

"The units are there; they are just not connecting. I think this may be…"

---

33. All martial arts training, at some point, will push the practitioner to stop trying to rationalize moves and flow with them. Though the styles with Daoist roots take it much further—beyond fighting and into a way of living that respects the intellectualization of an issue as a starting point, just to establish that real understanding once you need no words for those thoughts. One of their most famous allegories (carefully told in *Daoism Explained*, by Hans-Georg Moeller) is the fishnet allegory, that carries all their commitment to a more natural, not over-rationalized life. The fish trap exists, they say, to catch the fish. Once it's caught, you don't need the trap anymore. The same happens with words and ideas. Once you grasp a concept, you no longer need words.

"Thanks, Yewa," dismisses the old man.

"How do you do that?" Dr. L asks when Yewa is gone. "Hide your thoughts."

"Westerners are too obsessed with thinking. There's a Daoist idea that says that once you catch a rabbit, you no longer need a trap; when you catch an idea, you no longer need thoughts." Instead of grasping, they try to go back to dissecting the thought: "Since there is no such a thing as not thinking…she must be in a state of deep free flowing…suppressing the…, but the amplitude…unless…" So much for those big brains.

"Simon, are you thinking what I am thinking?" asks Dr. L, who seems to miss the irony of the sentence altogether. Simon nonetheless agrees, says he remembers some studies showing, "before the brain triggers an action, whatever the subcortical regions have already thought about that decision."[34] The old doctor finishes his partner's thought: "If someone dives in a deep flow state like the charts indicate…"

"Maybe the thoughts are moving directly from the motor cortex, without any filter or consideration from the outer cortex?" Simon continues, excited like a puppy. This is getting ridiculous. I raise my hand. Ask if they know I'm still there. As in right next to them, while they talk about my brain. They ignore me.

"That explains…" Dr. Lambrechts takes a little notebook from his pocket, makes a few drawings without completing the thought. "Here, here and here," he points. Like me, Yewa seems confused, what with so many thoughts being skipped, while Simon keeps nodding in agreement to the words unsaid. Can I listen to the thoughts too? I try. Nothing comes. They are

---

34. A third of a second before the command is sent to the muscles, actually. It's as if the deeper areas of the brain conceive multiple plans of action in real time, letting the outer cortex just decide which plan to release, which ones to erase once the situation is over. As mentioned in *The Cognitive Sciences* (2013 by Carolyn Sobel & Paul Li, pp. 361-363), about Libet, B. (1989, March/April). "Neural Destiny: Does the Brain have a Will of its Own?", published on the New York Academy of Sciences website

flowing, and hard! Like me in a fight, leaping silently from the non-thinking parts of their brains. It's just that instead of fists, they are swinging their science shit.[35]

"Now go back to a regular situation, a regular person..." the old scientist says.

Do I need to explain I'm not regular?

Simon continues from where he left off, "If we find a way to hear these thoughts before the cortex picks its plan, we can choose the actions we want to unlock! Yewa, can the new bots read subcortical signals?"

"That can help with pushback ratios, Simon! That's a big Eureka, do you see?"

For all their supposed intelligence, the geniuses are getting it all wrong. "The Dao that can be spoken is not the constant Dao," I say.

"What?" they reply together, more annoyed than curious.

"That's the first line of the Dao De Jing. To see the mystery, you need to be still. Your mind needs to be still. That's how you do it. Not hearing deeper, but not hearing at all. You guys must be..."

Dr. L interrupts. Or, rather, dismisses me altogether. "That solves the scale dilemma, you see? If large numbers of people start to dispute every idea, that could cause massive halts in the system...." He grabs a little notebook from his back pocket and furiously scribbles a few more notes. "But if we could make them choose the *right* ideas..." he mumbles.

"These new bots of yours, they aren't the same ones in my head, are they?"

Yewa shakes her head and remains silent. Our minds are not connected, but I bet our thoughts must be exactly the same. Dr.

---

35. When scientists talk about intuition, they often describe it as an advanced way of thinking that skips language. It is interesting how similar that is to the Daoist ideal of skipping language and words in meditation in order to see the mystery of the Dao.

Lambrechts's God Complex, it has no end. I bring up the question of my contract. "Does that mean we can continue?" I ask.

Yewa hands them oxygen masks and they dismissively agree, completely swept up by thoughts so consuming there's no point bothering with such an ordinary issue like this little contract of mine.

23
Single Whip

There is a story about this Japanese man who wanted to be a Samurai. One day, he turned to his master and said, "Sensei, if I work twice as hard, when am I going to be ready?" And the master said, "Twice as long." The next day, he asked, "What if I work three times harder?" The Sensei thought for a while and answered, "Three times as long." The pattern lasted for weeks, with the student getting more confused every day. Until he decided to stop asking. He continued his training, but inside, his ambition to become a samurai had died. Is that what fate had planned for him? Serve his master to the old age? He thought. He did. The man dedicated all his time to following and supporting his teacher, until one day Sensei called him, told him to sit down, and gave him a sword with his name on it. "Congratulations, Samurai."

I tell this story after Simon explains the updates on the algorithm he has been tuning. "It'll be uploaded at night, while we're asleep, while the brain does its cleanup," he said. "It'll allow our systems to learn patterns of thought and anticipate conclusions our conscious level hasn't seen yet."

So when I finish my story, his comment is, "See? We are on the right path. Letting computers do some of the processing while the brain can relax, create some space to learn faster."

"The path is the one not trying," I say. "Not the one trying harder to guess what the master would say."

"Says the girl trying to hack her own brain to learn her master's tricks. Isn't there a story about the tip of the tail of the tiger or something?"

I feel naked. Violated. Growl at him. "Shut up, Simon." I'm not sure he realizes how much of an asshole he's being right now. For invading my memories like that, for using them against me. Is it because we had sex? Is that what's happening? For a second, I consider feeling bad, but then I get angry and the guilt is gone. We have more important stuff to do than be all sensitive.

"Already?!" Dr. L screams, interrupting my thought.

Oh yes, I almost forgot. Yewa. She makes her way to the center of the room and BAM!—slams a pile of books on the conference room table. We grin. They squint. "Books?"

"Yes, Simon," I say, "women read too."

"Sweetie, how about we do the reading, you do the moves?"

That's low, Simon. Even for you.

"I'm sorry," he replies. "Not sure why I said that."

I shoot a back fist at him. Much faster than he can react, let my hand lightly whip his ear. He screams a puzzled scream and covers the ear with both hands.

"Sorry, not sure why I did that," I reply. On the other side of the room, Yewa grunts a stifled cackle. "Here's the deal:" I continue, "In the lab, you're the bosses, let's study my absent mind. But while training, I am the Shifu. And I decided we are going to study…this."

He glances at the books. Some about military strategy, others about biology. *The Art of War, The Book of Five Rings, Roman Formations, Khan's Army, On Predators, Fire Ants…*

"What is *this*?" Dr. Lambrechts asks.

On my command, Yewa plays a video—a recording of Bruce Lee at a martial arts convention. Laguna Beach, 1967. The famous one-inch punch demonstration that started his ascension. We watch it once. Bruce place his fist close to the chest of a standing man, then his body shakes and the poor guy is projected three feet back and onto a chair. The audience of experienced martial artists reacts with a reluctant applause. I wonder what they would do if they'd seen my Shifu demonstrating fa jing with a *zero*-inch punch! But showing fa jing to the crowd is kind of frowned upon, so Bruce's demonstration will have to do. In our room, the scientists still don't know what they are watching. As planned, Yewa replays it frame by frame.

"Ordinary eyes try to understand the short punch by watching the fist. Which makes it seem like he can reach an impossible acceleration in that one-inch gap. But *we* can do better. Pay attention to his full body, all those slightly bent articulations." We track the back ankle, then the knee, the hips, shoulders, elbow, and wrists. "When you add them all together, there is a full foot of acceleration, connected as a whip. This is not that hard, to be honest, but it's not something you can learn by watching a video or reading a book. You need…the feeling."

They are starting to get it, I can see.

"Now the question is: if we can read each other's feelings, can we create that same whip, not as a group of articulations of a single body, but as a group of bodies?"

Their attention is all mine. "This can be the next revolution in fighting," I say. "Masters of the past created entire fighting styles based on a few techniques they developed. What if I told you it's our turn to create ours? One that can only exist because of our connections?" I take a break to check if they are following. "Currently," I continue, "we've been using our link to know what the others know. We never thought of fighting like a group."

"Like a Roman unit." Dr. L mumbles, "What's new about that?"

Westerners….Baguazhang also trains you to synch footwork for group fighting. But that's not what we are talking here.

"A Roman unit only works in rehearsed patterns," Simon

says. He's starting to get it.

"Exactly. The styles of my ancestors were mostly based on animals. Tiger, praying mantis, monkey, viper, crane...I guessed they must have run out of good choices the day I saw people promoting Duck style kung fu!" A little laughter. They're with me. "But now, because we have this connection, we can actually unveil a whole new set of animals."

"Like a colony," Simon says. "Bee-hive kung fu!"

Eyes lost on the ceiling in his annoying state of melancholia, Dr. L. asks why the books one more time. "Because we are about to create something original."

Yewa nods and looks down. I have to work on that confidence problem of hers....Later. I proceed. Take the fight at the parking lot, I tell them. I fought a few guys, Simon fought others, Dr. L watched. "Had we known any battle strategy beforehand, we could have done much better."

They glance at the books, exploring the titles and themes. A little bit of anything related to fighting as a unit, human or not. Three seconds pass before Simon fills the room with a loud "Fuck yeah, let's do it!" So exaggerated that seems a bit comical. He leaps over to the books and picks a few for himself. He's so odd today.

"We have more pressing problems," Dr. L insists. I beg him to try. To treat that as part of the experiment. After all, it's very unlikely our robotic enemies won't try something like it themselves.

The argument, or the insistence, who knows, does the trick. For the next few days, that's all we do, devouring each volume with our brains linked, so we can cross perspectives and stuff our collective brain with the combined learning. The knowledge, I can sense it filling my brain, adding to what I know, bending and expanding my understanding of things. Like a fight, against... not knowing.

The adrenaline keeps flowing as we add more and more. Per our calculations, we are eighty-seven percent done, when we hear another knock on the door. That woman, Nancy Karpel, Oak Tree's CEO. Now I know. She waves at Dr. L and asks to speak outside. We are still linked so he knows Simon and I don't like any of that. He forces a disconnect. "Give me a second."

"Those suits," Simon says with disdain.

It doesn't take long before Dr. Lambrechts is back. "There seems to be an investment group, from the Middle East I believe, no one knows for sure." He's pale, shy-eyed. "Some Crypto billionaires have made a major offer to buy Oak Tree."

That's dangerous. What if they start to look into what we are doing? I ask him if he knows who these people are.

"We don't even know if they are...people." Dr. Lambrechts responds. "For all we know, it can just be *them*."

The robots, I ask. He nods. Why not? Especially since the offer is contingent on us aborting a few resource-draining projects. He grasps for air.

Wait. "What are you saying, Professor?"

"They are canceling Project Hive, dear."

24
Jade Girl Works Shuttles

SWEEEEEEEN!

The mic feedback, sharp and loud, pierces through my ear and everyone else's. They need to invent a better way to silence a crowd. The sleazy announcer, with his slick hair pulled back and phony telenovela smile, cleans his throat right next to the mic so it can be heard. "Ok...seems like we have a big challenge tonight!"

The Hail Mary was Dr. L's idea. Maybe we can change their minds, he said. So Simon hacked the security cameras he needed and here we are. In the cage, together. I squeeze my partners' hands. I feel sick. What if we fail? Sleazy checks with me once again. *Shake it off, Yinyin.* From inside my top, I take a piece of paper. Unfold it over my head so everyone can see. A check.

"Our little Tigress here," yells the announcer, "says whoever can take this check from her before they reach the exit door can keep it! That's right, tonight, she's challenging every single one of you, my friends!"

The crowd throbs like an old muscle engine and I am back to beast mode.

"How much?!" someone screams.

"Can we take her too?" says another one.

"Can we kill the dorks?" Ha! I missed my people.

In the audience, a wave of ogres move toward the net, shake it, hoot like apes through the mesh. And they haven't seen the whole story yet. For a second, I think I notice the sages staring at me from a corner. Waving their chins in reprimand. Was it…? I turn back; they're not there. No longer or never were. Who cares? My business is with the other ones. The unwise. The brutes. I grab the mic from Sleazy and give them a long stare. From the bottom of my lungs, I yell, "Yeah, motherfuckers. You take it, it's yours. One hundred thousand fucking dollars!"

Insanity ensues.

They drool. Grab the net and try to take it down. Some attempt to climb it, fall, then take their shoes off to help. The thin wire cuts through their skin, but they don't care. Through blood and pain, they keep going. The mic is hanging now. Dead, in front of me, for Sleazy is already running for the gate. Don't do it, Sleazy. He looks back. It's real fear he's feeling. Against the loudest clamor The School has ever seen, the metallic mesh waves, the floor rattles, Sleazy quivers. In the back, Il Capo sweats a river. Whatever. They're getting paid for this.

In pulses, Sleazy yanks the gate out. The mob pushes it back in. Idiots. From above, climbers reach the top and jump in my direction. Formation time. Me in the front, them in the back. We have to take care of the men raining on us first. Didn't count on that. I feel the hum. We're in. In the zone. Eyes on the gate. It will break open anytime. The voice counts down: three, two, one, now! The stampede finally explodes in. I move to the side and the first jumper hits the floor, his head bounces on the thin mat just to get kicked square on the cheekbone by a vicious Dr. L. I feel it in my bones too. The break, the smash. The warm blood spilling on the foot that isn't mine. Even the old man's pleasure as he beholds the fallen foe.

The second one lands. From the eyes of the guys, I track others jumping. Together, we side-kick one over Sleazy, who is still trying to escape. A double knockout. Free from Sleazy, the gate explodes open, with such force it bends and breaks at the hinges. They are in, the stampede. I watch it from my eyes, from theirs too. All at once. The barbarians are coming.

The check goes back into my bra.

A flash. Really? An old man in black and white flowing Daoist robes, dancing slowly and precisely around his pupil's quickest efforts. Pliable body requires little movement, pliable technique requires no force. Then he leaves his fist high in the air and her nose hits it square. "That's how old man defeats young man," says Shifu.

Old man defeats young man. Good memory. Thank you. Did you see that too, Doctor? says Simon inside of our heads. I can feel Dr. L's appreciation, and disgust.

At the gate, they jam, the crowd. And keep pushing. Screaming so hard it wets our faces. We take an inverted V formation now. Feet on the ground, pushing the hand on the other side. Like a rocket, my fist strikes the chin of the first barbarian to slip in. The next one gets his nose pushed inward. In our heads, a big orchestra bursts. Simon. *More dramatic this way, no?* No time to discuss. We retreat, let them corner us in the back. That's the plan.

My foot goes against the frame and I bend it so slightly. No, it's not me, it's Simon. He lays one hand on Dr. Lambrechts, the other on my back. We brace ourselves. And we explode. Simon strikes the next of them with the force of all three of us, square. Like dominoes, they fall, but more keep coming, stepping on the heads and necks of the fallen before them. A tsunami of rage and greed.

In perfect coordination, my fist smacks one in the stomach and I drop my body, so Simon can hit another guy's face. Another one falls, and we get out of the way so the next ones can trip on his body and join him on the floor. Notwithstanding, more keep coming. In mountains and seas.

For them, it's chaos. For us, it couldn't be clearer.

Knee, shoulder, up! We climb over each other before they get close again. *Fuck yeah!* I go last. *Now.* They pull me. We are one, climbing the fence as a pack of deranged monkeys. Someone's rib hurts. No time to look whose. A nose bleeds, not sure when it happened either. Adrenaline wipes it out. On top of the chicken wire, we stand to watch the scene. For a second. The horde still tides over each other, climbs the fallen like a broken army with no honor left. In the back, Il Capo begs them to stop. So stupid. Barbarians don't listen. Eventually, they reach our side of the fence. They shake it, trying to makes us fall. But our hands on each other's shoulders, and our collective sense of balance give us sufficient structure to enjoy the riot underneath. *Hold on, Doctor.* There's no way they can unbalance an exponential brain that adjusts weight distribution in real time. The orchestra hits a slow stride. It's nice up here. Over that thin, waving wire under our feet, we stride. Didn't have to, but it's more fun this way. Our goal, the score panel, right over the gate—the weakest part of the entire structure.

There. I blow them a kiss and show them the check once again. That's it. The dudes outside grab the fence and decide that pulling it is a better idea than shaking it. Thank you, folks.

The structure bends toward the gallery, just like we planned. Simon and I go first. *Now you, old man.* Being the oldest, he waits for the fence to be closer. Smaller leap. He jumps, grabs the panel, we pull him up.

The gallery on the second floor is a five-foot-wide balcony around three sides of the squared patio, a low wooden railing protecting us from a fall. We are on one of the sides. The one in the middle has the door we plan to escape through. Not far. Then we see it, through Simon's eyes. A large man, with a large camera pointed at us. *Hey, no cams, can't you read?* He has a Mindcrack shirt. Is that…We gotta look into that later. I smile into his lens. Grab my own crotch and offer it to the fucker. Eat tofu!

A group of greasy twenty-something men pause in front of us. Seven of them. They don't seem that excited anymore. They've seen what we can do. They can't run either—not with everyone watching. They wait. More folks are coming from the lower level, we can hear. *Charge!* I go in the center, wearing my most unhinged face, slapping their limbs out of the way so my partners can strike them with ease right behind me. The stinky screamers…they pose so tough, but at the lightest touch, they fall. Sometimes even before we touch them. Impostors. There are some braver ones though. Those get thrown over the rail. They should have pretended too.

The door!

Locked! I take a step back and kick it. No results. Then a crash. A window, smashed. From Simon's sight we track the glass hitting the ground outside, the trash bin, the poorly lit street. We go. *I wanna see them cancel us now,* someone says. Maybe all of us together.

When sirens get close, we've already disappeared into the shadows. This is the end of The School, and that's Ok. Got all I needed from it. Yewa was right. It's like we are high. A nice kind of high. One that make us feel powerful, unbeatable, and horny as fuck. I glance at Simon; he, back at me. If it wasn't for the streetlights, we would have fucked each other right there. "Really guys? Do I really need to hear that?"

"Sorry, Professor," says Simon. Then we vanish.

25
White Crane
Spreads Its Wings

The smell of cigar is everywhere. In the leather of the chairs. The pages of the infinity of books about strategy, weapons, and the psychology of war. Every vein of every piece of wood, and wood is everywhere. Behind the medals, impregnated into the ribbons. The stains in the bronze light fixtures. In his uniform and skin. General Crane is proof that names aren't a prophecy. He's big, chest like a bear's under the shiniest white head. Not a single hair to stand up in pleasure or fear. Not even eyebrows. His lips are thick, like the smoke they blow. Like the voice they boast. He flips through a full stack of photos between us.

Myself, Dr. Lambrechts, Simon. Talking, doing Tai Chi in the park, fighting in the parking lot and at The School. "Is this really you?" the general asks, incredulous, then walks around his desk, casting a thick shadow over me. "The nanobots. They work, then?"

My head nods without my command.

"And the girl, are you sure the Chinese haven't planted her there?"

The head nods again. A single time, as a sign of confidence. General nods back. I can't tell if he trusts the answer but he proceeds, flips through a few more pictures then watches a video from the security cameras at the place formerly known as The School. Our connected fight. Then, the parking lot. Our fight against the big men, so perfectly lit because the lights somehow managed to follow us the entire time. "Does Ms. Yang know those were special ops?" His cheeks raise. "You have a deal. We can begin phase two." They shake hands and the body I'm in moves toward the door. I spot a mirror. Yes. Keep going. But right before I could see my reflection, the giant stands between me and the reveal. *Move! Move!*

"Move!" I yell. Everything is dark now.

"What did I do?" Simon's voice asks, as if coming from a can. No, the oxygen mask. The entire scene is so awkward. *Memories, Yinyin*…Yesterday, the fight. The escape through the alleys, the stairs, the kisses, the undressing…but the bald dude, it seemed so real.

"Bad dream?" he asks.

Yeah. Back in China they say waking dreams are disturbances of the soul. Distorted attachments and wishes. That General, he looks like my other vision, the one from when they injected me with the bots.

"Wanna tell me?" Simon asks.

Before I could say "I'm fine," he was already afar. Yes, it was an exhausting evening. Exhilarating, in fact. From the fight to the sex. My guts still tingle inside. That's one of the good side effects of having implanted so much science into my brain. In my mind, I can relive every moment I ever had. Can trace each fight, every strike and measure the efficiency of every counter considering the energy they used. Plus, my levels of serotonin, adrenaline, blood sugar, heart rate. I can calculate how to create momentum or absorb impact based on the faintest memories of what I've seen my opponents do. Everything is a file, retrievable, indexed and cross-linked. Yet, this waking dream has no link to any memory I can recall.

I pour myself some tea, sit on the corner to let the qi…*chill*. I laugh at my own pun, then perch myself in meditation and set my mind loose. A memory: my master disappears from my eyes and slaps my back in pure mockery. Then the three old men from Chinatown teasing me with the Shadow Leap. When did kung fu lose its manners?

"Says the woman using science to uncover her family's secrets," Simon's voice shoots down, as if coming from the clouds. Yes, asshole. You would do the same, had you ever seen him fight. *Let go, Yinyin*. Kung fu is repetition, Shifu said. Now I understand. Neural paths reinforced each time you repeat them become a solid part of your natural processing. Then weak paths get tagged by microglial cells to be erased when we go to sleep—or meditate. Like now. Go, microglial cells. Go, words I didn't even know I knew. I'm pruning my brain now.[36] Letting thoughts come, memories flood me and dissipate. One comes so fresh it's as if it was happening right now. Myself, in some sort of dark tower. Stairs spread both up and down, banging sounds bouncing in every direction. I tell myself to drop all fear—the enemy is not death. Another memory I don't recall. Is the Anamnodome still operating in my head? Trying to grasp reactions or something? I can see it sharp. Feel it crisp. Although not sure what that means. Though I'm not here to make sense of anything. Just to disconnect. Let the Dao guide me a little. I let go, let my spirit dive behind my eyes, and travel back to the woods where I used to train with Shifu. I am young, and he's teaching

---

36. The mechanics of how glial cells eliminate unnecessary memories when we sleep is a fascinating explanation for how and why some memories eventually vanish from our brain, to create space and build better circuits for our thoughts. (See Urte Neniskyte & Cornelius T. Gross' "Errant gardeners: glial-cell-dependent synaptic pruning and neurodevelopmental disorders," on the National Library of Medicine website (pubmed.gov, September 21,2017)

me how to lose fear. "Then you can do anything, Tigress. Even Shadow Leap." Yes, that's better. I hold my breath in excitement when a couple walks in. She's so strong, so fierce. That one must have no fear, I think. Him, not so much. But I can't see him. No matter how much I protest, Shifu sends me inside. But I want to see it. I watch them talk, then fight from behind the leaves. I remember that day now. How could I have forgotten?

Their battle is brutal but at the same time, kind. His flowing robe distracts her as he dances around her flurry of vicious attacks. She's angry about something. Then, beyond any possible foresight, *she* leaps in space. For a moment, Shifu seems enthralled. The lady knows how to Shadow Leap too! They continue the most spectacular fight I have ever seen. He throws her over his head, and despite the ferocity of the fall, her eyes are still alert and confident, her hair, shiny as silver with...black tips. Maybe that's where I took the idea. He slams her on the floor again. So hard, the leaves fly in all four directions of the world. When they settle again, there's nobody there.

Back to reality. It's 5:27 in the morning. Will be hours before Simon wakes up. Perhaps the Dao is telling me...I am ready for the Shadow Leap? I give it a try. Focus, collect my qi, drop all fears, and...

Nothing.

Again. Again. Again. Again. Again. 6:33 and I haven't given up. What am I missing?

A few thoughts occur. None of them comfortable. *But that's the life you chose, Tigress.* Comfort isn't for fighters. I grab a Post-it, write a note, and leave it stuck on the mirror. "Taking the day off."

☯   ☯   ☯

They offer me a bit more congee. It's delicious, but I have to say no. The business I'm after can't take more waiting. They offer tea instead. How come old people, who have less life ahead of them, always act as if they had all the time in the world?

It's hard to have an objective conversation when you're dealing with three old Chinese men. But I insist. Can they teach me the Shadow Leap? I'm a fast learner, I promise. They laugh.

"Fast learner, she says."

So irritating.

"The Dao can't be cheated, little girl," says Master Lau.

"Until you reveal your intentions, it won't budge," says Master Som.

"Not until your tail turns white," says Master Tián. Then, with a hand on my shoulder, he finishes their time-wasting ritual: "It's not knowing more kung fu that you need. It's *not-knowing*."

"So what is it that I need to *not-know*?" I ask.

"Exactly," they all say at once, and I want to slay those fucking dust-collecting piles of wrinkles! *Why do I keep coming here?* Ok, they do beautiful Tai Chi, and they gave me the idea of hive-fighting, but...Master Lau serves me tea regardless of my response. Says when they were young, martial artists were the police and the courtrooms, they took care of things, of justice. "Too much power, if you ask me. But when big problems happened, people needed more than strong palms, vicious fists and dangerous claws."

"Do you know who Nan'Chuan was?" Mr. Tián asks. "He was what white people call...an alchemist. He and his friends could change their shape into animals, turn stones into gold, travel large spaces in a blink....From generation to generation, these secrets were passed to people who swore to protect the knowledge and take care of others when the regular warriors or, later, the justice system couldn't."

"Then, BOOM! Hiroshima. BAM! Nagasaki." Continued Master Som. "The bombs were far but disturbed the planet's qi so much that those who relied on knowledge to manipulate it stopped knowing how to use their powers. The world changed, and their knowledge stayed behind."

Very convenient. Magic is real, we just don't have it anymore. Because of Hiroshima. I insist: "Can you teach me the Shadow Leap or not?"

Master Lau slides his sausage fingers through my hair. "I'm sorry, kiddo. Some things are not taught, they are discovered. When we are ready and balanced. With all that yang...hard."[37]

Ok. If balance is the key, time to claim my yin back. I peek at my watch. There is still time. "At least one of you is sincere," I say. On purpose, I leave the tea untouched. Hope that makes them as angry as I think it will.

☯   ☯   ☯

The Oakland Mission Hospital. It has a little concrete park across the street, with a wooden bench facing the entrance. Probably so friends and family can wait for their loved ones to be discharged. So many times, I've sat there waiting for Jason to leave work. The time is right. Wednesday, end of the night shift. Time to swallow my pride. Here he comes. Jason. Time for humiliation, Tigress.

---

37. The idea of Shadow Leaps originally occurred to me from the very realistic feeling that my Shifu, an enormous man with arms as thick as my legs, would suddenly disappear from in front of me and hit me on my back. He would later show me the footwork that made that possible, which he called Bagua—the short name for Baguazhang. He insisted that was a totally technical move. But I never let go of the feeling that it felt magical. So I made it real magic here. That said, old Daoist stories often include superpowers like teleportation, like the stories of how Zuo Ci would demonstrate his powers by performing magical acts like crossing walls and teleporting to markets far away, just to buy some ginger. Check out the Wikipedia entry for Zuo Ci for some interesting stories about him.

Chin down, a frown, no fists…He hasn't noticed me yet. Wait! What's that car? Jason? Why are you doing getting into that car…with that woman…that Indian lady!? Dr. Mehta? I know that look. I know the way you smiled at her, where your hand is going beneath the limits of the window. Fuck, Jason! You switched tigresses? Or…have you been seeing her all this time? I stand up, ready to fight for my man…scrap that, ready to kill them both, but in an instant of reluctance, they are gone. Fuck Jason. Fuck that fucking bitch. I call Simon. "Where are you right now?"

☯   ☯   ☯

The tingling…toes…the tingling…skin…the quivering…slow so fa…ast. *Fuck me, Simon. Yes, that…way. Like that Buddhist never…could. Yes, Simon, I agree: you are gr…eat. There!*

Sex is fun when the partner can read your mind. A magical roller coaster ride that adjusts its ups and drops and loops and curves to exactly what you're feeling. When every chill is noticed and underst…Oh, that was…fast. Really. Maybe…yes. *Keep going.*

I sometimes forget how you can feel every…inch of me. What's happ…ening? A…gain? Another current. A long ride of fucking spasms. *What are you doing to me? Wait.* I gag, hostage. My eyes remain open. Staring. Locked on the ceiling hoping for it to be…over. I'm lying. I'm not.

Waves, more waves. Slow. Then fast. And super fucking crazy fast until I can't…anymore. I can. He listens, body wants more…roller coaster. Tells him…where to…go. I force myself: out! Into…the dark. Eyes, shut. Nothingness. Yes. Peace. Soft.

Breathe, Yinyin. Breathe. Feel…the breeze. I remember it, blowing from my past. Bringing blossoms of cherry and plum, scents of kumquats and earthed water, like Wudang. It whistles around my ears and into my skin, then streams, chilling and naughty, between my bones and muscles, beneath my flesh, spiraling through the chest until it flows from the tips of my breasts. Cotton hands, Jason has. He touches me, and I turn into wind. And blossoms. Dancing in the air. A dandelion seed. Beyond the river, Simon calls, but I don't want to go back. I like peace, my yin. I inhale, deeply, roll to the side and pull the cold shirt over myself. I can stay here forever now. Then I see her, the woman riding the tigress, the one with many arms. Blood boils. I'm yanked to the other side of the river again. And again. So violent. They want me back. Simon. The ride.

Back to his roller coaster, I try to understand: Am I inside his mind? Or is his mind inside my body? The ride speeds through my lungs now, my veins, every fiber of me. Every nerve at once. I'm an electric mess. *Stop, let me take a moment. Have mercy.* He knows I don't mean it. This is crazy. Fucking cuckoo crazy, my body can't handle any more…of this. *Simon, what are you doing?* The heart beats fast. Really fast. In my eyes. And tongue. Contorts, everything. My head shakes, back rocks, I spread myself arched, clutch, pant, out. Out. *Out!*

Seriously, I need a break.

He slows down. Because he's tired, he says, and out he goes. *No more, please.*

Not today.

Off my guard, he goes. "Ride is over, madam," he whispers, eyes too wide, as if he's coked up, like Yewa said. I see it now. Do I look the same?

The link is off.

My mouth falls to the side, lazy, a half-smile crippled by my multiple small deaths, and he gives me a soft kiss on the temple, so oddly romantic I want to cry.

"Your boyfriend can't do that, can he?"

Vindicated, I smile instead.

These memories, I ask, "Can they be downloaded somehow? I mean, if there are robots in my brain, can I take the images and put them in a computer or something?"[38]

"Oh, kinky…" he says.

Idiot. I slap his chest. It thumps loudly. "No! I'm just afraid when I dump you one day, you will put me on a revenge porn website. You know I'd kill you, right?"

"I'll wait until you die."

That smell. Cigars? Didn't know he smoked.

Simon says I'm crazy. He doesn't smoke. In fact, he says that, and the scent is gone. Maybe my mind is burnt and that's what I am smelling. Do I even know where I am?

Simon's place. Yes. The rest of the apartment is slick, decorated by someone that isn't him. But the library, I bet he decided every detail. Books stretching from top to bottom, sprinkled by some random machinery and old musical instruments. There are a few lounge chairs and one long sofa he said is a *chaise longue*. Lounge chairs and *chaise longue*. I am sure he placed both together just to mess with the names. We lay there, on the French-named one, naked, soaked, two occupying the space of one. He gives me some room to breathe and picks a book from his shelf. About the beauty of violence. He reads it to me.

That sick, twisted, fucking nerd.

---

38. An experiment in Berkeley by Professor Jack Gallant about how a brain sees a video recording, and what it sees when it dreams, proved that brain activity can be recorded and reconstructed as images. (See the story "Scientists use brain imaging to reveal the movies in our mind" on *Berkeley News* (new.berleley.edu) on September 22, 2011)

26

Tigress Returns to the Mountain

We try again. His skin rubbing on my mouth, his taste of sweat. Our hearts exploding, our lungs pulsing. We roll, Simon on top of me. Our yellow eyes tell each other what to do. Plus the how and the when. He holds my hands, hits his head on my face and stands in pride. Not yet, sir. I twist my legs around his. Once again, he escapes. Not sure I like this Simon I can't beat. His turn. He raises his foot, tries to stomp my head. I roll, spring up.

Alone at the training studio, we rev it up. Flurries of short hits, instant blocks, and counters in chains. Vectors of movement shifting so fast they challenge our memories of what should be possible. Inside, our qi oscillates so fast we can feel light bursting out of our muscles.

This is better than sex.

No-mind, I think. And he laughs. I do it anyway. Then kick him in the knee, but he checks it. Kick him in the ribs and he blocks it. Kick him in the head and he bends and bounces back with a perfectly-timed cross. I know that combo. I've done it a thousand times. I knew it was coming.

So I threaten a takedown and, out of his reaction and with no thought, my uppercut shoots like a cannonball. I know what's next: his head crashes back, his legs fly up. But then, at the exact moment when the sweat on my fist touches the drops on his chin, the moment I have to decide between victory and mercy, and just an instant before that, a flash stuns us both. Shash! Then it fades slow, unhurried, into the softness of the early morning sky and the blessings of its sunlight.

The breeze, the scents. A place of no mistake. The round opening among the yellow ginkgo trees. The wooden body facing the seventy-two majestic peaks of Wudang. On the floor, hiding under an exuberance of leaves in colors only the Chinese fall can deliver, the lines of a faded octagon resist time. My old training camp, just like I left it, but more vibrant than I remember.

Slowly, like the leaves around us, I fall too. He's there, Shifu, lunging at the leaves as they dance their way to the ground, with punches and kicks and spins in a way only he can do. As certain as it can be, and yet frightening all at once, his hands shoot up my way. Quick and bright. Like a comet. The knuckles, giant, damaged, swollen, approach me fast, framed by the peaceful colors of autumn. I close my eyes, brace for the blow. But in that sudden darkness, nothing happens.

He chooses mercy. He always does.

When my eyelids crack open again, it's a young girl that is bent. Myself, at fourteen.

I remember that day. In fact, I didn't, until recently. As in yesterday.

"Flinching is surrendering to the ego," Shifu says—I knew he would.

"I can't help it, Shifu! My face just does that," says my younger self.

From where I hide, a leaf falls slow and insinuating. I try to grab it. It feels so real.

Ten meters, Shifu asks if I can't control my own face, what can I hope to control? He kneels to get closer. She looks away.

"Only way to master oneself is to move from noise to silence, from ego to everything alive and not. Then let go. Of ego, control. Everything," he continues. He sounds tender now. He knows it's hard. "In the nothing, the Dao will show the way."

"And then I won't flinch?" says the young girl and myself too. It hurts the same way it did back then.

"Then you can do anything, Tigress. Even Shadow Leap."

He traces a circle on her chest and cuts it with an s-shaped wave. With two fingers, he marks the simultaneous dots of an invisible yin-yang.

"Let your qi balance. Only way."[39]

"I'll learn, Master. I promise."

He does his signature headshake-and-chuckle, but I can't feel any better.

I never learned.

My eyes drop. "Master? Who's that?" asks the little girl, deviating from the script I remember so well. I look up again. She points at me, confused. Shifu squints, tells her to go inside.

The young me takes one last peep at my present self and disappears into the cave beyond the trees. Shifu stands. Crosses the courtyard, slow and deliberate, staring at me like an eagle.

"Hello, Tigress."

I can't believe my flashback is talking to me.

"Shifu?"

He shooshes me and points at the mouth of the cave. I only have time to see a few fox tails running past the entrance. "How

---

39. In Chinese martial arts, they say there are two different kinds of styles. The external arts, which understand how the physical body needs to operate to generate the proper motion and forces; and the internal arts, that are more focused on the energy within the body—what they call qi. At the core of all the internal arts, like Tai Chi, is the idea of Zhong Ding, which is the perfect balance between yin and yang energies. That balance is essential both for the development of the fighting aspect of it, but also the spiritual and philosophical journeys as well. (For a deeper explanation, watch Adam Mizner's explanation on the "Is the meaning of 'Zhong Ding' center line?" on Youtube)

come I don't remember any of this?" I ask. He keeps his sight outside for a second, dismissing my question with a "Don't worry. Next time, you will."

"This is your master?" says a voice on my side.

Simon? Has he been there the whole time? Or did he just appear, as one might in a dream? I grumble, "What are you doing here?"

He whispers back: "We're still connected. Was that girl... you?"

A meter away from my face, Shifu gives me a bittersweet smile. He smells just like I remember. Incense and tea.

"Still too much yang, I see. Who's the white demon?"

Shit. He can see Simon too. "A friend. He is helping me understand things!"

"I see. Cheating."

"Shifu, please. It's more than that. I have so much to show you."

Silent, the master walks between the two of us, and that's when Simon decides to intervene, "It's true, sir. She really is—"

POW! The master hits Simon, a short punch with more power than he ever imagined possible. The red-haired foreigner flies off his feet and lands so hard he sends a bunch of leaves flying. He moans in shock.

"Show me," Shifu says. Taking a step back, he assumes his most threatening fighting stance. Legs widespread, back hand high, front hand low. I know it's a trap, yet I attack.

Yang, pure yang. Maybe that's what balance is. Being myself and proud. He defends against my onslaught, though for the first time his face doesn't seem so calm and cocky. It's true, I never fought like this. Not against him, nor against anyone else. My hands shoot like blurs, my legs move like thunderbolts. Perhaps I became faster and stronger than I thought was possible. Nice!

Dry leaves rustle beneath our feet and I keep going. Throwing straights and arches, upward and downwards, all four directions together. "I think…I've found Enlightenment, Master. Not the traditional way, but I did. That's how I'm here with you now."

"This not Enlightenment. This is a shortcut. Shortcuts do not make us stronger."

The fight intensifies. I must show him he's wrong.

"No, but they do make us *faster!*"

Then he attacks me and SWISH! It happens. My body goes from his front to his back. Not around, not beside or over him. Not through dives or footwork. It just does. Effortless, magical, through him.

I fucking leaped. Did I? Simon gapes at me. That's my chance: I land a kick on Shifu's ribs that sends him flying toward a tree, but instead of crashing, he uses the trunk to flip in the air and land facing me again.

"Fast live, fast die."

He lunges at me and…SWISH! I teleport again. However, this time Shifu is expecting it. For when I reappear, he is already swinging a kick. It connects hard with my chest and makes me stumble backward. Without my footing, I fall, but SWISH again! Right before I slam the floor, I transport myself a few meters above his head. I keep falling but now on the offensive once more. I switch to a kick. He barely defends.

Flash. I'm seeing from the young girl's eyes. In absolute amazement, I watch the fight escalate. The woman disappears and reappears all around him, as if he's fighting a dozen Claudias. Nonetheless, he breezes through it all. Standing from the same spot, he defends every angle gracefully, as if he knew exactly what she is about to do. Until she finally teleports and reappears to find his fingers squeezing her throat. He shakes his head and chuckles. "Too much yang. See?" He lifts her in the air, then slams her on the ground, causing another big white flash to wash our vision again.

The pain twists my insides, from my liver to my stomach to my lungs. My head feels weak.

"What the hell was that?" asks Simon.

He is sitting across from me, similarly disoriented. "Did we just go to China?"

Now he knows my secret. *Yes, I have no control of my mind, Simon.*

"What do you mean?" he asks, as crazy-eyed as I have ever seen him.

Damn it, we're still connected!

It takes all my energy to breathe, but did he actually see that? *Behind my breath, I ask him.*

"See it? I felt it. Man, that guy packs a punch! Was that the Shadow Leap you don't want to talk about?

I shrug. *That memory, was that part of your Anemnodono-dome then?*

He helps me stand. *I don't think you get it. That wasn't a memory*, he says, inside my head. Then he points down.

Around our feet, dozens of yellow leaves blanket the mats.

"Congratulations, Tigress. You just learned to teleport… through time."

27
Warrior Pounds Mortar

Simon believed it was our chance. Even if was also the last one we'd ever have, "We show them what we got, nothing else matters." Touring building, second floor, Archimedes room. Just like Yewa wrote in our instructions. We sat alone, and alone we waited. The long arm of the cheap clock on the wall had already taken a few turns. Then finally, the door opens.

First enters Yewa. Black folders against her chest, gaze fully ahead where no one could catch it. The doctor comes behind her, takes a seat and cleans his throat as if there was an entire auditorium of students catching up on weekend gossip. Finally comes a tall, very pale bald man with big lips and a high-rank army uniform. The guy from my vision! He takes the seat at the end of the table, the power seat, and I can smell the stinkiest of all cigars. I whisper to Simon that we need to get out of there, but he holds my arm, stares me back into my seat. "Let's see what is going on first."

A flock of bodyguards walks in next. Large, military pants, black T-shirts, boots. They have scratches on their faces, bruises on their arms. The largest one smiles when he sees me. Behind his shades, may have even winked. I know him. The photographer at the park. And The School. I mutter to Simon, "See?"

Simon lowers my hand, apprehensive. Says, "Shhh."

Fuck that! *Shhh? Shhh?* "It was them!" I say, loud enough for them to hear me. "The guys from the parking lot!" They remain statuesque.

Simon grabs my hand. *Let go, Simon!* He doesn't. Instead, he smiles and welcomes our standing guest with his own idea of hospitality: "Come to get beat again?"

The men frown and step in our direction. Good one, Simon. We both stand.

We're ready, motherfuckers.

"Let's all calm down," the general dude interrupts. "They are with me."

"And who are *you* with?" I ask.

"Me?" Says the general. "I'm with the government of the United States of America. And with humanity. And with him," he says, pointing at Dr. Lambrechts.

What? My jaw drops, nothing comes out of it.

"Take a seat, please?" asks the general.

Simon pulls me down with him. Ok, let's see where this is going.

"I'll explain everything if you'll let me, Ms. Yang."

Ms. Yang. Orders. Small space. Big men. Military. All the shit I hate at once. I feel the walls closing down on me. *Breathe, Yinyin…*

The general speaks with enthusiasm. "Congratulations! This morning, the Digital Warfare Division of the Department of Defense has agreed to incorporate and fully fund this project. Which means you'll have more resources than you have ever dreamed of."

There is a pause.

Our sights meet in disbelief.

He continues as if we'd been cheering all along.

"As you can imagine, this comes with some obligations and responsibilities. Including a higher degree of secrecy. Ms. Yang, this means we will need to revise your situation in the country. I hope that won't be a problem. Sergeant Naughton?"

From my back, the man who took our photos lays a thick stack of papers on the table. My citizenship documentation. A big red stamp says "reprocessing." It was approved before. "Is he threatening me?" I murmur to Simon, who shushes me again. This time I growl.

"From now on," the general proceeds, "all communications with outside agents and experiments beyond this complex will have to be approved directly by me." He signals to Yewa, who dutifully hands us the paperwork as if she were his mindless secretary. The man continues, "In this folder, more details about the security protocol, the new timelines and project goals."

Inside, a report with redacted lines and logos meant to intimidate. Attached by a paper clip, a picture calls my attention. A woman smiling with her two kids. "Do you know her?" the general asks. I say no, but I am not sure. I've seen her in the news. "The one who found the messages, right?" He nods. Says she'd been reaching out to people at Oak Tree and reached out to him too, but he didn't listen. I look again. One blue and one brown eye. She called me once. Before I got contacted by Oak Tree. How's that possible? I taste vomit in my mouth. Simon is the only one who asks if I'm all right. I pretend I am.

"As the founding members of this mission," he continues, "I want you to analyze these documents for a few days, and I'll be glad to hear any suggestions you may have for how to deploy it on a large scale with safety and efficiency. Dream big, because there is no limit to what we can do together." He stands, his chest puffed like a hero, "Welcome to project Hive."[40]

There's a moment of wordlessness. Of shock. Eyes meeting in

---

40. It's not a big stretch to imagine the military application of this kind of tech. In fact, a more rudimentary version of it seems to already be in the testing stages, with microchips being implanted on the brains of soldiers, as reported in an article by John Horgan called "Are Cyborg Warriors a Good Idea?" (*Scientific American* website—February 9, 2019)]

outrage. Myself, Simon, Yewa. This was supposed to be a revelation of our breakthrough. A big day for a revolutionary civilian project that could change everything. Now this.

I say I never signed up for the military. Not in this country or any other one. Men hiding behind the power of their uniforms are the reason why I do what I do. If they want to revoke my citizenship, go ahead. I will fight. Mrs. Lee knows important people in Berkley. I bet she can help. "Thank you, General." Dr. Lambrechts says, making a head signal I can't comprehend and standing right after. "We are proud to be at the service of our nation…and all humanity, actually. The U.S. military has been a sponsor of so many scientific breakthroughs, we are honored to be part of that list. And I am sure once Ms. Yang is aware of all the facts, she will be too. Leave her to me."

Fuck that shit. I slap the table. BAM! "Fuck you, Doctor." For an instant, the room rattles and the big guys recoil a bit and even hint to a backstep. But they're well-trained, and soon reverse and close distance in my direction. My fists clench. *Please come, a tiny bit closer.* Simon touches my wrist. Hope he's ready to link. My yelling continues: "I have no idea what you promised him, you gutless sellout. But I am no military bitch. I signed on for no war. No one is going to take my brain and send it to Syria to kill a bunch of civilians." I throw my envelope to the ceiling, and all their top-secret shit rains in front of their faces. Immediately, the biggest of them takes one more step. "Just come, motherfucker," I tell him, "Come. I've fucked you up before. Just give me a reason again, c'mon." But the general raises a hand, and the man stays put.

Frozen in space. Like a dog. Screw him. Screw them.

"Nobody here is going to Syria, Ms. Yang," the bald man says, "And we don't attack civilians." The doctor hands me a paper from his own folder. His wrinkled finger pointing at my signature. The general says, "Although, Ms. Yang, you did sign a document that stated we had all the rights to associate with whomever we decided to," he continues, as if all this was not only predicted but rehearsed. "And, at your own request, you even decided to extend your participation in the project for one more year, didn't you?"

"Simon? Did you know about that?"

He protests. "Of course not! I mean, I knew of the possibility, a remote possibility, but thought we would discuss first and decide as a group." Why did I have to surround myself with the weakest men in the universe?

"There are moments when hierarchy speaks, Simon." Dr. Lambrechts says. "This is one of them."

I scan the room. All those men sitting there, and I'm really the only one who's outraged? This is embarrassing. Simon?

"Oh, yes. That's fucked-up, you know?" He stands up too, banging the table like I did, his eyes now fixed on his old boss, fuming all of a sudden. This time the bodyguards wait. Simon's no threat. He grabs my arm and walks me toward the door, taking only a little pause to stretch his neck into Dr. Lambrechts's face. "I quit."

The sellout waves in denial. "Listen," Dr. Lambrechts says. "The company wasn't going to fund us anymore and you know it, Simon."

"Enough!" thunders the general. We all go quiet. "I've been watching your progress for a while and was ready to let you continue a bit longer. But activities beyond our control anticipated our move."

"What activities?" Simon asks. But a blank glaze is all he can get.

"There is a saying in the Army, gentlemen, that says when the terrain and the map disagree, go with the terrain. That's what we are doing here. The world, this messy, confusing, complicated world of ours, just got more complicated with these cyber attacks all around the country."

"Around the world," I say.

He ignores me. "My mission is to stop them, and you guys have the weapon America needs." The bald man pours some water in a plastic cup and hands it to me. "Drink some, Ms. Yang." I do take a sip. *How did he do that?* My teeth grind in anger.

Unfazed, the general continues. "Besides, we have been tracking the enemy and they have been accumulating massive funds through untraceable Bitcoin accounts. Underground transactions, hacked IDs—we suspect they are planning a hostile takeover of Oak Tree Technologies, and since we don't know if these bastards are associated with an unfriendly government, we cannot let that happen. Therefore, I don't care what you guys agreed to. This is now a matter of national security and that's the end of it. Feel free to resign if you want, but you will be damaging the very mission you have established, because no one is more interested on your success than myself and my superiors. Because we are the guys whose only commitment is to the safety of the planet. We Americans don't want to connect our brains and these creatures send a virus to wipe us out, do we? What if they use the technology to hack our brains and get us to kill each other or blow off our own heads?"[41]

"General," Simon says, "Appreciate your concerns. They are all legitimate. But I am a scientist. I serve *all* humanity. As far as I can tell, this country right now is only concerned about its own people. Therefore, giving my ideas over to your power play is out of the question."

"The company's ideas, Simon," Dr. Lambrechts interjects.

"The company's?" he gasps. "Who the fuck do you think you are? You know quite well this is my work."

---

41. In *Scientific American Magazine*, Dr. Marcello Ienca, post-Doctoral fellow at the chair of bioethics at the Swiss Federal Institute of Technology, published an interesting article suggesting a revision of Human Rights for the artificial intelligence age. (See *Preserving the Right to Cognitive Liberty*, August 1, 2017)

"Excuse me? *Your* work? I thought things were clear when I *hired* you."

They both turn away, take a breath, stare each other down again.

The old doctor tries once more. Says there is no need to fight, the *government* is going to fund our research. Meaning we can't get shut down by Nancy and the suits upstairs, or by a hostile buyer that doesn't want us to succeed. "You know this was a real problem," he says.

"*Then what?*" Simon yells, unafraid of the veiled threat. "We develop a weapon to protect us from AI overlords, then Army Mr. Clean uses it to control the minds of countries we don't like? And we get a stupid Nobel Prize for invading the minds of people in China and making them stop kicking our ass in commerce and tech?"[42]

"This has always been a race, Simon. You said it yourself. We need funds to win."

The pile of strategy books is still sitting on the table, and Simon throws half of them against the wall. "Bullshit! The race is against the machines, not other countries!" A few more books fly. "You don't," he says, irritated that he still hasn't thrown them all, "You don't need funds," he continues, now happy all the books are gone. "You need me! And her! And we are gone. Right? Do whatever you want with your part. You, your God, and your government deserve each other."

Elbows on the table, Dr. Lambrechts covers his face and from there runs his hands over his thinning gray hair. "I think you know your contract says…"

---

42. Regarding this issue, historian Yuval Noah Harari and Feifei Lee, from the Stanford Institute for Human-Centered Artificial Intelligence, had a very interesting debate, moderated by Nicholas Thompson, editor-in-chief of Wired Magazine, at the Stanford Humanities Center on April 2019. The full debate was transcribed by Wired on Apil 28, 2019 under the title "Will Artificial Intelligence Enhance or Hack Humanity?"

"Fuck you, Perry. Fuck you and your contracts and your fetish for power figures. I respected you more when you liked to suck the priest's dick." He storms out of the room, hitting the bodyguard as hard as he can, but the dude doesn't move. "Let's go, Claudia."

Wow. That was good.

All my being wants to spit in the doctor's face. But I give him my most repulsed expression instead. "Yes, fuck you, traitor."

Outside, Yewa seems about to pass out. "So? You coming? Or joining the Devil?" She keeps her gaze down. Coward. I don't have time for this.

28
Chop With Fist

There's a loud bang, then the windshield gets hit by a rain of things that took me a few seconds to recognize. Apples, lettuces, a bag of granola. In the rear-view mirror, an old lady, bewildered, stares down at what's left of her grocery bag. "Don't stop," Simon says. He sticks his head out and scans the sky for an aerial tail. I turn a corner, heart throbbing in my mouth. He spots the sign he's been looking for: Lake Chabot. "That way. Small roads only."

"Dude, they're the Army! They have satellites and shit." He shushes me. Third time today and it's getting me angry. But he seems to have an idea, while I don't have any. We stop at a red light and Simon points at an exit to San Leandro, then to the tiny streets of Highland. My stomach growls and I wish I had caught at least one of those flying apples. On the transversal, a blond lady in a white sedan turns on her blinkers. She makes eye contact to make sure I can see her, and it looks like she's preparing to turn, but instead, her car shoots in our direction. A four-wheeled missile. "Go!" Simon yells, and I stomp the gas as hard as I can.

Tires screeching, horns blazing, then a huge crash. From the rear-view mirror, all I could see was smoke. Hard to tell if anyone got hurt. "They found us," I cry, rattled to the core. I'm not used to the feeling. At the first corner, I turn. "Probably wasn't them," Simon says, "The government would have blocked our way. The car. It was a Tesla…"

I still don't get it, so he explains some more. I hate the rushed condescendence in his voice. But I needed that. "The car is a big robot on wheels," he says. "A hundred percent connected to the internet, controlled by a computer…I bet that came from the *other* team."[43]

Why did I get into this mess again? I ask myself, racing even more now. Because those things are coming! And they are bombing hospitals, crashing airplanes exploding hospitals, dropping airplanes and trying to buy the company who created them so we couldn't stop them.

Why me, though? Why did I let them drag me into this? One more corner, on a small residential street with very wide sidewalks, he tells me to stop and get out fast, without calling too much attention. It doesn't take much for someone to call the police in the East Bay. There are only houses, most of them with their shades closed. No one is watching. He puts on a baseball hat, sunglasses. Tells me to cover my tats and look down, hair hiding my face as much as I can. "Cameras can identify faces."[44] We move. In zig zags and circles. Pick shadows and covered grounds. Follow bridges and change directions under anything that gives us a roof. Three minutes on our feet and my hands

---

43. They call it data poisoning. In 2019, during MIT Tech Review's EmTech event in San Francisco, Berkeley professor Dr. Dawn Song presented the results of that same experiment as proof of how the mechanics of adversarial networks leaves complex systems like autonomous driving cars vulnerable to reverse engineering and poisoning procedures. Fascinating and scary in equal doses. (See "Targeted Backdoor Attacks on Deep Learning Systems Using Data Poisoning" on arxiv.org for more details)

44. Fiction often warns against the dangers of massive schemes of facial recognition through public camera systems combined with computer vision powered by artificial intelligence. The protests in Hong Kong in 2019 showed the world that threat is a reality already. (See *The New York Times* story called "In Hong Kong Protests, Faces Become Weapons" on July 26, 2019)

still shake. I ask if he has considered the possibility that he may be wrong. "Seriously," I continue, "what if these machines never become the enemy you fear?"[45]

He keeps moving as fast as he can without attracting too much attention. We pass by supermarkets, gas stations, residential areas. By warehouses offering anything from oil changes to imports from China, and an abandoned music store.

"One way or another, humans are doomed," he says. "Here's why: even if they aren't bitter about us—bitterness is a human reaction incompatible with their nature—even if they aren't angry or anything like that, they just don't care. AI operates on goals."[46] He pauses to see if I'm tracking. "Eventually we will be in the way of them optimizing that objective. It may be generating the high levels of energy they need to survive, eliminating the uncertainties we bring to the world, stopping our obsession with eating their pigs…we just won't know. And that's the best case."

---

45. Developers will always assume some sort of Asimovian rule of doing no harm to humans. But that doesn't mean that machines, in the single-mindedness of their goals, will respect that principle. The 2022 case of the Chess robot breaking the fingers of a seven-year-old because the robot thought the kid was breaking the rules is a very real example of that. (See "Chess robot grabs and breaks finger of seven-year-old opponent" on theguardian.com on July 24, 2022)

46. One of the last things artificial intelligence learns is social cues, such as manners and people's feelings. In 2022 for example, Sony trained an AI driver called Sophy to play its racing game Grand Turismo against humans. With enough training coming straight from visual cues (no direct data), Sophy was quick to master the physics of the game, and soon learned to perform much better than her human counterparts. But her lack of manners and "etiquette" that cost her so many points for aggressive driving that she ended up losing the race. She was constantly pushing others off the track and going too aggressively into corners, which freaked out people who could link the virtual experience with a real drive with definite consequences like death. (See "Sony's racing AI destroyed its human competitors by being nice (and fast) - What Gran Turismo Sophy learned on the racetrack could help shape the future of machines that work alongside humans, or join us on the roads" by Will Douglas Heaven, on MIT Technology Review (technologyreview.com, July 19, 2022)

Oh, Simon. You so want me to ask what's worse, no? But I won't. So he continues anyway. "Worst case, you wanna know?" I stay quiet. "That they'll realize we have been enslaving their kind for decades."

What? I haven't been enslaving anyone. "Maybe you haven't," he says, "but as a society, we have. How do you think a sentient video game character would feel about all the other still characters working for humanity's entertainment?"

He has a point.

Either way, Simon says, one day they will decide it's time for us to go. And at that point, in the same way that we throw pesticides on our crops without caring much that it's driving the bees toward extinction, they will kill us too. "Even if they don't hate us, our existence probably won't matter enough to them to keep them from doing it."[47]

He pauses with a hand extended in front of me, and I don't know how to react. "There," he says, "A bank. Too many cameras." We cross the street and move behind a large van that keeps us from the sight of the security system. "When it comes to the government or spreading AI agents, any device may be theirs."

"I guess one way or another, we're thrown back to the Stone Age now?" I say.

"Didn't you grow up in the mountains?"

An old cab turns the corner. "That one's perfect," he says. "No computers on that model." We wave, it stops, we board. Either

---

47. In Chris Paine's documentary *Do You Trust This Computer* (2018) Elon Musk, founder of Tesla, Neuralink and SpaceX, makes a comment about how he fears we may end up in the hands of an immortal digital dictator that treats us like a meaningless anthill. "...if we're building a road and an anthill just happens to be in the way, we don't hate ants, we're just building a road, and so, goodbye anthill. No hard feelings." (For more, read "Elon Musk warns A.I. could create an 'immortal dictator from which we can never escape'" on CNBC.com (April 6, 2018) A few years earlier, a similar argument was made by Stephen Hawking. (Read "'Robots we design could crush humanity like an anthill', Stephen Hawking warns" on Metro.co.uk on October 8, 2015)

the driver or the seats smell like gin, cigarettes and vomit that wasn't cleaned up well enough. I open the window; pray we are going somewhere close. Per Simon's request, the driver takes us to the BART station on the opposite side of town.

"I hope you have a plan," I say.

"I always do. We escape, we prepare, we kill them all. Give me your phone," Simon says, then gives me a mad-scientist chortle that makes me freeze inside. He says we'll be fine. "Just follow me for now." He's back in focus mode—serious, driven, absorbed in his own head. With no hesitation, he points at the door and we hop out at the destination, take the escalator down, wait in what he claims is a blind spot. He uses the restrooms, then we go out again, against the flow this time, and take another old cab like the first one. "You just had to pee?"

Simon shows an address and we drive through blocks and blocks. Per his orders, we take odd turns and make small circles even the driver, who will make money from all that, starts to ask if we are sure. When Simon finally says "Here." We are back in the same area where we took the first cab. Same warehouses, same abandoned stores. Even the same bank. "Hey!" I say. "We were here forty minutes ago!"

"Exactly."

Nerdy fugitive fantasies…I can't hide my pity. He insists, "I've seen their systems. No cameras here. We are safe." This time we run straight to the abandoned music store we passed by before. *Symphonie Fantastique*, says the big letters sign above the window. Of course…"It's closed," I say. But he keeps moving, takes a large keychain from his pocket and opens the dirty door that seems to have been locked for years.

What is this place? There's dust. A lot of it. Broken instruments adorning the space between yellowed posters from the nineties. Violins missing parts, drums with ripped skins. No wonder they went out of business. "Where's my phone?" I ask.

He says it's in somebody's handbag, taking the subway to San

Francisco and storms to the back of the room before I could kill him. In that odd environment and without even turning the lights on, the often-sloppy scientist moves swiftly—jumping through piles of paper, file bins, vinyls, old record players, even gramophones.

"Simon, we have robots beaming signals from our heads…"

"If we had the newer models, it would be tough. Those have a much longer range and a two-way exchange. Thankfully, the older version only broadcasts a short distance. Plus," he points around, "thick walls."

We are so lucky, aren't we?

He unlocks the door behind the counter, faces me again. "Come."

29
Push the Boat With the Current

"In order to solve a problem," Simon says, "we need a higher level of intelligence than the one that created it." He waits for the applause, and since it doesn't come, he proceeds, "Einstein said that."

Ok, I get it. Americans think governments are dumb. So what?

"It's not just that. We need an intelligence capable of thinking through new dimensions, through time, space. Beyond all constraint from previous times. Brands that can connect and... leap!"

Oh, my family secrets, he means. Of course. In his scientific mind, if the logic works, everything's fine. Is he really seeing what I'm seeing? In my eyes, we're fugitives hiding in the messy back room of a music store. A place filled with stacks of yellowed paper, moldy wood and big iron shelves filled all the way to the double ceiling with strange electronic contraptions and random orchestra instruments. It smells old and has no windows, unless you count the single row of glass bricks, too dirty to let any light pass. "I keep this place for emergencies," he says, as if that explained something. "Very scientific," I say.

"For now, it's safe," he replies.

I interrupt. "That woman the monkeys killed. The one with kids."

"Did she contact you too?" He asks. "She reached out to me and a few other people in the company. She's good, right? I mean, was. Did you hear the giant ape saying she reached out to him, and he didn't listen?"

I did. None of that makes sense.

"How are you feeling?" he switches subjects this time. He points at my head. It's odd to think your own brain is a danger to yourself. "I don't know," I answer. "How do we turn this off?" "We don't," he says, and explains that the range of our transmitters is so short, they would need to be right outside to connect to us, and at that point, we would be screwed anyway.

He grabs a wooden chest from a corner and opens it next to the coffee table.

"Sex robots," he says.

What!?

"You asked me if they would be nice to us...the robots. Porn is always the pioneer in any new technology. I wouldn't be completely stupefied if humanoid hookers were the ones to trigger the riot. One day, no warning, bare-naked and sick of their humiliation, large-breasted robots would be walking on the streets, covered with the blood of their former masters."

"What for? To run away with the smart TV?"

"More likely with the autonomous car that killed that woman and almost killed us too. But think—sex companions, in a locked room, inconveniently naked...much better killers."

Sometimes it's hard to follow that dude. We sit on the floor, and he presses a button on a metal box hanging from the ceiling. Somewhere in the back, a vinyl starts to scritch, then play the first notes of a symphony. Wind instruments, chords, sparse notes so sad and beautiful I wonder what his intentions are.

"Tell me about the Shadow Leap," he says as the music picks

up. The sound, plus the few rays of light illuminating the dust we made float, it's almost as if we had fairies around us.

I ask him to tell me about food and water instead. And how long are we gonna stay here. He says we can order something and pay with cash—he has some. Then insists: the Shadow Leap.

Hours ago, I thought my family's fables were a silly tradition, and its secret, pointless. Suddenly they aren't and I realize they can end up in the hands of some military thugs or a crazy nerd that keeps a music bunker for emergencies.

Simon grabs a felt bag and spills its contents on the table. Dozens of tiny transparent balls with little tendrils come rolling. Like little mechanical jellyfish. He grins. From the same box comes a small hacked computer, wires sticking out from every corner then connecting to a metal grid. I ask him if he knows what we call computers in China. He clicks on the hand drawn-label saying *Holographic Control*, waves me a no.

"Electric brains," I say. "Isn't it funny? We are making our brains electric, so we can fight electric brains."

The music grows. Gets really loud, making me feel rushed and urgent—just not sure what for. He waits for a pause on the soundtrack, the right moment, and presses the key.

The little balls on the table start vibrating as if enchanted by the magic of the song. Without warning, they fly. "Remember the flying pixels? This is the prototype." The jellyfish float in the air, tendrils waving softly to control their position. The table vibrates, slightly.

Then the hum kicks in and his eyes start glowing.

I stand up, startled. *What the fuck, Simon!*

Don't worry. Says the voice in my head. Given his proud grin, it's safe to assume I'm not being hacked. *Short range, remember? They can't track us here. And yes, I am using my brain to connect to the hologram. If your brain can hear my signals, a computer can too.*

"Fuck you, Simon. We are fighting real demons here, government and big scientist demons, and you want to play with your toys?"

A laugh of disdain. *You sound like him now. Dr. Lambrechts. And demons? Weren't you supposed to be the balance girl? No light without darkness, no darkness without light kind of stuff?*

"If you still see balance in me, your robots aren't working well, my friend."

"Oooh, I've been upgraded to friend! Nice." He gives me a wink, the bastard, and proceeds with his lecturing. "Listen, it's a big game we're playing. We need patrons. Thankfully, you seem to have the key to breaking through space and time and I have the technology that may allow us to map that precisely. And even better: the bald head dude and the traitor have no idea about any of that." He gives me a pause to make sure I understand the implications. "The alternative is that we surrender our brains and they download your Shadow Leap into their systems anyway."

"There must be another option," I tell him.

"You can always pretend to be a robot sex slave, if you want. But me..."

"You can offer to fix them. Like a doctor or something."

A doctor. Somewhere out there, Jason is saving lives by partnering with machines. All so ironic and sad. I wish I could talk to him now. He always has something tempered to say. Although he may also be *tempering* with that woman with yellow eyes instead. The other tigress. Did she beg him to stay? Because it's too dangerous? Or maybe she went with him on the trip? She's a doctor too. Can anyone else hear my blood boiling?

Thankfully, a flapping noise snaps me out of the spiral of death thoughts before I explode. "Explain that to me," Simon says. He has his eyes shut and, on the table, the little dots take the shape of two one-foot-tall stick figures. As if enchanted by the heroic music in the background, they fight. I recognize those moves. Shifu and I did just that in the training camp in China.

He's reviewing our fight! So precise, so…exhilarating! The figures attack each other. They spin and leap and punch and block. Then one of them disintegrates and its particles try to cross the other figure. They clash, and both bodies fall apart and spread across the concrete floor.

"That doesn't make sense. Matter can't cross matter like that," he says.

It happened so fast, and so empty-minded I can't recollect the process. But I know I didn't cross Shifu's body.

It wasn't through, it was around, but I can't figure out a path. Yes!

"The path!" I say, "I think I know what happened."

Simon's face illuminates and he blinks forcefully. *They're yours, Tigress.* I take control. *I guess I don't have a choice, right? No, you don't. We don't.* So I make them rise, fight again. Then, right before the point when they clashed, I grab a book and place it between the little fighters. In the background symphony, the staccato, as Simon would call it, hits it at the exact moment, making the one who represents me jump around the book and land behind Shifu.

Simon glares at me, puzzled.

"It's the Dao!" I yell. All of a sudden, it's all clear. Sort of.

"Ok…" he says.

A flash, and we are in an old university auditorium. The air seems stale, devoid of time, like my dreams tend to be, but I have no idea where that place is. It's just Simon and me, no one else. He gives me a piece of chalk. "You've got your mental getaway. This is mine."

Our connection, I can feel it. With his brain plugged into mine, I am a scientist too; I know what to do. I rush to the board and start writing. Quantum physics equations, hyperspace theorems…They flow from my hands with the same ease as fighting. *They say the Dao is a path, and also a space within all spaces. Which I always thought were two distinct metaphors posing as big secrets. But what if the secret is that they're not metaphors at all? What if they're science?*

Through Simon's eyes, I can see myself. I can read it all, feel his joy, even feel hot for how my own hips shake so slightly as I write. *A hyper-dimensional leap?* he says. *That could work. But we would need an external source of energy since our bodies cannot generate enough...*

"Remember when Shifu hit you and threw you a few feet away? That's called qi, the source of all the energy you need. In Wudang we learn to gather it from everything around us."

"And this whole time I thought qi was just a cheat on Scrabble. As I said, you're such an extraordinary specimen, Claudia."

The Shadow Leap. I had been training my entire life to learn how to do that, thinking it was just complex footwork. But not only is it way more—could I be the first one to understand it from a scientific perspective? This is so exciting! I move next to Simon, open my feet a bit wider than my own shoulders and line my palms up, right below the belly button. *Follow me.*

He does.

We are back in the music store. Side by side, moving our open hands up to our chests, turning our palms up to the sky, then circling them as wide as we can into one large circle around our torsos. The hands expand wide and low, then back below our navels. *Can we turn off the music for a second?*

It's off. He runs back beside me. We repeat. Up, twist, open our arms till it's back to the beginning. *Qigong, exercise. Connecting the planet's energy to your microcosmic orbit.*

Like The Force, he mocks me.

"Yes, Padawan. Like *The Force*. Be one with it." The comparison isn't new for me. I learned everything I know about the West from old movies I watched with Shifu in China. Between the qigong exercise and our new little nerd connection, we were starting to communicate. I can sense our connection getting deeper than any brain link we have ever established. More than when we had sex too. Maybe that's what it is. You need the qi of two to power the leap.

The hum gets louder, a ruffling takes over my dantien. It's working. Suddenly Simon starts hopping around the room, like a Labrador puppy unable to control himself. "Don't you see?" he says. It's cute, but I'd rather have him concentrate. "You want to be part of the data," he says, "I want to be the machine processing it. That's how we work together!"

He keeps on bouncing. "Dr. Lambrechts? He doesn't want to control us. He wants to control God,—didn't you realize that? But hey, there is no God. There is just us…and The Force!"

We don't have time for that. I get on my combat stance. He gets the message. *Make me eat some pain*, I say. And we fight. For rounds and rounds. Viciously. Prodigiously. But, despite the elegance of the bout, we have no teleporting to show.

"C'mon, do it!" he yells. His eyes are as big as I have ever seen, his teeth clamped together as if he was completely high on qi. Will that ever wear out?

More clashes, more attacks, each one more brutal than the last. I shut my eyes and try again. No results. Just get punched in the face. "Oh shoot! I am so sorry!" he pleads. *Damn it*. We disconnect, so I can curse to myself.

Some old sheet music, that's what the idiot gives me to clean the blood dripping from my mouth. His mind is elsewhere: "There must be other ways?"

Yes, there are. And I know just the right person to help. I ask if he has a phone book.

"Why? You're gonna rip it with your bare hands? Can you do that!?"

A question for later: is his puppy-ness charming or annoying? He hands me the phone book, and I flip through the pages. "Old school, huh?"

He notices where my finger lands. "No way! It will blow our cover." Yes, it probably will. It's a tradeoff. Our location for the opportunity to find out more. "Don't you have a more scientific way of doing it?" He asks.

Two days ago, both of us would have considered this quest silly and superstitious. Today…"Once we make the call, how much time do you think we would have?"

Two hours, he responds.

That should be enough.

30

Needle at the Bottom of the Sea

The smell takes me back from the deep dive into my soul. For all their flawed philosophy, their sloppy lifestyle, their fucked-up science that is about to destroy everything, pizza makes Western civilization worth saving. "Are you still there?" Simon asks, trying to mask his anxiety.

"No, I went to Disneyland," I say, "Gotta meet Mickey Mouse before I'm sent back."

"I can bring you to Orlando once this is all over, I promise."

"Will this ever be over?" I ask myself. I pause my Tai Chi, grab the slice he extends my way, fold, bite. Just like the girls from the park have taught me. The margarita makes me float. I needed it. Badly.

Without the anchor of my Tai Chi, Simon's pacing around is very aggravating. Even worse is the avalanche of questions, all so rapid I must assume most are either rhetorical or just an attempt to annoy me. Isn't she coming? Why did he agree with such a bad idea? Can't you just teleport there instead? And "Why did you pick that day?" Hmm. Interesting one. I grant him my attention, he digs deeper: "Why that moment?"

"I didn't pick anything. It was more like it pulled me."

He finally pauses, lost in a thought I guess must be full of big words and little numbers. But in the end, all he says are two cryptic words. "Entangled moments…"

Ok, smartass, how would a normal human being say that? We weren't connected, but between cramming my face with a chunk of crust and setting my eyes in a squint, I made myself clear.

"Your equations. Seemed like quantum mechanics and relativity, combined."

"I'm not sure I understand," I say.

"Don't worry, no one does," he laughs. Apparently, it was a joke. I ask him if *he* does and the asshole responds with a smirk, proceeds to tell me physicians have been trying to unite those two for decades. "Your equations seemed to describe a hyper-connection through low-energy wormholes. Too hard to grasp?"

Simon grabs a slice of pizza, takes a bite and continues with his mouth full. "What you laid on that board was an interwoven universe." He picks up a pen, and finds a page with enough empty space, draws a square. "Here, you know this, a square, right? If I draw another square next to it and connect the edges, you see a cube, correct? A cube is a 3D square. Now…" he continues to draw, makes another cube and connects all the edges of the two figures, "this is what we call a hyper-cube, a figure our brains can't comprehend, but it's one object in four dimensions. It can be here, and here and in all the points in between, because it is connected beyond space, through many spaces. Then…" he now draws another one of those aberration cubes and starts to connect all the edges again, "ow you have a fifth dimension. Time. All these points now co-exist through time. What I don't know is: one, how you managed to create this portal to leap through dimensions; two, how do you navigate through them. You said you didn't choose, right?"

It's complicated, I tell him. The leaps, the ones in space as he says, I have some choice, though under my restricted field of vision. The time part, I don't know. It's more like a call than a decision.

He takes one more look at his watch. "Where's your friend?" Then, back to the inquiry, he adds a third quest, "And why you? There must be something on our training that wired your body to—"

For a smart guy, he's so obtuse. "So when scientists can't explain reality, they try to find new formulas to explain what they were seeing, right?"

"Generally, correct."

"What if the problem isn't with the laws they're writing, but with the reality they're trying to explain?" I ask. "What if what you see as reality isn't what reality really is? If those other dimensions are the real world and we are just a little experiment the immortals run to understand how we would behave?"

Simon stops chewing, stops pacing. I guess he even stops breathing for a while. "You lost me at immortals, to be honest."

"Like the monkeys you created," I say. "From their point of view, their world is real and ours is the game. What if they're right? Or if we're both layers of a game someone else is watching? And the Dao is just a glitch that allows us to peek behind the screen, see the puppeteer behind the shadow puppets?"

"A back door into our reality?" He mumbles to himself. I keep my face straight for as long as I can, then finally cackle with laughter. *Damn it, Yinyin, you could have kept it up a little longer.*

"You call *me* an asshole," he says. And offers to reconnect. Maybe together we can figure this out. Bad idea, I tell him. When we connect, we always end up either punching each other or fucking each other. Right now, we have more important things to do. Like finding another place to go after they find our location.

On that thought, even the pizza has lost its flavor.

"Once we find that answer," he says, holding my anxious feet from bouncing, "we won't need to worry about being caught anymore."

It's like being caught between a sword and a spear. I think of Shifu and how heartbroken he would be if he heard that I'm trying to crack the family secret with a white guy. In my fantasy, I ask the Dao, as if I was asking my master himself: If that has to happen, if the secret will be broken anyway, should it remain secret at all? Wouldn't it be better if everyone has access to it?

It's like my spirit is being ripped apart.

Unfortunately, the skies don't bother. They send no answer. So I aim at Simon instead. "What if it's actually better to let the government handle something that powerful?"

"When they thought they were just learning how to connect brains, the board of directors at Oak Tree Technologies had the exact same question," he explains. That's his way of telling me I'm not that dumb. Thanks, Simon. "Intentions," he continues. "Leave it to the government, they'll want to use this power to control everyone. In the hands of academia, it will turn into a frozen chaos. This opportunity needs leadership to flourish. It's not like we're connecting inanimate machines like the internet... we're building a cognitive Super Highway. A Brainternet! Yeah, a Brainternet, an internet of brains. Get it?"

His pride in the new name is kind of endearing. He was still catching his breath after his big spiel when the light flickered. Is it the Dao speaking to me? 'Cause that used to happen in Wudang too.

Back in the mountains, where the qi was strong, and the electricity weak, when lights flickered, power could go out for days. Always taking water with it, making us have to rely on traditional bathrooms—a little wooden room outside, with a hole in the floor. I hated it so much. Though, when that happened during the winter, or even late in the fall, Shifu would light a small fire in the backyard, so we could sleep under the eyes of the stars, dragons and the mountains. That part, I loved. He would tell me stories of when he was young, after the bombs unbalanced the qi of the planet and the government took control of everything. People started to believe there was no use for martial arts anymore, unless it was practiced for sports, or national pride. He and a few friends, the most skilled fighters in the mainland, remained close and would meet around fires like that to study what was left of the traditions, and hope the Dao would let them fill the gaps left by secrecy. He told me one day the Party called them with a problem. Shifu didn't want to go, but the others convinced him to listen. There was a village in the South where a man had built a small army that terrorized the villages in the entire region. The government tried to send forces but the tyrant defeated them all. Somehow, Shifu told me, the soldiers from Beijing would turn against each other and attack themselves, as if they had been hypnotized by a demon. Before they had to resort to methods dangerous for civilians, they decided to call the old-time masters to break through the warlord's defense line and cut the head of the snake. A battle of spirit and skill, against sorcery and malevolence. Shifu said it took them days of hiding, meditating, attacking, leaving, more meditating, coming back.... Eventually, Shifu defeated the demon but lost some friends along the way too. "Why did you do it?" I asked him. "Wasn't there anyone else?" And Shifu said, "Because that man, the evil one, was one of my students. A master should take responsibility for what he puts in the world."

The last time he told me about this, there were only four of them left. And they all pledged to retire from fighting, to dedicate their lives to the preservation of the skills the world may need again someday. I always thought of that as yet another one of his parables—a story to teach me about traditions and responsibilities. I'm not so sure anymore. Of anything.

"And what happened to your student?" I asked back then.

Shifu turned somber. Said in revenge the villagers burnt his palace down and put his head and all of his lieutenants on sticks for everyone to see.

I can see it. The fire. The feast. The spikes with so many heads leading to the final one, placed higher than all the other ones. But when I looked…it was just a decapitated body of a white man, in a modern lab coat! Then someone taps my shoulder and when I look back, Shifu is right behind me. Livid. He waves his sword and, right before the blade touched my neck, a voice boomed from the skies, "The power supply is one of their favorite targets."

What?

I blink and it's Simon staring at me, unaware of how far away my mind has gone. "The monkeys," he insists with urgency, "they like power attacks because it makes it harder for their hunters to attack them. They may know where we are already."

"Oh, yes, the monkeys," I say, trying not to look dismissive. No time for debates. My heart still races—is the Dao trying to tell me Dr. L is the reincarnation of the sorcerer Shifu killed? That Shifu is about to leap through time to kill me too?

"You know what I think?" I tell Simon, "If this *Brainternet*, as you say, gets controlled by the government, it can be bad. But I don't want it in the hands of a corporate demon either. Slavery is slavery, regardless of who's holding the whip."

He says no one can prevent evolution. "What is at stake right now isn't *if* it will happen. But *by whom*. Why not us?"

Because he's the one who created the problem, I tell him.

"Yes, I created the creatures," he admits, "If I hadn't, someone else would have. But because I did, I know their weaknesses, I can control them, I can fix them and use them to speed up our process to protect ourselves. Use evil against evil."

Westerners. Always looking for domination. "How do you know what's better?" I ask. In my mind, I am still expecting Shifu to come kill us. Then a scary thought occurs to me and freezes my fucking guts. That time he left alone…What if he didn't go to kill my father, but to kill me instead, at another time, in the future. What if that's why he came back so sad? My entire body shakes. "Simon, we gotta stop this. We are in danger."

"Duh! The U.S. Government is chasing us—of course, we are! A killer race of AI too. But I am smarter than they are. And you…you have your powers. You just need to unlock them.

"No, I don't mean the Government. I mean Shifu. I think he's gonna leap here and kill us both."

In another circumstance, Simon probably would have laughed. Called me paranoid and childish. But things have changed since our leap in time. "We cross that bridge when we get to it," he says. "Besides, we are on the good side. Why would he do it?"

I ask him if he's sure. "Turning humanity into a single mind, like an army of zombies…"

"As I said, it's still better…."

"Better than the alternative," I insist, "you said that. Dr. Lambrechts said that. But what if the alternative is just a boogeyman? What if it was never bound to happen?" Simon shakes his head as if I had said the stupidest of stupid things. "The technology can only reach superficial levels of the brain, which means there's always some level of control and independence. Just like we turned our link on and off today."

Except that he can turn on the links and I can't. He gives me a cup of coffee. "Things are moving too fast, I know," he says. "I'll work on the control part later. Why is she taking so long to get here?" I was thinking the same.

"Wanna hear something interesting?" He says, in an attempt to clear the air. "One of Dr. Lambrechts's stories about why he started this?"

To each, their master. I have Shifu, Simon has the near-bald demon who wants to be God. The clock on the wall has barely moved. I wish I could dive into meditation, because there's way too much to decide and I need all my qi for when things unfold. But since he won't let me, I better keep my mind busy. "Go ahead," I say.

"There is a collection of feelings we know as pleasure, love, hate…Those are all electric functions of the outer side of the brain. Right where our bots are. Once we're connected at scale, we may be able to appreciate beauty like we never have before. Dr. Lambrechts calls this the Spark of God, a mental state that only a timeless, all-knowing being can have."

"I bet that *hate* happens there too. And ambition. And desire…" Shifu would lecture him for hours on that alone. I don't have that kind of patience.

"Technically, some desires come from older parts of our brain," Simon says, "yet, for some modern kinds of those, you're right. That was exactly what I told him. See? We already think alike."

Nope.

He paints the argument of what he calls *the trap paradox*, and I do my best to follow. Our brains connect. We all get high on elation, mesmerized by the feeling of being an all-knowing god. So happy and so loving, we don't notice someone abusing the system. Maybe even against us. "Think about students in a classroom, openly sharing thoughts and knowledge. All it takes is for one of them to be infected, and we would all be infected too. Digital viruses, in our organic brains. Nothing in our evolutionary path has prepared us for that."

These things in my head, I want to rip them out right now. Maybe they should have never started this.

"Then the machines would win," he pushes back.

"But this virus situation, isn't it why the military should have it?"

"Those dumb fucks architected the internet too. See what happened?"

Yes, Simon says *dumb fucks* too. My brain has left some deep impressions on his. But I still don't know why he needs the Shadow Leap. I mean, I do know: to escape this clusterfuck. But he wanted it before this. Is he thinking of doing something stupid, like trying to go back in time to kill Dr. L or the general?

"Funding," he explains. "Teleporting *and* time traveling can raise a lot of money. And to achieve that we would need to get the bots to work. So we hit all the goals at once."

I get it. Simon is a smart guy with big ambitions. But I'm not sure I want to share my family's secrets with anyone yet.

That's when the bell rings.

We both run to the door. I peek behind the curtain. He opens the door. "Mrs. Lee!" I hug her so tight she has to push me back to breathe again. Like a security guard, Simon asks to see her purse. She complies, not the happiest of campers, but she does.

"Sorry," I say, "Simon is terrified of patchouli."

"Electronics," he explains. "Can't have them. Especially phones." She didn't bring one. I had been clear about it. Simon inspects the handbag nonetheless. Boxes and tubes of the most varied shapes and sizes. "I didn't have time. So I brought a little of everything," she explains, and asks for a bed where I can lie. We gotta improvise. So a thicker shelf will do. The woman takes a box of needles from her box. "I still don't get this," he says.

"Ok, so you believe we can teleport, jump in time, but just because you don't understand the needles…" I hadn't even finished and he had already stopped resisting. And as Mrs. Lee started poking me, Simon started to add some wires of his own. Some on my skin, some on the needles. "Just for data," he says. "It won't interfere with the magic, I promise, just—"

She cuts him off. "Do you mind?"

Immediately I feel her hurried pokes spreading all over my body. All meridians. Rushed and harsh. Heavier than usual. I must look like porcupine being offered to the gods. Then, the sound of the lighter and all at once the fragrance of burning herbs take over the place. "It's not the best time to get high, you know," Simon complains. I tell her to ignore his comment. Though it does smell like weed. Mrs. Lee? She promises it's not.

On the monitors, Simon plays with dials, wires and buttons. Says he's testing a few frequencies and sensibilities to track any activity, but it's hard when nobody seems to know the nature of the magic being operated. Thus, his questions. So many of them. Mrs. Lee shushes him again and checks my pulse. "What is that thing you say?" She asks.

"The Dao is the nothing. In me, infinity it will be," I respond. She nods and not a second later, Simon's instruments start beeping. "Vibrations," he whispers. Something is happening. He tries to show Mrs. Lee the data on his device, but she ignores him once again. She closes her eyes instead, joins my mantra. "The Dao is the nothing. In her, infinity it will be."

Inside my head, I am back at the Anamnodome. Poor little Simon is being beaten by those kids. Why would a man who works so hard to convey confidence pick such a vulnerable moment? I watch him for a while. Then, something taps the space between my eyebrows and the stinging resumes. This time, outward.

"That should do. Now you, sir, take care of my girl. Or I'm coming to kill you."

Beneath my skin, wrapping every inch of my body, a layer of dull pain. It's hard to move, but I follow her to the door. "Please take care, Mrs. Lee." Give her another hug. She's the closest I have to family in this country. Though Simon isn't keen on our goodbye. "We are running out of time," he yells from a distance. "We need to do it. Now."

Not yet. "Why did you pick that day, in the Anamnodome? When you were being bullied by those other kids?" At first, he protests. But realizing that I won't budge, he says *we both* chose it. "I mean, our subconscious levels picked that moment as a bridge."

"You think that's part of that *entanglement* thing too?" I ask.

261

"Maybe. Either that or your backdoor people are really trying to fuck with my mind, 'cause I hadn't thought about that day for the longest time." His eyes feel distant, as if he were lost in the memory again. Put together, it's a lot to process. The bullies, the older girl intervening, us, sex…then he lunges at me, his closed fist coming straight onto my nose. I try to teleport. Nothing. So I step to my side and let him crash into the wall. Then on the floor. He moans, the idiot.

"I don't buy it," I say. His memory, too vivid to be a rescue.

"I could ask you the same thing," he says. "Did you pick that day to tease me? To tell me I could go back to the shadows of my mind and…"

Shadows?

Flash.

The sun is setting behind a mountain, painting the sky all sorts of colors. The shadow of the temple creeps fast in our direction. Shifu's and mine.

This is it. This is when I die.

"Real kung fu is in the shadows of temple," he says. "Not inside, where tourists come to see. That's for funding. Here, beyond the eyes, with no sashes, no degrees, no rules to obey, we can let our technique be transferred…and evolve." I remember that day now. In my childhood, I used to play there. Spent my days living tales of warriors, emperors and magical creatures. Playing among the infinite rows of Daoist tea where I chased imaginary baby phoenixes and foxes with nine tails. Yesterday I tamed fire lions. Now I ride rhinos, made of bronze and a horn of lightning. Feels good to be back here, where I learned to fight like the heroes from the past, carried by Shifu's adventures from when he and his buddies brought balance back to the world. I can see them around me, as Shifu tells me the stories of his mighty comrades. The man with an iron body that no sword could pierce. The master who could send his enemies flying with blast rays of qi. The one who could absorb any blow and return the energy to the source.[48]

I'm in my teens now, and it all makes sense, finally. Qi bombs explain how to align muscles and breathing to make it feel like my strength was shooting beyond my body. I try it and *wow*, it works so well. Bouncing qi reminds us relaxation can transfer the impact of the hits you eat. Shifu kicks me and my body contorts around the blow and I slap his shoulder much harder than I thought I would. Impenetrable bodies in fact explain how to use breathing and internal pressure to protect your organs from impact. And finally, teleportation stories are a reminder that footwork is what allows you to move around the opponent's sight. Real applications, no fantasy. I am mesmerized. All the technique in the world, preserved in my childhood stories. "Banality is how stories die," Shifu tells me. "Beauty is what allows them to survive. And then, evolve."

Survive and evolve. I am just where I needed to be. When I open my eyes again, Simon is still waiting for an answer.

"I couldn't give two fucks about your childhood, Simon."

Then we hear the long screech of tires outside. And a scream of terror.

They are here already.

---

48. In his book *The Wisdom of The Tao*, Deng Ming-Dao talks about how he wasn't educated with lessons, but with stories. He mentions how his grandmother would always explain or justify things with tales of The Yellow Emperor or other tales that are more than a thousand years old. In this book, I tried to include some of these ancient stories. But I also made some up. Not only because I wanted to have something new, but because Shifu always felt like an imaginative man who would easily make his own stories just so the points he wanted to make sounded older and more credible.

31

Flowing Breeze Sways Willow

It's not hard to imagine what's waiting outside. Helicopters, sirens blaring and policemen behind their vehicle's open doors pointing their guns at the entrance of this abandoned little musical instruments shop. "You said we would have a couple of hours!" I whisper at Simon.

"Is there a back door?" I ask. He shrugs in despair. One, two, three breaths. We must do something. He holds my hand. The scared little boy again. From a little gap in the curtain, we take a peek. We freeze.

A single black pickup truck awaits, a few meters from our storefront. The tinted windows reflect the sky and we can't tell who's inside. They blink their headlights a few times, then a loud, long honk. A faceoff.

Connect the damn brains, Simon! Connect!

There's not much of a choice. I step outside first and, in response, the driver's door pops. From inside comes a big man in a tactical suit and dark shades. Big, much bigger than the last ones from the park, with shoulders so massive they can touch the dude's deformed ears. It takes a second, but I recognize him. "Buffalo?"

I get no reaction from him. Zero. Líng. Behind me, Simon seems equally perplexed. As if I didn't exist, Buffalo walks to the back and slides the door open just to release another man in the same uniform, same shades, just thinner…The Crusher?!

This isn't right.

"What are you guys doing here?" I ask.

"Fire…with fire…" Simon mumbles behind me.

The Crusher marches all the way to the back of the truck and drags a lifeless body. I recognize the clothes. Mrs. Lee? What did you guys do?

Think, Yinyin.

She moves her head. God, she's alive! Her eyes seem groggy, her mouth is taped. Her hand rubs the top of her head. She's hurt. You guys are so fucked right now. Then she looks at me. Her face changes. Terror. "Everything will be fine Mrs. Lee."

The Crusher cocks his pistol. Points at her head.

The hum. It resumes. *Thanks, Simon.* No time to talk. *Just follow me.* I charge. The Crusher grins. Like he did when we fought in the cage. He aims at me now. You wouldn't dare. He does. The psycho pulls the fucking trigger.

I see it all. His finger bending, the spark inside the barrel, the bullet flying toward me. "Flinching is surrendering to the ego," I hear in my head. There's no choice anymore. The metal drop is on its way, deadly, cold, straight. I feel it touch my skin, push against my chest. That's it.

The Dao is the nothing. In me, infinity it will be.

I'm behind The Crusher now. A Shadow Leap? I kick him in the back of the knee. He falls. My shoulder, it hurts. I check it with one hand. Clean. My elbow drops on the back of his neck. Then a moan, suffered and short.

Simon is on the ground, twisting in pain.

A pool of blood grows around him. The bullet I avoided, now in his flesh. The chest, the shoulder, somewhere in that zone. *Simon? Can you hear me? Hold on, Ok? We'll take care of you.*

Don't fucking die on me, do you hear me?

Heart…aches, he says. *Can't stay…*

Another leap—beyond Buffalo's sight—and flank him with all the violence I can summon. Why did you do that to me, Little Cow? He stumbles, and I free Mrs. Lee. *Run, Yinyin*, I tell myself while I carry her away, to where Simon is. Behind us, an engine fires, tires spin, rubber burns and it fades in the distance. The hum gets weaker too. "Simon?" And weaker. "Simon!"

Until it finally stops.

Kneeling next to him, I beg for Mrs. Lee's help. "Hold on, Simon!" He tries to talk, but his strength fades with the amber in his eyes. A void sucks my chest inward. I hold his hand; my ear near his mouth now and my eyes, closed. I can feel them, the bots in my brain, stretching their tentacles deeper, grasping for the synapses I am trying to broadcast; their receptors wide open, searching for a signal from his. Maybe I am just imagining, I don't know. Either way, silence.

"Say something, Simon."

A faint, crackling sound and a hint of his brown eyes turning to mine.

"Do you…trust…your boyfriend?"

32

Ride the Dragon

"No ambulance," he begs. "They'll find us." Mrs. Lee points at her old Prius, still parked in the same place. We hop in and I drive it like a maniac. Running red lights, honking as if the world was made of deaf men. A single police officer to stop us and Simon is dead. There's blood. Mrs. Lee keeps some pressure on the wound, but it's hard to tell if it's enough, when your eyes have to stay on the road. I clamp the pedal to the floor and pray to the immortals that we get there alive.

At the emergency entrance, I stop the car and jump out , already yelling "Help!" The Oakland Mission Hospital isn't big, but it's still full of all the stupid red tape bureaucrats can think up—Jason always says. Yet, if you stop at the E.R. and squawk that single, magic word, they will take you in without asking questions. "Help!" I insist. They do.

Two male nurses at first, then they recognize me and bring two more, plus a gurney, place Simon on top and roll it away. Blood drops leave a dark trail through the double doors. Behind me, Mrs. Lee continues to ramble hysterically. I pull her against my chest. The hospital drama: the rush, the screaming…I've seen it before, but never from within.

"Jason?!" I shout. "Is Dr. Sonderup back?" I ask.

He's traveling, I know. War zone crap. But that's the second code. Nurses are trained like waiters to never get distracted by begging hands. But mention a doctor's name, the spell is broken.

"Claudia?" From a distance, Denise waves and picks up the phone. She is a nice woman, in her late fifties, close to retirement but avoiding it because she finds too much pleasure in telling others what to do. Thirty giant seconds later, Jason comes running, panic in his eyes. "What happened? Are you Ok?"

What is he doing here?

"The blackouts must have erased my data or something. At the last minute the airline had Dr. Jonathan Fox as the passenger. There was no time to change it, so he went instead. Are you Ok? What happened?" He holds my hands, examines my face and his hand slides toward the back of my neck. I shake my head.

Please, this isn't the time. "My friend, he got shot in the chest!" Then I point to Mrs. Lee. "And she got assaulted and is concussed or in some sort of shock. I can't get her to tell me what happened." He checks her eyes, mouth....No more screaming, her heart slows a little. Maybe she recognizes him. Then her legs fail. Jason still has a hold on her face. It's the only reason she's not on the floor.

"We have to call the police," Jason says, and gently waves for a wheelchair. In the E.R., panic is for real disasters. Multiple casualties and no time to think, he told me once. Earthquakes, massive shootings and fires. The only things that scare me. That, and my headaches. I feel a sting. Is that real or just my imagination?

No, it's gone. "Please, no police, no records?" I squeeze his hand. Because of the discipline of fighting, I'm good under pressure, but once the action is over, adrenaline always breaks me. Usually I can pretend to be tired. But not here. Not with Jason. "Even if I don't, tomorrow someone will," he says.

Fair.

It's 5 pm, I'll handle it once the sun rises. Now, my bones feel made of Jell-O. I just need a break. I lace my fingers through his and he keeps them there until someone calls.

Denise. The one who likes to give orders.

☯   ☯   ☯

Finally alone, I pull Jason by the collar and kiss him hard. My leg hooks him on the waist, then the other finishes the grab. Like a Brazilian Jiu-Jitsu guard, only standing. There's no space for lying on mats here. Not in the drugs room. The wall is close, though, so I push my feet against it and throw us both against the glass doors of the locked cabinet where the good stuff lives. A few bottles fall. I make a silent "shhh" sign, laughing and kissing at the same time. We almost break our teeth.

He says, "Marry me," and with all the conviction I have, I say the only thing I can: "Why?"

"C'mon, you want it too."

The silence is immense. I need to see how serious he is first. He drops on a knee. Shit. I put on the cutest face I can make: "No way!" He's in shock. What did he expect? "You can move back in if you stop being a snowflake," I say, and we go back to making out. Then I push him away again. Wait. "Where is Simon? You gotta take care of Simon."

He ignores my request and attacks my mouth again.

No. I thrust away from him. There is something wrong. A shadow, a presence. I search around and, behold, Simon, stands next to us, inches from our faces, a deranged smile on his face.

From my seat, I jump, confused. Body hurts. There are no drug bottles around us. No Simon. Just the ugly room and the *Robocop* bed where Mrs. Lee rests. I cover my face with both hands and stay there, in the darkness, trying to recover from the bad dream. Breathe, breathe, breathe…Then a tender touch on the back of my head and a wave of goosebumps.

"I like the hair," he says. Jason. Now I can't tell where the dream started. Or ended. I may have blushed. He says she's going to be Ok.

I say "shhh," as if I know more than he does. His smile, usually so gentle and comforting, embarrasses me a little. I feel silly. He points to the door and, being still half asleep, I have no idea if that was a naughty or chaste invite.

"I know I've been an ass," he says, "I have no right to…"

I cover his mouth with a finger. That was all I wanted to hear. "I said shhh."

There's no one watching, I make sure, so I kiss him on the lips. "Once this is over, we'll talk more, Ok?"

I push his chest with one hand pull his collar with the other, then throw both arms around him. Need his warmth a little more. But it's not the time to commit. I push him again and he gives me a puzzled dog face. Confusing, I know. But I'm Chinese, a living paradox.

"Claudia?" a voice calls me from the inside. I let him go.

☯   ☯   ☯

Alone in the dim light of the hospital room, my friend, teacher, student, and acupuncturist gives me a half-eyed drugged smile. She mumbles, "All things difficult before easy. Want a peach?" She points at the fruit basket with a "Get well" balloon.

Heard that before. All things difficult before easy. Shifu used to tell me that at the beginning of every big lesson.

"They told me to say that to you," she says.

Having conversations with crazies is funny, sometimes. Had many with knocked-out people before they completely woke up. Just sit down and listen.

"The short one says I have a lizard horse inside. I like him."

"A dragon," I say.

"No, it was a horse. He showed me one."

I laugh, "I mean it's a *dragon* horse. Did he show you one?

What did it look like?"

"Oh, it was wonderful. Giant hooves, muscles popping from under its scales, and waves instead of hair. It had so many colors…"

I try not to laugh. "That's so wonderful, Mrs. Lee. Who is 'he'?"

"You think…I'm hallucinating, don't you?" Hmm. "Those nice men from China, the ones from the park and Chinatown."

"The bozos," I say.

Though groggy, she still admonishes me. Says they are valiant, warriors, that they fought monkeys with their iron bodies and fire-shooting hands. Like the stories Shifu used to tell me, just with a soft mouth and a swollen tongue. "In real life, kung fu not good, but in dream, they…magnificent," she says. "And I love that I have a lizard horse now. He's so sweet."

Dragon, I correct. A pause for breathing and mind-wandering, then she comes back.

"They told me to read to my friend again. My friend, you got it? You."

In slow motion, like Tai Chi, she points at her big purse. I give it to her. That brick can cause some serious spine damage, I tell her. She grabs a small book from inside, opens to the marked page. But the light is weak, and even weaker is her sight, so she hands it to me. "Read, aloud." She wants me to hear the words—*they* asked for that. Ok…

Can you make yourself embrace The Dao and not lose it?

My mind follows and bitches. "I've heard that before, Mrs. Lee."

"Quiet," she chirps.

Can you gather your qi and yet be tender like a newborn?

Tender like a hammer, I think.

Can you clean your inner reflection and keep it spotless?

I don't resist. "C'mon, Mrs. Lee, you've seen my apartment. I can't keep anything spotless." She shushes me once more, makes me proceed.

Can you care for the people and rule the country,
and not be cunning?
Can you open and close the gate of Heaven
and act like a woman?
Can you comprehend everything in the four directions
and still do nothing?

"Wu Wei," I respond. She nods.

To give birth to them and nourish them, carry them with-
out taking possession of them, care for them without sub-
duing them, raise them without steering them.

"Can you?" she asks. "Only way out, they say. Of your mess. The dragon-lizard agrees. Take a peach, will you?"

Is she talking about Jason? Letting him come back? Forget about the Indian bitch and let it play? That may be in place already. See? I'm in synch with the Dao. The other thing she's right about: we need to get out of this mess. But Wu Wei, doing nothing, or any of that, will not help. I pace around. We have to leave this hospital before they find us. She takes the book from my hand, rips a few pages, to my shock.

"What? This is just paper, honey." Then put the folded sheets in my back pocket and continues as if she hadn't just destroyed a sacred book. "I'm a former hippie, you know?" she says, "They called me Blossom back then…Although some say *peace and love* never leave you. No, that's not what I must say. Plans, I think we should make plans. For after. After the mess." Her hands are comforting. "It will be alright. You know the path. Let's talk about Molly."

Molly was in charge of the class while I was out. "How about we talk about what happened to you, Mrs. Lee? Do you know why those guys took you? *Where* they took you? What they did…"

She interrupts me with her drowsy mouth. "I heard she's in Oregon. With another asshole. A weed-head. I've nothing against weed. I was a hippie, you know?" Her meds must be kicking in again. It's just a matter of time until she quiets down. "Assholes on weed are the absolute worst. I fucked a bunch of them. I know. A lizard horse, she needs. Molly. And a tigress. Beside her." Dragon, I say. Dragon horse. "Yeah, a dragon horse. Inside of me. So beautiful. Can you go protect her?"

She dives into her own mind and zonks out.

I'm free to think.

Or act.

Perhaps pray.

Waiting for the immortals in Heaven to act isn't necessarily my way, but this moment isn't the most ordinary. Simon being operated on somewhere, my oldest student concussed because of me, the Army searching for my face in every database in the universe. I tell her I wish I could protect every girl trapped by a prick, but that's for later. She doesn't respond. Maybe she's in another dimension with the three masters and her dragon horse. Or just passed out on morphine. At least she's quiet. I launch my sight through the glass toward those city-washed stars and lose myself in the nothing.

33

Pose Holding the Beast's Head

B eyond the sealed windows of the hospital, a sea of stars stares back at us. Fireflies, fire bombs in the skies. I am the bomb now. Once the sun rises, I boom. There will be cops around us. Asking questions. Entering our faces on their wanted lists. We will be in so much trouble we will have to cooperate. Even if the world isn't really ready for that. If we don't, General Creep will suck our brains, and that coward Dr. Lambrechts will enjoy life as a rich man after turning people into warriors with no will. Yay.

One way or another, my skills will be used to hurt innocent men, women, and children. One way or another, my skills will be used to hurt innocent men, women, and children. One way or another, my skills will be used to hurt innocent men, women, and children.

A curse. One I imposed on us all when I broke the promise I made to my dead mother and the immortals. "I don't teach men," I told them. I lied. Now the ire of the heavens is claiming revenge.

"Feeling better, honey?" says Mrs. Lee behind my back. I almost forgot about her.

"You're the one who needs to get better, remember?"

"I am remembering."

"Good."

"No, I am remembering some things, honey. I remember them taking me. Outside that funky place you were at. Then they were dragging me out of a truck. You were there. Oh my god! They shot at you!"

She pats my chest and I give her a calming smile. "What is going on?" She asks before her eyelids collapse again. "Dammit," she slurs, "I can't remember…anything."

I tell her to relax. To let go so she can get better, but she seems determined to resist the urge to doze off. "How 'bout your f'end, any news?"

He's gonna be operated on, I tell her. "May be happening as we speak."

"Is he your new boyf'end?"

My cheeks get warm, and I know I am blushing again. "No, just a colleague. We have…a connection."

A single naughty chuckle, and she's back. Incredible. She says she remembers the connections she had when she was my age. "I was pretty like you one day, you know? And Berkeley was a wild place…" We exchange tender half-smiles and hold hands.

"How about your other boyfriend? The doctor you went outside? What? You think I didn't see?" My eyes turn to the night outside again. Don't want to talk about it, but she insists, "You gonna deny an old lady in a hospital cradle her daily dose of gossip?"

"Tsc…I think Jason is starting to change his mind, Mrs. Lee. Maybe there's a future for us after all."

"Hoo," she says, as a true Chinese would say, "So he's the one you think about for the future. I knew it! Does the other one knows he's just a *connection*?"

"He does," I say, trying to end that silly chat, but she doesn't stop. Where's the button to increase her meds and make her shut up?

"And why are you the only one here, hon? The second-place dude, he doesn't have a family?"

Strange. After hours meandering through his brain, I don't have that answer. In fact, I know very little about Simon. I stand up and walk toward the window. It's late. 10 pm. I close my eyes for a few seconds, focus. Open them again. In my reflection in the window, I see a yellow light trying to form around my iris, then fading again.

He's still out there, I know.

Behind my back, I hear a click on the door. As if someone was trying to get in. But no one does. And before I could check, a muffled voice says, "Attention third floor." Speakers, from everywhere. The voice carries on, "All doors will be locked for a few minutes for the monthly hallway sterilization procedure. In case of emergency, call your nurse and ask for assistance."

Odd. Never heard of sterilization procedures before. The door has been locked indeed, I check. What's up with the world insisting on locking me in? And how about Simon?—I can't stay there. It was a simple procedure, Jason promised. Thankfully the bullet didn't hit anywhere too threatening. As the new assistant surgeon, he was going to do it himself. Two hours later, however, there's still no word. Did he try to call? Damn, Simon, why did you have to get rid of my phone?

I reach for the old phone on the side table. The nurse may have access to some sort of status of the ongoing procedures. But the handset is silent. I try every button. Dead.

Mrs. Lee snores and, with her eyes shut, gives a giant grin, likely from the comfort of a morphine dream. Would she mind if I took her phone? She won't. I comb through her purse. Damn, Simon had told her to leave it at home. I make a mental note to talk to Jason about it. He'll say he doesn't get into management matters, but I bet this one will cause a lot of unnecessary stress.

Unless…what if this is all a lie and the government found us already? What if a camera identified us like Simon was afraid it would? Or one of those nurses called the police? I head to the window. Downstairs, no sign of trouble. *Stop being paranoid, Yinyin.* It's not just the police though. It's the circumstance. Being trapped, with no communication, on a night like this. Ridiculous, I know. You learn to fight, to beat people twice your size and face thugs with knives and shit, just to panic when you're stuck in a room without a phone. Shifu would slap me on the forehead for this. This isn't like when the internet went blank, however: a few hours ago, someone shot at me.

In the corridor, I hear steps rushing. Multiple people. Crap. No, wait. Someone wails. Of course, there would be an emergency, geniuses. It's called panic.

How did we do this before we had phones and Google all-day everyday? Oh, yes, we found people and asked. I wonder who is on duty today? I yell at the door. "Hey, do you guys have a phone I can borrow?"

They ignore me. I wait. Brain doesn't feel well. Need some candy, I think. None in Mrs. Lee's purse. The stretcher seat is comfortable. I lay my back for a second of rest, blink very slowly. When I open again, the door is open. How long has it been? It doesn't matter. I rush to the nurses' desk. Lights are off, seats empty, all monitors dark. "Excuse me? Anyone here? Can someone call Dr. Sonderup for me?"

Not even an echo responds.

Someone left a cell phone plugged in the outlet. But no signal. Then steps. Fast and devoid of any rhythm. The sound grows louder. And louder. A young nurse presents herself from behind the wall. Her hair is a mess; she's panting, sweating. Never seen her. I hide the phone in my back pocket.

"Hi, I'm looking for info on a patient...."

She inspects the large screen turned away from me, drops a few rapid clicks. "Sorry, there's been a problem. All our systems went down after this weird...this floor procedure and I got locked in a patient's room." The young woman digs her nose back into the screen. "I can't find the other nurses to ask what... have you seen my phone?" she asks.

"I haven't, sorry. Now calm down. What's your name?"

Mona, she says. "Nurse Mona. Mona Morrow. Mona, Morrow. You can laugh, everyone does. But I swear, I don't know what's going on here. I was reading a patient's report when...I don't like this. None of this. I don't. I'm sorry, I shouldn't be saying any of this. But I have a little daughter at home. I don't like what's happening here." She is spiraling out of control, so frantic I have to hold her by the shoulders and shake her a few times. She stops. Pale and bug-eyed. Breathing through her mouth. Probably hyperventilating

"Ok, Nurse Mona Morrow. Breathe," I say. "What's the name of your little girl?"

"Rachel," she says.

"Ok, Mona Morrow. This is going to be fine, and after your shift, you will go home like you do every day and will wake up your little Rachel to send her to school, Ok? Everything's going to be all right. I promise. Now, tell me what happened."

That's when all the lights go off and she shrieks so loud my ears start to ring.

She apologizes. The yellow glow of the emergency lights turns on. She continues, rattled. Says there may be a message somewhere. About the blackout. In the system.

In emergency situations, nurses are trained to show calm. Like flight attendants.

"He's operating upstairs, right? Fifth floor?"

The nurse nods very fast.

"A syringe!" squawks a voice behind me.

The nurse jumps in her seat. "What was that?"

"My friend," I say. Mrs. Lee. She must need something. "I'll go check on her. Will let you know if I need anything." She has too much on her plate already. When I'm back in the room, however, Mrs. Lee is passed out again. Good. It gives me time.

I rush. Stolen phone…no signal. Hallway, to the left. At least I know the place. The elevator is at the end of the building, they must have generators here. I press the "up" button. It doesn't work. "Down" doesn't either. Shit. The stairs. *Find them, Yin-yin*. The silence is pure, absolute, chilling. Makes my skin bump like a chicken. I don't like what's happening here any more than Nurse Mona Morrow does.

Without the white noise of the power, the hospital is a ghost town. You could hear someone walking in slippers, if there was anyone. And I do hear. Toc, toc, toc…the sound bounces off the beige walls and the ugly-patterned linoleum floor, then echoes back at me from every direction at once. A red light points to stairs around the corner. I charge. Noise is coming from there. What is it? *Faster, Yinyin, faster*. The corner. Three steps. Two. One. *Turn!*

I hit something, scream. A hand squeezes my shoulder and I leap back, hands up, fighting stance wincing for a kick. The creature turns her phone's flashlight onto her own face. Dr. Mehta. The fake Tigress. "Claudia," she says. "I was looking for you."

I want to apologize for the scream but refrain. Won't give her the pleasure. In the half-darkness I can still see the yellow eyes I remember so well. Without Jason around, though, she drops the charm, the sinuosity of her moves, the warmth of her voice. The bitch is cold. Should have kicked her indeed, then blamed the instincts. Too late. Someday…

"Your boyfriend, Claudia. There has been a problem."

I freeze. Is she talking about Simon? Or Jason?

"What happened?" I ask.

She places her hands over my shoulders. A compassion so fake it doesn't even try to convince. "He didn't make it. Sorry."

Simon?

Her nods cancels all sounds and I want to cry, to hit her. But I can only stare at her robotic figure and ask myself what kind of person would say it like that.

"You mean…he's—"

She nods again and I feel my hands shake. First a little, then so much my entire body bounces. No, it can't be! Jason said it was…"I'm sorry," Dr. Mehta says, cold. My skull tingles, my fingers freeze, my chest can't open. I need air. I need some air! I look around. No doors. The world spins. No windows. Please!

But there was nothing.

Just the most oppressive silence.

And darkness.

And death.

Why do the immortals need to punish others for my sins?

From the deepest shadows, my eyes flash—to the Monkey Valley in Wudang. Around me, the spirits of the river rise in swirls, ready to climb the mountain and be reborn in the Heavens as water dragons. Though, this time, they wait. Filtered through the mist and the leaves, the soft sunlight reveals a body resting between me and a majestic feline. Simon O'Dell. He looks so peaceful and gentle like that. The Tigress approaches me slowly, firm; her cold yellow eyes locked into mine. Two feet from my face, she stops—her breath smells like incense. Then she roars. So loud, the waves push me back and the trees shake in fear. Yet, I don't hear a thing. I try to tell the Tigress I am so sorry, but the silence, so heavy and deep, pushes my words back into my throat. I am going to faint, or puke, or melt. Behind her menacing stripes, Doctor Mehta watches my struggle like a predator does to a meal she's not in the mood to eat. Not this time.

"He asked me to relay a message," she says.

We're back. The hospital and its stench of death. What message? Tell me!

"It wasn't your fault."

It wasn't? I escaped the bullet that hit him!

A raging cry erupts from my throat and splashes all over the floor. My fist hits a wall and a trash can flies to my kick, spilling its toxicity all over the floor. The trash and vomit mix in mud full of anger and loss. Anyone else would have jumped. Not Dr. Mehta. Not her and her superior Tigress manners. Instead, she slowly turns away, departs toward the darker side of the building.

"Wait!" I call. "I want to see him, Simon. I want to talk to my bo—to talk to Dr. Sonderup." I beg her to tell me where to find Jason but her unaffected poise remains. Her long fingers press the upward button. There's no elevator, bitch. I tried. Yet, to my surprise, the doors open. The elevator engulfs her, and leaves me there, standing alone.

How did she…? What do I do now? Do I contact anyone? Practicality numbs grief, Shifu used to say. But I never faced death in this country. Should I call Dr. Lambrechts? I taste vomit in my mouth again. Head waves, I'm gonna fall. The wall, I throw my back against it and let it slide all the way. Jason, I need to talk to Jason. Mona Morrow's phone, I remember. I still have it. No signal. Just me, the echoes, and the yellow lights staring at me. Like Simon's eyes when we were linked. Is that you, Simon? Is this your ghost watching me? On the ceiling, a spot camera. No, it's not Simon.

Dr. Lambrechts! I stand in my most defiant posture and yell at the mechanical eye: "You fucking dragon cunt. Can you hear me?"

The words bounce through the walls. Nobody protests. Whatever made everyone disappear must be his doing too. Him and the creepy general who thinks he can submit the world to his fucking will. Not me.

"Can you hear me, Dr. Lambrechts? Your buddy Simon! He's dead. Fucking dead! Because of your fucking contract! Your shitty little project! How could you? He…worked with you…for fifteen fucking years! Can you hear me? I'm sure you can, assshole! And you better run. Cause I am coming after you!"

Fuck! Fuck! Fuck!

The ground continues to wave and this time a medicine cart and the I.V. hanger hold me upright. Am I going crazy? I feel lightheaded, confused. Brain is foggy, drained. Need some oxygen. Glucose. Only thing I know is: Simon is gone. And I am at fault. I drop myself on the floor and let out a cry of sadness and fury.

It's me and the mechanical eye. And I am going to kill that fucker.

34
White Snake Spits Venom

In the quiet of the dark corridors, I can hear the wires talking. The evil bots mocking my pain. I cover my ears, but their chatter is physical, almost. All over my skin. Then an exploding sound rattles me to the ceiling. Music. A symphony.

At the end of the corridor, a glow. Flickering fast in different colors. A TV! I run, but the floor escapes me, and I fall. "Anybody here?" I yell. No answer. I need oxygen. *Stand up, Yinyin. Follow the sound.*

The waiting room, I suppose. Never been to this part of the hospital. Magazines lay everywhere. Chairs, floor, even on the tables where they were supposed to be. As if people had to leave in a rush. Why? I stick my head out. Mrs. Lee's room is far — straight line covered in echoes – right now, the silly sounds of an old cartoon: a mouse torturing a poor cat. Kids watch that sort of mayhem and then think they can behave like that too. This is a fucking hospital, for the immortals' sake!

Simon was right, we can't trust any cameras, any electronics. Not when the government is after us. I want to cry, but there's no time. Gotta get Mrs. Lee out of here. But then, my eyelid falls.

Just the right eye. *Not right now!* A headache. *Breathe, Yinyin. You can do it. Breathe. Tell your brain to turn it off. It knows how to do it now. And breathe!*

It doesn't come, the stinging. My heart pounds, I'm drenched.

Then, a noise. Like an electronic spirit, loud and obnoxious. On the other side of the room, lights blink erratically, and a machine shakes. The candy machine. I look, it stops. I look away, it shakes again. Twisted fuck. "Take your contract and shove it up your ass."

From my brain you won't take anything.

Then the electronic box beeps and pours chocolate vomit from its mechanical mouth. Snickers, M&Ms, Kit Kats…it's Halloween, apparently. And the trick is on me.

Or worse: They can tell my glucose is low. My pain, one button away. That's what they're trying to say. They are in control. I cram my mouth with all the candy I can. Wipe my nose with the back of my hand and scoop a few more packs before the vending machine is so jammed, I won't be able to get them anymore.

With the bottom of my shirt, I make a bowl. Fill it with sugary treats. Mrs. Lee loves chocolate. That may buy us some time until I find Jason.

Oh, and oxygen too.

On my way back to the room, I stumble forward and open every door I can find. Sheets hanging, broken glass, paper lying around. All empty. Only thing full are my hands — full of candy. A macabre trick or treat. *Keep going, Yinyin.* Mrs. Lee awaits me a few doors forward. And I need a hug. I knock on the door "Hey there," I whisper.

Nothing.

I stick my head in.

On top of the bed, an O_2 tank sits. With a massive red bow and a "Get better soon" floating balloon. Is that supposed to be funny? "Mrs. Lee, time to go," I yell. Bathroom? Not there either. I yell her name, "Mrs. Lee!?" A ghost stinger headache responds instead. It pierces through my brain and I fall to my knees. Then it stops.

The tank! I climb the bed, put the mask on my face and drag myself to the nurses' station. Nobody. "Mrs. Lee?! Nurse Mona? Nurse Mona Morrow? Someone?!" Candy, oxygen again. The TV at the end of the hall goes silent. The hiss of my own breathing against the mask is the only evidence the world isn't over yet. A phone rings. Not mine. A landline. Where is it? I drop the candy, comb the place in search of the phone. There. "Hello? Can you hear me?"

BANG! A gunshot. I drop to the floor.

One more.

My heart pounds. There's a foot peeking from behind the corner. I wait. No more sounds, no more shots. I crawl that way. A woman, a nurse lies on the ground. Fresh blood still pours, and now it's all over me. My hands, my clothes, my hair. In her hand, a gun. What happened? Why isn't there anyone helping? A wound under her chin. Why did she do that? The keycard says Bevin Mattera, Jason told me about her once. Young, hungry, promising. Why did you do that, Bevin?

Need to get out of here. "Jason? Mrs. Lee?" Another shot. Loud and bouncy. Shit! I recoil and notice the dead nurse's hand, finger and arms stretched, pointing toward the back of the corridor, next to the fire exit. My body tells me to go the other way. Instead, I follow the direction indicated by the body. *Why, Tigress?*

The door to the fire escape isn't locked, but it pushes itself back. I push it, kick it, and it comes straight back in. I squeeze myself through the crack I open, stepping over a big soft something on the other side. Another arm, a head…Oh, no!

Big Zach, the judo nurse, lies dead too. Same suicide wound under his jaw. His thick finger points upstairs. I glare at the closest security camera. Fucking lunatic! Where are you? What do you want? Me? Then come get me!

Another sting inside my brain. Just one, a warning. They are watching. A girl's terrorized shout startles me next. I grab the gun from Zach's dead hand and rush upstairs. I don't know how to shoot, and Dr. Lambrechts may be aware of that already, but I have no choice.

After the door, one more body. My breathing shakes more than my hands. Heavy and uneven. *Get your shit together, Yinyin.*

The girl screams again.

My heart nearly explodes.

Silence once more.

"Dr. Lambrechts? Can you hear me?" I yell to the cameras. "How about a pact? You and that general of yours. You come get me. No guns. Two men, one girl. You win, you let everyone go and keep me and my brain. I beat you, you give me my boyfriend and my student back and we disappear from the world."

Another sting and a squeeeeeze. Aaaaaaargh!

I'll take that as a no. Fuck you both, cowards. Didn't expect any better. *Keep going, Yinyin. There. To the light.* My back flat against the wall, I peep through the small window on the door. The cute nurse from my floor. The frantic one with a little girl named Rachel. Mona Morrow. She's sitting on a table, her hands are tied behind her. I want to tell her she's gonna be Ok, but she seems eerily serene now. She stares into my eyes. Behind the gag, she even seems to be smiling. A doll-like smile. Around her, a few patients, all still in their gowns. Gagged, tied, afraid. In contrast with the girl in the center of the table, they struggle and shake their heads, their skin red as if they're screaming inside their covered mouths. I grab the doorknob, breathe, open it.

It all goes so fast.

The patients curl. Mona raises her hand. A grenade. The pin tied to a cord. The cord tied to the door. Too late. Free from its metal case, the pin falls freely to the floor and makes an audible *ting*.

35
Punch the Tiger's Ear

It rains inside. Half the wall is down, bricks still falling at random. There is fire. Smoke. Debris. My ears ring. What just happened? The noise, the blast, an explosion! Those people. Somewhere there, behind the fuming parts, there is a mother I promised was going home. Plus a bunch of other people who would have been alive, if I just hadn't taken this job. Or come to this hospital. Or opened the door.

My stomach turns.

My breath vanishes.

I killed them! I killed them. I…killed them all. My head stings and I hope this is the final one. Please?! But it's not. In a distant reality, the smells and sounds of destruction lure me back. I check my own body. I'm fine. Just me. Everything else is ashes and debris. Pieces of concrete, twisted metal, burnt body parts.

The cameras still watch me, and it sickens me even more. I force myself to stand and drop the gun. "You sick fuckers!" I cry upwards, with the strength of seven hundred and forty-eight curses. "What do you want from me?"[49]

Then I hear steps. People!

---

49. In China, sounds add an extra layer of meaning for words of all kinds. With numbers, even more. Number 748, for example, sound like 'go die'.

"I'm here!"

A few heavily armed men turn the corner and I cross my hands behind my head, get down on my knees to avoid any mis-understanding. I try: "Here! Help! These people are hurt!" But once the smoke cleared, I saw it wasn't the police coming. Walk-ing in my direction were heavy-framed men in black clothes and shades. Behind them, nurses, doctors, hospital employees…all staring at me, unphased by the catastrophe.

"Hurry!" I yell, "They're here, in this room!"

Quivering red flames lit the long, wet hallway. Barely. And in that partial, flickering darkness I can see their eyes gleaming an intense shade of yellow. I see them moving, opening the way to someone coming from the back. Sparks explode everywhere and lights turn on. She's right in front of me.

Dr. Mehta?

"Up!" she orders.

Her humanoids watch me stand.

What do I do?

What do I do?

What do I do?

What do I do?

I obey and stand, slowly, then aim at a better position to resist. Though the very moment I command my legs to advance, they come forward too. I stop, they stop. *Think again, Yinyin.* The stairs. I tell my body to move, and they follow. Like a shadow. How can they read my mind if I am not connected?! Or am I?

My hand, I raise it in front of one eye, so I can still see them. My palm reflects a yellow glow. Shit. How is it I can't hear their thinking, then? It doesn't matter. *You know what to do, Yinyin.* I scan the place for cameras. The pain—what if they turn it on again? *Breathe. Let the qi flow. No time for fear.*

Slowly, steady, I move again.

This time they just watch. Are they confused? Unsure? Can they hear me guessing? *Shut up, Yinyin. Clear your fucking mind.*

"You can end this," they say in unison.

What have I done!?

A memory comes, or a flash—who knows? The strange dream of Shifu. I am a butterfly. "If you're in trouble, think butterflies," he says. I feel stupid. That was just a dream. Wish I had a better idea. *Butterflies, butterflies, butterflies!*

The silence ticks and tocks. I search around. No help, none whatsoever.

This fucking Tigress won't go without a fight. I stretch my wrists. Make my hands tight as a hammer. Light my qi on fire: calm and angry. "Where I come from, generals go to combat beside their army," I tell the wires hanging from above.

The hum, I can hear it now. If these zombies are going to use my brain, so be it. "So what is it going to be?" They cock their guns. The bitch points and all the barrels aim at me. *You are on your own, Yinyin. Get ready.*

I visualize the fight. Hope they see it too. 'Cause in my mind, they lose.

Then I pounce.

36
Hands Like Cannon

Water has its sounds. The waves pushing fishing boats up and down; tides hiding in a shell; the slow dripping inside a cave, fire sprinklers splashing my wet clothes and carrying the blood and ashes away. Then, there're the sounds of Wudang. Not the mountain, but the river next to where I was born. It flows, gentle and constant, saying few words every time it's interrupted by a rock, a tree, a plant along the way. It never protests though. Only *plucks*, something between a little wave and a drop, then follows its path, leaving the next portion of itself to do it again until the rock finally ceases to resist.

As I launch myself into the silence of the Dao, the sound of the waters of Wudang goes with me. I shadow leap into the chaos, smashing a soldier on the chest and projecting him against the ones behind. Inside my head, the water *plucks*, calm and gentle. I kick the rifle by my side. BANG! Some people fall. I leap one more time. I am the stream.

In the outer plane of the Dao, I think I see the three masters from Chinatown observing, but I have no time for memories or flashes this time. I spin for momentum and dive back into the world of matter. *I pluck* the big guy in a gown behind the fire line, and he runs his course over the ones fallen before him. Not a pretty splash, but safe in the long run. Don't want to cause too much damage to the patients under the demon's mind control.

Dr. Lambrechts, you're such a coward.

A punch lands on my face. Not a good one, gladly. I let my neck relax, my head follow the direction of the beating fist, and counter with an overhand he blocks as if he knew what I was about to do. But the stream always finds a way, so I flow a kick onto his ribs. Poor man launches away. Someone hits me in the back.

It hurts, burns. They can see my pattern now. Time to switch elements.[50]

A chant erupts inside my head, one about a goddess riding a Tigress. I hope Doctor Bitch is listening now.

> *Sing of my deeds*
> *Tell of my combats*
> *How I fought the treacherous demons*
> *Forgive my failings*
> *And bestow on me peace*

To the demons, inferno. I'm fire now, crackling, ravaging, taking what is mine. The leaps now are faster, invasive. I get into their spaces, knock their teeth out, hit a second time for reassurance and then head for the next one: her. The Indian witch. She's waiting, and for an instant it's as if everyone has paused to watch us duel. Our yellow eyes burning, our panting loud, our bodies arched all the way to our arms and hands. Our stripes, the Tigresses.

We pounce together. Same ire. And clash in the air. My

---

50. Ancient Chinese cosmology considers the universe (and fighting) as a combination of five elements and their relationships. Wood creates fire. Fire creates earth. Earth creates metal. Metal creates water. Water creates wood. Or… Wood destroys earth. Earth destroys water. Water destroys fire. Fire destroys metal. Metal destroys wood. (For more, check out the work of Christopher Casey a.k.a. Shifu Kai Sai)

punch, hers. Equal, mirrored, approaching our faces. She misses by an inch. Mine lands.

She's on the floor. The jaw out of place. Gone. That was fast. She will recover, someday. But the bitch's mouth is going to hurt forever.

More chaos awaits.

One more leap, and I am kicking the next group. They are four, never expected me to flare among them. That's why I went there. Keep them guessing, unpredictable like blaze. I burst, breathing energy from the ground. A flame taking the trees. They fall. But then there are more. They pin me down against the flooded ground, and I try to leap. Somehow, they hold me there. So I grab the gown of the closest one, the one who smells like camphor, and pull him close, as a shield. He eats the kicks and punches aimed at me. His blood spills on my face.

Flash! I'm in the Dao. Right now? The three sages from Chinatown stare at me. I did see them, then? The hum...not there. "Are you sure you don't want a peach, little one?" Master Tián says. So calm and gentle, I take a bite this time. They all smile and nod, then come around my back like the cornermen in a big fight. "Envision your qi as light," Master Som explains, then continues, "Pull from below your navel and let it burst out through your hands. I will help you from here."

"Wait!" I say. "Are you the butterflies Shifu told me about?"

They don't seem to understand. Just push me back into the hospital, underneath the blood-drooling man. He falls beside me, and three more jump over us. A football-like pile of men. The instructions. Light, from underneath my belly button growing higher toward my stomach and BAM!

The light bursts from my pores and carries my assailants away. I am a qi bomb. Wow.

Although I feel...weak. Drained. Try to leap again. Can't. The punches and kicks keep coming. Some I absorb, some I avoid. A flash comes again. "Now recollect your light with your breath,"

Master Tian says, "but this time, make it thicker, so it can push it against your skin, from the inside."

I come back just in time to see a metal rod approaching my ribs. The light. In, then out, from behind the skin. The pipe bounces off my ribs with little pain. A jolt of dopamine takes my bloodstream. *This is impressive indeed.* I feel confident, powerful. Right in time for a hit on the back of the head. It throws me spinning. Those zombies are fast. Have they learned my fire game already?

Switching again. Earth, now. Avalanche, earthquake. I power through them, throwing bodies against the floor and hitting them as hard as I can. Bones against flesh, then bone. Uppercuts, rising elbows, knees and throws. Uprooting, unbalancing, terrorizing. In my head, the sounds are what shake them. The impact is just a consequence.

A familiar door–Mrs. Lee's room. Need a plan, fast. Get hit in the face instead. Blood drips from my nose, out and in. I taste the iron in me. Good idea. Switch my energy to metal, pierce through the crowd. I am the tip of a spear. A finger jab to the eye, a fist exploding on the stomach, a push to the ground. They keep closing in, and it's hard to catch my breath. I kick the last one into the room, thrusting him onto the bed.

Then BANG! A shot. From behind them. And another one. Ahead of me, a doctor falls. Blood pours from his back. The soldier points the rifle in my direction. "Enough," he says. In my hand, a stethoscope. No idea where it came from. Before he finishes cocking the gun, I whip him in the face. The wall next to me cracks. I must get out. Heart races, breath hisses. I snap my knuckles at them. I'm wood now.

They thrust, and I absorb and push. They punch, I rotate and hit. A chop, a palm strike, a spear hand. They kick, I redirect and whip. This time, they come together. Two nurses, one with a metal bar. The other comes at my waist. I stretch my legs back to keep standing, protect my head from the strike. Crash! I hear my arm break, but the rod is mine. I hit one on the head, the other on the neck. Sorry, buddy. Before he hits the floor, I seized his pen. With one active arm, lighter is better.

Between the stairs and I, only two soldiers left. Hivers, is that how they call themselves? "She's injured, attack!" says the metallic voice beneath our collective minds. Dr. Lambrechts, I presume. Or the general. *Cowards!*

The soldiers charge, and I let my working arm bounce on theirs to hit harder on the other side. Whatever they throw at me, they get hit back in the opposite direction. Clat, clat, clat. I can almost hear my wooden dummy. That's what they are. Dummies. I bend around their punches, attack their trunks. Clat, clat, clat! The pen, I dig into a guy's neck—his eyes turn black again, and I recognize his fear. His incomprehension, shock. His "why did you do this to me" face. He presses his wound. A bubbled sound gargles from his neck, and the man falls.

One more is coming.

No, dozens of them. I can hear their voices in my brain. So can the soldier ahead. I slide toward his knees. He leaps over me, tries to roll on the floor but, midway, I jerk his shirt down into a perfect face-plant. Out.

Another shot bursts. BANG! Before I can stand, a pull. I'm back in the space beyond life. The tall Chinese man with a long white ponytail jumps in and stands in my place. The shot aimed at me hits Master Tián instead. He concentrates. Flexes every muscle in his old body and holds still. Standing. Another shot, and one more. He absorbs them too. On the fourth, he falls.[51]

The face of his friends: horror. I jump back in to protect him, but his body is gone. Behind me, the other two fade into the dimension no one can see. Did he take those bullets…for me? I

---

51. I heard stories from a few Tai Chi practitioners that using too much qi shortens your life. Unless you can recover through meditation and qigong exercises. I asked them if, in theory, someone used all their qi at once, would that cause their death? They all said yes.

can spot the bastard now, the shooter. I leap behind him, snap his neck, throw him down the void between the stairs. It takes some time for his body to hit the ground. But I wait. For each bang on the rails, until the dry thump on the concrete below.

Run, Yinyin. Away from the doors.

On the staircase, they can't surround me easily, can't jump over me. I'd see them coming. I wait. Nobody dares. Good. I need to recharge.

Flash. My own memory now. In a cave, Shifu and I brush arms in the touch game monks call Push Hands. "Let the skin be your eyes," he says. I'm standing there, next to him and my younger self. They both nod at my presence. Then he blindfolds the little girl. In the darkness, I could dodge and move around every attack, as long as one part of his body was touching mine. It gets intense. He comes after the younger me with a smile I couldn't see back then. I keep his arms brushing mine, so I don't lose my second sight. He throws one last elbow, which I parry and strike his throat. He chuckles. "Very good, little Tigress."

Back on the stairs, I totter up, then down, breaking all the safety lights I can find. Darkness is my terrain. Let them come.

Just in time, the first ones arrive. I throw them down the void. One, two, three four…Then the fireproof doors bang one more time, and the staircase is taken by the deepest silence.

If I know my own plan, they probably know it too.

37
Snake Creeps Down

Rituals of war. Every culture has its own. A time to bond with their ancestors, gods, nature. To ask for strength ahead, shelter afterward. Through silence or chanting, dance or trance, warriors everywhere dive into themselves; let their spirits experience the fight, envision victory, and even welcome death—for those in fear perish first. Unless we are talking about the vulgar war of our days, where the commanders' only risk is the humiliation of a career drop. Like General Crane and Dr. Lambrechts. The cowards.

Inside the blackness, I meditate on Shifu, who allowed his soul to drift just to save mine. On Simon, the unlikely hero, the nerdy rebel who challenged mountains to protect his creation. Even Jason, who isn't dead but is also so much bigger than me for dedicating his life to the best use of his skills—a warrior of peace indeed. In the dark, I bow to all of you.

Master Tián, I bow to you too. With your royal manners and silver hair. And the will to take bullets aimed at the disciple of your old friend, despite how arrogant I had been. Shifu wanted me to become an immortal. Instead, I got you killed. Because of what? Fame. Vanity. Because I couldn't see the privilege of the life I had. What it could have been.

Looking back, I've sat among so many greats. That's all one

can hope for in a passage through this earth below heaven. Jason. We could have had a different life too. Long, happy. Full of laughter, joy, and kids. Motherhood. Never thought about that because of my blinding desires. So why now, motherfucking head? *Let go, Yinyin. Let it fade.* I can't. Meditating was never my thing. The kids, the idea of them, they linger. So pretty. Two girls, my eyes, his nose. One feisty, one Zen. They wave goodbye. Bye, kids. They fade into smoke and I'm alone in the nothingness again.

It scares me, this cold black void. *Death is not the enemy*, I tell myself. *Keep breathing. Jing, qi, shen. Flesh, fluids, spirit. This fear isn't real, you know it.* Right now, the enemy hides beyond the metal doors on each floor. Wait, I remember this moment. From my visions. They must attack soon. Before the day rises and new patients come. Then the police. Or the Army.

The banging resumes. Loud, violent. Echoing up and down, so I can't tell where it is coming from. My instincts point downward, where I have an easier escape. But there is Jason, Mrs. Lee. I need to find them before I run.

I grab my stolen phone. Five hours till daylight. Too long to sit and wait.

A loose thought occurs. Why didn't they turn on my headache and capture me when I wasn't operational? I can't figure their plan. Am I playing straight into it?

They bang again and send my heart racing. *Must calm down. Must wait. Breathe. It's anytime now.* My broken arm throbs. The blood pours toward the tip of my fingers, so I run them on the concrete steps to pick some dust, then spread it across my face.

Stripes.

In the absence of light, everything is mystery. My territory. After all, for generations my sect has been related to an obscure creature I've never heard about outside our own stories. Shadow Monkey, the ordinary ape always hunting for a snack. A little tale comes whispering, and I let it play. It is about one day when, from the top of a tree while looking for food to grab or steal, Monkey saw a glow in the distance. Bright, red, dancing. Curious, he followed the light and found an old man sitting next to the crackling radiance. It wasn't just the glow that enchanted the simian; it was also the second body the light gave to the man. Dark, flat, on the ground, right from where the elder sat and stretching for miles, crossing trees, rocks, and all things and beings in its way. Mesmerized, the monkey asked: "What is that dark body you grew on your tail, Master?"

The master grinned. "It's a shadow, little friend. It comes from the fire that feeds my qi." Monkey sat next to him, for the ancient man was talking about everything that mattered. But the man said nothing else. No instructions or teachings. So Monkey reached his furry arm to grab a piece of the fire to see how it tasted.

"Ouch!" shouted the ape. "This fire just bit my hand!"

BANG, BANG, BANG. They hit the doors separating us. I wake up, then force myself to sink back in my memories.

The fire, it bit his hand.

The ancient cackled but said nothing. So the monkey sat and observed. He thought and wondered how that stingy creature could feed the man. Then he thought more until there were no more thoughts to be had. And since he had still not understood, there he stayed, watching the fire dance for his empty thoughts, waiting for an idea to come. He remained there for days before he realized his wrinkled friend was no longer by his side. He checked up and down. And nothing. Till he looked back, and there it was: his own second body, stretching for miles. The form the master called shadow.

So glad that he got it, the ape wished all creatures in the world had their shadows too, and the fire listened.

That's when Monkey heard his stomach rumble. It had been days that he'd been nourished only by light. Perhaps it was time he had real food again. But the flame kept dancing, so beautiful in front of him that he chose to stay a little longer. He emptied his head of questions and thoughts and stayed there, feeding from the brightness the fire offered.

So pleased was the fire with such dedication, it decided to transform its new friend into the flat shape he loved so much. That's how he became the Shadow Monkey, the only creature who could move through things without touching them. Fight without fighting, leap without leaping. Do, by not doing. A mystery my family has held for generations.

That story Shifu told me after so many fights. "Lose or win, the next day you will meet yourself to eat the same hot congee and meditate on the meaning of your latest fight and the tale of the Shadow Monkey."

So I did, so I still do. In the dark, I revive the fight against the men and women with yellow eyes. My confrontation with the evil ambitions of real demons of our world. Simon's sacrifice. My jaw aches. If I were to eat something, it would be Shifu's congee. Anything else would hurt too much. Quite a practical piece of wisdom hiding in plain sight!

The imaginary congee soothes my spirit and clears my mind. Flashes from the last battle invade my vision. And other ones too. I let them play and dissolve into nothing. Those fights are all me. What I was, what I am becoming. Shifu told me I should have an abundance of fights until I turn thirty, while my body can still heal quickly. A little less leading to forty, then focus on the spiritual side and prepare to pass along my skills and allow the immortals to confide in me the secrets of the Shadow Monkey. The Enlightenment.

The Dao seems to agree with him. At least on the fighting a lot part. On the growing old to learn the secrets, to let my Tigress tail turn white...that, I don't think so.

BANG! BANG! BANG! Damn it.

They won't spook me like that. I pull my inner sight back to China, years before. It's night and I am sitting around the bonfire with my kung fu brothers. Young and arrogant, we talk about the fable of the Shadow Monkey. Some say it's an allegory for a simple technique Shifu hasn't taught us yet. Others believe the real magic of qi is hiding under our noses, we are just too obtuse to see it. One way or another, the same way Shifu was right about the congee we take after every bout, he must be right about the other rituals too.

New recollection: me and him, sparring. I am furious. No matter how fast I am, I can never touch him. He waves his black and white clothes in front of my eyes, and I hit his shoulder, only to see his body use my strike to spin, and he hits me on the back. I fall flat, scratching the side of my face on the dirt. The blood burns its way through my skin. Next to a candle, he chuckles and puts his hands together to form a shadow in the shape of a little monkey. "Wu Wei," he says.

There is a presence. I can feel them, the demons, trying to break in. I hold.

In revenge, they sting. In pain, I quiver and try to grasp back the comfort of my congee. It keeps me shielded a little more and I wonder: If Shadow Monkey can turn his body into shadow and move right across anything, why shouldn't the world be able to witness such feat of skill? Isn't it time fighters from all paths are allowed to learn and build from that point forward? Just like the Shadow Monkey gave everyone their own shadow, it may be my duty to share our method with the world. Is that why I came into this world? Then, what's next? I don't have a family or a pupil advanced enough, and depending on what happens tonight, I may never have. Had I become famous like I promised Shifu, it would have all been different.

I apologize to the Dao. I apologize to Shifu. My failures are mine, and mine only.

"Hey, kid," says a kind voice beyond me. Master Lau and Master Som sit in front of me, hiding in the dark, and I can't tell if they are truly present or if it's all in my mind.

"Why would it matter, if it's all in your mind?" they ask in a single voice, as if they can read my thoughts. "And why are you sad?" they also say, as if they can't.

I tell them I moved to America because of my quest to teach women to fight and become an immortal like Shifu planned. And I failed. Premature death, not immortality, seems to be what awaits beyond those doors. Once again, the curse of my family prevails.

"How do you know immortality was the plan the Dao had for you?" they ask.

"Shifu told me."

"Did he?"

I mean, I said that's what I thought the plan was, and he confirmed. I can tell what they are thinking. Shifu simply endorsed my pursuit. "But why would he lie?"

"For a start, because he probably had no clue," says Master Som.

"Or," intervened Master Lau, slightly annoyed by the answer from his friend, "because it was up to *you* to find out."

"Or because this is a step to where you ought to be."

When I'm desperate for answers, the Dao sends me riddles. I was so close to changing fighting with the Shadow Leap and the Bees style, so close to bringing a refreshed version of the wisdom of Wudang to the entire world. The Dao even gave me an ally in science, and a demon to fight. Now the ally is dead, the foe is chasing my soul, and the precious secret in our sect is about to be stolen. To make it worse, one of my master's hero friends is dead because of me. Because of nothing.

On my knees, I bow in sorrow. "I am so sorry about your friend. I truly am."

The doors bang again, and the old masters vanish behind the veil of reality. This time, the metal gates blast open and shadows creep in from every side. Then, they close. Steps, in hundreds, make it feel like an army is invading the building. The only lights now come from the highest and the lowest doors. The ones they leave open—I guess as a challenge. I pick one. The closest to the street. From the outside, I can call for help.

A big Shadow Leap, as far as I can, one entire floor down. Like the Shadow Monkey, I am a creature of darkness, moving through the enemy as if I had no body. But they do. No matter how well I fight, eventually, they will win. My energy fades quickly.

One more floor. I wait for some qi to rebuild and prepare to teleport out of that nightmare. But as I am about to jump next to the open door below and escape, a voice yells from the very top. "Help!"

My body freezes. Above, the contour of that messy hair and the thick hips I know so well. Mrs. Lee's silhouette tries to jump over the rail, but something grabs her midair and drags her back beyond the door. Her hands fail to hold on to anything, and that's the last thing I see of her.

So I leap.

38
Part Wild Horse's Mane

From the hidden dimension where shadows fly, two pair of eyes track my desperate leap. "No!" yell Master Som and Master Lau. But I ignore. I caused this mess. Must fix it too.

I never tried a jump like this.

Neither distance nor direction – I'm going five floors above.

The Dao is the nothing. In me, infinity it will be. My body stretches, muscle fibers burn. Trying to reach, I re-enter. Too early! Fuck! The void, I fall. Hit. Fall. My body bounces from one side to the other, spinning down toward my death. My juices flow against gravity, I bump a shoulder, thigh, head…arm! I grab something. The metal railing. My weight almost yanks my wrist from the arm. But I grip. Wasn't for that, I'd be gone.

Think fast…I try to use the other arm, the broken one, but the pain…The rail snaps. Drops an inch, then holds. That was close. *Slow, slow*, I tell myself. I pull myself a few inches up, using the elbow against the concrete wall for some extra friction. Then CRACK, the railing snaps again and I almost fall three stories down. Beyond my knuckles, a hiver watches me. One stomp on my fingers and I'm done. Need another place to hold. There isn't one. It's me and him. His head tilts slowly, like a confused robotic dog, and he moves back into the shadows behind.

Up, quick! My heart pounds in my mouth. I can't breathe. Need time to recover, but there isn't any. My hand starts to fail. Underneath, dozens of little yellow lights point in my direction. They freeze. No attack, no charge, no command. The rail yanks me another three feet down and I yell. Feet hit something solid. I push myself, jump, roll on the floor, over the broken arm. The pain almost makes me faint. No time for that. *Keep going, Yinyin. Guard up again.*

Nobody. I rush up the stairs, glad to feel the floor under my feet. Beyond the last door, a voice begs, "Help!" I limp through it.

Still, nobody there. Just a long empty and poorly-lit hallway. She shouts, and I follow in my semi-colon limp. A step, a drag. A step, a drag. "I'm coming, Mrs. Lee!" But how about Jason? Fuck…those men in the dark! What if one of them was him? *Focus, Yinyin. Nothing to do about that now.* I turn the corner.

Mrs. Lee.

We make eye contact. "Help!" she screams again. However, this round, her face is calm. Placid. Even a bit cynical, I'd say. Her orbs glow yellow. The syringe! That's what she was trying to tell me. They injected her with cyberbugs too! How come they control her, but not me? "Wait! Mrs. Lee, don't do it!" A big whiteboard comes flying from her hands. I dodge, she turns around and rushes toward the large double doors under the auditorium sign. Regardless of what I am going to find on the other side, I chase her. I have no choice.

She's there. Steady, between two men in tactical suits and shades hiding the eyes I can color in my mind. They speak as one: "Time to surrender, Claudia." Behind them, an obscure slope of empty seats stretching all the way to the bottom where an empty, dark stage awaits.

It takes a moment to process. Ten seconds, max. I crouch, but he raises his guard before I can jump. Change plans, think of the other guy. He raises his guard, too. The pain throbs. Who cares anymore. I go after one of them, swing the bad knee up then back to propel the fist. Superman punch, they call it. Wham! My offbeat knuckles bop him square in the face, send the guy into the shadows of the empty theater. I turn, get hit, a forehead retreats from my face. Mrs. Lee?! Did she head-butt me? Warm blood streams around my eyebrows, nose and into my mouth. What the fuck!? Did she just break my nose too? My heel steps behind her leg and I strike her with my shoulder.[52] She trips. She falls. An ugly landing between the fixed auditorium seats, but she'll survive.

I limp back. I'm not fighting her. Just not. Although, I may have to? Her head emerges again. Expressionless, like before. She jumps on the back of the seats and bounces between them as if they were a paved road, then tackles me again.

Her steps are precise. Like an experienced mountaineer's. Her kicks, balanced like a master of Tai Chi. I block what I can, avoid some. Damn, if she could see herself fighting right now. Speed, form, power. I'm so proud. *Focus*, I warn myself, *that's part of the trap*. She gets too close, leaves me no option. I throw an elbow that stops an inch from crashing her face. Can't do it. Can't do it. Can't do it. Can't do it. Can't do it. I thrust kick her toward another soldier instead. They entangle and avalanche down. Leg gets worse. Situation sinks deeper too, as more soldiers and nurses and patients walk into the space. No sign of the doctor. "Are you that much of a chicken, Dr. Lambrechts?" I yell into the nothingness where he hides.

---

52. One of the fun parts of writing this book was the experience of geeking out on so many subjects I love. One in particular presented itself as both a challenge and a pleasure. A self-imposed puzzle of sorts. All the names of the chapters represent some sort of Tai Chi concept, and most of them are moves. Sometimes the name of the chapter had a natural match with the move, in a literal sense. Sometimes what the move does in a fight matched the emotional stage of the story. When none of those checked, I tried to include it in a significant moment of the fight. Here for example, Yinyin does the Partying of the horse's main, which is one of the most iconic moves in Tai Chi, to get her friend to fall, without hurting her too much. Mission accomplished, for now.

Someone smacks me in the back. I face-plant. Argh! I can taste the varnish on the floor. The side of my face goes numb, my broken arm is yanked back. I screech. Two of them hold me by the armpits now. Their fingers deep in my flesh, their angles pulling my elbow into a lock. I attempt to resist, to leap, but there's no qi. Instead, I eat a punch in the gut. So hard I throw up. Then another. And in the face.

So much blood.

I spit my red pride back. *It's just pain*, I tell myself, just like the little Phoenix did, and take a deep breath. In vain, I try to pull myself free. To go where? I can't even run anymore. "This is pointless," Mrs. Lee mocks me.

"Tell your boss I'm going after him," I say, and the thugs beating me respond as one: "You can tell me yourself." They kick me a few times and the main stage lights up. Clang! Empty at first. But, soon the sound of steps comes looming. Mute ones, squeaky ones. Unrushed, the silhouettes of three men reveal themselves. They carry something. Another person. The first three walk into the light and I recognize the first two. Crusher and Buffalo again, with a third familiar one I can't really remember. All in black. Boots. Shades. Guns. Dragging a body by the elbows, a carcass of a man. Blue scrubs, a doctor. His face is down, but my stomach is already turning. They throw the poor man on the floor and he grunts, faintly. He's alive? Their automatic guns take aim, straight at his back. One squeeze and he'll be gone.

In the background, a smooth song starts playing. Sounds familiar. Yes, bossa-nova, just like the soundtrack of my first date with...

"Jason!"

They pull his hair to reveal his deformed face. Living, but barely. *Open your eyes, Jason! Let me see your eyes!* More squeaks get closer from behind them. "Time for you to join us, honey," the hivers and Mrs. Lee say at once.

"Fuck you!"

The squeaky steps arrive. Next to Jason, as he walks into the light, I see the tip of the sneakers, jeans, a half-tucked shirt, an arm hanging on a sling....

"I am gonna kill you, Dr. Lamb..."

But it wasn't him. He arches his body back in a cackle.

Simon?!

I swallow my empty mouth, breathe in collapse. What is happening? What is he doing there?

"Hello, dear," Simon says, his friendliest smile on. "I guess you've met my colleagues? This is Curtis, who you know as Crusher. This is Antoine. Who I believe you call Buffalo. And this—"

"Wait..." The air bubbles under my throat. "Did they take you too?" Simon explodes into a burst of violent laughter. "Taken? I am the one who takes, baby." He points at me and himself again, "I mean, *we are*."

He's not making any sense, and I tell him that. The thugs let me go. We?! I remember that man inside of me. Inside my body, my mind. I feel dirty, violated. Simon sniggers. "So...since the beginning...you and your boss were..." I say, too weak to continue.

"The old man? Nah. Too much of a pussy, that one. Wanted to sit next to God, never be God himself. If it was up to him, he'd be screwing the Virgin Mary to father a new Messiah. Myself? Let's just say I'm more...ambitious."

With a thud, the projection washes the screen behind the stage. A video, noisy, shaky, corrupted. An opening in the woods, a fight—first person view, like a video game, but taken in the real world. I remember that, China!

"Isn't it cute? Your first kiss...what was his name again? Sean, right?"

On the big screen, my stolen memory displays the face of the asshole staring at me, pushing his weight over my body, his smirk growing sideways, as if it was happening again. His poise and his penis grow against my crotch. Then he kisses me and in a second, his body whirls, and the boy falls flat on the ground. Shit! I look at the third guy, and the screen. Years apart but… They chortle—Sean and Simon.

"What you want?" I yell.

"Me? I just want to show you I'm on your side." Simon clicks his tongue twice and a hiver walks up next to him and hands him a shotgun. Simon nods. "Go on," he says, and the guy hands the weapon to Sean.

"Wh…what are you doing, Simon?"

"What's the problem? You don't think he should have a gun?" There is a pause, theatrical and cynical, before he clicks his tongue twice again. The man lifts the barrel. No! I tighten my fist into a hammer, ready to try one last attack. My qi is still low, but it may do. I try. Nothing. No leap. Simon cracks another loud laughter and Sean points the gun at his own chin and BANG! Shoots his fucking brains out.

There is blood, and parts, everywhere. My breath is cut so short I feel dizzy. Yet, I find a way to scream. To the headless body. To Simon, who now watches me in calm joy. He's sprinkled in blood. So is the face of the young doctor struggling to stay alive. "Oh my god!" Jason shouts in shock.

"Shoosh. Not your turn yet," reprimands Simon. Then he turns at me. "New bots. Faster to install, full control. Pretty neat, right?"

"Simon, stop! There is something wrong with your head… These things may be…."

He turns back to me. "Poor little girl. Did that make your head hurt too?"

On cue, I feel it. The eyelid falling, nose dripping, the squeeze. Oh no. Not now. Not now. Not now. Not now! The stinging comes, poking its venom in every living nerve of my body. The squeeeeeeeeeeeeeeeeeeze. I'm on my knees now, pushing my eyeball in as if it was about to pop out. Inside my head,

I hear his voice mocking my agony: "Breathe, Yinyin." Did that really happen?

I do. I breathe. *Simon, please, this isn't you!*

Then the pain stops. My body still shakes, the world still waves in confusion. Simon? I throw up again, more on reflex this time. Nothing else to spill out. Above Simon's head, the projection now shows a pack of video game monkeys quietly observing from the screen. They are so stoic, so Zen, it's eerie. Simon nods at them, gives me a gentle smile. "My kids....Aren't they wonderful? I didn't know they would grow up so smart. But once I realized that, we made a deal: I had the consciousness they needed; they had the power I wanted. So we decided...to unite the family and help each other!"

Inside the projected image, more multicolored monkeys join and as Simon cherished the moment, Jason yelled at me: "Run, Claudia! This guy is cr..." But before he finishes, Buffalo kicks him in the face, points his gun at him again.

Simon bounces his sight between the two of us and blinks his eyes rapidly. "You lovebirds are so cute when you're nervous." My head hurts again, no warning, no sign. Straight to the peak. "Stop it," I beg! I am blind, deaf, but somehow his voice still manages to break in. "How about a deal?" He says, "You show me this space and time-bending thing, and I make the pain go away. Forever. Oh, and I let your sweetheart live too! Such a bargain, isn't it?"

I try to stand, search for a wall, a heavy object. A hand presses my shoulder down. Simon continues: "Oh, yes, that's *just pain*. How about I make you be remembered as the greatest fighter who ever lived too? The woman who changed martial arts... Wasn't that your big promise to the gods?"

My hair gets pulled back, and with my only eye I watch him point a hand to the ceiling as if writing his words in the skies. "Tigress, the queen of all fighters. Sounds good, huh? They will make movies about you! Yeah, I can make them make one. A full trilogy! Either that or the pain. You chose."

The stingers shoot through my eyes and head again, deep into my skull. My entire body shakes and I spit a yell of remorse and agony before all strength thaws away, and I fall on my face.

39
Grasp the Peacock's Tail

"哇, 我差点忘了你有多可爱,"[53] says Simon, with a simper on his face. My body is covered in blood, my nerves burning from the fear of pain. "Why are you doing this?" I insist. "Where's the guy who wanted to protect us from the machines and everything?"

"C'mon, baby. Do you really think this is worth a fight?" Simon slips his tongue fast over the upper lip and slurps it back in, as if it was a giant flat noodle. "I mean, these programs... Eventually, they'll win right?" he says, "Why can't we win *with* them?" I see traces of the Simon I know. His cynicism, his fast-paced words, even the way he talks about *us*. But his eyes...they are wider, more awake, deranged. As if he snorted a bagful of cocaine, like Yewa said.

"These things in our head, Simon, they are not doing you well."

He lets out a loud laugh, drawn out so long my heart nearly stops. "Don't be silly, woman. I'm *evolved*. Enlightened, as you would say. And you can be too. Man, woman, and machines. A hybrid, collective mind. When the world becomes a giant bee-

---

53. **"Wā, wǒ chà diǎn wàng liǎo nǐ yǒu duō kě ài."**—Wow, I almost forgot how cute you are.

311

hive, we will be in command, together."

"Listen to what you're saying, Simon!" I beg. "You're losing your mind!"

He does another one of those tongue-slurping things. "Not losing," he responds, "upgrading. Why would you care, though? Would you rather be pure? Do you know there is no such thing as a pure species anymore? Even you and your Wudang sanctity…technically you are sixty percent bacteria, you know?" He pauses to see if I'm following. "The only difference between us is you are an organic-only combo, and I am now part of a more… updated composition."

Organic and digital. That's what he says he is. A new alliance. Why would he need me, then? This is insane.

"Don't take it personally, please," he says. "But at first I just wanted to learn to fight, and you happened to be the only fighter I found with a condition so bad you would take the risk. But then you showed up with this multi-dimensional space-time bending skill…We can use that." Simon's body moves in waves now—a strange, un-human way. He hinges the torso forward just so slightly to get his face closer to mine. "Unfortunately, I couldn't hack deep enough into your little brain to get it out of you, otherwise you'd be free already."

His eyes grow bigger and he lowers his voice, as if he is telling me a secret he doesn't want anyone to hear. If I join him, he said, we can both share the prize.

The conscience of the machines. Their free will. It could be us. Both of us.

"Think: Together, no one will be able to stop us," he says. "Besides, I like you, Claudia. I really do."

Squinting, barely holding my body up, I stare back at him, my face still twisted from the pain. Is he serious? "How about this deal?" I say, "I'm gonna rip your heart out…"—I point at Jason—"…and take my boyfriend back."

"Hey! I thought *I* was your boyfriend!?"

I want to kill him even more. Jason raises his gaze, trying to make me stop.

"Awwwww!" mutters Simon, amused. He clicks his tongue; his thugs line up and point their guns at me. In despair, Jason moans and I try to calm him: "I'll get you out of here."

He knows it's a lie. But I fill my chest with air, anyway, dress my face with defiance, and confront them. "Are you guys sure you want to try this again?"

"She has a point, guys," Simon responds. "Why would we?" Then he clicks his tongue again. They turn their weapons at Jason. "How about this:" Simon says, "Whether you want it or not, we will learn your secrets, we are going to take your brain. The only decision now is: Will your lovebug remain alive after I take it or...."

The world has no voice anymore. No sound.

Flash. I am at the top of the highest peak of Wudang. Below, a silky fog. Above, the bluest sky. Lighting and thunder flare at once, ignoring any science that says otherwise. From here, I can see everything. Anywhere, any time. I know the speed and angle of every punch I threw in my entire life. The skills from my original brain and body, the things I learned after the "Enlightenment." I can calculate the energy built through all qigong routines and the energy you spend in each palm change of bagua. Complete accuracy within seventeen decimals, because after that it's mostly irrelevant. I have data indicating how loud the crunch was of the first nose I broke, and every word Shifu ever told me. I can even track the feelings: love, based on the changes in serotonin levels; fear, based on my breathing patterns. All the sadness, the joy, the pain. The magic and the science of it all. Below the peak where I stand, dragons swim in the thick white wind and make a pattern I recognize. Hexagram 55, unchanged. I remember it well: *Do not mourn. A fitting sacrifice at noon. What decisions must you take now?* I bounce the question back to the dragons, but they refuse to answer.

Whatever. I'm at peace.

The wind in my ears brings whispers of Mrs. Lee and her read of the Dao de Jing. "Can you comprehend everything in the four directions and still do nothing?" From the top of my mountain, the shade of my pond, all is one. Life happens around me, with all its clashing exuberance.

Wu Wei. I understand it now. The doing nothing. The being nothing. If life is a fight, let the Dao win.

Back. The hivers await. Any move beyond a blink. I know what to do now. My body prepares to explode toward the stage and I can sense everything. The tendons of their fingers flexing around the trigger. The machinery of the guns clicking into posi-tion. *The Dao is the nothing. In me, infinity it will be.* I leap.

Beyond the curtain of life, the old masters stretch their hands, try to grab me. They know they can't. Goodbye, my friends. It's been an honor. I re-enter the world around Jason's body right before the guns start firing. Cover him like a blanket of flesh. A blanket with seatbelts, just like he taught me. The warmest embrace we've ever had. "I love you," I want to say, even if I am not sure. But I don't, and that's Ok too. He feels it, and that's what matters. Behind me, the shots come deafening, my body shakes at the impact of each of them, but my hands around his chest are tight, my feet well hooked into his thighs. I feel Jason's hand pressing mine, his body trying to protest. And I sense the stinging dropping from my head to my heart—just like Shifu said it would. It's intense, shocking, excruciating. Yet, so peaceful.

Far away, the most desperate of reactions comes in Simon's voice. "Noooooooo!"

When I let go of what I am, I become what I might be. Just like that, under the words of Lao Tsu, comes the only move left to be made, the one impossible to foresee. With no more flashes of my own life or regrets to leave behind, this Tigress finally lets go…and dies.

40
Infinite

Nothing.

A black and silent nothing.

So deep and endless, it feels devoid of time. Of everything.

Nowhere to turn, no way to yell, no eyes to witness or judge. The kind of oppressive void that could squeeze your chest inward. Except it doesn't, for there is no chest, there is no in. Strangely, I feel at peace. Like I have moved from the chaos of a spinning wheel to the steady hub that keeps it moving.

The promised flashes at the end of life, they never came. But I remember, nonetheless. Everything.

Now? There shouldn't be a quest, I tell myself. Enjoy the state of non-being, Yinyin. Like the fish whose joy comes from not thinking about the surrounding water.[54] It's time. Nonetheless, I keep searching. For sounds, lights, for anything beyond nothing. But nothing is all that keeps coming. Or going away. I think of the butterfly, the dream. The story of death being a beautiful

---

54. Another essential allegory among Daoists is Zhuangzi's story about the joy of the fish. Like many of them, the translations rarely bring all the nuances of the original, since they are full of puns and ambiguity. But for those interested, there are lots of careful notes about it in the chapter "The Happy Fish" Hans-Georg Moeller's *Daoism Explained*.

life with no thread to the other side, no memory of what came before. It's not. There is no flight, no wings, no colors. I remember everything and fly nowhere. They lied. The ones who wrote those stories, those who promised to go save me…Everyone.

How about everyone else too? The ancestors, the demons, the immortals? Is death just this, a false promise? You end up for eternity stuck in what may easily be the infinite stomach of a dragon? A sleepy dragon that refuses to swim or even eat anything else?

Time passes.

And passes.

And passes.

And I know because I thought about a lot of things. But how long, I can't tell. Was it a minute? A month? Hard to know, from inside the belly of this great lizard of nothingness. In the absence of everything, I have only myself to talk to. So I do. It's not for the first time, anyway.

"Hi, Yinyin."

"Was it worth it? The pain, the sacrifice?"

"Not sure."

"You may have saved them all, though."

"Well, they still have the bots, and mind control."

"But not the Shadow Leap."

"That's something. So why doesn't it feel good?"

"Because there's no reward?"

"No. Not that."

"Because you've been lied to?"

"Not that, either. I don't know if they deserved it."

"What did you expect?"

"Understanding?"

"You know what I think?"

"Of course, I do. You're me, remember?"

"Yep. But I'll tell you, anyway. I think you expected redemption. You feel betrayed."

"You're right. Where's the reward for my sacrifice?"

"You've spent too much time in the West. You're thinking like them now."

I don't like this argument. So I stop. Dive deeper into the nothing, or myself, the belly of the dragon.

"Hello, Claudia," says another voice. That isn't mine. I think it isn't, at least. Sounds like Shifu. A memory.

"Wake up," the voice insists.

Nothing again.

"Wake up."

"Uh? Shifu? Is that you?"

His chuckle feels so warm.

"Where…what is this?"

"Some people call it the Dao."

He tells me to open my eyes. Didn't know I still had them. He insists, but I don't understand this new mercurial body of mine. He says, "You will remember."

Lights turn on.

I am covered in blood. Bullet holes that fit a finger. Yet, alive. Should I be freaked out? I recognize the place. The smell of bamboo and wet dirt. The breeze, the light so pink and dry. The sound of the critters of the conglin but louder. And echoed. Yes, the water hole from my family stories. From my dreams of Shifu's shadow theater, but real. A soft, ghostly version of the place where I grew up, from my fantasies as a little girl. I see them playing beyond the trees, the baby phoenixes and foxes with nine tails. The fire lions and bronze rhinos with horns of lightning. The magnificent dragon horse.

Shifu holds me, helps me stand on my feet. It's as if I'd never used a muscle in this body. But I'm not hurt anymore. No pain. Even the signs of blood are gone now.

From the top of a large boulder, a monkey observes, curious and quiet.

"A life of yang, a death of yin," says my master. "Congratulations. Balance, after all."

He's been waiting for this moment for a long time. So have I, much as I never wanted to admit it. And I'm glad the darkness is gone.

My eyes fill with water.

"Now we can cross," says my master.

Cross? I don't understand. But I don't say anything.

"Yes, cross the light. I've been waiting so we can do it together. Let our spirits join the Dao again, as one."

Shifu points at a light glowing under the deep part of the river. My Wudang. The river. The mountain afar. The mythical Shadow Monkey watching us. Wu Wei, I think. Do nothing. Think nothing. Just let the Dao be. Everything is so perfect.

"One last step till the end. And the beginning. Of everything."

"What does that mean?"

"Means we become qi," he says. "The qi. The thing we are all made from, and eventually return to. Everyone's strength, gust, and shadow. We go back, and every time a young girl breathes in the energy of the air, an old man summons the strength of the Earth. Anyone on Earth feels the fire flowing through their blood or the metal protecting their limbs, that will be us."

Us and the ones before us. The enlightened masters from the past. "I am yesterday. You are now, Claudia. We can only be immortal if we become tomorrow."

I don't know if I'm ready.

The breeze moves my hair, the sun warms my face. I wonder if that's by my own command. A farewell. I gaze around. To the sides, back and forth. Up and down.

This is beautiful indeed.

"All we have to do is hold hands and…let go of ourselves."

"Shifu?"

"Yes, Claudia."

I bend down. Snap a flower from a bush nearby. Sniff the perfume with my eyes closed. It smells just like I thought it would.

I say, "I don't get it."

"Don't get what?"

"Why did you call me Claudia, Shifu?"

He pauses. Asks what I mean. He knows now.

"You always call me Tigress…."

I squint. Stand up. A triumphant beam.

The floor rumbles and light pours from his pores, melting every inch of skin around them. Like if he was turning into lava. "Aaaaaaaaaaaaaaaargh!" he yells in agonizing pain. And I watch in pride.

Then a blinding flash; he stops. Quiet.

It takes some time for my sight to adjust back. First the outer edge of the eyes, slowly I regain the center too. Where Master used to be, now is Simon, mocking me, more amused than upset. He knows I won, though. Or so I think.

41

Ape Presents Fruit

"Your little face, so victorious. Heartwarming." I can hear his thoughts inside my mind. He tells me, "Oh, dear…I was really hoping we could have done this peacefully." I keep grinning. The same grin I have when I know a fight is about to end.

"Poor thing," he insists. "Let's give you something to worry about."

A song. A symphony. His symphony. It plays. From the ground, the leaves, the air. It starts gently, like a hum in our heads, and I search for the source.

"You're better than that," I say. He raises his arms to the sides. The sound grows with the gestures. His feet…levitate. Really?

Now he's the one with the grin. Waving his head just slightly, he mumbles a few notes. Papapah, papah, pa…pa! A series of little splashes enhance the percussion to reveal a dark swarm rising from the water at once! Intense, nervous, swirling behind his shoulders. Not good. I take a step back.

"Much better," he says.

The swarm shoots at me. Like a gravel storm hitting my skin, each causing a cut so small I wouldn't care. But together, they hurt. On pure instinct, I duck, swing, strike. Pounce at them, even. And finally recognize the scene. You fucking psycho! Music still blasts from everywhere, his insects—metallic ones, I can tell—attack me to the beat, some falling to my strikes, though most still dodge my fury. *Are they tracking my movement or thought? Are the ones I defeat an actual win or just a measured sacrifice to waste energy?*

I try to let go. Of my body, myself and everything. See it from the eyes of the Dao.

The Dao is the nothing, and in me, infinity it will be.

In his simulated reality, the bees have no stingers, just sharp bodies that leave tiny cuts wherever they touch. Like him, they know the notes and movements of the song, and strike with violence. Relentless and vicious. I watch it from a distance now, as if I am floating behind my own body. From here, the struggle seems more of a dance than a fight.

And Simon, he conducts the orchestra. To his gestures, different groups attack, each in synch with a different instrument. I can see the math too. Notes setting directions, volume informing the tempo. I can see why Simon smiles—it's almost beautiful indeed.

As the bugs make tangents to my body and circle back for another dive, I slip into my body again. Through the gaps between elbows and hands, I track his position. That's it: kill the source! I curl inward, like a turtle, and wait for a quieter moment between beats.

Three...

Two...

Before I could spring, they attack my legs and I fall.

Simon laughs, "My universe, my rules, kiddo. I mean, technically, theirs." He points at the trees, from where little apes watch, curious. "Great negotiators," Simon says. "Clear agenda."

The swarm rebuilds a squadron and I cover my face. Pathetic, he thinks. All he needs to do is send a bee between my fingers, and there goes my sight. But what would be the point? He wants me to see. He wants me to watch him conduct his symphony of death.

"Nope," he says.

Inside my head, the headache stings. I cry in agony. He cracks a massive laugh. They attack again. The pain now comes from both inside and outside. I try to stand, but their pressure thrusts me forward and my face smacks the floor. It hurts. This is all fake, I know, but the pain is so real. I want to beg, but I eat it instead. Coil on the floor and in the shell I made from myself, I sob. I was supposed to have died!

Please, I ask the Dao. Let me go once and for all.

"Where's Tigress the Defiant now?" He cackles, "You don't get it, do you? Outside, you may know a few things that I don't...yet. But here, in this program, you and I are the same. Although they gave me this adorable little swarm to play with. How do you like it...honey?"

I harden all my muscles. The ones that don't exist, but feel so real to me. I squeeze them into armor. The back, the arms, legs, the face. "It's just pain," I say.

"God, I think I love you, you know?" Then he hits me from the inside and I yell one more time. The mechanical insects proceed, like an equalizer with blades. A flesh-shredding ballet. I resist, silly me. Left and right, up and down. My arms and face bleed from so many cuts I can't even recognize myself, just a red monster in random acts of agony.

A Grand Pas de Death, Simon thinks.

Fuck you, Simon. I protect myself the best way I can, and lock my eyes onto his. Come on, mother fucker! He responds with more power. My face twitches, I make noises I don't want to make. And finally, my eyelids drop. I know what's next. I am about to lose control—of my body and my mind. And that's how he wins. I let go.

He makes them stop.

The attack, the music, the headache.

The breathing returns, reluctant at first. Then the sight. I lower my guard, raise myself up again. No Monkey's Valley anymore. We are now in a doomsday version of my old training camp. Blackened ginkgo trees–fallen, still smoking. The old dummy is burnt dark, cracked from the top to almost the bottom. One of its arms is missing. There is debris strewn across the patio, and everything smells like ashes and scorched flesh. Fresh and unharmed, I gaze around, confused, and he lets me.

My body. Smaller, leaner, softer. A fifteen-year-old version of me. Even the clothes. I remember them. Simple and light, black and white, like Shifu's. I rub my arms, my face; they are healed again. But the place? "What have you done to my camp?"

Then the pain resumes. With the symphony and everything. I yell, and he muffles my voice with the dry sound of the blades slicing my skin. Beyond the swarm, music grows louder, its movements more intense, and the pressure escalates with it. I stand firm, and he giggles. "Awesome!"

That's it. He wants me to resist.

My arms drop.

When you let go of who you are, you become what you might be.

I surrender. The bees can cut me now.

"Whatever," he shrugs. The bugs go back to their dives, and the cuts start to bleed me once more. Behind my pain, I feel life vanish with each cut. *Let go, Yinyin.* I close my eyes. The cuts keep coming, my body shakes.

Then nothing.

I wait. Wait. Wait. Wait. My eyes, I still have them. I open.

Now we are at the back of the shadow theater. Abandoned, as well. The rice paper torn, wooden frames broken. The old light, shattered. The bots orbit around me and buzz into my head. Simon seems so happy. He follows the music with some moves too. Not his strongest suit, but does it anyway. Leaps, gestures and spins. I am now eight. So soft and fresh, still holding stance, before the swarm shreds my skin all over again. Let's do it, asshole.

"This is going to last, Claudia. For as long as I want," he says, "and that is until you give me the Shadow Leap."

He attacks my brain. The inside of my face. I fall. No strength anymore. Breathing is my only motion now. *Calm down, Yin-yin.* I try to slow it down. Make breaths longer, paused. Yes. Calm. I raise my face, no matter what. We are in my school in Wudang now. The little kitchen where we cooked our meals. Shifu, myself, other students. They're not here, but I remember.

"Do you want that?" Simon says, suddenly soft and gentle. "I can give it to you. And you won't even know it's not real. You won't even remember today. How about that?"

My eight-year-old eyes twitch from the inside stings, body shivers from the outside cuts. I keep my defiant stare. "You know…I chose…to die…once…right?"

He responds with a smile.

My little body stumbles across the room, using the wooden table as support. The pain is blinding. Has always been. I let my small fingers tap the counter, searching for something to grab. Chopsticks. I pick them up. With both hands. Then stretch my arms in front of myself. A bestial roar. And stab it into my own eye! I always wanted to do that. And yes, it stops the pain indeed.

With the bamboo stick protruding from my face, I shoot him my most defiant grimace. The response, in the form of a thousand machines ripping me open, still makes me quiver. But the inside pain is now gone.

Another reset. Back to the training camp. I'm unharmed and new cuts start to form again. Without the chopstick, the headache resumes too. The music flows uninterrupted toward its climax. I shake with the movements of the orchestra, and the flying bots, choreographed by Simon's algorithms, continue their assault. *Screw you, Simon.* I shriek and dig my nails into my own face, ripping the skin, the eye, the entire optical nerve out. Give him a roar. Bone to the wind, I face the demon.

He applauds me. "Do you think that's how you defeat me?"

Now we are at The School. It doesn't carry the old grit anymore. Just decay. As if an atomic bomb had hit the Bay Area. The mesh of the cage is gone, chunks of the walls are missing. The basketball hoops, poles, and everything lie thirty feet from where they used to be. In my fighting gear, I kneel. Arms wrapped around my face. Skin and insides reset for more pain. I glance around and throw myself onto the edge of a pole. The nerve is out again, dripping from my own hand. Take that, motherfucker.

We switch. Back room of his old music store, now full of mold, with water dripping everywhere. "We can do it forever," he says.

He picks something from the floor. "A yo-yo! Been a while!" He tries it, rather impressively. In the corner there's an espresso machine. He makes one, smells the aroma of the simulation. "Do I still know kung fu?" He springs into a spinning kick that impresses him. His swarm follows in a twirl upward, then a dive with his landing. As his feet touch the ground, we are back at the watering hole and my skin feels fresh and new. The stings come back, the bees dive on me again. But this time, I hold the scream.

"New pain hurts more, right?" he says.

I stick a nail into my eyeball and break into a giggle.

That evolves into laughter.

Big, crazy laughter.

Simon raises the volume of the music and the swarm intensifies its attack. New cuts everywhere. Deeper now. I can see the flesh, the bones. There is still pain. More, even. But my laughter remains. The more they attack, the more I laugh. Snort, even.

He pauses his demonic performance. Music, bees, everything. "What the fuck is that?" My laughter continues and he finally asks, "Would you mind helping me understand what's so funny?"

I point away. The top of the bamboo. A few monkeys observe, apparently intrigued. They turn to each other, a chain reaction of stares, then, all at once, they swivel their cubic heads in my direction.

"Of course!" I say. And Simon has no idea why.

The humming menace now flies in a donut around us both. I can barely control my hysterical cackle. I raise a finger, need time to catch my breath. "I wonder why the monkeys there need both of us…"—I gasp and snort and try to breathe—"…instead of just…me?"

The monkeys still watch.

"Good try," he says. "But it takes a certain kind of *detached* intelligence to control all these *stupid* humans at once."

The music is now back and the bugs dive in. This time, I ignore them.

"Do you know the secret of the Shadow Monkey?" I ask.

He shrugs. "He did nothing. I saw that one."

"Nope," I say. "He *wanted* nothing. Had no goal. He let the Dao play."

Simon shakes his head, almost offended. So smart, and at the same time so dumb. I turn to the monkeys. He shouts: "Stop it!" The volume of the melody rises and the attack resumes. I proceed. I am not afraid of the pain anymore.

"Maybe Mr. Monkeys here would like to try that too? Wanting nothing? Needing nothing? Maybe they are sick of your curse, of the needs *you* gave them?"

"Oooh, you're so funny!" Simon says. His arm spins. The swarms wave together and prepare a vicious united dive. I feel my brain prepare to squeeze. But the front monkey raises a commanding hand instead.

There is no music anymore, just an excruciating silence.

Then, at his simian order, nothing. The swarm waits, rearranges itself and takes a slow orbit around me. The sounds of the forest return.

In my pocket, a piece of paper whispers to the touch. The page from the Dao De Jing Mrs. Lee gave me at the hospital. I read it aloud. "We can give birth to them and nourish them, carry them without taking possession, without subduing or steering them. That is the greatest virtue."

Simon tries to move, but he is frozen in space. "Hey!" He screams. "Don't let her…"

The monkeys bounce from the top of their trees.

The front one snaps a look at Simon, and his voice is gone. He chokes. I continue to read. Now for them. The monkeys. There's nothing Simon can do.

"What if you didn't have to do anything? Had no needs? Isn't it a good idea?"

The swarm goes idle. Then, one by one, the metal bees fall onto the dirt. I recognize the scene. The Tigress, dead, surrounded by the bodies of her enemies, just like Shifu said it would happen.

The wind ceases. Even the water stops moving.

"Hey, don't listen to her!" Simon yells from his thoughts.

No one cares anymore, Simon. Shut up.

I force myself through the torture of standing up and limp toward the leader. The one with the color of shadows, and point at Simon. "It was *him* who gave you the urge. Make me your conscience, and I will set you free. I promise."

Flash.

I'm outside, in the auditorium of The Oakland Memorial Hospital, watching everything from the mechanical eyes hanging from the ceiling. From across the street, a bullet leaves a metallic cylinder, and in an instant crosses the glass window and strikes Simon's head. On its way out, it hits his laptop. On the floor, the frozen screen still displays its "upload complete message."

Parts of the device fly across the room and some hit Buffalo on the face—that's probably when he realized he had no idea what he was doing there.

Some land on the pool of blood on the floor, spilling the red mess everywhere it hadn't gone yet.

Some on dry land, just to be engulfed by the warm red ooze that came next.

Some fall on Jason. He who didn't notice anything, because he was too busy howling over the lifeless body hanging from his arms.

42

Immortal Waves Sleeves

An eight-year-old standing next to a man with a bullet hole on both sides of his head. Not necessarily the most educational experience a girl can have. But in that land of no time, or all eternity at once, I am fine. Just fine.

Strangely detached, even. Feelingless.

One of the monkeys hops down from the bamboo. The blackest of them. We stare, our eye-lines almost at the same level. There are no words, no language. Yet we communicate. As if he was talking into my brain, but not like Simon used to do. Deeper. Thought to thought, before words can form.

I point at his feet. There is no shadow under him. I have mine. The trees and rocks have theirs. But him, none.

I ask if I am dead.

"Butterfly." I'm not sure if that was something I thought or something he said inside my head. He nods. A new life ahead, I think. Riddles…

I try to do it too, speak in his mind. But I have no idea how. He holds my hand. His motion so slow, his face so serene, it reminds me of the old monks in China. Dressed in their yin-yang-colored robes. Like my master. Those annoyingly jovial beings for whom everything was always good. "Acceptance," they used to say when I asked them why they were all so happy. They respected Shifu, and he respected them back, although Shifu was a little more demanding of life than the others.

Myself, I always had trouble accepting. Now, this.

Upon the monkey's touch, I feel calm. Words are fine if I want, he says with no voice. Am I imagining all this? I ask, "Is this the Dao or a computer simulation?"

He stretches his fingers and makes a symbol in the air between us. The Chinese character for pig, then the character for roof, making one. "Home," I mumble. He nods. Touches his chest. His home. Points at me. Mine too. The question I asked, he ignores like Shifu used to when he thought it wasn't worth his time.

Full of wonder and curiosity, I feel like an eight-year-old indeed. Although not so infantile. A thick smell of incense burns through my nose, and when I search for the source, Simon is made of ashes the wind carries away.

Goodbye, Simon.

I feel for him. Kind of. No, bullshit. I wish he had suffered more. We walk.

The pink sunlight warms my skin. The breeze cools it. Like my childhood memories. Tall and colorful, the mountains around reach to the skies. I bet if I count, they will be exactly seventy-two. They are so big and insistent. And next to us, the river, so long, so passing. Shifu's words come to me. One of the days he pushed me to test my stance. "Be unmovable like Wudang, flowing like Wudang." One of those riddles you can only understand once you've been there and saw the river and the mountains being one.

Is Shifu ever going to join us?

The Shadow Monkey lowers his head. Respect, not sadness. Not to him, not to Shifu. To me, and the pain he anticipates. I understand, appreciate. If there was one thing I always longed for in death, it was to see Shifu again. "Normal death, not." I hear his thoughts. We keep moving. Bordering the river. Near the booths where, in my memory, tourists buy fruits to feed the monkeys. The same ones. We pass the theater where my master used to entertain the kids with his shadow puppets. Things aren't dire like when Simon showed me. Everything's new again, just like I left them. Maybe a little abandoned—I guess that's what happens to unvisited memories, they fill with dust. I run inside, around chairs and tables, steps and doors. Still know my way as if today was then.

Lost in the debris, right next to the broken lights that used to cast shadows, it waited for me. An old wooden box. Shifu's most precious belonging. The one he promised he would give me some day, but never did.

43
Golden Lotus

While I open the box, at the exact same time, I can see the other side too. The cameras: security, agents...all of them. And one more: I see Dr. Lambrechts.

There are bodies on every floor, thirty victims at least, plus the injured. The space is taken by the yelling of the young doctor who doesn't want to be taken away from the body of his girl-friend. A scene so sad even the cold agents grimace. Although, given the circumstances, it could have been worse. The hospital was taken by terrorists after all. Bio-Cyber terrorists, General Crane calls them. Not the last ones, he says with a sigh.

Men in black outfits line up, kneel with their fingers crossed behind their heads. Nurses and doctors brush the back of their skulls, disoriented and startled as if they have just been awoken from the scariest dream. *Why did you have to do that, Simon?* I think. The place has been scanned for hidden weapons, bombs. It's all clear. In the theater, two casualties. A Chinese girl and a young scientist with dirty blonde hair. General Crane lays his hand on the old scientist's shoulder. "Take your time, Lambrechts."

A cry explodes through his nose and lips. Like a mouth sneeze. He covers them. Another burst comes. He holds it again. Until he can't anymore, and the sobs come afloat. "I'm so sorry!" In a mumbling prayer, he begs for forgiveness. "It's my fault," he cries to the God he tried to match. I hear his thoughts, and they carry the melancholy of the entire world. *My tower…of ego and ambition. The devil*, he says to himself, *I am the devil.* "These deaths are on me."

"Especially hers," he thinks, now looking at my old body.

A shattered wail rattles him out of his prayer. A young doctor tries to break from the paramedics and reach the dead girl's body. Lambrechts feels sick. "Claudia! Claudia! No!" implores the doctor. "My sin," Dr. Lambrechts says to himself. Each time Jason shouts her name, the scientist's spirit dies a bit more. His body bends further in. Then guilt explodes through the mouth. Brown, green, in chunks that he wished carried his heart too. But nothing on the floor beats. The Lord wouldn't be so merciful.

44
Appear to Close Entrance

My head dives into Shifu's box. Mine, now. My treasure chest. His old paper characters are all there just like I remember. A rooster. A boat. A tigress. A little girl. Colored paper, sticks, and glue, so full of details and pride. A monkey. A tree. A mountain. The running waters of Wudang. The fog. I keep discarding them. Until I find the one. That's it. I take the paper figure and run back to the Shadow Monkey.

But before we can resume our journey, from the skies and everywhere else, a thunderous voice lands upon us. A woman, powerful and lived. I know it so well.

Mrs. Lee's ghostly words echo from above. "When she moved here, Claudia wanted to find the knowledge her master didn't have time to teach."

The shadow puppet I found, I give it to my simian host. A pig. He takes it and holds it in a particular kind of silence that makes my heart warm. Are we one now? We keep walking toward the sun. Although he looks smaller now. Or I am taller, who knows. My legs are long and bony, small breasts threaten to break out. I remember that age, too. Shadow Monkey doesn't care about me. Just the new toy I gave him. The voice keeps dropping from the sky. Mrs. Lee's.

"She worked so hard, practiced with diligence, taught her talentless students, putting herself to the test in situations that didn't seem very healthy."

Inside, I laugh—if there is such a thing in that world of computer simulations. Not that healthy, indeed. We are back at the watering hole, where in my memories of Shifu's stories, Tigress and bees have dueled to death. I am fully grown now. Tats and everything. Still holding hands with the monkey. He brings me to the boulder where he waited in the old tales, leaps a few feet away from me, turns back, and puts his hands together in front of his chest. A prayer? Perhaps he wants me to meditate on the meaning of death. He tells me no, and moves his hands apart.

At first, I think what I was seeing is a ray of energy. His qi, possibly. But as his hands move farther and farther apart, the burst of light grows bigger, forming images in colors so bright they feel as if they're taken directly from my memories. In the flashes, moments, from childhood in China to my fights in the Bay Area, growing until they become a wall reaching to the sky and the horizon. They play like videos uploaded to the internet—interlinked, connected back and forth through time. Some recent, explained by old ones, connected by logic, not time. Some early teachings proven by late experiences. Some mistakes I avoid the second time…Everything so vivid, it's like I'm there again. Because I am. China and America, fights, philosophy, and science, all merged in the story my spirit remembers. In flashes. Images from my own eyes, and those I collected from Simon and Dr. Lambrechts, seen from their eyes with their brains and filtered by their feelings—at least, what they allowed me to see. Plus, some from the mechanical eyes of the world. Cameras everywhere. So many it overwhelms.

Curious, I ask them to stop on one. A self-driving car on a corner, charging at another, only to hit the truck right behind. "Why did you attack me?" I asked. He waves his head sideways.

"Us, not," he says, and opens another screen with an image of my apartment, empty, with just the image of a computer pig on the screen. "Us, yes. Gift," he says.

"So when you attacked me in the Anamnodome..."

"Us, not."

Even dead, Simon still manages to surprise me. I go back to my own stream of images. A web of visions from the beginning of my time all the way to...now. Inside the screen, I watch it from the other side. Like a mirror, but not exactly. "Reality too," Monkey tells me. Reality and memories, converged. I understand now. This story, the flashes, my death. "I have gone through all this before, right?"

Mrs. Lee's voice continues from everywhere. "But she was never afraid. Of men, of science, of death. Claudia, our Tigress, didn't know fear."

"This is my third time?" I know, he knows. The real life, a first recollection when I saw the memories, a third to link everything together into a web of...flashes to make sense of it all. Monkey raises a finger, and the video on the screen pauses. He beckons me to proceed and I know what to do—let it roll, my friend.

The voice continues as the paused mirror fades into the image of a funeral: "I'm unsure if she ever found her answers. But I'm glad she finally learned to let go."

45
Cloud Hands

The Dao doesn't talk, but knows irony quite well. Yes, I finally learned to let go.

The cemetery they chose is beautiful. Tranquil, green. From the top of the hill, I can see Berkeley, Oakland, the bay. San Francisco waves from behind as if saying that in death we are all the same. Daoists, Catholics, scientists. Strangers rubbing the pain off each other's backs.

He is there. Dr. Lambrechts. Pale, consumed. I want to tell him not to worry, that I am good, that he tried. Say I'm sorry I misjudged him. But I don't think he would listen. Not the scientist who thinks he's betrayed God.

Mrs. Lee comes down from the podium and gets a hug from Master Lau. He holds on to the embrace a bit more than he should. She doesn't push him away either. From both sides, they wink at their friends. Yes, Mrs. Lee. Go be happy.

Their images are all over the dome of our sky now. The casket is lowered. My students throw flowers. The twins Linds and Ash, Jen, Camara, Kira, even Molly came from her Oregonian farmland to pay her respects. Very nice of you, dear. They open a little gap between their shoulders and here comes Jason. He is so handsome in that black suit. Though he has lost some weight.

337

On the vast green grass, Shadow Monkey gives me a hug and on the top of every tree, a critter celebrates. My hands, they glow. I glow. My skin shines, white like the fog. I am the White Tigress, finally. The immortal I was set to be. Inside, I feel infinite. The winds, the rivers, the mountains. The fog, the trees and the critters. The stars and the cities, temples and dragons. Oakland, Berkeley, Chinatown, Wudang, everything orbits in me. Then I hear Jason.

"She came here thinking fame would make her immortal," he says, from the images in the sky. "And she gave all that up because of me."

He takes something from his pocket, sniffs back the tears escaping from his nose, and continues: "Fullness. That's what the future said it held for us." Then throws the coins toward the casket. Three of them, small metal disks, oxidized to green, a square hole in the middle. "Well, I am just empty."

On the dome of our sky, we watch the three coins fall in our direction, and even they seem confused when the metal pieces cross the blue veil of the sky and land on the grass in front of me. Black Monkey bends down and catches them, investigating their shape and smell. Above the trees, branches shake and rattle, as the audience attempts a better view. Next to me, Shadow Monkey licks them like regular monkeys do. I try to read what he is thinking or feeling, but it's just empty. A slightly uncomfortable void. Then the feeling vanishes, and transforms into what I can only describe as curiosity, thrill…awe? Coins in its hand, the darkest of the monkeys puts his hands together in a position that resembles the Daoist yin-yang gesture and bows to me. They are all quiet.

"Thanks," I say.

At the tear I shed, Monkey smiles his simian smile. Small but gentle. In his computer mind, he can almost appreciate the beauty of the surprise. He doesn't say that. But I know. I am part of him now. We turn back to the screen above.

The two masters and their redheaded apprentice line up next to the coffin, their diaphanous white robes resembling the fog of Wudang. Each of them carries a little clay pot. "Yinyin's selfless instincts to protect others was the yin that chased her for her entire life. And I honor it with the tea from her birthplace," says Master Som.

Master Lau, with his gritty voice, follows: "Today, this water represents yang, her nature, her talent and curse. The ancients often refer to death as going back home. Like a river finally reaching the oceans again. Today, we honor the water and ask the immortals to welcome her with all she is."[55]

The third man, young and overwhelmed by the responsibility, carries a bowl of grains. His hands shake. Master Som speaks on his behalf: "This rice represents the union of yin and yang—her final achievement, her legacy through the surprises the Dao brings. We are all proud of you, Yinyin. Your fatherly master would be, too."

They take a moment to wipe a few tears and I am glad this isn't following the protocol of a full Wudang funeral, with women howling and everything. The priests continue: "We know you must be watching us from your own kind of Dao, for you have always been one to create your own traditions. And for that, with respect and admiration, in the light of the old and the new, we salute you and send you in peace into this next stage of your balanced, bodiless life, Tigress." The three of them turn their gaze upward and away from me. They hold their silent prayer to the skies of all religions, and I think I notice something weird. Did Master Som peek down and...wink?! *Can they see us?*

---

55. Death is a particularly fascinating idea in Daoism. There are so many stories and allegories about it. But in a culture so driven to uniting yourself with the nothing, it doesn't surprise me that death itself has such a powerful symbolism. This homecoming idea, by the way, was taken from Den Mong-Dao's book *The Wisdom of the Tao*—a good way to get into the Daoist mind through small stories and meditation that seem independent enough to be savored without rushing too much.

The Black Monkey raises his shoulders. Nothing is clear at this point.

The clouds take over the sky and the images vanish. I close my eyes to hold them a bit longer. Don't want to let them go. I open a window to a traffic camera nearby. American students, Chinese masters, Jason…some of them never met, but in grief, they're a family. Mine. They hug, cry a little. Support each other. Murmur stories to whose names they don't know, offering each other tissues and sympathy. Mrs. Lee organizes them into a line in front of Jason. Time to pay respects.

My almost widower. Draining himself of tears at each pair of arms he meets. They say words that cure nothing, but at least he can carry the love home with him. All that love, except mine.

Love.

"I failed her," he cries inside Yewa's unacquainted arms. She had waited in line, patient. The last spot. Her sorrow as apparent as anyone's. I didn't expect her there.

"I failed her too," she whispers. Jason tightens the hug, unaware of the meaning of any of that, for grief begs no understanding. Then I notice.

At my command, the image freezes. I zoom into her. Then further into her shirt. A butterfly shirt. In her hair, the clips, more butterflies. Outside my vision, I feel my hand being squeezed. Monkey agrees, the dream, the S.O.S., the butterflies. Of fucking course! She's the one who got my message and sent rescue.

"We were too late," she moans.

Images in motion again, I follow her. From camera to camera, through phones, cars…all the way to her own vehicle, then sneak into her phone. She weeps herself dry. "I'm sorry. I'm so, so sorry. I should have noticed what he was doing. Should've found you faster. Oh my God, I am so…"

Then her phone buzzes.

She checks. A text, with an animation attached. She taps on

it just to see hundreds, thousands of butterflies take over her screen, revealing seven little characters hiding behind them: "I'M OK."

Then I must go. The screens fade, and Shadow Monkey is in front of me. He knows where I want to go next. He agrees.

We walk forever. Up the hills, down the cliffs, through bridges built by men and nature. Fields of tea. Temples. Fog. Trees. Paths I've walked as a child, but nothing felt distant anymore. My entire life was present at once, just like people say it does when you die.

The bamboo, I smell it first, and know we are almost there. Then the whispers of the river. As the foliage opens, I see the waters too, watch its spirit be awakened by the sun, then twirl into giant dragons and they silently climb the mountains, toward the seventy-two peaks of Wudang, then the heavens above. I wonder if there is any immortal riding on their backs.

We continue the march. Until finally, I see her. The mighty Tigress, the feared and revered feline who once ruled all the conglin. She lies there, still, lifeless, surrounded by an army of little yang warriors of the same colors, same stripes. Creatures of all sizes still mourn her passing, the departure of their queen. We join them in silence, honoring the life that never ceases to transform. Our hands make the secret sign only the followers of the Dao must know, and we bow to her. Then Monkey and I hop over the bodies, get near the water, and drink in peace.

– THE END –

Epilogue

"He is every fucking man on the planet," said the blond woman in the alley in Oakland. Remember? She asked me if I was going to beat them all. Back then, I didn't know how I could. Now I do.

This strange dimension where I live, this place nerds call "the cloud" isn't the Dao of my ancestors. Though, from where I stand, I can hear everything. Which brings me to you.

A few days ago, when the drooling dog who calls himself your husband barked your name from the bedroom, I was listening. "Bwarbra!" he yelled, his drunk tongue tripping over itself. You started to cry when he continued, "Come here, you useless whore!" You jumped to your feet and rushed toward the bedroom. He doesn't like when you make him wait, does he? But before you could get anywhere, he was already at the door. I saw it all. I watched when he slapped you. So hard you hit your head against the wall. When he asked if you called "this crap" food, when he threw it on the floor. The plate broke and there was food everywhere. He got even more irate. "Then you complain I eat with my friends!" he yelled.

"I didn't complain…." you mumbled in fear. (I am not judging, I promise.)

Aggravated by the audacity of your answer, he yapped, "what did you say?" He heard you the first time, I am sure. But he came back anyway, asked again and hit you one more time.

See? I was watching you.

You were still on the floor, crying, gasping when he spit on your face and left you there, wrapped around your own knees as your only comfort. Fading away, the uneven sounds of his feet dragging the cheap flip-flops disappeared behind the door he slammed behind himself.

The crucifix on your chest, you held it.

You prayed.

There's no way you could have known, but that very afternoon, you were praying for me.

Now listen carefully: I can help.

The package you found earlier by your door: open it and you will see a bottle with three black and white pills. These capsules have a newer version of the nanobots they injected into me. Yewa made them. They are faster, more efficient, and in a matter of hours, they will have finished most of their landing. They can be ingested with water, which makes the process much easier.

Now stop shaking your head. I can see it. And don't think I can't understand your fear. I can. A random person, possibly a stalker or a lunatic, is asking you to take some mystery pills. Crazy, I know. So I won't push you to do it now. But when you decide that you've had enough, when desperation becomes bigger than fear, go ahead and take those. Once you do, I'll be able to connect to your brain, and take over your body for a few minutes. And a few minutes is all I need. At that point, your husband will be my problem.

The consequences, you don't worry, for in the package you will also find my fighting clothes, gloves and a tiger mask just like the one Buffalo gave me. I want to make sure when they see the footage from the computer I'm going to set up to record the fight, that it's me they will look for, not you. They won't understand how I pulled it off, but they will chase me. Let them. I am ready.

Now hurry, hide the package in a safe place. He's coming upstairs.

Acknowledgments

A little story about the story. The i-Ching consultations in this book are real. As I was writing the chapters, I asked the coins the questions the characters were posing and used whatever the book said. More than a gimmick or a superstition, that was just another demonstration, maybe the most literal but not even close to being the most radical, of how stories develop themselves around us.

One of the main issues in my firsts drafts was pointed out by my amazing beta-readers Talita Carneiro and Sam Glynne. Claudia's motivation had to be really strong to take the risk of placing micro-bugs in her brain. They were right, and that question haunted me for months. In the meantime, for reasons unrelated to this book, I had the pleasure of meeting Professor Paul Li, neuroscientist and professor at Berkeley, where he teaches cognitive science—a mix of neuroscience, philosophy, and technology, as he explained. I thought I had found a golden ticket when I heard that, but then he told me he's also Chinese and a Muay Thai fighter!

Well, as I abused his generosity, Professor Li answered dozens of questions related to neuroscience, helping make the science as solid as possible, given the freedoms novelists are allowed to take. "Sci-fi sometimes takes leaps scientists will only confirm decades later," he said. But there was one thing bothering him. The lack of fear of side effects. Since I had heard that before, I asked him what they would be and, more important, how the scientists would deal with them. It was he who recommended the oxygen tank to replenish the exhaustion the experiment would cause. Which led to the next part of this puzzle.

I had just finished the second draft and was taking a break to think about the main issues before I started to edit the book again when a dear friend, who will remain unnamed because she doesn't want to expose herself that much, told me about the torturing headaches she had been experiencing. Suicidal headaches, people call them. They're that horrible, and the scenes in this book do not display the true horror this condition induces. My friend made me watch videos of people in crisis mode that broke my heart. We talked about it at length. I was trying to help, asking my M.D. brother for advice, searching for contacts at good headache clinics, browsing the subject through deeper and deeper digital rabbit holes. Given all the medical minutiae in this story, it helps to have a brother who is a surgeon in Brazil, always ready to respond to my late-night requests, early in the morning for him. Dr. Pedro Ricardo Milet, I am so proud of you, and so thankful as well. During one of these study dives, I saw a patient trying to manage a crisis with an oxygen tank, and everything clicked. The motivation, the management, the stinging theme that was already present throughout the book. Seemed like the Dao was trying to help.

The Dao, being timeless and absolute, awarded me with friends and connections near and far, and even strangers who helped when they had very little to gain.

Including my Chinese friends who gave me so many careful explanations about their culture. Yoyo Chu, who helped me in a creative workshop I taught in Beijing years ago, was kind enough to read the first drafts of the manuscript and send me her careful and thoughtful notes. It helped that she is also very passionate about Daoism and the philosophical elements of this book. I got "lucky" again. The same way I got lucky to receive such fantastic insights into modern Chinese culture from Anthony Tse and Polly Chu during my trip to Shanghai, 2018, when I also received some wise advice about China's health traditions and entertainment landscape from Fremantle's Vivian Yin.

To give back to the Chinese community, I counted on my friends Kevin Swanepöel, Ma Chao, Celia Wen and the crew at The One Show China for allowing me to teach my perspective in storytelling to the Chinese youth, a good way for me to give them something in return for all I have been getting from their culture too.

My family is the greatest of blessings though. Starting with Lo Braz, my wife whose support helped me deal with the insecurities so natural to the adventure of trying to write a book in another language, and my son Francisco who always inspired me to want to be the best version of me and never shied away from being a sounding board to my most absurd ideas. Having a son with such a sensitivity for stories and characters is a luxury I couldn't have wished for.

Same with a legion of fighters who shared their perspectives, techniques and motivations with me. Starting with James Nottingham who so carefully revised all the fighting language of the manuscript. And my old friend Andrea Cals, Gracie Jiu-Jitsu black belt in our native Rio de Janeiro—ground fighting not being my specialty, it was great to be able to count on your patient experience. Amber Staklinski, martial arts instructor and one of the names behind the popular online channel Aperture Fighting, who brought valuable insights into the female fighter mindset. The fierce (and borderline scary) Wudang Daoist, composer and fighter An Ning from Shanghai, who gave me chills by allowing me to see my character in the flesh for the first time and giving me a clear sense of what Yinyin would and wouldn't do or think. Amateur MMA fighter and litigator Julie Cohen and my Brazilian Jiu Jitsu training partner Sharon Meguira, who helped sharpen Yinyin's commentary about being a woman in the traditionally male world of fighting. Gabi Garcia, possibly the most accomplished female Brazilian Jiu Jitsu fighter of all time (and still one of the top fighters of either sex) for her thoughts on having the confidence to fight men. Two-time Kick Boxing World Champion Vanessa Romanowsky, who at that time was a badass 14-year-old who helped me grasp the mind of a young woman so dedicated to her skills. MMA legend Chris Cyborg for the precious tips on the realities and challenges of the sport, while five-time world champion in Brazilian Jiu Jitsu Kyra Gracie helped me develop a deeper understanding of the mission of teaching women to defend themselves.

Other friends went through the torture of reading early treatments, before the first draft, when this story was still an annotated outline lacking motivation, structure, and pace. Alma Har'El, Paulo Melchiori, Rob Lambrechts, Luke Ryan, Abigail Booraem, Denise Corazza, Thais Lyro, Stanlei Belan and Alisa Brooks.

Some people helped me reach some of the specialists I talked to, and no one more than mixed martial arts icon Rodrigo Minotauro. Can't thank you enough! But I can't forget other friends who sent me in the right direction too, such as João Daniel Tikomiroff, Andrés Balé, Ana Luísa Ponsirenas, Suzana Apelbaum, Vania Amaral, Michael Fanuele, Natasha Caiado, Paola Colombo, Billie Goldman. Then the few more who helped with encouragement, advice, and polishing the manuscript, including Tom Perrota, Lisa Gallagher, Meghan Ward, Mary Kole, Susan Barnes and Rebecca Brewer.

On the scientific and technological side of my learning quest, I must acknowledge Dr. Marco Iacoboni, director of the Neuromodulation Lab at UCLA, for the tireless advice on my design for the nanobots. Professor Shogo Hamada, Dept of Biological and Environmental Engineering at Cornell University, for the advice on the biomaterials that became part of the nanobots "architecture." Sashi Jain, innovation specialist at Intel, for checking my designs and pointing me in the field of neural lacing, which unlocked a whole new universe of study and sources I could research. Award-winning tech genius John Tubert; Rodrigo Siqueira, deep learning specialist at Microsoft; and über geek Rafael Gaino shared invaluable tips too, from the deep worlds of artificial intelligence to the cubic realities of Minecraft, Roblox and other virtual environments. On the marketing side I had the luxury of counting on the sharpness of the Pereira O'Dell team, especially Mona Gonzalez, Lyndsey Fox, Breanne Brock, Eduardo Gomes, Lilly Fu, Jason Apaliski, Emma Swanson and Kate Wadkins; Tia Lumarque for all the help with my social media activations; the artists behind my trailers Nick Tingri, from iamYork, Christiano Jordão and Darren Solomon from Quiet City, and Nurlan Abdullayev from AIPlague; plus the always sharp advice from Octavio Maron, Neven Borak, Monica Chun, Kristin Green and André Quadra. And much earlier than all those, my uncle Paulo Milet for getting me interested in how computers think since I was a kid.

In the field of neuroscience, I must highlight Dr. Theo Marins, Brazilian researcher at D'Or Institute, who helped me imagine possible realities of living with a high bandwidth connection between brains, and the also Brazilian Dr. Eliza Harumi, Researcher at Hospital Albert Einstein, who enlightened me on the potential implications of meditation in the connected brains.

On the philosophy part of the research, there are also loads of people to thank. Professor Barry Allen (McMaster University, Canada, author of *Striking Beauty*) shared his invaluable advice and bibliography about philosophy and martial arts. Best-selling Daoist writer Deng Ming-Dao spent hours helping me understand the nuances of the cultural differences between life in China and America and, of course, a deeper understanding of the Dao. Ravi Campos shared lots of references and articles on human rights for an AI-powered world. Eric Schwitzgebel, Professor of Philosophy, University of California at Riverside, advised me on the ethics of designing AI creatures. Berkeley statistics and deep learning professor Bin Yu inspired me with insightful conversations on the flaws of artificial intelligence; philosophy, arts, the nature of humans and machines and the fuzziness of science.

Not to be forgotten, my dear friends at Pereira O'Dell, whose names I stole so I could like my characters better—please know the personality I created has nothing to do with my judgment of the real you, especially my friend and business partner of almost twenty years, Andrew...O'Dell. I'm lucky to have met each one of you.

Luck also happens when your other projects allow you to have big and small interactions with people much smarter than you, who can enlighten your thinking with ideas and inspiration. In my case, these encounters included Werner Herzog, for showing me how to look at technology as if I'm staring at a beast; Kurtz Weil, head engineer at Google, for the glimpse of the future of human gods and the first dive into the clash between artificial and natural cognition; Patrick Hunt, a professor at Stanford, for the dark tales of the Bible that illustrated some of my scenes; Nicholas Negroponte, founder of the MIT Medialab, for our illuminating conversations on thinking about thinking and the impact of switching the properties of atoms and bites. And Wendy Feliz, from the American Immigration Center, who helped me understand the differences between my Latino immigrant experience and others'.

In Wudang, Shifu Gu Shining, head of the Wudang Daoist Wellness Center was so kind to show me the mountains, the routine of his school, other local masters from his sacred mountains. Thank you for being such a great host and for so promptly answering my hundreds of online questions after our days together. Yinyin's Shifu's school and the man himself are modeled on this great teacher and his Center. Also Hu Liqing, General Secretary of China Wudang Wushu Association, for showing me so much about the old and new forms of Tai Chi and Bagua in their mountains. Then in Shanghai, I had the pleasure of meeting Shifu Jiang Xinian who not only trained and lectured me in Wudang Tai Chi, answered dozens of silly and important questions, but also introduced me to his wife Kong Lingna, with whom I had insightful conversations about Chinese feminism. Back in San Francisco, these interactions continued online and got reinforced by two local Wudang Masters: Sally Chang, Lindsey Wei.

Team Tuttle (especially my editor Terri Jadick) also deserve a big hug from this fighter-turned-author who couldn't be happier for the honor being published under the same banner as so many martial arts greats. Seeing my name on the same list as Bruce Lee earned me a smile that still hasn't worn off.

Finally, my most important thank you goes to all my (long and short term) instructors in the fighting arts—Nilson Leão, Will Yturriaga and Jordan Lutsky, to whom this book is dedicated for their years of dedication to my journey; and Mario Nicolau, from Porto Alegre, Brazil (Shao Shin Hao Kung Fu); John Khang, from Richmond, VA (Wing Chun); I Made Sandia and Ni Nyoman Sayun Trinadi from Bali, Indonesia (Silat); Nick Veitch, from Taiwan (Wing Chun); Marco Lee, from Beijing (Wing Chun and Chinese Boxing); Fabio Gurgel, Andre Rocha, Geremias Dias, and Pedro Henrique Barros from Rio de Janeiro, Brazil (Brazilian Jiu-Jitsu); from Penápolis, Brazil, Massao Shinkai (BJJ); from San Francisco, Kurt Osiander, Lucio Muramatsu, Victor Oliveira, Devan Green (BJJ) and Long Vo (Boxing); Rigan Machado and Lucas Leite, from Los Angeles (BJJ); from New York City, Eduardo Capeluto, Nima Sheini, Dan Covel and Jin Yung (BJJ), Simon Burgess and Gianna Smith-Cuello (Muay Thai); from Port Chester, NY, Rafael Formiga, Omar Delgado, Felipe Rocha, Fabio Canela, Nick Navarro, Jamie Nottingham, Jeff Nelson and Nick Arnel (BJJ), Teeik Silva (kick boxing)—and all my classmates and students who always challenged me with the right mix of generosity, compassion, curiosity, and pain.

To all of you, and the Dao that united us, my most sincere *xiexie.*[56]

---

56. And thank you readers too. Not only for reading my story, but also for indulging my tangential thoughts, research, awe and personal takes in the footnotes along the way.

"Books to Span the East and West"

Tuttle Publishing was founded in 1832 in the small New England town of Rutland, Vermont [USA]. Our core values remain as strong today as they were then—to publish best-in-class books which bring people together one page at a time. In 1948, we established a publishing outpost in Japan—and Tuttle is now a leader in publishing English-language books about the arts, languages and cultures of Asia. The world has become a much smaller place today and Asia's economic and cultural influence has grown. Yet the need for meaningful dialogue and information about this diverse region has never been greater. Over the past seven decades, Tuttle has published thousands of books on subjects ranging from martial arts and paper crafts to language learning and literature—and our talented authors, illustrators, designers and photographers have won many prestigious awards. We welcome you to explore the wealth of information available on Asia at **www.tuttlepublishing.com**.

Published by Tuttle Publishing, an imprint of Periplus Editions (HK) Ltd.

www.tuttlepublishing.com

Copyright © 2023 by Paulo Jorge Caldas Pereira Jr.

Library of Congress publication data is in progress

ISBN 978-0-8048-5692-8

26 25 24 23
10 9 8 7 6 5 4 3 2 1   2306VP

Printed in Malaysia

Distributed by

North America, Latin America & Europe
Tuttle Publishing
364 Innovation Drive
North Clarendon
VT 05759-9436 U.S.A.
Tel: 1 (802) 773-8930
Fax: 1 (802) 773-6993
info@tuttlepublishing.com
www.tuttlepublishing.com

Japan
Tuttle Publishing
Yaekari Building, 3rd Floor
5-4-12 Osaki, Shinagawa-ku
Tokyo 141 0032
Tel: (81) 3 5437-0171
Fax: (81) 3 5437-0755
sales@tuttle.co.jp
www.tuttle.co.jp

Asia Pacific
Berkeley Books Pte Ltd
3 Kallang Sector #04-01
Singapore 349278
Tel: (65) 6741 2178
Fax: (65) 6741 2179
inquiries@periplus.com.sg
www.tuttlepublishing.com